The Secret of the Bird God

Book 3 in the

'Remember the Future'

Time Travel Adventures

by

Evadeen Brickwood

Remember the Future® youth-series book 3:
"The Secret of the Bird God"

This book was first published as a paperback edition by
Evadeen Brickwood at CreateSpace

First paperback edition
2017 by Evadeen Brickwood at CreateSpace

ISBN:
ISBN: 978-1-548-266882 with CreateSpace
ISBN-13: 978-0-9946918-4-2 with NLSA

Cover Design by Yvonne Less, www.art4artists.com.au
Source for cover images:
'Depositphotos.com' licensed
Book layout: Birgit Böttner
Map illustration: Birgit Böttner
This edition was also printed in Cape Town
Marketing: Alphalogic International

Finding their way back to Alesia and their home in the future, turns out to be more difficult than the time travellers imagined. War breaks out in the Mediterranean Sea and forces Katherine, Trevor and Chryséis to flee inland. Nothing here is the way they thought it would be, and who has ever heard of Egypt without pyramids? Here, they discover unbelievable books, a school of magic and that virtual-invisibility coats come in handy in prehistoric Egypt, now called Ta Mery. Somebody seems to be standing in their way and eventually, they find out the shocking truth. Can the elusive Bird God help the children get to safety in time?

Acknowledgements

A big thank-you to Peter Böttner, who patiently test-read the manuscript one last time after the last re-write, four years after the book was completed; to all my editors and proof-readers and to everybody, who gave their valuable input during its creation.

Map of the Atlantean Sea

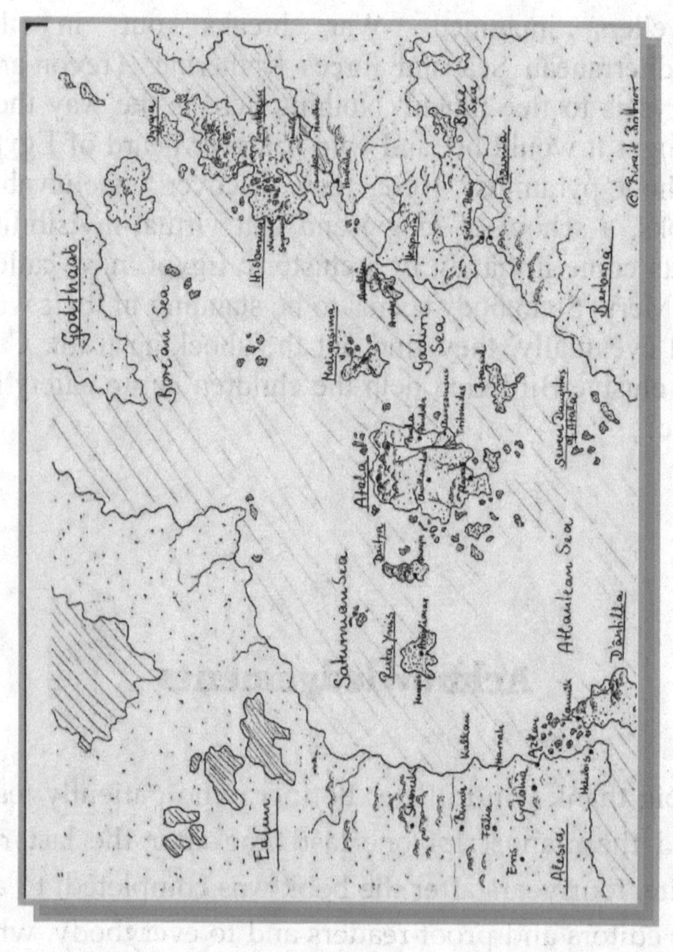

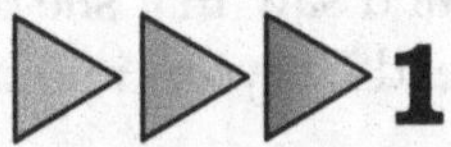 1   A VILLAGE OF BIRD NESTS

Chryséis had the most wonderful dream. She was riding a horse in the open fields back home. Her parents were there, with Cassie and Jason. They were laughing together. Suddenly, she jumped onto one of Túvar's swift, white horses and rode on and on, across the fields outside Cydonia. In the background were the rushing sounds of the ocean... the ocean?!

She opened one eye just a little. Trevor and Katherine were fast asleep next to her in a large oval basket, covered in feathery blankets. Warm and soft. Everything was fine!

Chryséis felt so comfortable, that she soon fell asleep again in the large nest. Half an hour later, she woke up with a start, confused by the smell of the ocean, the sound of the surf and the growing daylight outside. Outside the... the... where exactly was she?

Someone kept tapping her shoulder and tousled her hair. "Chris —"

"Leave me..." she mumbled. Her leg felt a bit sore.

"Chris, wake up, it's getting late!" Katherine's voice was urgent.

"What is it, something wrong? Are we there yet?"

"Something wrong? You bet there is something wrong!"

Alarmed, Chryséis sat up straight, rubbing her eyes. "Why? What is it?" Then yesterday's memories came flooding back with terrifying speed. "Oh no!" she moaned and held her head.

They had been on a ship back to Atala, then the terrible storm... and so much lightning! The ship tossing helplessly between high waves. They had to swim for their lives, struggling onto the beach in the pouring rain and... now this... nest.

Her leg was sore. She looked downed and saw that she'd had scraped her knee. It was enough to send Chryséis into a state of panic.

"I've had it!" she groaned. "I'm out of here! Where is the TPF?" She groped for her backpack and found her time-portal finder. A flat, pear-shaped metal object. "We are going back. I mean it!"

Katherine was shocked. "But Chris, we can't just..."

"If you don't want to come back with me, that's fine. I'll go on my own. I've had enough!" She yelled.

Chryséis pointed the TPF quickly toward the wall and pressed the big white button. A blurred image appeared on the woven wall that was fastened to the rock. There were oscillating waves that formed a vortex.

"No, you can't do that!" Trevor tried to grab the TPF from her.

"Watch me." Chryséis moved the device out of the way.

Everything happened so fast! She pressed the red button, programmed to the reference point in the future - back to Carter Valley and... before her startled friends could stop her, Chryséis jumped. She jumped into the vortex, disappeared into the basket wall and was gone!

The vortex spun round and round and Katherine wanted to follow Chryséis, but Trevor held her back by her elbow. "No, don't!"

"Why... we must stay together," Katherine cried.

"Too late. It's too dangerous." The shimmery image began to fade.

"It's not too late. I want to go with her!" Katherine tried to free her arm.

"No!"

The vortex disappeared and with it – Chryséis disappeared.

"Let me go, Trevor! Oh, why did she do that? She knows that she shouldn't do that. She knows that." Katherine sat down and began to sob. "What if she...? What do we do now?"

"I don't know. We'll think of something." Trevor stared at a faint shimmer that began to appear on the basket wall. "What's that?"

"What's what?" Katherine lifted her eyes.

"The vortex is coming back."

"What?" Katherine cried. The image kept oscillating stronger and brighter now. "What does that mean?"

"That can mean only one thing." The vortex reappeared, churning round and round in spirals. Chryséis was pushed out and landed on the thick seaweed rushes on the woven floor.

"Oh Chris! You came back!"

"Ooh, oh," Chryséis moaned a little and held her head. "Ouch!"

"What did you do that for?" Katherine shouted at her and began to cry.

"What's wrong with you, are you crazy?" Trevor was angry. "You could have killed yourself. You could have killed... all of us!" He wrestled the TPF from Chryséis' hand. "Give me that."

"What's wrong with your head? Let me see," Katherine sobbed and crawled over to Chryséis.

"I'm sorry." Chryséis groaned, "I'm such an idiot!"

"You can say that again," Trevor muttered.

"You have a bump on your head." Katherine declared and slapped Chryséis on the arm.

"Ouch!" Katherine slapped her again.

"Don't kill me. I didn't think clearly, that's all."

"That's all? Well, that's not good enough. We are scientists, in the middle of an experiment. You can't just lose your cool. It's dangerous. For everyone... " Trevor was running out of words. Why did girls have to be so hysterical?

"Give me a break, I'm just a kid. And I said I'm sorry. Oh Katie, stop crying. I won't do it again, I promise."

Katherine wiped her eyes and slapped Chryséis again on the arm - just for good measure. "How could you do that?

How could you do that?"

"Ouch, stop it! My head's already hurting. And my knee." She had hurt her knee the day before during the storm.

Katherine took a deep breath and stood up. "Good!" She reached back, but Trevor grabbed her hand. Then a thought crossed his mind.

"Listen, where did you go? Did you go back... home?" His words came out in a rasping sort of way. Katherine swallowed her tears and pulled her hand free. Her anger was beginning to dissolve.

"I... I think so. I didn't really look. Everything seemed... normal. I just pressed the reverse button as soon as I got out and came back through the vortex. Just like you did the first time you tested the TPF."

Trevor nodded. "And a good thing you did! Imagine the time loop you could have started - for all of us. Then we would never be able to go back home."

"Yes. Sorry." Chryséis looked rather guilty.

They all calmed down, but Trevor still held tightly onto the time portal finder, the TPF Chryséis had used.

While Chryséis had slept, he and Katherine had already unpacked the soaking backpacks. They had taken the virtual invisibility coats, or VICs for short, and the other devices out of the sandwich bags, that now lay scattered on the floor, more or less dry. Trevor's toothbrush was nowhere to be found, but that wasn't so important. The digital camera still worked. They had switched on the palmtop and the vacuum batteries were in working order.

"On the bright side, at least we know that the time portal finders still work," Trevor said sarcastically. "Thanks for testing the reference button. I'm sure we can get home from any other point, not just from Shepherd's Hill in Cydonia. Why didn't you look around a bit? Then we'd know for sure," Katherine said.

"What? I'm glad she came back straight away." Trevor shook his head.

Chryséis pointed to the nest-like bed. "I don't even feel like carrying on with our project. I just want to be normal again. Not almost drown or be eaten by huge birds."

Katherine giggled. "I doubt that birds live here. They don't normally sleep in beds or weave baskets out of bamboo."

" — or have trap doors in the floor," Trevor said. It was important that they came to grips their current situation.

He inspected the basket walls. They were covered with a clear substance to make the room watertight, effectively protecting it against the ever-present sand and wind and water. The walls came together in a seam above, forming the ceiling.

"This was made by humans," he said.

"True," Katherine mused. "I wonder how they fix the baskets to the cliff, though." She combed her hair into a high ponytail and put her sandals on.

"Hope they like us, whoever they are. At least they kept us safe from the storm."

"Or… they keep us caged as living meat provisions," Chryséis said. "What if they are cruel giants or something?"

"Oh stop it already! It's bad enough that you gave us a fright like that, jumping into the vortex and all!"

Chryséis shrugged her shoulder with a guilty expression.

Trevor scratched his head. "Wait… remember the flying Nepeshai people? It could be them."

"Could be, but there were people walking on the beach," Katherine said. "I don't think they had wings. Whoever they are, it's best to be careful."

"Right." Chryséis was still not convinced that they should continue with their project.

"Where's Tepi?" Katherine suddenly realised that her yellow dog was not in the basket hut with them. A tear rolled down her cheek. Had she drowned in the storm? Tepi just couldn't be dead… that would be too much!

"She was with us on the beach when we were running for shelter. There were fish drying on racks… Tepi was right next to me."

"Do you think she's still out there somewhere?"

"Probably… we should go and look for her. Wonder if the crew from the ship is also here," Trevor said. He peeped through a crack in the basket wall. "We must be high up on the cliff. I can see the beach and the sea down there."

"We are high up on the cliff?" Katherine asked astonished.

Before they could discuss their situation further, there was a scraping sound and the trapdoor swung open with a loud clatter. A smiling young woman appeared. She had smooth brown hair and looked at them with very blue eyes. The woman pulled herself up with ease and put down a ceramic pot before lifting herself up and sat on the woven floor.

"Sha'anti athenai," the woman greeted them. "My name is Nerilee of Berberia." She had a somewhat whistling accent, but the children could understand what she said.

"Shelanti!" They said and stared at her.

The young woman smiled broadly and nodded. "You are well, athenai?"

"Yes, we are. Thank you for… saving us on the beach."

"Ah yes Rimmon, the god of rain and thunder, has thrown quite a tantrum yesterday. The elders say it is time to appease the deity."

"Yes, it was a very bad storm."

"Eat… breakfast now... and come down later."

Nerilee's cheeks and chin were decorated with tiny tattoos: always three dots in a triangle. She stood up nimbly, walked to a wall shelf and took down three small bowls. She had no wings and was definitely human.

"Where are we, Nerilee of Berberia?"

"In Tãzilian village in Berberia. Means the 'Foreign Land', far from Atland. You lucky, come land here, not farther down the coast."

"Oh, and why is that? Being shipwrecked is not very lucky, no matter where," Katherine replied.

The woman threw back her long, dark hair and ladled

steaming fish soup into the bowls. "Oh, but it is. Nereus and his daughters be thanked for your good luck. Down south, the coast is marshy and — there is the village of Nahuatlacas."

The saltmarshes to the south, where a land bridge had once connected Punt with the mother continent, were now the home to flamingoes and many crocodilians.

"Nahuatlacas?" The time travellers tried to pronounce the word. "What's that?" Trevor asked.

"Bad people," Nerilee said with disgust. " a tribe from Atland, also survivors of the Great Deluge just like the Tăzilian tribespeople, but they are bad people, the Nahuatlacas. Started calling themselves 'crocodile people' and don't mind a bit of human flesh now and then."

The children were sitting there, mouths agape.

Had she said too much? *No need to worry them even more,* Nerilee thought. The 'crocodile people' marked the skin on their backs with stone blades, so the scars resembled the backs of the crocodiles. They also filed their teeth to sharp points in order to make the resemblance perfect. The hearts of shipwrecked sailors were often sacrificed to a cruel deity called 'Hummingbird to the Left'. Nerilee shuddered at the thought, but kept quiet.

Tăzilians were of the great clan of Guan-Chez or 'Men from the White Mountain'. A proud, slender and fine-featured people. They kept well away from their cruel southern neighbours, for the Nahuatlacas had lost their civilized ways.

Cannibals! "The Earthmother be thanked," Katherine said quickly.

"Yes, the Earthmother be thanked." Nerilee put wooden spoons into the bowls and set them down onto the floor. Then she smiled at them and withdrew, climbing expertly down the ladder.

The children began to eat hungrily. What Chryséis had done and their tiff earlier was all but forgotten.

"It's fish soup, but it tastes good," Trevor praised.

"We've had far worse than fish soup for breakfast. Chryséis

said. We should have asked her about Tepi."

"You're right, but we'll go just now and look for her."

"There are cannibals around here?!" Katherine asked and pulled a face.

"Thank goodness not here in this village." Chryséis had nearly finished her soup.

"Are you sure? Maybe she's just trying to butter us up," Trevor said ", and they fatten us up like the witch in Hansel and Gretel?"

They laughed uneasily and ate the rest of the soup.

"At least these Tassils seem friendly enough," Chryséis said, still chewing, as they got ready to leave the basket hut. She handed the dishes down to Trevor, who had climbed down through the trapdoor. Chryséis und Katherine followed him.

"Nerilee's okay, but the other villagers might not be so friendly when they see you with your hair in all directions." Trevor and Katherine grinned. Blonde strands had dried into an odd shape on Chryséis's head.

"No offence, but you look like some kind of Rutian forest elf…"

"Can you fix it?" Chryséis asked impatiently.

"Sure," Katherine said and quickly braided her friend's hair. Trevor peeked down, to get the lay of the land. There were other baskets on the cliff that were connected with rope ladders.

"They must be using some sort of glue to stick these baskets to the cliff," he said. "Well, something like that. Come on now, you're taking way too long." Trevor hurried them on.

He didn't know what to do with the crockery and put the bowls down on the wooden platform.

"Okay, ready," Katherine said. "Let's go and find Tepi."

"Wait before we go…" Chryséis stared at her feet. "Am I forgiven? For just taking off earlier…"

"I guess," Trevor grumbled.

"I need to know, we're okay!" Chryséis looked at her friends and bit her lower lip.

"I guess," Trevor repeated in a dull voice.

Katherine showed a different reaction. She glared at Chryséis. "If you ever do that again, I swear..."

"I won't! I promise. I was just so confused and... I won't do it again."

"Well then - I guess we're good," Katherine grunted.

"Thank you..." She didn't mention that her knee began to hurt again.

"Yeah, yeah." Katherine was suddenly not so sure that she should have forgiven Chryséis so quickly, but it didn't matter so much now. They had to go and look for Tepi.

Climbing down wasn't as easy as it had seemed at first. Not looking down helped, because they were really high up. There was a rope ladder leading down onto another platform. While they struggled to reach it, children in loincloths with wild, unkempt hair stared down at them from above. Way above. They shouted and grinned and let themselves glide down on ropes.

"They don't seem to worry much about hairstyles around here," Chryséis grinned.

They stared at the children's nimble movements. Should they wait for them or go ahead?

Although they looked wild, Tăzilian children had good manners and helped with chores. School was out for today and the children were curious about the strangers that had survived the storm. They were taught in their mother language with the help of letters written on small ivory tablets and sand drawings.

A group of women in rough cloth saris looked up at them from the beach down below. They were tattooed like Nerilee and seemed friendly.

One of the women gestured for the wild-looking children to stay where they were and waved the time travellers down. They copied the village children and glided slowly down. They reached the sand and waited patiently for the women to say something.

An older woman put her fingers on her heart and then her mouth. It was a well-known gesture, they understood.

"Sha'anti, athenai. My name is Tewannakit of Berberia. Village elder. Welcome. The two sailors tell us that you are from Cydonia."

So only two of the sailors had survived the shipwreck! The children felt sad for the rest of the crew. "Yes, yes we are..." Katherine said.

"We will hold a ceremony for the drowned later," she said. "Right now, let us take care of that leg of yours."

Another woman pointed to the dried blood on Chryséis' knee.

"Oh, it's not so bad," Chryséis said lightly, but was grateful for the attention.

They followed the women down the beach to a shed that was open at the back. It was probably their 'House of Life'.

Chryséis' knee was bandaged with a green salve and seaweed, which felt a bit awkward.

"Shukri," she thanked Tewannakit of Berberia and the other woman, who had not introduced herself.

"It should heal quickly, child," she said and the other women nodded.

"Can I ask you something?" Katherine began.

"About your dog?" One of the women asked.

"How did you...?" But then Katherine remembered the telepathic abilities of many people in the Known World.

The woman waved for them to follow. They went to a large shed, where fish were drying on strings and smoked fish hung from wooden racks. The Tăzilians lived off the fruits of the ocean.

Fishing gear was stored under the racks in an orderly fashion. Harpoons, made from sturdy whalebone, three-pronged spears and angling rods of walrus ivory, right next to piles of fishing nets.

Out of the shade, something golden came hurtling toward them. It was a barking and yelping Tepi, who almost knocked Katherine off her feet.

"Oh thank goodness, Tepi!" Tears streaked Katherine's face as she squatted down to pet her dog. Tepi whimpered at the sound of her name and wagged her tail even more.

"Is she hurt?" Trevor asked.

"I don't think so," Katherine said and wiped her face with the back of her hand.

"Tepi must have spent the night here. Probably couldn't resist the fish heads on the heap over there." The heap emitted an unpleasant odour and Tepi looked gleeful. "I'm so glad, you're okay." Katherine gave Tepi a good scratch and looked up.

"My goodness, just look at that cliff! That's what they call a village."

The cliff stretched as far as the eye could see. Elongated onion-shaped baskets were moulded onto the vertical crevices and held in place with a clay-like substance. Steps were hewn into the rock, supported with timber.

"That's more like a city!" Trevor said.

"More than one village," Tewannakit said and the women laughed. As the women spoke to each other, the Tăzilians whistled and chirped among themselves.

"They talk like birds," Trevor whispered.

"Yes, they do," Katherine whispered back.

These beach dwellers didn't seem able to fly like the Nepeshai people did, but if they spoke like birds.

"We are going to cook now. Do you want to come with us?" One of the women said.

They went down to the beach, past the altar to the Earthmother, made of driftwood and glittering objects. On the rock behind the altar, a slow but steady trickle of freshwater gurgled into a long trough. Two laughing women fetched water with sealed baskets and carried them on their heads to the cooking fires.

The wild-looking children were now all around them. They chattered and twittered and reminded the time travellers a bit of the merpeople they had met in Alesia.

There seemed to be only women and children around. Katherine saw boats, sails flapping, cheerfully bobbing on the gentle waves. The men were probably out at sea, fishing.

But it wasn't always this picturesque.

Rimmon's whimsical temper was well-known to fishermen along the coast and on the islands not far from the coastal waters where the Guanchis lived. The fishermen of both tribes knew how to read the weather signs and when the storm was closing in, the wailing conch-horn signal was sounded. "Whooa, whooa, whooooa!"

Yesterday morning, there had been just enough time to secure the boats and fishing gear and to settle around filled supper pots in cosy huts before the rain began to pelt the coast. They could hear the thunder and waves rolling ashore, exploding on the rocks by the beach and felt safe inside their basket houses.

A group of dawdling boys had spotted a passing sailing ship and saw the mast splinter to pieces as it drifted toward the dark rocks.

The good fishermen sent prayers to the gracious Earthmother for the welfare of those aboard. Strangely, a number of Ioannu had been sighted out at sea before the storm, surrounded by tame dolphins. As if the Seaborn people were expecting the ship to appear, but in a furious storm such as this one, it was dangerous even for the Ioannu to linger around sharp rocks.

Some passengers had managed to stumble onto the beach. The fishermen abandoned their evening meal and had come to the rescue the survivors.

Today the skies were clear again and the weather would hold. A group of older men was busy repairing fishing gear next to overturned boats, while the women cooked by the waterside. A group of children were sitting by the cooking fires and practised with alphabetic and numerical symbols in 'Tifinar', the written language of the Atlandian Guan-Chez tribes.

"Come over here," one of the older boys, who was apparently the leader, called the three friends over.

He showed them the ivory tablets that were laid out on the

ground. The symbols could be combined into words and sums. This was the best the Tăzilians could do to keep a kind of citadel-school going.

"That's not Akkadian," Trevor said.

"What's Akkadian?" The boy asked.

The time travellers looked at each other. "The language, we use in Alesia."

"Where is Alesia?" One of the girls wanted to know.

"Far across the ocean," Chryséis explained. "Beyond Atland in the west."

When they realized that they didn't know each other's written languages, the village kids taught them a few words and phrases in Tifinar.

"That means three ships on the horizon," the leader of the children said and pointed to a row of oval tablets in the sand.

Chryséis rearranged the tablets. "Then that means three new people on a ship." The children giggled.

"No, it means three mokis on a ship."

"Close enough," Chryséis grumbled. They all had a good laugh and tried out other phrases.

The aroma of a delicious stew wafted over. Fish and meat were also grilled over a fire on a wooden grid, called a barbacóa. The women worked to the rhythms of traditional songs that sounded more like birds chirping. Tonight they would be able to pay their respects to the departed souls from the shipwreck on the beach, just the way it should be.

The time travellers observed the peaceful activities and were glad that they hadn't ended up in a village of cannibals. At least nobody here made an attempt to include them in the menu. On the contrary, the children brought them good luck.

Trevor didn't want to admit it, but he also had enough of dangerous adventures in prehistory and missed the quiet life at their boarding school.

For now, he just enjoyed the beach, feeling carefree and safe.

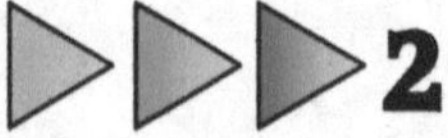 **2**   # CYDONIA CALLING

At the citadel in Cydonia, the Lady opened her eyes and took a deep breath. She was still trying to make telepathic contact with the three children from the future. The Lady had tried ever since they disappeared on their way back to Alesia across the Atlantean Ocean, but there was still no response.

Not since the disturbing news had reached Cydonia that the ship they had boarded in Caradoc, had been lost in a storm at sea with all hands aboard. The 'Navis Terumal' was last located before the Berberian coast, just after passing the island of Breasal.

The Lady's gaze caught the outline of Shepherd's Hill on the opposite side of Vallé Cydonia and her heart grew heavy. The afternoon sun bathed everything in a golden light and she leaned on the window frame, surveying the city. It was on Shepherd's Hill that Trevor, Chryséis and Katherine had arrived in the 'Alesian Epoch' only this spring. She had taken them under her protection and grown rather fond of the smart kids.

She had also promised them protection from other Ladies governing the Known World and even asked the merpeople to look after their welfare at sea when she herself could not.

"Oh dear Earthmother, please let them be alive and well." she murmured. "If anyone finds the letter of passage on them, they will know what to do."

The children had learned to send and receive telepathic messages and there was still a flicker of hope. She proceeded to send telepathic messages to the merpeople and to the Ladies of citadels in Northern Punt and Breasal: to look out for three children, lost after their ship capsized in a vicious storm before the coast of Berberia.

The letter of passage, however, had disappeared together with the ship, swallowed by the swirling waves.

*

"We have to go back to Alesia," Katherine said to Nerilee, who was scrubbing root vegetables by the water trough. "Can we take one of your boats?"

Nerilee didn't quite know what to answer the shipwrecked children. Taking a boat on their own? Had madness seized their minds? There were only fishing vessels here. Surely, none of the boats was strong enough to sail across the tricky waters of the Gadiric Sea. Especially during the stormy season of Rimmon. The larger boats were only readied later in the year when a group of Tăzilians was due to visit their Guanchi relatives on the islands.

"No, athenai, I believe this is impossible," she said. "The elders must make a decision like that."

"Can you ask your elders, then?"

"The answer would remain the same, I'm afraid. I have to go now and help with preparations for tonight. Please don't worry. A way will be found," Nerilee said and walked off with her basket full of vegetables.

"Don't worry?" Chryséis repeated. "Of course, we worry."

"What should we do now?" Trevor thought that simply taking a boat and sail west would be the answer to their problem. It shouldn't be too difficult to catch a ferry from one of the islands.

"I'm tired of this nonsense, I wanna go home!" Katherine complained. "Should we just use one of the TPFs?"

"I don't think that's necessary, and it might land us in some other time in the past now. If we go home just like that, everybody would worry about us and that's not right." Trevor fiddled with the wooden drain, leading from the trough toward the basket houses.

"Didn't you hear what she said?" Chryséis said

19

impatiently. "We cannot just take a fishing boat and sail across the sea. It's too far and too dangerous. All we can do is wait."

"Yeah? Look who's talking," Trevor smirked.

"Oh, yeah, right. I won't live that one down in a hurry," Chryséis moaned, meaning her ill-considered trip through the vortex.

"And there are no proper ships here," Katherine sighed. "So waiting for the elders it is." She swallowed back a tear, turned around and wiped her eyes as casually as possible. *They would find another way to go back to Alesia. They simply had to.* It didn't enter their minds that they might telepathically contact the Lady of Cydonia.

"I'll see if they need help with cooking," Katherine said and followed Nerilee down the beach.

They were here now and it wasn't too bad. The Tăzilians led a peaceful life in their bird nest village. Every morning at sunrise, the men floated their sturdy boats out to sea, where they would spend their time fishing until after midday. The Berberian coast brimmed with fish and the community was thriving.

Tasty smoked fish, the Tăzilians called sprots, were a delicacy, they sold to inland dwellers. The villagers exchanged them for cloth, building materials, spices, leather, grains and utensils that could not be provided by the sea. Together with sea salt and garum, a fish sauce made from fermented scraps of fish, smoked fish was one of the most popular trade goods on market days.

"I think I saw some Ioannu sitting by the rocks," Chryséis said to Trevor. "Wanna come check it out?"

"Sure, why not."

Katherine was busy helping a group of women clean and string fish for drying. She didn't see her friends waving and so they decided to explore without her. Tepi, however, sprinted across the beach to join the two children. They jogged over the flat boulders until the rocks became too spikey to negotiate.

Chryséis had been right. Three Ioannu males were sitting

on a flattened boulder in the water while their dolphin steeds squeaked excitedly in deeper water.

They had come from a sheltered bay up north, where their small community lived. The Ioannu waved to the children, who balanced as far as possible toward the flat rock. Ever since the storm, Tepi didn't like being close to seawater and stayed on the beach. She was chasing her tail for a bit before settling down.

"Oh, it is wonderful to see you." Chryséis gushed at the sight of them. "Shelanti!"

"Shelanti, athenai," the tallest of the mermen shouted merrily. "You are the foreign children from Cydonia, I presume," he said in a squeaking voice. "I am Tarit Maredit, 'Protector of the Sea'."

"Shelanti, Tarit Maredit," Chryséis said.

The Ioannu had come back to find out whether the three special children had survived the shipwreck and were in good health. The entire Ioannu community had promised to watch over them anywhere near the oceans of the Known World, after all.

"The honourable Ladies of Cydonia, Algiras, Anaá and Caradoc inquire after the well-being of their young friends'," the leader of the mermen continued. "The good Lady of Cydonia is requesting thought-communication if you please."

Of course, telepathy!

"Sorry, we didn't even think of it. Please let her know that we are well. Even our four-legged friend Tepi is here." Trevor pointed to the dog on the beach, keeping a close watch.

"I see," the merman said and smiled when he saw the funny land animal.

"We want to go home," Chryséis said, "but we are not allowed to take one of the fishing boats. There is a ceremony for the departed sailors tonight and we hope that the elders will make a plan for us."

"Your joyous news shall be made known to the Ladies, athenai," Tarit Maredit squeaked and dolphins chimed in.

They chatted to the mermen for a little while, but the

Ioannu had to leave when the tide was turning. It was dangerous to remain by the sharp rocks for too long.

"We will be back in the morning and perhaps you will come with us."

"That would be great!" Trevor grinned from ear to ear. He'd always wanted to ride on a dolphin.

The two time travellers would have loved to leave with them, but that wasn't possible without Katherine and their belongings. They also knew that it would be a very wet trip.

"On second thought, perhaps it's better to speak to the elders first. Maybe we can take a ship from the nearest seaport."

The Ioannu agreed that it would be better to speak to the elders.

"We will see you later, then," their leader called out.

They let themselves slide into the water, climbed onto their dolphins' backs and were gone in a flash.

Trevor and Chryséis walked back to the village with Tepi sniffing excitedly at every piece of driftwood and seaweed. Now, that the Ioannu had restored the link to their friends in Alesia, things looked up.

They found Katherine in a sheltered spot behind a rock wall. Some boys were playing Balôta, the Tăzilian version of Pigsnout. Balôta was pretty similar to the popular Alesian ball game: whacking a small soft têrakhon ball against a vertical wall with large wicker spoons. There were only two players per team and there were no holes in the rock face either. The point of the game was to keep going and outplay the other team.

Sometimes games were held between the Tăzilians and their island cousins, the Guanchis.

Trevor joined in the next game. Katherine was busy scraping fish as if she had never done anything else.

"Oh, that's so great, guys. They haven't forgotten about us!" she cried. "I wish I could have gone with you! We have to contact the Lady of Cydonia telepathically, then." She stared at the pile of fish in front of her, then at Chryséis. "I really have to clean this lot," she sighed. "If you help me, we'll finish sooner."

"Okay, then," Chryséis said without much enthusiasm.

It didn't take them long and they were done cleaning the fish. Just as they wanted to leave with Trevor, Nerilee and Tewannakit came to speak to them.

"Athenai," Tewannakit began, "the elders have decided that you and the mariners should accompany the next moki-caravan to the market at Bilbá soon." The children hadn't seen the two seamen yet, who were still recovering from the ordeal of the shipwreck.

"Around the waning moon two days from now. From there, you will be taken to the nearest port and hence make your way back to Atala." The woman pointed up to the top of the cliff.

A herd of dark, shaggy mokis was grazing on the plain above the cliff. They were looked after by young Tăzilian herd boys. The large three-toed animals with their odd short trunks were used as beasts of burden.

"Sure, there's no rush," Katherine mumbled to herself.

"Thank you very much, Tewannakit. Shukri. That is kind of you," Trevor politely answered for all of them.

"Make ready and wash yourselves now. The feast will start when the sun reaches this point." Nerilee's arm described a low angle.

"We will do so," Chryséis said, and they strolled back to the water trough, where they washed their hands and faces. "The Ioannu will be back tomorrow morning. Then we can tell them about the new plan."

"How will we know when they will come?"

"He'll let us know telepathically. You are so good at it, Chris, so you'll tell us when."

"We won't have the time to speak to the Lady of Cydonia now. We'll contact her tomorrow."

"Sure thing," Trevor said.

A group of boys came and asked the children if they wanted to play Balôta. Trevor jumped up with a delighted expression.

Their journey through Prydhain and Lyonesse to take back the Speaking Stone had not allowed for much time for play and Balôta was a welcome distraction.

"Don't take too long, Trev. You'll have to wash again."

But Trevor and the other boys were already running away.

Soon, the memorial festivities began in honour the souls lost during the shipwreck. It was the first time, the children saw the two seamen, who had survived the sinking of the 'Navis Terumal'. They numbly followed the prescribed rituals for the dead at the small shrine of the Earthmother. During the ceremony, incense was lit and prayers were said. Then the festivities began.

The villagers sat in a large circle around a nice fireplace where delicacies, such as raw sea urchin eggs, fried fish, roasted saurian and turtle meat were laid out on platters. Everyone gathered around, chatting, or rather chirping, and dining on the bountiful fare.

The time travellers were amazed at the bird language the Tăzilians spoke. Although they tried to keep speaking their the Akkadian mother tongue, trilling, twittering and screeching allowed them to communicate from cliff to cliff.

Girls and boys performed the 'Song of the Spirits above the Waters' and the 'Ode to Bhûranyu'. Then young dancers were accompanied by two female imsad players and energetic drumbeat.

After the meal, there was more chatting and laughing and the music played until it was time for bed.

The villagers closed their eyes, the music ceased and in the background was only the rushing of the Atlantean Sea. One of the elders spoke and asked for Rimmon's wrath not to return for a while and for a speedy journey home for their guests.

The day after the feast, the time travellers had met with the Ioannu by the rocks again and told them about the decision by the elders.

"It is decided then. I will let the Lady of Cydonia know. She wishes to speak to you directly, soon."

"Yes, we will speak to her. We are just always so busy," Trevor said.

For starters, Nerilee had woken them with breakfast and mentioned that the fishermen offered to take them out to sea on a boat. The children had declined, but the two sailors accepted gladly. They felt out of place when staying on solid ground for too long.

Then Chryséis had urged them on to the meeting with the Ioannu.

"They are already waiting for us," she had said.

When they returned to the village, a group of boys asked them to come and stalk flying saurians with them, while Tepi sat at the bottom of the cliff, waiting.

The saurians that nested on the rock above, away from the basket village, were quite small, compared to the ones they had seen so far.

The boys effortlessly climbed up the steep rocks with woven pouches slung across their shoulders and the three friends followed them a bit out of breath. Soon, they came across feathered nests with eggs that disappeared into the pouches. Then one of the boys brought down a male flight saurian with his sling. The crested flight-saurians tucked their dark wings under and made quite a racket as they hobbled along the rocky shelf above. Their young were just learning to glide off the rocks all the way down to the sea.

Some of the parents came rather close to the children and screeched and they climbed down swiftly. None of the boys wanted to lose an eye.

Tepi sat where they had left her, tail wagging happily. She had collected the flight-saurian and was guarding it.

They took their catch to the cooking fires, where they placed the eggs and the slain saurian on a bed of seaweeds. The women praised the children and sent them off to study in one of the lower-lying huts.

Later, the three friends sauntered down the beach and watched the salt-making plant for a while.

Tepi got all excited and barked when she saw the salt-encrusted cloths flapping in the breeze over large, shallow pans filled with seawater. Pieces of stiff white cloth were hanging in the water to absorb the salt as the water evaporated. It was the older children's job to scratch the salt off the cloth every few days and collect the white substance in tightly woven baskets.

"I think we better go back to the village," Chryséis said. "I don't want to meet those weird cannibals." They were still within safe limits but turned back anyway.

Later, Trevor and Chryséis helped to dig out crabs in the shallow water, while Katherine made herself useful by helping to prepare glasswort salad, a raw sea urchin egg dish and steamed beach spinach. Tiny raw sea urchin eggs tasted a little like honey melon and cooked with scrambled saurian eggs, they tasted like shrimps.

After the evening meal, they were so tired that they went up the ladder to their basket hut high above the beach, even before the sun had disappeared behind the horizon.

When the flaming sun dipped into the ocean, Chryséis made telepathic contact with the Lady of Cydonia at last, as tired as she was.

'They are taking us to a marketplace in Berberia soon and then to some seaport. We'll take a ship to Alesia from there.' Chryséis sent the thought out, concentrating on the Lady's face.

The answer came quickly. 'It is best not to wait. Leave tomorrow morning. I wish you all a good trip and we will communicate again, soon,' the Lady had thought. 'Good night and shelanti, athenai.'

When they fell asleep in the large bed, the time travellers didn't feel quite so lost and lonely anymore.

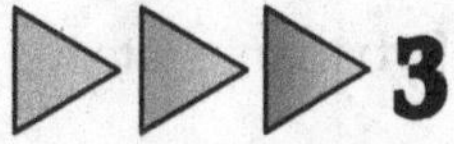 **3**   WAR OF THE GIANTS

On the third day after the shipwreck, it was time to say goodbye to the hospitable Tăzilians and the caravan made ready to leave just before daybreak.

Tewannakit and three men took the young time travellers and the two seamen to Bilbá in the Land of Sybaris. From there, they would travel by vimaan to the seaport of Hyela up north. The Lady of Hyela would arrange their sea journey back to Alesia from there.

Their guides donned long travel tunics, made of chamois leather that was embroidered with small seashells and shark's teeth. The children packed all their things carefully into the dried daypacks and made doubly sure that they hadn't forgotten anything.

The tiny caravan consisted of three sturdy mokis, carrying salt and sprots in baskets strapped to their flanks as well as longish amphorae with the prized garum fish sauce. The goods would be exchanged for much-needed rope, cloth for dressmaking and for grain and honey.

The mokis wobbled in single file along a narrow path, winding up the low hills to the south of the Tăzilian village. Tepi trotted placidly alongside Katherine's moki, stopping now and again to sniff the air and the ground.

It didn't take long before they saw Berberi nomads, tending a herd of fat-tail sheep with curious long legs. Dwarf elephants grazed nearby, but the three children were no longer surprised by such sights. Had they not seen much more exotic animals before?

Farther up the path, the Tăzilians took only a short

moment to greet distant Berberi cousins from the Tamashek tribe before they pressed on. If they wanted to sell their goods today, they had to make haste.

After another hour through the bleak Sybarian plateau, they arrived at the marketplace.

Many Berberis and local farmers had already set up in the marketplace, offering their goods. Trading was brisk. Mokis, screeching harpees in cages, crockery, articles of food and tools. Everything exchanged hands.

The Tăzilians and their guests rode up to their usual spot and tethered the mokis to short poles behind an open tent that always served as their stall.

"We are late. Let's quickly unpack," Tewannakit said. As soon as the goods were laid out on large, embroidered cloths, the children walked around and watched the people at the market.

Young children in loincloths ran about playing with sticks and balls. Berberi women, their faces adorned with dotted tattoos, wore simple lengths of cloth wrapped around their slender bodies like saris.

The Berberi were a superstitious people. Pouches with good luck charms and little magical objects were dangling from belts and around their necks, and they wore a single large blue bead on wristbands. The blue cat's eye was supposed to avert ill thoughts.

On opposite corners of the main square sat two popular storytellers, called rawis on large quilted blankets.

One of the rawis entertained traders and village folk with stories of Guanchi island-priestesses, called the Magades. In one story, they cast themselves off the cliffs into the sea as a sacrifice to the sea deities. In another story, a priestess found true love with a Berberi man and left her island on the back of a large bird that her lover had sent.

They strolled around a bit.

"Did you understand, what he said about the ocean draining and forming a desert?" Trevor asked as they walked back to the Tăzilian stall, hungry and tired.

"I don't think he was talking about the ocean, but a large lake," Chryséis said.

"Okay, a large lake, then."

"I'm starving..." Katherine walked faster.

By now, they couldn't wait to see the great city of Hyela on the Blue Sea coast. After a simple meal, the Tăzilians, overnighted at the only inn in the village.

For breakfast, they were given dried fish and some kind of gruel. Provisions for their trip to Hyela consisted of a packet of sprots and saurian eggs, filled with fresh-water and closed with cork stoppers, that were carried across the chest.

"The vimaan is ready and waiting for you, athenai," The maiden, who ran the inn told them eventually. The hospitable Tăzilians had already said goodbye and left at daybreak with their packed mokis for their nest village by the Atlantean Sea.

The vimaan turned out to be quite rickety with a twirly picture of an Ankh El. The two seamen jokingly called it a leftover from the 'Dark Age'.

"It's definitely better to take an old vimaan than walking all the way to the Blue Sea coast," Trevor said.

"The seaport of Hyela is on Cape Peloron due north and a long way off. We can only hope that the vimaan will make it there today," the seamen still laughed.

The maiden, who steered the vehicle smiled encouragement, as the five survivors of the latest shipwreck and their dog, climbed into the single cabin. Sure enough, the vimaan made it to Hyela in one piece.

Closer to the coast, the vimaan floated above cedar and strawberry trees and finally, the Blue Sea coast appeared. Large mountain goats grazed on the rocks below, while the maiden tried to stay away from flying saurians and falcons. There was much forest in the foothills of the green, misty Mother Rock Mountains.

"Look at that!" Katherine cried and pointed to pygmy

elephants, herded along a steep slope by a group of Berberis.

"Oh, another observatory," Chryséis said as they flew over large white egg-like buildings. An ideal moment to take a picture with their little camera.

In the country of Oinotria, the vimaan followed the meandering Medsherta river for a while in a northerly direction. Hyela was the capital of Oinotria.

A herd of mighty aurochs crossed the river below and Trevor pressed his nose against the vimaan's têrakhon hood to watch the splashing antics of the powerful animals.

Chryséis and Katherine fell asleep on the way to the Cape. Trevor felt hungry and opened one of the food parcels, they had received in Bilbá. It contained smoked sprots that he shared with the two silent sailors and Tepi. The girls woke up just before the vimaan entered the city.

They could have been fooled into thinking that they were back in Algiras. The same type of buildings, squares and harbour-fortifications. Trevor even spotted a couple of toboggans, just like the large wickerwork baskets they had seen on the island of Avallûn and the citadel complex was also situated on a small hill not far from the harbour.

But some things were different here in Hyela. People wore Greek-style robes, brightly-coloured in the latest Blue Sea fashion. Men were shaved and their hair cut short, while the topknot hairstyles with polished sticks, the women wore, resembled Asian hairdos and their shoes had looped wooden heels in the shape of a teardrop.

When they arrived in the citadel yard, their vimaan was welcomed by three singing maidens and a small group of officials. They were shown to their rooms in a tower and from there, they had a fabulous view of their surroundings.

"Let me take a picture of the harbour," Chryséis said and leaned out of the window on the tower's northern side.

"Do you see how people are running up and down the streets?" She rubbernecked to get a better look.

"Why? Do you think something's happening?" Trevor

looked worried.

"I can't see much, but there's a lot going on in the harbour," Chryséis said. The tense atmosphere was some cause for concern, but it would take a while before they found out the reason for the commotion.

Before long they were called to dinner. It consisted of sesame-covered bread-rings and slices of Luni, a giant cheese that was laid out on its own sturdy table. They couldn't believe the size of the humongous cheese, but it actually tasted quite good. Maidens cut slices off the cheese and served them at the table. Even Tepi had her own bowl. At dinner, the children learned what the commotion in the city was all about: A war had begun!

The giant king from the nearby island state had mounted one of his surprise attacks on the Oinotrian coast and was threatening Hyela!

Sankhasura was king of a tribe of warrior giants, who lived on a group of Blue Sea islands just off the coast. They were not well-liked by their neighbours for causing a terrible war many sheaves of years ago. The fierce giants had lost the war and had been banned from most of the mainland along the Blue Sea ever since. Understandably, the giants didn't like their confined existence on the islands and King Sankhasura now tried to expand his territory.

The Ama-zûnas were a warrior-tribe and tasked with patrolling the coast as they were allies to Oinotria and all civilized countries in the region. They would have preferred to get rid of the Guebras once and for all, but this would have been seen as a crime against civilisation. It was also a well-known fact that those victorious in war assumed the traits of the defeated nation. Nobody wanted to assume the traits of the giants.

However, not all giants around the Blue Sea were in favour of war. The Kabiri were related to the 'Children of the Moon' and wanted nothing more than to live in peace with their neighbours.

They were allowed to trade with the Oinotrians and other Blue Sea nations and fought by their side if need be.

This time, king Sankhasura seemed to have found allies in the Gorgonas of Hesperia, north of the 'Passage of Golden Pillars' that all ships had to pass on their way into the Blue Sea. A battle seemed imminent. Therefore, no sea travel was permitted inside the 'Passage of Golden Pillars'. No ships were allowed to leave Hyela.

The time travellers were shocked. They had made the unpleasant acquaintance of the Gorgonas before.

"No guesses that the Edfunians might also be involved. Stubborn buggers," Katherine said.

"That means, we can't go back to Alesia," Chryséis stated.

"Oh, great!" Trevor mumbled. "From the frying pan into the fire."

"Can't they let us go on one of the large continental vimaans?" Chryséis had tears in her eyes.

"I don't think, we are important enough for that," Katherine said.

"Although the seaport is protected by a strong electromagnetic shield, all sea traffic has to be abandoned until peace is restored," The Lady of Hyela explained.

"Honourable Lady," Porsenna from Algiras, one of the sailors addressed the ruler of Oinotria. "How long will this situation last?"

The Lady looked at him with a frown. "The most recent battle lasted no longer than three phases of the moon." She tried to sound encouraging.

"Oh, is that all?" Trevor and Katherine said in unison.

Everybody at the table stared at them for showing bad manners. The two of them looked at their plates and made it through dinner without saying another word out loud. That's how Oinotrians liked children best: seen, but not heard.

"Oh, brilliant," Trevor whispered. "What are we supposed to do now? I thought we had left the evil Edfunians behind once and for all. Now they have evil family members right here,"

"Bummer," Chryséis whispered back. "Three weeks in this place? Is there no other seaport around?"

"We have to wait and see what they decide, Chris," Katherine said softly. "There's not much we can do."

"Yeah, whatever..." Chryséis felt tears welling up again and Katherine squeezed her arm a little.

It wasn't hard to guess that Chryséis was homesick.

Tepi planted her head on the girl's thigh and looked at her with big puppy eyes. Chryséis patted the dog's head and passed her a few morsels of Luni cheese under the table.

After the dinner, Trevor addressed the citadel officials again. "Athenai, Is there no other way to get back to Alesia? We don't have very much time on our hands."

Trevor feared the officials would reprimand him again with their stares, but he had to know what they could do.

"Very well then," a bald official, called Rissa of Hyela, said in a haughty tone. "You may stay here in Hyela and wait, athenai or..."

"But we have to go back home..." Chryséis interrupted.

Such insolence, such impatience! The bald man closed his eyes as if Chryséis had given him a booming headache.

"... or we will find another solution for you. War is no pastime, child. You must leave it up to your elders, what to decide." Rissa would act as warlord soon and had other things on his mind than babysitting foreign children.

"I see," Chryséis said. "So there is nothing that we can do?"

"No, there is not."

"Nice guy," Katherine whispered in Trevor's ear.

The two sailors seemed to take the news with indifference. If it was the Earthmother's will to keep them longer in a foreign land, then that's how it was. They felt more at home close to the sea and would wait out the battle. The local sorghum beer was also really very good to these men, who spent most of their lives at sea.

"Honourable Lady..." The soon-to-be warlord Rissa wanted to complain about the insolent children. "Dear Lady..."

But the Lady of the Citadel held her hand up and the Rissa fell silent at once. "There is no time for further discussions." She was itching to end dinner and return to a conference with the elders of Oinotria, but before then, she had to find a solution for the children from Alesia.

Rissa couldn't deny that the children were annoying him. They obviously didn't accept their fate in the same placid manner as was expected of them. Had the Lady of Cydonia failed to teach them how to talk to their elders?

Obviously, he didn't know that they were not from Alesia or even from the same epoch.

The Lady of Hyela knew this, of course. To everybody else, the children were just three young Cydonians with a strange accent, who travelled on their own. This was not a topic to be debated at dinner and especially not with a stubborn man like Rissa.

She had been contacted by the Lady of Cydonia and had discussed the situation telepathically with other Ladies right before dinner.

Therefore, she asked them to join her alone in the audience room.

"I know of your situation, athenai. Please forgive Rissa's ignorance. He will be acting as a warlord and, I'm afraid, it doesn't make him any kinder than usual."

"Okay..." Katherine said. The warlords in Cydonia hadn't been much friendlier.

"I have decided that you should accompany our maiden Tafawana to the country of Ta Mery, where the 'Festival of Sokhar' will soon be held. We attend the festival every year and as for you: one can never get enough education —"

The faces of the three time travellers lit up.

"So we don't have to hang around here - sorry, no offence, Lady," Trevor said.

"Nobody will hang around in Hyela, I can assure you," The Lady answered. "The annual "Festival of Sokhar" is held in Ush-bantoun, a rather new town in Ta Mery, the Black Land."

The children already battled with all these new names of countries and cities... and they had no idea, where this Black Land was supposed to be.

"So it is settled then. You may join the maiden Tafawana on her journey to Ush-bantoun. There you will be safe for now. Come to think of it, stop in the Mâ-Rock Mountains on your way to the Black Land. The hot pools of Felsina should be interesting for our young visitors," the Lady concluded.

"Sure, hot pools sound interesting. And then we come back here and take a ship to Alesia when the war is over?" Katherine said.

The Lady of Hyela gracefully rose from her chair. "That is what I propose. Or perhaps you could take a ship from another port anywhere along the coast if you wish. All ships have to sail via Hyela on their way through the Golden Pillars. We shall see how long the war with the giants will take. Right now, it is important that you leave this town. The Lady of Cydonia will never forgive me, should harm come to you."

She ordered that the children were issued with paizas, small clay disks that served as travel documents and were stamped with the seal of Hyela. They were inscribed with information on the bearer and intent of travel.

Since they had lost their letters from the Lady of Cydonia in the storm, another type of identification was needed.

It didn't take the citadel scribes long to produce the three clay medallions. Even Tepi was mentioned on them.

Then things went from bad to worse around the Blue Sea when the Gorgonas warships joined the ships of the giants. The warlords feared that they might be able to breach the strong shield that lay invisibly over the Oinotrian coastline. The vimaan that would take the maiden and the children out of Hyela had to leave immediately as the shield could only be lifted for a short moment.

As the vimaan was leaving the coast, blood-curdling war cries could be heard, coming from the islands, where a gruesome sacrifice to the war god Xipe Xolotle took place.

"Lord of sacrifice, how can you be
known in this body
at the time of death?"
"Ari-sûdana!"
"Ari-sûdana!"

*

Soon, the three friends sat in a comfortable, rather modern vimaan and were on their way to the Mâ-Rock Mountains.

Mâ-Rock meant Mother Rock. It was the oldest and highest mountain range in the region.

The first stop on their trip was the town of Felsina, right in the heart of the highlands. From Felsina, it would be straight on to Ush-bantoun in the Black Land. The Black Land was the northernmost province in the country of Ta Mery. That much the time travellers had learnt by now. Pity, they couldn't just google where this Black Land was.

At the citadel of Hyela, Rissa the presiding warlord was giving a speech when a death ray, coming from the Blue Sea, struck a house on the Oinotrian coast far to the east. The house exploded, but the attack was immediately registered and the hole in the protection shield mended.

What the time travellers could see from their lofty position in the vimaan, was a bright flash that looked like a lightning bolt - then they felt the pressure wave.

"I think there's another thunderstorm underway," Katherine said and settled back into her seat. "I don't like storms. I'm glad we are leaving the coast."

"You must not fret, children. Felsina is far from the coast." Another lightning bolt lit up the sky, but they barely felt the pressure wave when their pilot pulled on the steering rod and the vimaan swerved inland.

"Shouldn't we be going west?" Chryséis asked.

"No, athenai, we are going east. To Ta Mery and the large lion," Tafawana said patiently and gave the pilot instructions to travel at a lower altitude.

"A large lion?"

"Yes, you know..." Tafawana sighed.

But the children didn't know. "Didn't the Lady of Cydonia tell us about a country called Ta Mery?" Trevor asked. "That they are experimenting with lifting large rocks, there?"

"You mean..."

"Yes, it's Egypt. How could I forget? She told us about Egypt! And Kem was called the Black Land in ancient Egypt," Chryséis said all excited.

"What? That can't be true. That's way too far away from Alesia," Katherine moaned.

"Oh, stop it already, Katie. I'm sure we have a better chance of getting back to Alesia from Egypt than just sitting around in this... this... fishing village – waiting until some war with those dumb, big giants is over."

Trevor didn't notice that he had switched to English and Tafawana gave him her most disapproving look.

Chryséis couldn't be bothered with the maiden's huffing and puffing. This time travel adventure had been really great, but now she wanted to go home now.

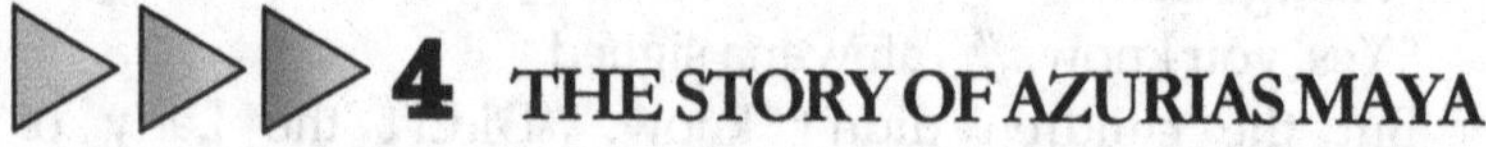

4 THE STORY OF AZURIAS MAYA

The the time, when the Blue Sea coast was on the brink of war, another ship-wrecked traveller left a village in the south of the Puntian continent.

He was about to cross a hostile stretch of wasteland that separated him from the civilization he needed to find. He had lost his memory after finding himself stranded on a beach, but now he needed to find a citadel and people of his own kind up north. That much he remembered.

Many moons ago, his swift Atalian ship had been on its way to Mintaka in the country of Ta Neteru, when a hurricane caused it to drift off course before the Puntian coast. A powerful wave had hurled the vessel against sharp rocks before the storm blew itself out. The next morning, members of the Ogudoni tribe found the injured man while combing the beach for useful items. There had been no other survivors.

The Ogudoni quickly bagged what they needed and picked up some driftwood before heading back home. They carried the man and a flat leather case, filled with parchments and strange instruments that he was holding to his chest.

During the weeks that followed, the tribespeople nurtured the 'Lucky One' back to health. Little did he know how lucky he had really been. The ship had drifted far south to Yam, the 'Land of the Horizon Dwellers' and out of the grasp of a cannibal tribe in the marshland up the coast.

In the care of the friendly Ogudoni, the man slowly recovered from his injuries. The shaman did his best to revive him with herbs and potions, but although he awoke after one moon, his memory remained lost for some time.

The Ogudoni came from Atlantean stock, black of face and knowledgeable in the ways of civilization. Generations ago, they had ventured across an ancient land bridge to the continent of Punt to explore new lands. Further inland, the Ogudoni had battled crude cannibals and herds of large lizards.

They had survived, but many, including the sages, who knew the traditions of old, had perished in a cataclysm. The Ogudoni were forced to retreat to the coast and the following generations knew little of their clan's heritage. During the cataclysm, the land bridge to the west had disappeared beneath the waves together with the part of Atland, they had come from. Only legends of a homeland across the great water remained, and the echo of a once-great nation.

*

The traveller slowly regained his memory and even learned Izi-Dogo, the language of the tribe. He remembered his name - Azurias Maya - and that he had once lived on a big island far in the north-west. Understanding the language allowed him to listen to the rawi in the village square tell of fertile plains around an inland sea, the Mer Wer, at the heart of this paradise, teeming with wildlife.

They told of happiness and abundance among the people in the land. Then the billowing sea engulfed the greatest cities of the Known World, the ground shook and gave way. The bottom of the Mer Wer lifted up, draining all its waters into a flood plain, cutting off southern Punt from the northern territories Where the swamps had dried, only a few acidic lakes remained.

The fruits of the earth were spoilt and many lives had

been lost. A few crocodilians, giraffes, hippopotamus and saurians had repopulated the hostile marshes and stories of ghosts abounded.

The ship-wrecked man listened spellbound and soon knew the story by heart. The Ogudoni showed him the leather case, with its mysterious scrolls and instruments, they had found on him. Luckily, the scrolls were only slightly damaged by seawater.

As soon as the man was well enough, he studied the artfully drawn maps of the sky. He had a faint notion that he was supposed to understand them somehow and that he himself had drawn them.

His hosts were curious about the complicated-looking instruments and especially the drawings. It was obvious to him that they showed the stars in the sky, but Azurias Maya could not yet understand their meaning.

The Ogudoni told him that he, the 'Lucky One', would remember in time, and indeed, soon much of the buried knowledge began to return.

Vaguely at first, then more and more pieces of the mosaic began to fall into place. What Azurias Maya remembered was astonishing: He was an astronomer from Algiras, the capital of Atland. This was the island in the northwest, and that he worked at the great observatory in the hills outside of Algiras.

During routine observations of the firmament, something very unusual had caught his eye. His calculations indicated that in a faraway solar system, one of the heavenly bodies was moving in the opposite direction around its sun. The other planets moved in the same direction. An unbelievable discovery! To share his exciting findings, with the most eminent astronomers of his generation, he had set ship for the country of Ta Neteru in Eastern Punt. It was a centre of astronomy with its large libraries and universities.

Every day Azurias Maya remembered a little more and

the desire to go north and find his own people grew stronger inside him.

The Ogudoni were not willing to accompany Azurias Maya. The fear of ghosts and the Badlands was too overpowering. So he decided to leave on his own. To repay the good people, who had saved his life, the astronomer taught them what he knew about the stars.

He drew pictures of heavenly bodies in the sand and taught them their names.

The villagers had never heard of such things before and found the dog star most intriguing. Soon they began to enact the stories in dances, with costumes to match. The chief's son, a rawi in training, was selected to memorize the information. It was the only thing he had to give in return for the hospitality of the Ogudoni people.

Soon, the famous astronomer Azurias Maya from Atala prepared to leave the village on the coast.

The only problem was that he had to pass through the Badlands and the torrid hot centre of the Badlands.

Whether he would find support or would have to defend himself, was anybody's guess, but Azurias Maya had no choice. There were no seaports along the western Puntian coast and if he ever wanted to see his people again, he had to cross the Badlands.

He left the village of the Ogudoni on a waxing moon. The Ogudoni gave him last words of advice: Cannibal tribes, who had taken the land from early settlers, and herds of great lizards were to be expected en route and he had to brave these hazards on his own. Azurias Maya promised to be careful.

Soon, he crossed hills, rainforest and reptile-infested rivers and finally the swamp and sand dunes that encroached on fertile farmlands.

He encountered herds of dangerous saurian and barely made it across the river alive. Instead of cannibals, he met friendly locals, who helped with food and shelter and refilled his hollowed-out gourds with fresh water.

Azurias Maya pressed on and soon approached the edge of the Badlands.

A flock of vultures alighted suddenly from a group of dead trees, giving him a mighty fright. The large birds busied themselves with the remains of an elephant that saurians had killed and left half-eaten.

This place was a far cry from the gentle, rolling hills and flower gardens of Atland, he wished to see again or even the land of the Ogudoni.

Over the ages, harsh rains had gouged out deep grooves and ridges from the stone to form strange shapes and valleys. The water had evaporated and only acidic pools were left.

As he entered this eerie place, he walked past a skeleton. Human by the looks of it and bleached white with time. The air was fetid and Azurias Maya skirted a shallow, foul-smelling lake. Its shores were encrusted with layers of salt and the water was not fit to drink. Skeletons lay half-way inside the water as if they were ready to drink. The sight made his skin crawl.

It's still time to turn back, he thought to himself, but decided to keep going. Not far now, he convinced himself, not far.

A black dog suddenly emerged from a rock formation straight ahead of him. It had pointed ears and a long snout and its master had died of thirst a fortnight ago. The animal had somehow managed to survive. Nervous and alert to noises, the dog instinctively located another living soul.

At first, Azurias Maya shooed the dog away.

"Go, go!" He yelled and threw stones. Perhaps it was diseased and might bite. Then he got used to the animal and even welcomed its presence in the wasteland. He had even named the dog Nubi, for no particular reason.

The animal had learned to seek out hidden water and help himself to small lizards and rodents and this was now to the man's advantage.

When they rested on the third day, he poured a little water in a depression in the rock for the dog to lap up.

Overnight they had become friends.

They shared dried strips of meat for supper and half a fat cake full of nuts, grains and dried berries in the morning, but Azurias Maya didn't find water even on the fourth day and his provisions began to dwindle. Without water, he would not make it to the other side of the Badlands. Then his situation became even worse.

A sandstorm swept over the dry land and man and dog raced over the crunchy salt crust just in time to hide in a cavity in the rocks before the stinging cloud of sand reached them.

Sand began to pile up outside the cave and the scientist desperately tried to dig the mound away from the opening. The space inside was too shallow to hold much air and after a few hours, the man began to lose consciousness while the storm blew itself out.

Nubi whined and licked his hairy face, but the man would not wake up. So the dog began digging. He managed to work his way through the pile of sand and stormed out of the small cave, sniffing the air.

Azurias Maya had not been aware of it, but he had almost reached the other side of the Badlands by now.

It smelled like - humans. Nubi barked and barked and caught the attention of two desert dwellers, who were inspecting their far-flung fresh water wells after the sand storm.

The men were wrapped in wide tunics and veils against the gritty wind and harsh sun. They drank from the well and offered the dog some water. Nubi drank thirstily, then ran forth and back and made a racket, so that they eventually followed him back to the tiny cave. The dog began to dig and the men helped him.

That's how Antar, the desert prince, and his man found

the famous astronomer from Atala. Azurias Maya came to and sat in a stupor.

"Shelanti athenai, shelanti," he kept saying. "Shukri, you saved my life."

Azurias Maya had escaped certain death for the second time.

Antar and his men lived in the settlement of Engaddi, a jewel-like oasis on the northern edge of the Badlands, not far from the town of Sakhara.

"We'll take you to Engaddi. To safety," Antar said.

He placed Azurias Maya on his horse and took him without delay to a gorge halfway to Engaddi, where wild camels had found a home. Long ago, settlers from Bakhtria had brought a handful of the animals with them. Uncomfortable with the humid conditions, the camels had escaped south and found a new home in the cooler gorge, protected against the scorching sun and searing winds. Small caves in the gorge, still covered with drawings of animals and dancing people, were no longer inhabited.

Freshwater pools lay hidden among the rocks, sustaining them. A lone mastodon family also dined on gigantic ferns and grasses on either side of the pools. It was a holy place to the oasis dwellers of Engaddi.

The men dipped cups made of dinosaur eggs into the cool water and gave it to Azurias Maya to drink. He drank until he could no more. The last thing he saw was the view of the mountains turning dark one by one in the sinking sun.

He awoke in Engaddi with sore eyes and a throbbing head. Long shadows of the date palms were slanting across a dusty road and green fields. A woman drew water from a well outside and a group of children played a noisy game of Pigsnout. It reminded him of his home in Atland.

Nubi, the dog, slept on the ground next to the comfortable hammock, he was resting in. The colourful door screen was pushed aside and one of the men, who had rescued him, entered the room. He removed his headscarf and smiled broadly. "Shalantai, my name is Antar of Engaddi. Are you feeling better?"

"Shelanti, athenai. I am Azurias Maya of Algiras and much indebted to you for saving my life."

The desert prince bowed slightly and flashed his white teeth. "You shall repay the favour to another worthy soul one day." He said, as was the custom. Antar's men had come to the rescue of many caravans in the desert and saved many lives.

"For sure, for sure," Azurias Maya said.

Nubi pricked his ears, facing both men as if he understood their conversation.

"As fate has it, a north-bound caravan will be leaving for Sakhara in the morning. Azurias Maya and his four-legged companion may join the caravan," Antar said.

He indicated the time of departure by stretching his arm out at a flat angle. At sunrise then.

"The Earthmother be thanked," Azurias Maya sighed. "Shukri, prince Antar. Shukri merbani."

The sun had barely hoisted itself over the horizon when the leader of the caravan, a veiled Konk by the name of Tomi, gave the signal for departure. A long line of rather small elephants, a few saurians and shaggy mokis laden with goods, fell into step behind each other.

Azurias Maya rode on the back of a placid moki that sometimes looked woefully back at him during their journey. Nubi trotted next to the moki and barked a little with excitement now and then. It wasn't difficult to keep up as the caravan dawdled leisurely along the narrow path.

The astronomer didn't mind the slow pace. Riding was better than walking anytime and at last, his strenuous journey was coming to an end. He would request help from the Lady and maidens of Sakhara and then return across the Atlantean Sea to his home in Atland.

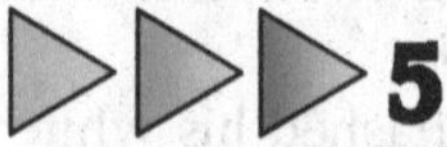 **5**   **ROAD OF NO RETURN**

The pilot had been told to offload Tafawana and the children in the town of Felsina in the Mâ-Rock Mountains and return with the citadel vimaan to Hyela at once. Warfare was no laughing matter and the warlords needed every available vimaan in their battle against the Guebras.

They landed smoothly in the misty yard of the citadel. In a few days, the time travellers would board a vimaan to the city of Kem-Oun, where the blue Nila River split up into a great delta of rivers and rivulets.

"The three children will explore the land of Ta Mery and its culture at the invitation of the Lady of Cydonia," Tafawana explained to the Lady of Felsina.

"Very well if the good Lady of Cydonia so wishes," The Lady said. "Her guests are our guests. May you all be welcome."

"Thank you, honourable Lady. First, we will travel to Kem-Oun, then on to Ush-bantoun to visit the Festival of Sokhar and later to Rostau, down south along the Nila River."

"Such a long journey for these three children from Alesia?"

"That's what the honourable Lady of Hyela agreed to. Surely by the time they return to our lovely port city, the troublesome giants will have withdrawn to their wretched islands again. The children will board a ship and safely return to Alesia."

It was the end of the spring monsoon when frequent showers in the foothills soaked the green slopes for weeks at a time. Soon they would make way for a fairly dry summer before the cold winter rains returned in autumn. Felsina had greeted their vimaan with mud, mist and rain. Lots of rain - and it didn't get any better.

Felsina was surrounded by a dense green mountain forest, full of horsetail ferns, mosses and liverwort, which enveloped even some of the houses. A constant trickle of spring water dripped down from higher-lying ground and one small river had decided to change its course and now ran right across the main road in town.

"It's really wet here," Chryséis said and shivered.

"Well, we won't stay here for long. Tomorrow morning we'll be off to a warm and dry Ta Mery," Tafawana said in a reassuring tone.

But when they were preparing for the night, unsettling news reached the citadel: King Psammetich of Felsina got himself killed while pursuing a wild boar in the thick forest.

He had been a good king and there was much weeping and mourning among his loyal subjects. During preparations for the funeral, nobody was to leave Felsina, especially since foul play was suspected.

The day before, the rains had stopped for a short while and King Psammetich had ridden out with a small hunting party to bring back wild boar and fallow deer for the citadel table. For this purpose, he often employed the help of friendly forest fauns, who lured the animals towards nets between the trees. The fauns played enticing melodies on their double flutes and fine harps that the curious animals followed.

But this time, something had gone tragically wrong.

The king's noble steed of excellent breeding had suddenly reared, spooked by a sudden movement in the underbrush. The trusted animal stumbled on the slippery rocks and the king was flung against a boulder. That's how he met his untimely death. Then it began to rain again. It rained and rained and the rain came down in long silvery threads. Humidity hung thickly in the air and a grey sun showed itself only here and there, veiled in clouds. The happy twittering of forest birds had died down and all the usual sounds were muffled.

Rumours began to spread: had there not been talk of too much hunting in the forest? Had the forest elves turned against their human neighbours with black magic?

Obéa was as much feared in the Mâ-Rock Mountains as in the rest of the Known World. People became distrustful of the forest dwellers.

"The 'House of Truth' will act fast. There will be a funeral, then we will be on our way again," Tafawana assured the children. "Surely you can see that it would be improper to leave Felsina now."

Chryséis rolled her eyes. "I can't believe this. Is our trip jinxed or something?"

"Nah, just a minor glitch," Trevor said. "In any case, it gives us a chance to catch up with our log book."

It took the 'House of Truth' exactly three days to establish that no magical elfin arrow had found its way into the king's heart. The findings of the 'House of Truth' were beyond question. The forest fauns were vindicated.

The Lady of Felsina apologised publicly to the faun king to keep the peace in the realm. Now the funeral preparation could begin. It rained during the announcement and did not stop and while all of this was going on, a successor of the good king had been found by the senate.

"At least, it didn't take them too long to come up with a new king," Trevor said.

"A stupid idea to come here in the first place," Katherine complained. "I'm going to climb out of my skull if this rain doesn't stop."

"I thought you were used to the rain," Trevor grinned.

"That doesn't mean, I must like it."

"And I don't like funerals!" Chryséis moaned. "It's always so sad - and what are we supposed to do there? A wedding would be better. Remember how much fun we had in Cydonia?"

"This funeral doesn't sound like much fun," Trevor said.

"But we don't have a choice. So we have to go to a funeral."

The official, who had brought the news of the impending funeral rites, had heard those last few words as he was about to leave the room.

"Fun? What is fun?" He looked miffed.

He didn't understand what the children were babbling on about, but he thought, he should let them know, how impolite they were. Trevor remembered the Akkadian word. "Ehm, I guess you would call it jollity."

The official was puzzled. He frowned. The children looked at each other. People in Oinotria were so touchy! What was wrong with the word 'jollity' now? Adults in Hyela had also been so serious about everything.

All three of them tried to speak at the same time. They explained how much they regretted the good king's demise. Really. The funeral would be very solemn and festive, no doubt. Just being confined to the citadel quarters by the constant rain, was not very uplifting.

They saw the frown on the official's forehead disappear. He unruffled his feathers and gave them a weak smile. Children!

"Athenai, we do have jollity in Felsina," he said. "We might not be in Ush-bantoun or Hyela or even Rostau… but there are plays and concerts and festivals. During more appropriate times."

They looked down at the ground and mumbled. "Of course, athenai."

"We have heated pools," the official said proudly, "…and a 'House of Knowledge," he paused. "…and good food."

The time travellers were nodding to everything the man said and took mental notes. Heated pools and a library? That sounded interesting. But the man wasn't finished yet.

"…and what greater jollity is there than a purposeful life?" he said, creasing his forehead again with an air of propriety.

"For sure, for sure," Trevor said. This guy really went off on a tangent! But it was important that the citadel official seemed appeased.

"Very well then, athenai. I must be on my way." The official nodded and left.

"Close shave!" Chryséis said. "Imagine we get arrested for not being sad enough about their dead king."

"Yeah, imagine!" Katherine said and watched the rain drip off the overhanging roof outside their window. "I'm tired of just updating our log book. We have to do something or I'm going bananas."

"Can't risk that now, can we?" Trevor said.

"Oh, you think..." Chryséis said. She referred to her crazy decision to time-travel alone. "Perhaps, I was also a bit nuts then..."

"Yes, you were," Katherine said. "You could have at least done something interesting in the future and told us about it."

"I'm never gonna live that one down, am I?"

"Nope."

"Alright then," Trevor cut in. "We should do some exploring in this place. That's what we're here for, right?"

They decided to give the Felsinian hot pools a go. One of the maidens gave them dark cloaks to wear, called chitons or raincoats, and somewhat garbled directions.

There was much hustle and bustle in the yard, where the crowning would take place. Everybody was busy with preparations and didn't pay attention to the children.

They left through a side gate and Tepi got all excited to be outdoors. She chased the muddy road up and down and didn't give a hoot about the rain.

"Did you understand, where these hot pools are supposed to be?" Katherine asked. "I don't want to walk around endlessly in this drab weather." She threw a stick for Tepi to fetch. Chryséis and Trevor walked ahead of her on the wet main road and jumped over the little stream.

"She said we'll see the sign down there at the crossing," Trevor said, turning halfway around. Katherine also jumped and nearly fell on the slippery road.

"Careful," Chryséis cautioned and took Katherine by the

hand.

There was hardly anybody in the streets or on the square. The walkways around the square were roofed-in and fairly dry. An interesting feature, apart from the mossy statues and gurgling water features.

Water features - as if this town didn't have enough water already! They tried to ask somebody for directions, but the few people they saw, hurried past with their hood pulled down over their faces.

"So helpful," Katherine moaned.

"We should look around for the street sign," Chryséis said and sure enough, they found the sign. It had three wavy lines on it and a hand pointed to the left. Felsina was not as small as it had seemed at first. There were rows of moss-covered houses on the entire eastern side of the hill. They walked down the road and soon saw the entrance to the heated pools. Another sign with three wavy lines was held up by a statue of the god of health. It was a big building under a high tunnel-shaped roof.

They saw a long pool with lanes and small round pools filled with steaming water. The pools were fed by a bubbling fountain and against the walls were wooden stands, covered in clothing.

"Is that, where we are supposed to change?" Trevor asked.

"Are you shy?" Chryséis asked him.

"No," he lied.

"We'll just change inside our towels," Katherine said. "They are big enough. People are wearing some kind of swimsuits. I'm sure that the maiden packed some for us."

"Okay."

There was soft lighting and music seemed to waft down from the roof. And there were people everywhere!

"That's probably, why nobody is out on the streets. They're all taking a morning dip in the heated pools to warm up," Trevor stated.

"Looks like it. Not a bad idea." Chryséis started to undress inside her towel and put her clothes and shoes in a small pile on the stand. The others copied her.

They decided to let themselves down into one of the small pools and stood in the hot water for a while. It smelled faintly of lavender and of the sea.

"Look, there are stone benches along the pool wall," Katherine said.

They sat inside the round basin while Tepi guarded their things. She growled at everyone, who came too close and the Felsians walked quickly past. After about an hour, they left the pool feeling warm and very clean, and the rain didn't seem quite so unpleasant anymore.

It was barely noon when they left the pools, and the rain was still pouring down. A cooking house had opened on the square and they bought pancakes filled with fried mushrooms. They sat down on one of the benches under the roof.

"Not bad, the food," Trevor said. It was also fun to study the square and the few pedestrians walking past.

"What's that over there?" Chryséis pointed to an illuminated building with a statue in front, holding an open scroll. The statue looked like a cat on two legs.

"Must be the library." Katherine mumbled.

"Come on, finish your pancake. Let's go explore the library," Chryséis said. The only library they had seen from the inside was on the island of Atala. They had a lot more time on their hands now to look at books and scrolls and mirages. Trevor would have loved another one of those tasty rolled-up pancakes, but that would have just held them up, so he trotted after the girls.

The têrakhon windows in jewel-like colours were bright and welcoming and the tableau of the cat-statue read 'Sekmet Welcomes You'.

"Okay then, let's go in..." Trevor said and ordered Tepi to stay outside. The dog plunked herself sullenly next to the statue and didn't look up when they closed the door.

The children walked straight to one of the viewing tables that were arranged in a semi-circle. They had seen tables like that in the 'House of Knowledge' in Algiras!

"Shalanti, how may I be of assistance?" A surly-looking librarian accosted them from behind some type of counter.

He was stocky and bald with a white toga carelessly draped over his left shoulder. He gave them not his friendliest look. In fact, the librarian had hoped for a quiet afternoon with his feet up, a cup of mint tea and reading a romance scroll. Now he had to do his best to be polite and helpful to a group of children.

"Shelanti athenai, we would like to read some books, please." Katherine couldn't think of anything else to say. The librarian snorted and looked down his nose at the obviously foreign children, but he was expected to help all visitors. Even the obviously foreign ones.

"Some books, mhm, I see. Anything specific? Science? History?" Some books, I'll say! He thought to himself and sniffled a little.

"Science... and mathematics," Katherine and Chryséis said at the same time. They looked at each other and grinned. Snap. The librarian grunted and took them to one of the kidney-shaped tables with what looked like a magnifying glass mounted over it on a movable arm, just like a modern desk lamp. This was so exciting!

Books were stacked against the side of the table. The librarian seemed to disapprove of this and made a move to take them away. People were so careless, leaving books lying around like that.

"Oh, please, could we take a look at them?" Trevor begged. The librarian looked up in surprise. These books were not adequate for older children. Although the Felsinian library couldn't quite rival the famous library in Lukania or the great 'House of Knowledge' in Innu, it had certainly more to offer than this.

"So you do not want to see books on science... and

mathematics?" He mocked them.

"We do, but we want to start with these ones," Trevor said.

The librarian shrugged, adjusted his garment and mumbled something to himself. He shuffled off to fetch adequate books on science and mathematics, avoiding a book about the size of a flat washing machine that was lying on the floor!

Trevor hardly noticed it as he studied the table in front of him. He was fascinated by the table surface: rough as if a fine golden net had been welded onto it.

Trevor picked up the book on top of the stack. It looked like an open scroll and there were drawings on the parchment and large writing. They recognized some of the characters and symbols. The book was for young children, telling the adventures of a little boat on the blue Nila River.

"Whoa, look at this!" Chryséis caught a glance of the boat through the oval lens suspended above the scroll. The polished crystal lay flat in a cradle, attached to the jointed metal arm. The crystal could be taken from its fitting and laid directly onto the books, but the children didn't know that yet.

"I don't believe this —" Chryséis pulled the crystal lens closer. There it was again...

"What?" Trevor and Katherine stretched their necks to get a look through the lens. Something moved.

The little boat began to sail on the waves. The children couldn't believe their eyes! Then the scroll began to 'play' a melody - rocking the boat gently on the moving waves. The book played a boat song! With a sudden jerk, the boat sailed up into the crystal lens, making the children jump. Then it moved down the blue river again, until it was out of sight. The boat music had a lulling effect. Katherine couldn't help herself and yawned broadly.

"Must be a bedtime story. A lullaby maybe," Trevor yawned too. "Interesting."

"Do you think people can take the books out?" Katherine asked and yawned again.

"Doesn't look like it. I don't believe that everybody has a crystal like that lying around at home to read them."

"Maybe not."

The librarian suddenly appeared next to the table. A storybook for little ones, how inappropriate! He thought and placed two books on the table.

"What is that?" Katherine asked him abruptly, pointing to the magical lens.

"You ask what the reading-crystal is? Every child knows what the reading-crystal is!" The librarian scoffed. "Whatever would we do without a Ze-phir?" He shook his head. "These are made from the best su-kitok crystal." The librarian pointed to all the other tables in the empty library. "Every table has got one."

"Of course." Trevor nudged Katherine in the ribs. "It is a Ze-phir. We knew that. It's just, that we have been in Prydhain for so long... and there was no 'House of Knowledge' nearby..." He realized that he was oversharing with the unfriendly little man.

"Prydhain? Hmm." The librarian knew that a group of Cydonian children stayed at the citadel. The cobbler had told him yesterday. There was no mention of Prydhain, though. Didn't they have libraries in Alesia or even Prydhain for that matter? To his knowledge they did.

"Here children," the librarian said pointedly. "Next time you should pay better attention during your lessons – in Cydonia." He plunked a bound book on the desk.

They read the cover of the thick book: 'Science of Mathematical Expression'. The book had a striking cover made of crocodile hide. The little, bald man opened the book and waited. "You know how to use the Ze-phir, I trust?"

"Yes sure... of course. You hold it over the book and look through it," Trevor answered.

"Oh, you can do so much more than that. But it will have to do for now," the librarian said haughtily and shuffled off.

The pages were covered in mathematical symbols. Some of

the symbols and equations looked unfamiliar. Then the crystal lens began to do its magic.

The symbols began to change, paired up into equations, only to separate again, revealing incredible colours. The equations burst into sprays like miniature fireworks. They vanished and reappeared from a hundred points merging into musical compositions and kaleidoscope images. New combinations spiralled upward through the crystal, only to recede into glittering swirls.

The children stood open-mouthed. Mathematical symbols translated into colours and melodies? They had never thought of maths like that before.

Trevor cried. "Wow! That's what maths can look like?"

The bald man looked up with disapproval. Had these children been raised by Edfunians?

"Can you do that with other books as well?" Katherine blurted out. The librarian scratched his nose.

"Why of course, child." He didn't understand their amazement over something so ordinary. Thankfully, another surprise-visitor to the 'House of Knowledge' demanded his attention. The librarian adjusted his white garment with an important air and walked toward the man.

"That was so cool! I wish I could take one of those crystals with me to Pemberton. Just imagine what our schoolbooks would look like through this Ze-phir," Chryséis gushed.

"I guess nothing mind-boggling would happen. Our books aren't written that way." Trevor put a damper on her delight.

"Pity!" Katherine said. "These books here are fantastic! Couldn't we just take one of those scrolls with us?"

"No, you can't steal books from a library, Katie!" Chryséis said. Trevor tried to cheer them up. "Did you see the look on the librarian's face? I'm sure he thought that we were incredibly stupid."

"Can't blame him for that," Chryséis said. "Oh, let him think what he likes. I don't care."

They soon left the library and it began to rain heavily again as they walked back up the paved road to the citadel. Tepi trotted behind them, looking like a wet rag. She had given up on chasing imaginary rodents and wanted some food.

"I wish I had my toothbrush with me," Trevor said randomly. "I really want to brush my teeth." He'd lost his toothbrush when their ship sank during the storm.

"What is it with you and your toothbrush, Trev?" Chryséis glared at him and Katherine tried not to giggle.

"I would just like to brush my teeth sometimes, that's all…" They began to laugh.

People, coming from the citadel, whispered about the death of their good king and stared at the giggling children with disapproval. The rain nearly stopped and was only a light drizzle.

They passed a low tree with a broad crown and noticed something strange. Trevor stopped first, then Katherine and Chryséis. Was there somebody sitting in the tree? Nothing to see now - but wait - slowly, a shape reappeared on one of the branches. A man by the looks of it. A bearded young man with a turban on his head, waving at them. Tepi started barking, but stopped when the strange man with the turban held up his hand.

"Young friends," he addressed them. They looked around, but he was clearly not speaking to anybody else.

"Emm, yes?" Katherine answered slowly.

"I heard a wish uttered loud and clear," The man with the turban said, lifting his eyebrows.

"I… I don't think so. Sorry to trouble you, sir." Trevor started to walk past the tree.

"Stop right there, athenai," the man growled and waggled his beard. "Are you rejecting a Djin? A servant of the Gods?"

"A Djin? Did you say you're a Djin, as in genie? But that's not possible. They exist only in fairy tales…" Trevor stuttered.

The Djin looked somewhat puzzled.

"As far as I am concerned, fairies do not have tails. At least not the ones I know of…" he sniffled.

"No, not those kinds of tails…" Chryséis tried to explain.

"Perhaps we could hurry this up a bit. I heard a wish uttered by this young man?" He pointed at Trevor then wiped tiny raindrops off his purple velvet waistcoat. "Regarding the cleaning of teeth… with a brush?"

Trevor stared at the Djin. What? Then his face lit up. "Yes, of course, my toothbrush, I lost my toothbrush."

"Aha, I knew it. How may I help you, athenai?"

Katherine and Chryséis looked at each other. Trevor's wish must have somehow activated this genie on his tree. Maybe some type of mirage, Katherine thought.

"I lost my toothbrush during a shipwreck and I really need to clean my teeth," Trevor explained. "Can you bring it back?"

"Hoho, young man, a foreigner by the looks of it." The Djin grinned knowingly.

The drizzle stopped. Bright orange stripes stained the sky, then turned grey again while the Djin contemplated the fate of Trevor's toothbrush.

"No, I cannot bring back your toothbrush," the Djin said, "but I can show you, how to make a toothbrush." His hand swept down and broke off a twig.

"You mean you are sitting on a toothbrush tree?" Chryséis asked him wide-eyed. The tree looked small, but just like – well – a normal tree.

"Yes, indeed I am, young friend."

It was the Djin's turn to stare at the children. Didn't they know a toothbrush tree from a cedar?

He chewed the thicker end of the twig until it looked like a frazzled paintbrush. Then he held up the twig and threw a second twig to Trevor. He caught it and copied the Djin. The twig had a slightly minty taste.

Then he showed Trevor how to brush his teeth with the shredded end. He spit onto the ground and bared his – visibly - clean teeth. Trevor did the same. *Hmm not bad,* he thought, *possibly antibacterial properties.*

"What is the name of this tree?" Katherine asked the

helpful genie.

"Danticlos," the Djin mumbled with the twig-toothbrush in his mouth, "or simply toothbrush-tree."

He tossed the twig over his shoulder and folded his arms again. Assignment completed! "You will always have a toothbrush if there is a Danticlos tree around."

"What I like is that you don't need water to rinse. What if I can't find a toothbrush-tree?" Trevor frowned.

"Any fruit tree will do. Not the same, but good enough."

It started drizzling again and the Djin looked uncomfortable.

"May I now ask to be released from my duty?" He shook himself. "You may call me again when in need."

Trevor stared at the Djin "Really? Ah, yes, yes, of course, you are released…" he said. *A toothbrush tree*, he thought, who knew! Trevor was still impressed with the reading-crystal and now this. A toothbrush tree. The Djin began to fade. So he was only a mirage, after all!

"Wait, how do we get you back when we need you?" Trevor called out after him, but the Djin had already disappeared. "There must be hundreds of things he could teach us…"

"Let's go, Trev. The forest is magic. Remember? Like the one on Ruta Ynis. They also have fauns here, and Djins and who knows what else."

"That's a scary thought," Katherine said.

"But he gave me a toothbrush," Trevor grinned.

"Yes, he did - if he was real at all."

"Real enough for me. How else would I be holding this toothbrush now if he wasn't real?"

Katherine and Chryséis also tried out twigs as they walked back uphill to the citadel and wondered how a genie could just appear and disappear like that.

 **6**   # A STRANGE VISITOR

They were just sitting down to dinner in the hall when a man and a black dog arrived at the citadel. Both of them shivering and dripping wet. The rather hairy man requested hospitality from the Lady and desired to be taken to the nearest port as soon as possible. Hyela, perhaps. He looked ragged with his long, light-brown hair and rough beard and exuded an unpleasant smell.

He was possibly a hermit and had definitely not cut his hair for a while, but wore typical - if tattered - Atalian travel clothes, with fine embroidery around the neck. He had to be civilized, then. Two gourds and an obsidian knife were fastened to his belt and the colourful woven blanket around his shoulders was distinctly Puntian.

"Let me introduce myself. I am the astronomer Azurias Maya of Algiras. This memory returned to me only recently, after the ship I was travelling on capsized on the southern Puntian coast. The Ogudoni people nursed me back to health and I made my way through the Badlands to get here. I wish to return to my homeland."

"Welcome, Azurias Maya of Algiras," the Lady of Felsina greeted him. "Be our guest."

Azurias Maya inclined his head. He wasn't used to speaking so much and took a deep breath before he continued. "I must apologise for my appearance, honourable Lady, as I was taken only to the edge of the forest by a merchant from Sakhara. My companion and I have been walking through the rain for hours. Kindly allow me to dry off and change my clothes."

In order to prove that he was indeed the long-lost astronomer Azurias Maya from Algiras, he showed them drawings and instruments from a leather case slung across his chest.

So he hasn't forgotten his manners, after all, the Lady of Felsina thought and said, "I am sorry to hear your story. Many ships have suffered a similar fate on the western seacoast. These three children travelled on one of those." She waved her hand towards the time travellers. "You have my permission to change your clothing."

Azurias Maya nodded to the children in greeting. His dog began to wag his tail as soon as he became aware of Tepi, but Tepi ignored him roundly. He listened to the name of Nubi and was the exact opposite to the fluffy, light-coloured Tepi, but roughly of the same height. Nubi was black and smooth with a long snout and pointed ears that he pricked at the slightest sound and seemed rather devoted to the man.

Trevor nudged Katherine with his elbow.

"What?" She hissed, but instead of answering her, he said to the traveller, "Excuse me, sir, I mean athenai. I've heard your name before in Algiras. We learned of your unfortunate sea voyage and saw the square that was named after you. The Algirans think you are dead."

"Oh," Azurias Maya said simply. "I see. I will have to prove them wrong then."

"I guess, you will, athenai," The Lady of Felsina said.

Two servants took him to a guest room and the man returned cleaner and drier, but just as hairy as before.

Everyone around the table stared at him, as he walked to his seat at the end of the table. He removed the water containers, and his knife. Only then did he start to wolf down his food. He fed his dog morsels of venison pie and Luni cheese under the table and seemed content enough.

"Athenai, you say you hail from Atland and were shipwrecked like our young guests here?" one of the senior maidens asked.

"Yes, I am from Algiras. You hail from Atala, also, athenai?" Azurias Maya asked the children and stopped eating just long enough to ask the question. He seems to have forgotten his manners again, as he stuffed a big piece of boar meat into his mouth.

"We were visiting Algiras, honourable astronomer," Chryséis answered politely. "We are from Cydonia, travelled to Prydhain and only stayed on your beautiful island for a couple of moons. We took a ship back to Alesia one moon ago when Rimmon decided our fate on the Berberian coast." Chryséis was proud of her long speech.

"Hmm," the man with the bushy beard grunted, and that was it. After a few attempts at making conversation, the maiden gave up. He didn't seem like a famous astronomer to her at all, the way he looked and behaved.

The Lady of Felsina had his story confirmed later in the evening via thought transfer and summoned the traveller to her audience room.

While Nubi was waiting outside, Tepi had become curious and found him in the company of a junior maiden. The two dogs struck up an immediate friendship, whined and smelled each other's backsides.

"Greetings from the Lady of Algiras, honourable Azurias Maya." The Lady in the audience room inclined her head.

The astronomer settled into a comfortable chair and took a walnut biscuit from a wooden bowl on the table.

"I am told that you are indeed the same scientist, who the people of Atala assumed lost at sea and that you had been on your way to Mintaka in Ta Neteru many moons ago," the Lady of Felsina began the conversation.

"Yes, dear Lady," he said and inclined his head as well. "Had lost my memory... and now cannot communicate by thought anymore."

"That explains a lot of things," the Lady said. "We will

do what we can to reunite you with your people. In the meantime, please feel free to cleanse yourself as you see fit and visit the famous hot pools of Felsina."

A hint at his appearance, no civilised man would have missed. Azurias Maya, however, was too tired to bother right now and felt more like sleeping until morning.

The Lady read his thoughts. "Very well, honourable scientist," the Lady said. "Have it your way. Just know that Hyela is currently embroiled in a war with giants. All sea-traffic has ceased until the war ends. You are welcome to wait things out in Felsina or travel by vimaan to Kem-Oun with the maiden Tafawana and these three children from Alesia. The choice is yours."

Considering the climate in the Ma Roc Mountains and the situation in Hyela, Azurias Maya didn't have to think twice about his options.

"I will go with the maiden and the children and then travel on to Ta Neteru. Ships will surely be going west after my meetings with colleagues in Mintaka."

Things were peaceful at the citadel and Azurias Maya slept soundly. Trevor sneaked past citadel servants, who were busy decorating the hall and returned to the Danticlos tree to cut off a few twigs. He spent the rest of the evening carving toothbrushes with handles.

By the following morning, the rain had stopped and decorations were hurriedly moved back into the citadel gardens. Tafawana told her guests over breakfast that it was the day of the funeral and that the funeral rites were followed by the coronation of the newly-elected king. The new king was apparently a brother of the good king Psammetich by the name of Takelot.

"We might have to postpone your departure until the mist lifts," the Lady continued. "It is too dangerous to fly among the trees."

Back in their quarters, Katherine flopped into an upholstered chair, looking depressed. She couldn't believe their bad luck. If it wasn't a war, it was dense mist!

"Crikey, not another problem!" She said. "I'm going to grow old in this place. Perhaps this whole trip is jinxed." Even Tepi looked depressed as she rolled up in a corner of the room.

"Get a grip, Katie! I don't think we'll spend our entire lives here. And since when do you believe in such things as a jinx?" Trevor asked her. "There must be another reason."

"You don't need a reason for a jinx!" Chryséis insisted.

"Thanks a lot, Chris," Trevor said. "I say we go for a walk. Maybe to the marketplace or a concert.

Chryséis agreed. "Anything's better than sitting around, moping when it rains!"

They put on their chitons and walked down the road past the library that appeared to be closed. Then they went on to the swimming pools. It was the only way they knew. The marketplace was completely deserted and there was no concert to be seen anywhere.

"Where is everybody? The funeral is not until late morning," Chryséis wondered. "I'm sure there would be concerts all over in Algiras."

"It's probably still too wet outside," Katherine sighed. "I don't feel like going to the pools. Can't we just sit down somewhere?" They sat down on a bench by the closed cooking house.

"This whole idea of travelling to Egypt was a mistake right from the start. The port in Hyela is probably open again and we're stuck in this small rainy town," Chryséis sighed.

"If that was true, they would have taken us back to Hyela by now," Katherine said.

"What do you suggest, Chris? That we travel back to the future and forget about the Lady of Cydonia and prehistoric Egypt? Aren't you one bit curious about Pharaohs and pyramids?" Trevor shook his head.

For him, there was no contest between going back to boring school life at Pemberton and seeing ancient Egypt.

"It's too early for Pharaohs and pyramids, but I'm sure, it will be exciting," he said. "Things could be worse - like war for example. And the mists can't take long to lift."

But the mists didn't lift and by the time, they were back at the citadel, thick droplets battered the colourful têrakhon-windows.

"I'm tired of the 'Alesian Epoch'. We could be home by now," Chryséis lamented.

"Goodness, stop being such a baby. We can't let a bit of rain stop us. We wanted adventure and here it is," Trevor said. He didn't seem homesick at all.

"The 'Speaking Stone' said that… not everything that happens is predictable. And that we would have a safe if adventurous journey. And as long as we remember to be careful and trust the right people - we'll be okay."

"Alright then, here's the thing: we go to Egypt, have a good look around. Then we go back to Alesia and home through the vortex. That's it. No more adventures!" Chryséis said hotly.

"We could also stay here in Felsina and wait for the vimaan to return from Hyela," Katherine said, but she wasn't really serious.

"No thanks." Trevor looked out the window. "It looks like the rain is letting up." He shoved his hands deeper into the pockets of his chiton . The girls joined him by the window in the entrance hall.

"No, it doesn't…" Chryséis scanned the sky. "How can this be North Africa if it rains all the time?"

"Perhaps we should build an ark," Katherine joked.

"You're used to this kind of weather," Chryséis grumbled.

"Doesn't mean that I like it," Katherine said. "And as my father always says: there is no wrong weather, only the wrong clothing."

"Right, and who was all depressed just now?" Chryséis asked her.

They waited in the hall for somebody to call them

outside to attend the festivities and finally Tafawana came to fetch them.

"The funeral rites are performed at a roofed-in area by the forest, then we will take the vimaan right after the coronation here at the citadel," she said. "After the mists lift."

"I want to have her optimism," Katherine murmured.

They grabbed their backpacks and Katherine whistled. Tepi came running and they followed the maiden outside.

Suddenly, Trevor felt plucking at his sleeve. "Trev!"

"What?!" he said.

"I forgot the palmtop computer on the window sill," Chryséis said in an urgent voice.

Trevor glared at her. "Do you want to go and get it or must I go?"

"I'll get it." Chryséis sneaked back into their room without the maiden noticing. Katherine looked at Trevor, and he just rolled his eyes.

Azurias Maya trotted behind them, but he looked as unkempt as before and rather glum.

The rain stopped as they made their way along a narrow path through the mist. There were so many people under the roof by the forest that Tafawana had to push through the crowd.

A chalice with red wine was handed around and the funeral pyre was already burning when creatures of the forest appeared between the nearby forest trees. The Felsinians nodded at them and then the ceremony was suddenly over. The crowd left the smouldering pyre behind and went to the citadel.

"The king is dead, long live the king!"

The two dogs wagged their tails and performed a sort of dance, whimpering happily at each other.

The coronation site had been moved again to the citadel gardens underneath lengths of red fabric and everyone gathered around.

Nubi sniffed excitedly at the children's feet and jumped

up at Katherine to lick her nose. Katherine was surprised by the unexpected show of affection but had to laugh at the black dog's antics.

Some people laughed with her, but laughing was not right as long as the pyre was still in sight.

"Down Nubi," the hairy man said calmly and Nubi left Katherine alone and began sniffing Tepi's rear end.

"Where's Chris?" Katherine asked and Trevor shrugged his shoulders.

As the ceremony began, the first rays of sunshine broke through the thinning mist. A wonderful omen for the future of the new king's reign!

Takelot and his wife Bint-Anath held their hands up to the Lady of Felsina and swore by the Earthmother and the laws of the Known World, to look after the community to their best knowledge and ability.

The crowd jubilated and – unbelievably - the sun broke fully through the clouds, melting away the persistent mists.

Now serious celebrations started.

"Pula!" The crowd roared. "Pula!" Unsurprisingly, Pula meant both 'rain and blessing' in the Mâ-Rock Mountains. "Pula! Pula!"

"Time to leave," Tafawana said calmly.

"Got it!" a beaming Chryséis tapped on Katherine's shoulder and briefly showed her the palmtop before putting it into her backpack.

"You missed the whole thing! A minute later and you would have stayed behind," Katherine hissed at her friend.

And that's how the time travellers left this wet town in a bright red citadel vimaan, with the maiden Tafawana, two dogs and a scientist from Atala.

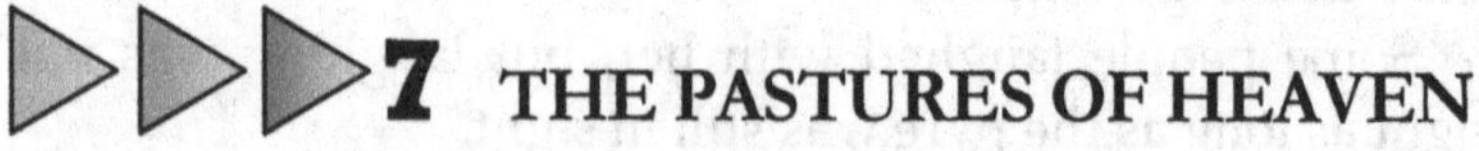

▷▷▷**7** THE PASTURES OF HEAVEN

The vimaan was on its way to Ush-bantoun even before the banquet had started. The two dogs were lying next to each other on the cabin floor and Azurias Maya was staring into the distance.

What a strange fellow, Tafawana thought. He didn't seem to listen at all when she spoke about the region they were passing through. Tafawana had apparently been raised in a farming area not far from here, before she had become a maiden in Hyela. She pointed here and there and the children tried their best to keep up with the maiden.

"This is the Vallé Silantris, famous for its bee-keeping. And over there, you can see the Vallé Cisra with large agricultural testing stations right next to the Vallé Wadjet, where the best Luni cheese is made."

As in so many countries of the Known World, the settlements were connected by a network of well-maintained roads. Now and again, flocks of birds passed the vimaan and caravans underneath. Thatched houses and bales of hay dotted the luscious fields and huts on elevated platforms were filled to the top with grains.

"I was born in 'the Pastures of Heaven' not far from here," Tafawana said with longing in her voice. "It's so nice there."

Katherine had to look twice before she realised that the hay bales were disappearing one by one from the field below.

"Tafawana, why are these bales disappearing? There is nobody on the field," she asked.

"That's because an agricultural teleporter is on the job, bringing in the hay. It's neatly stacked in barns and storage huts. Rodents and insects are controlled with crystal beams, see over there."

Agricultural teleporters? They hadn't really paid attention to such things in Alesia. They saw a net of beams running through one of the fields and Trevor took a picture of it.

"Shukri. That's very interesting," he said and pushed the micro camera back into his pocket.

The vimaan flitted past a small temple on a rise, surrounded by colourful scarecrows to keep birds away from the crops and orchards. Farm animals ripped at the new grass with great appetite and broad straw hats bobbed up and down in the fields below.

"I can't see any Konks," Katherine said.

"Maybe they don't live around here." Chryséis shrugged her shoulders.

"Oh, Konks live farther down south," Tafawana explained. "In the hills."

"Right." Katherine nodded. "This area is so green."

"Don't set her off," Trevor whispered, but Tafawana was unstoppable.

"Yes, this is a very fertile country, the 'bread basket' of the region," Tafawana said proudly. "In spring, ocean winds carry rain clouds inland. Then the rainfalls ease into drizzle just in time for planting and the villagers sing their age-old songs at harvest time, they thank the Earthmother with joyous celebrations again. What a wonderful life."

The maiden seemed to clearly suffer from home sickness.

The vimaan passed above some sort of enclosure. "The 'Sabre-toothed Cat Rehabilitation Centre' by Lake Acessa. It's one of a kind," Tafawana said. Were they sabre-toothed tigers? That was impossible! They should have died out a long time ago.

"There are only a few of those great felines left and our scientists put much effort into saving the animals. The breeding programme proved quite successful. Two of these fearsome cats will be released into the wild soon. A large reserve in the Koh Kaf Mountains has been chosen for this purpose."

"Look at that!" Chryséis pointed to an overgrown hill not far from a small lake. Huge brown cats with very long teeth rested in the high grass. They had obviously just devoured an antelope.

A large male cat growled lazily at the vimaan and three cubs played around the bloodied skeleton, pulling at the limp hide. A female stood up on her hindlegs and clawed through the air at the vehicle. This caused the driver to quickly pull the vimaan upward.

Alarmed, Nubi sat up and sniffed the air. What a suspicious scent! Tepi whimpered a little then both dogs started to howl.

Tafawana stared at them. "What din is that!"

They tried to calm the two dogs down. "Okay, okay, Tepi."

"Enough, Nubi. Down with you!" Azurias Maya ordered and the black dog lay down with a whimper. Tepi followed his example. It was the first time since they'd left Felsina that the astronomer had spoken.

Katherine chuckled. "Those are real vampire cats! No wonder, they don't like them."

"No, they are sabre-toothed cats," Tafawana explained slowly.

"Yes, they are," Trevor yawned. Not even He was suddenly hungry. "Are we going to have something to eat?"

"We will land soon and have a meal," Tafawana answered and Trevor smiled with content.

"It is not far now," the maiden told them. "To pass the time, let me tell you about the two falcon queens, who are still revered to this day."

The queens had apparently ruled side by side for sheaves of years after the Dark Age in the twin city of Ne-khen, an ancient centre.

"Ne and Khen are so close together that they are still simply called Ne-Khen. The city of Ne was ruled by the Lady of the 'White Crown' and the city of Khen was ruled by the Lady of the 'Green Crown'."

"There are pictures of the falcon queens, wearing their bird-crowns and winged bird gods painted on many walls in the 'Pastures of Heaven'. I will show you one in Ush-bantoun."

"Ah, interesting. They like birds around here," Chryséis said, but she could barely keep her eyes open.

Half an hour later, they saw a strange village with box-like houses and large windows appeared below. The houses were stacked on top of each other, and many of them had spacious, transparent domes instead of roofs. This made the clustered houses look like a pile of see-through têrakhon bubbles.

"Why are the houses stacked on top of each other like that?" Trevor asked. He felt really hungry by now.

"In the olden days, it was important for protection against surprise attacks by giant warriors. They were roaming the young countryside and took whatever wasn't tied down."

"Are there still giant warriors around?" Chryséis asked. She was wide awake again.

"No, not like in the olden days."

"That's good to know. We've had some problems with giants in the past," Katherine said and relaxed.

"Awesome," Trevor marvelled at the domes. He took pictures of the village and settled back in his seat. "What a nice village."

"Yes, it was nice, growing up here," Tafawana sighed.

"You grew up here? Who lives in those houses over there?" Katherine asked. She pointed to a number of domes on a hill, apart from the rest of the village.

"Do not point your finger, child," Tafawana reprimanded her. "Yes, I grew up here, and these are new settlers from the land of Bharata Varsha. The foreigners are… different. They keep their own company."

Katherine had no idea where these new settlers had come

from, but she didn't dare ask the maiden and listen to another lecture.

Suddenly, the vimaan started jumping around in the air. The dogs sat up and whimpered and everyone held onto their seats.

The time travellers stared at each other. In Prydhain, the vimaan they were happily travelling in, had been redirected to the Fûna Mountains by a bunch of sorcerers and they had taken Trevor prisoner. Was this black magic - again?

"What on earth!" Chryséis cried.

But this time the reason for the fault was not black magic.

Tafawana spoke briefly to the driver.

"Athenai, we are forced to land the vessel. Something is not in order," Tafawana said. She gave the driver a mental command to land the vehicle in the village of Urka, her home village.

Chryséis began to feel queasy from the sudden descent and the dogs barked as the vimaan swooped down before thumping onto village green.

"Now see what you've done," the maiden scolded the driver. "I told you to inspect this vehicle before we left Felsina…" She drew up her eyebrows.

"Honourable maiden, my apologies, there was not enough time…" The driver felt embarrassed. He knew that he should have inspected the vimaan, especially the energy cells. "With the passing of our good king Psammetich on so suddenly, the funeral and the coronation, it simply slipped my mind."

"Oh, I understand," Tafawana said grumpily. "Too late for regrets now."

A banner flapped proudly on a wooden pole. It showed a soaring falcon with one green wing and one white wing against a sky-blue background. It was the official flag of the 'Pastures of Heaven'. Every village around here had a similar flagpole on their village green. Trevor snapped a quick picture and let the camera it slip back into his pocket, before somebody noticed it.

Tafawana wasn't as cross as she acted. She knew the

village well since she had grown up here. Family on her mother's side still lived nearby and a long-overdue visit was now in order.

A number of villagers move towards the lawn as soon as the impressive red vimaan had been spotted. The see-through top opened with a smacking noise and everybody inside climbed out.

Tepi and Nubi stretched themselves at length and yawned broadly. The air smelled of moist earth, but the sun was shining.

"Stay with the vimaan, athenai, and oversee the repairs." Tafawana gave the driver a sharp order, then turned around and greeted the astonished villagers. She embraced every one of them as they were all relatives to some degree.

"What a rare pleasure, Tafawana," an elderly woman said.

"Well, it seems to please the Earthmother, aunt..." Tafawana said and introduced her travel companions. She answered questions from the village folk while they walked down the road toward a roofed-in square.

The white-washed houses were stacked on top of each other with bubble-roofs, just as they had seen from above. There were lawns and gardens on flat roofs and in the courtyards between the houses. These roofs could be accessed from the ground on narrow stairs and stepladders. Trevor was so impressed that he almost forgot his hunger pangs. "If there are giants around, that wouldn't help much," he said.

"True." Katherine waved back at a shock-haired youngster in a scarlet jacket on a garden rooftop by the square. Grazing goats and sheep climbed between rooftops and farm birds pecked the ground around the domed skylights. The animals knew their way up and down the stairs. They were looked after by shepherd-boys, who rested on the lawns, studying the shapes of clouds and chewed on long blades of grass.

The visitors enjoyed a tasty informal lunch with their hosts that tasted heavenly to Trevor. The meal consisted of cream cheese, flatbread, roasted nuts and dried mulberries.

Afterwards, the village elders studied their paizas and they answered curious questions. The children and the quiet man were given rooms in the large, multi-storied home of a village elder. The interior of the large house smelled of incense and beeswax. It reminded Chryséis of Etheridgeville far in the future.

"It smells like our townhouse back home," she sighed.

"Don't get all homesick on us again," Trevor warned her.

"I told you I won't use the vortex on my own again!" she said and inspected the carved rafters, made of scented cedar wood.

The daughter of the house, a lively girl of about fifteen by the name of Bibi Gul, was excited to see Tafawana. She was even more excited to have young visitors in the house and immediately took them under her wing.

"Ishpateh Tafawana, prusht taza?" Greetings Tafawana, Are you well? The young woman politely greeted the maiden in the local dialect.

The children didn't understand a word. The language and customs in 'The Pastures of Heaven' were Turanian. Asian in modern terms.

Bibi Gul eyed the three children curiously then asked "Kes-ke-hé?"

Who is that? Tafawana translated and answered the question.

Trevor swallowed hard, but couldn't stop himself staring at the pretty girl. Bibi Gul had the most amazing green eyes! Like deep pools, one could swim in and…

"Trevor!" Chryséis whispered. "Are you on your own planet?"

He felt himself turn red and grunted softly.

"Ishpateh baba! Ishpateh baya!" The girl said in a friendly tone and Trevor tried not to look at her directly.

Greetings sister, greetings brother.

Deep auburn lights shone in Bibi Gul's hair. What an unusual colour! He tried to listen again. The time travellers didn't understand her, but guessed that they were greeted.

"Shelanti, athenai!" they replied.

"Aah, shelaanti, shelaanti, baba, baya." Bibi Gul smiled and mirrored their greeting gestures while bowing slightly. She laughed happily. Her Akkadian was pretty good, because the village children learned it at school.

Bibi Gul took the guests upstairs to rather 'modern' looking bedrooms under têrakhon domes. Trevor had to share a room with the silent man and Nubi while the girls moved with Tepi into Bibi Gul's spacious room. The girl showed them where they could put their stuff then left the room. The view from the see-through the dome was amazing and one could even open a segment and walk onto the flat roof.

"If I ever have my own house, I want it to be like this," Katherine said. "With see-through domes and a roof garden."

"Of course, you will have your own house one day - back home - and I'll come to visit you. We'll sit on the roof garden and look at the stars," Chryséis said.

"With a telescope..." Katherine mumbled dreamily.

"A big one."

"I feel like a tourist here. No drama and no near-death experiences."

"Don't jinx it. Just look at those blue flowers out there," Chryséis sighed.

"And no rain!"

The girls were done in no time and walked down the stairs. They passed a small niche with the painted figurine of a smiling woman on a stone ball.

"Is this Aïma?" she asked Bibi Gul, who met them on the stairs.

"No, friend, the name Aïma is not well-known around here. The Earthmother is called Jestak. She protects the home."

"I see," Chryséis said and thought, why do they always have to rename their gods everywhere?

The pedigree of so many gods was still confusing to the

time travellers. The farther east they travelled, the more gods there were. Every country had a different name for the Earthmother alone.

They sat in the hall for a while and listened to Bibi Gul play the harp. Soon it was time for another meal and they sat down around a low table. . Bibi Gul's father joined them for the meal but he had to leave soon on important business.

Bibi Gul brought bowls with aioli, pickled vegetables, roasted walnuts pounded into a paste with olive oil and a plate with bread rings. Walnuts were an important ingredient in village cooking

Afterward the meal, Bibi Gul decided that it was time for a little sightseeing around Urka. She put on a loose coat and draped it carefully over one shoulder. She gave each of the children a coat and showed them how to put it on.

Azurias Maya had retired to his room, but Nubi, his faithful dog, followed Tepi and the children outside. Actually, Nubi needed to go outside rather urgently.

There were many walnut and mulberry trees in Urka, lining the streets along the village green. Each family cared for at least one of the trees and the village folk shared the nuts and fruits in autumn.

They walked past a patch with longish pumpkins and all sorts of leafy vegetables. Bibi Gul proudly told them about the time when pumpkins grew so big, an entire family could feast off a single one for a week.

"Can you imagine them as lanterns with cut-out grinning faces at Halloween?" He asked Chryséis.

"Sure, why not."

Bibi Gul took a paved road out of the village. Yellow fields turned out to be planted with wheat and sylphium, a yellow-flowering herb, next to blue lavender.

"Sylphium is very popular during wedding ceremonies," Bibi Gul explained. She became more talkative by the minute and asked questions about life in Alesia.

"What is Cydonia like? Is it strange to have so many

giants around?" She had never seen a giant in her life. "And what are the schools like? Are the teachers nice?"

She barely noticed that the Alesian boy didn't say very much but Katherine and Chryséis answered her questions eagerly.

This wasn't easy considering that they didn't actually come from Alesia. She found their answers very interesting and a lively conversation was underway when they passed the village necropolis. Generations of villagers were buried here. Round buildings with thatched roofs served as walk-in family tombs.

"Custom demands the breaking of dishes at the end of a funeral," She told them and actually opened the door of one of the round tombs for her new friends to have a look inside. Wooden statues of the ancestors sat in wall niches, painted and dressed all around the painted walls.

"Creepy!" Trevor mumbled.

"All the doors face west toward the 'Land of the Dead'," the girl said before they left the grave. Land of the Dead? That could be Atland.

They passed a farmer, who led a strange-looking beast of burden into Urka. The animal had a thick, green-speckled hide and balanced two baskets hanging across its back that contained large eggs.

"Ishpateh," he greeted them and went his way.

Bibi Gul showed them three greenhouses with large windows, where strawberries grew to the size of tomatoes. Most of the fruits and vegetables were unknown to the time travellers. The greenhouses were quite similar to the agricultural testing station in Cydonia, just that the plants were grown for food, not scientific research.

"So everybody can just walk into a greenhouse and take fruits they want?" Trevor asked.

"But of course, "answered Bibi Gul surprised.

The workers welcomed the children and gave each of them a strawberry to chew on. They were the best, juiciest strawberries they had ever tasted. They were allowed to stroll around the place by themselves. As it turned out, the people in the village were vegetarians, so the goats and sheep were used only for milk and wool. Baskets with blue eggs were placed outside the entrance of the next greenhouse. They reminded them of harpee eggs, just that they were much bigger.

Red berry juice dripped onto Bibi Gul's chin and she laughed at her mishap. They left the greenhouses and took another road that forked to the right, past a large windmill and blue flowering fields. Small sturdy horses and mokis grazed on a paddock and a water wheel clattered incessantly. Trevor picked some lavender and made the girls smell the fragrant flowers.

Then Bibi Gul had a surprise in store for them. She led her friends through an apricot orchard, where red butterflies fluttered between the fruit trees to another field. They saw people in white suits with helmets and rows of small cone-shaped huts. Nubi and Tepi gambolled between the trees of the orchard, chasing shrieking guinea fowl.

"I give up. Are those astronauts? No way!" Chryséis rubbed her eyes to make sure she wasn't dreaming.

Bibi Gul walked on and the time travellers soon realized that these people weren't astronauts at all, but bee-keepers. All around the lower part of the helmet was a broad flap made of fabric. Not exactly what astronauts would wear.

The beekeepers greeted Bibi Gul and her guests and went back to work. Honey farmers had their hands full at this time of year.

One of the bee farmers, Bibi Gul's uncle Naitan of Mimra, stopped to greet them with his helmet under his arm.

"Ishpateh Bibi Gul, prusht taza?" "Greetings Bibi Gul, are you well?"

"Ishpateh, uncle Naitan."

"Shelanti, athenai." He had heard of the unexpected visitors and greeted the children in perfect Akkadian.

"Shelanti," they greeted him back.

Bees hummed through the air, but didn't come near them. The bee-keepers used smoke of pine needles and eucalyptus leaves to calm the bees. Bibi Gul picked up a large spoon with smouldering pine needles and waved it carefully around. She took a honeycomb from a covered bucket and they were allowed to taste honey from a small earthen jar that was shaped like a beehive. Bibi Gul called the wax terâ and bees api as they ate more honey. The honey tasted of lavender and rosemary and they ate more of it. But then, bees started buzzing around the children.

"Is it safe to go near the bees without a suit?" Chryséis asked. She felt nervous with all these stinging insects around.

"It is quite unusual for them to behave like this," Naitan said. "If they don't feel threatened and don't swarm, there are no problems. I wonder what excites them so much." He gave her an encouraging smile.

"Unusual?" Trevor felt uneasy.

"Sometimes they take a dislike to electromagnetic frequencies, but we have it under control. Now if you will excuse me, athenai, I must go back to work. Not too close to the hives Bibi Gul ... bayartai. Goodbye."

"Do you think it could be unusual electromagnetic frequencies around us?" Chryséis asked Trevor.

"Could be, but I heard that bee stings can be painful..."

"Yes, and if one of us has an allergy, it could get dangerous."

They walked away from the beehives and to their relief, the bees didn't follow them. The buzzing faded.

"Wax is used to make têrakhon," Bibi Gul said, "but I'm sure, you already knew that."

Têrakhon was the mysterious substance the children had often come across in the Known World. Sometimes it looked like glass, sometimes like plastic or rubber.

"Sure..." The children nodded and looked at each other.

"Mastix resin is also used," Bibi Gul said. "Mastix or any

other type of resin, but how têrakhon looks in the end, depends on technology."

"How do you know all of that?" Chryséis asked. At last, somebody told them how têrakhon was made, and now they wanted to know more!

"Everybody knows that. The other ingredients and exact procedures are usually secret. There are technicians, who specialise in the production." That's all Bibi Gul could tell them.

"It would be great if we could take the formula for têrakhon back to the future," Chryséis said to Katherine.

"There must be a number of formulas, but where do we find them?"

"Maybe we'll find out at one of the libraries," Chryséis said.

"Hmm, could be."

"Honeybees are very useful," Bibi Gul told them and picked a ripe apricot. "Here, pick a fruit for yourselves... There is also têra-api, a form of medicine, used in the "House of Life" next to the bathhouse. Live bees are used to sting a patient's skin to cure illnesses."

They were back on the main road now.

"Ouch, that sounds painful!" Trevor said.

"It's good for rheumatic conditions. The bath master in every village uses bees' venom for têra-api."

"Ooh, just imagine..." Katherine shook herself. The thought alone gave her goosebumps. "I prefer the devices, medics use in Cydonia."

"A yes we also have those, of course," Bibi Gul said.

"Is there a 'House of Knowledge' in Urka?" Katherine asked. Might as well check out the têrakhon formulas while they were here.

"No, athenai not here. We don't have many books in the village. But there is a big library in Ush-bantoun. Isn't that, where you are headed?"

 **8**   **CAVE DWELLERS**

In the evening, they ate shishaou, a flatbread that was filled with goat's cheese and crushed walnuts then baked over open fire. They were also given wooden bowls with mashed pumpkin spiced with cinnamon.

After the meal, Bibi Gul's father joined his friends for musical practice.

"I have an idea," Bibi Gul said. "Let's go and explore a cave near Lake Dudaka."

"Sure, why not," Trevor said eagerly.

"She has so much energy," Katherine sighed.

"Beats sitting around in a citadel with nothing to do when it's raining cats and dogs outside," Trevor answered.

"Alright then, let's go."

Azurias Maya wanted to rest and Nubi stayed behind with him. Tepi was jumping around, looking forward to some exercise, even without her new friend! They greeted village women cleaning vegetables in flat colourful baskets in front of their houses, enjoying the warm sun rays before the dusk set in.

"Mind the weather, Bib Gul!" One of the women said. "It smells like rain to me."

"Rain? But there are no rain clouds in the sky," Bibi Gul answered.

"Mind the weather, children," the woman repeated.

They found a path over the rough terrain outside the village, up and down a few slopes, until they reached a low hill next to the lake.

Tepi began to bark and charged ahead of the group. She growled and barked a few times and ran towards a craggy rock. The rock was camouflaged with grey-green lichen and moss. They all jogged up the hill to see why Tepi was so excited. Before they reached the mossy rock, there was a hissing meow. Then they saw a large cat. An overgrown red tabby glared at the excited dog, baring its teeth. Ready to lunge, its nose and whiskers were quivering and its fangs were exposed. The cat looked dangerous enough.

Trevor positioned himself protectively in front of the girls, but Katherine pushed past him and whistled. The spell was broken. Tepi retreated and sat down at Katherine's feet. Looking up at the girl with big questioning eyes. The scary wildcat looked startled for an uneasy moment, then climbed nimbly up and was gone.

"Tepi, what were you thinking?" Katherine scolded. "This cat was much bigger than you. It's too big to chase!"

Tepi gave Katherine a heart-melting look with her tail between her legs. Perhaps rolling onto her back would help. They had to laugh and she was soon back on her paws, joining in with happy barking.

"That cat was nearly the size of a puma," Trevor said, "It would have made mincemeat of Tepi."

"Oh, I think you are exaggerating, Trev. It was more some kind of wildcat."

"Didn't look like a pussycat to me," he insisted.

Bibi Gul seemed quite used to such encounters. She turned around and waved them on. It was getting late and she wanted to show her new friends something. Why make a fuss about a wildcat? They ate rats and mice and this one had not been particularly big.

"Come athenai, I want you to see this cave!"

It turned out to be a roosting cave for bats. One of many in the area. The farmers didn't mind the bats. They ate obnoxious insects in the pistachio and laurel forests.

Sometimes after dark, entire armies of bats took to the

skies, chasing flying insects in long wavy columns and dipping into Lake Dudaka, drinking water in mid-flight. On such occasions, some of the daring bats fell prey to crocodiles, lying in wait at the far end of the lake, but it didn't seem to deter the bats.

Tepi growled. Without warning, a blood-curdling shriek came from the top of the hill. Then another shriek and another. The children flattened themselves against the rock, hoping that it would make them invisible. Bibi Gul pulled a startled Trevor back just in time as two eagles swooped on the bats as they sailed out of the cave. The eagles retreated quickly to lofty heights with two limp bodies in their sharp claws.

"Oh, my…" Katherine was deeply impressed. Tepi growled and let out a hacking bark. "Sshhh, Tepi. You don't want them to think you are prey!"

"Messengers of the Bird God," Bibi Gul said.

"There is a Bird God?" Trevor whistled through his teeth.

"If there are bird queens, why shouldn't they have a Bird God?" Chryséis asked, but the eagles stayed away.

They saw in the dim light that snakes were suspended from the cave walls, snapping at flapping bats. Other snakes just lay in wait on the ground. The stench at the mouth of the large cave was strong and Bibi Gul motioned that they should leave and they strolled back towards Urka.

Bibi Gul pointed to a strange landscape in the distance. In the failing light, crater-like pits looked like a lunar landscape. They saw something move around the entrances to underground dwellings.

"That's where the heavy-built, hairy Matmatis live", she explained. "Village kids sometimes dare to sneak close to the Matmatis out of curiosity. They return wide-eyed with stories of the Wildmen eating fried lizards and bats," Bibi Gul told them.

"How do they catch the bats, with slingshots?" Trevor wanted to know.

"I cannot tell you, athenai, but it seems likely. We better make our way back. It really looks like rain."

"Oh, not again. I think we've had enough rain in Felsina," Chryséis sighed.

It grew darker and they couldn't see how the two large eagles winged back to the Matmati village with their prey and dropped it off with a large Matmati man. Then they returned to the cave for more bats.

When the children reached the road, the weather turned and thick raindrops splattered onto the paving stones all around them, leaving dark marks. They began to run and soon reached the village. The children ran past the musicians, who had been practicing on the village green and were now fleeing from the rain into the safety of their homes.

Tepi charged ahead into the house. She shook herself dry and the children screeched.

"Don't do that, Tepi. Not inside!" Katherine scolded her. They took off their wet raincoats and Bibi Gul showed them, where to hang them up.

"What an adventure," Chryséis marvelled. "First the wildcat, then the bats, snakes and eagles and now we are all wet."

By now the rain came down really hard, drumming against têrakhon domes and windows, but it was cosy inside.

"Not rain again!" Katherine moaned. It felt as if they had never left rainy Felsina. "Is the rain going to last?"

"It usually clears up in the morning," Bibi Gul explained. "But you never know. Rain is good for the plants."

"I'm sure the vimaan will be ready soon. We should ask Tafawana when we can leave," Trevor suggested.

They hadn't seen the maiden Tafawana the whole day. Bibi Gul had told them that she was visiting her extended family. "She will be back tomorrow, I'm sure. Pity that you have to leave so soon, athenai. I liked having you around."

"Yes, we also liked being here and thank you so much for your hospitality, but we have plans as you know."

"I know." Bibi Gul nodded.

They joined her father and the two dogs in front of the bricked fireplace. He was polishing his wood instrument vigorously and wasn't in the mood to talk, so they chatted a bit and drank steaming cups of mint tea.

Azurias Maya had gone out to the hot swimming pools for a good bath and to see a barber and when he came back, they barely recognised him. His hair was cut in a short Alesian style and his beard was gone.

The famous astronomer looked much younger and truth be told, he smelled much better too. Nubi sniffed at his legs and frowned when he sat down on the window seat in front of the fireplace.

His attitude had changed with his appearance. He leaned back, held his teacup and was soon telling them what had happened to him since his sea voyage more than four seasons ago.

"Oh please, athenai, tell us more about your adventures!" Bibi Gul begged and clapped her hands.

"Very well," he said and thought for a moment.

He told them about the storm, the shipwreck, the Ogudoni people and the recovery from his injuries. How he had made his way from the 'Land of the Horizon Dwellers' to Northern Punt to find his people left them speechless.

"I wish this not on an enemy, for I had lost all knowledge of my origin, my family, my country. All memory had vanished from my mind like a small cloud from a hot summer's sky. The good Ogudoni people salvaged my leather case with drawings and instruments. Without them, I doubt I would have remembered and be here today."

"Hear, hear…" Bibi Gul's father said with compassion.

"Nubi, my dog, adopted me somewhere in the Badlands. A terrible place of death and sickness, I can tell you."

"You are a famous astronomer from Algiras. I'm sure, the people back home will be thrilled to have you back,"

Trevor said.

"I'm glad to hear that I am not completely forgotten... I must find a seaport where ships sail towards the sinking sun," the astronomer concluded.

"Tafawana said you'd come with us. We are on our way to Egypt... I mean to Ta Mery." Trevor caught himself just in time.

"Yes, athenai. I will go to Ta Mery with you, because the seaport of Hyela is under attack..." He said then stopped. His head was obviously aching again.

The others exchanged worried looks.

"Azurias Maya of Algiras, you should go and seek help from medics at a 'House of Life'. They will surely be able to help with your...condition of the mind," Bibi Gul's father said and put his instrument away. "My daughter can show you the way."

Trevor shot the pretty girl a sideways glance and turned slightly pink. Chryséis nudged Katherine and they both grinned.

"The medics in the Black Land might be able to help. I should rest now. Would you good people be able to prepare an infusion of willow bark? It usually helps with the pain."

Azurias Maya stood up abruptly, dropping his blanket onto the window seat, and withdrew to the room he shared with Trevor.

"Why don't you relate your own adventurous journey, young athenai?" Bibi Gul suggested.

So, Chryséis, Trevor and Katherine told of their own misfortune of being shipwrecked on the Berberian coast, about the Tăzilian nest village and how they had come to travel to this place instead of taking a ship back to Alesia. Bibi Gul asked excited questions, while Nubi stretched his limbs and yawned noisily. Tepi jumped to her feet and begged Katherine with big eyes to let her go outside with her new friend.

"Okay," Katherine said softly and smiled, stroking the dog.

"If the rain persists, swarms of thousands of locusts could descend on the farmlands any time. Not to speak of other insects," Bibi Gul's father changed the subject. "A serious cause for concern. The angle of laser beams needs to be adjusted, in order to compensate for an insect invasion. Our bats alone will not be enough."

"Yes, father. A serious cause of concern, but I believe that our guests are tired."

"Of course, my daughter, thank you for being so considerate."

"I should go and see where the dogs have run off to," Katherine said.

"I'll come with you," Bibi Gul offered. "You don't know your way around the village yet."

"I'll also come," Trevor said. He didn't feel like talking to the astronomer, in case his mood had changed again.

"I'm tired. I'll go to bed." Chryséis yawned.

Wet goats grazed peacefully on the village green. They hardly noticed the rain through their thick fur. It was so dark that they couldn't see much of the village at all, but the dogs were yapping at the goats. The children didn't notice how curious eyes were following them around.

"This is like Oxford in autumn!" Katherine sighed.

"Must feel like home to you." Trevor mocked her.

"Sure Trev, in Oxford, we also have houses with carved cedar beams, see-through domes and all that," Katherine grumbled.

Bibi Gul couldn't follow the exchange in English and began to chat in Akkadian, but it was soon time to go back.

In the morning raindrops hung from palm fronds and shrubs like tiny crystals. Trevor decided to take a short walk around the village. He bumped against a low magnolia branch, heavy with raindrops, and an unpleasant shower came down on his head.

Then the sun peeked through the thinning cloud

blanket and the boring grey receded as if by magic. Trevor saw a clutch of tiny pink blooms by the roadside and picked some of the fragrant gillyflowers on a whim. He heard singing coming from a corner of the square. The village choir practised for a competition with neighbouring villages. Tepi had joined him by now.

"Come, let's go back to the house and see if they have some breakfast for us. I'm starving." Trevor said to the dog. She looked up at the boy and started chasing up and down the road to the laughter of the singers.

Indeed, the others were about to sit down for breakfast.

At least not frogs and cockroaches, Katherine thought, as she made herself comfortable on a thick cushion. She hoped that she would never again be asked to eat a meal like the one they'd had in Prydhain.

After breakfast, which consisted of spinach omelette with chickpeas, Tafawana returned and announced that the vimaan had been repaired.

It was time to depart.

To say goodbye, the villagers rubbed their noses just like Eskimos. Trevor just nodded and turned around, while Azurias Maya mumbled something that sounded like goodbye.

Chryséis parted with her pink veil as a gift to Bibi Gul. The girl clapped her hands with delight. She rubbed her nose against Chryséis's nose and assured her new friend that she would cherish the veil immensely.

"Bayartai. Goodbye!" "Bayartai!" Some of the villagers had come to see the visitors off. They all climbed into the vimaan and the têrakhon top closed with a sucking noise. It lifted off the soft green grass and soon disappeared on the horizon.

When Bibi Gul went home, she found a sweet-smelling bunch of small pink flowers on her coat, she had tossed onto the window seats the night before.

Tepi wanted to lie by Azurias Maya's feet next to Nubi.

Katherine missed the silky warmth by her feet, but she understood that Tepi needed to be with other animals once in a while. Tafawana joined the driver of the vimaan in the front. They had overnighted at her uncle's house and become friends. The astronomer seemed to sleep, so the children were soon speaking English.

"I can't believe that we met the great astronomer." Chryséis almost whispered as if the sleeping man could somehow understand her.

"I wonder why they didn't locate him after his ship sank," Katherine said. "They should have put a tracker on him or something like that."

"How were they supposed to know what would happen?"

"What about telepathy?"

"Telepathy isn't fool-proof, Chris. The Lady of Cydonia couldn't zone in on us after the shipwreck, remember? Now we 'talk' to her more often."

"Probably. We can ask the Lady of Cydonia when we see her."

"I'm just glad we aren't stuck in the rain again. I can't wait to get to Egypt," Trevor said. "Just for a short while."

Katherine took a couple of short breaths and sneezed.

"Bless you," Chryséis said. "You are sneezing an awful lot."

"It's not so bad," Katherine said. "I had no idea it would rain so much in North Africa. But this village was great, don't you think? I'm glad we had to land here."

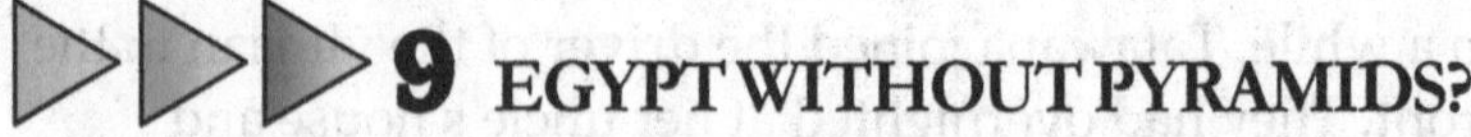

9 EGYPT WITHOUT PYRAMIDS?

The newly repaired vimaan took them farther east. A small cream-coloured vimaan passed them from the south.

"They are headed for Byrsa on the sea with its high-walled fortress," Tafawana told them. The drivers saluted each other. Down below, forested hills took over from cultivated croplands again. Large cedar and pistachio forests by the looks of it.

"Achoo!" Katherine wiped her nose with her sleeve.

"Katie, stop sneezing. What is the matter with you?" Chryséis was getting annoyed. Whenever she started to fall asleep, Katherine would sneeze again.

"I don't know what's the matter with me." Katherine sniffled pitiably. Her eyes looked red and swollen, and she felt like scratching her arms all the time.

"You could have an allergy, you know. Prehistoric grass or some animal," Trevor suggested lazily. He had been sleeping when Katherine interrupted his dream with her sneezing.

"Oh, that's great. Hayfever." She wiped her nose with the soft linen cloth Bibi Gul had put on top of some bread and cheese.

"Get a medic to check you out …" Chryséis mumbled and fell asleep again, despite the sneezing.

Way below, men waved their shepherd's crooks in greeting at the low-flying vimaan with the emblem of Felsina. The shepherds looked after herds of fat-tail sheep and grey cattle. They were skilled cheese makers and returned to the valleys at the end of summer with great wheels of Luni cheese.

Trevor waved back, then he had to look twice.

Unbelievably, there were stone circles on the heath. Not quite Stonehenge, but there was a stark contrast between the white stones and the purple heather. A long road lined with white rocks lead the way up a hill, where a star-shaped outline showed the evening star, a symbol of Atland in the west.

The girls were sleeping, so Trevor took a picture to show it to them later. The girls won't believe this, he thought.

There was no sign of a desert, just green hills and farmland. Straight ahead, the vimaan approached a network of rivers. This had to be the swampy delta of the Nila River.

The Blue Sea was to the left of them and from the right, the broad glittering band of the great river snaked toward the coast.

"Guys, wake up, we are nearly there." Trevor shook Katherine and Chryséis, but let Azurias Maya sleep.

"Look over there!" Chryséis yawned and pointed to houses and farms between the many smaller rivers. Herds of mastodon and hippos wallowed in the muddy waters underneath. Two mastodon bulls tore into each other in the splashing water with bone-chilling roars and crocodilians looked on from a bare sandbank, hoping for an easy meal.

"Do you think they are sarcasuchus?" Katherine asked.

"I don't know, but they are huge," Chryséis said.

Antelopes and graceful gazelles drank cautiously at the edge of the water side by side with buffaloes and wild boars, ready to bolt if the crocodilians moved.

"Oops, I think we're already landing." Katherine cried.

The vimaan began to descend. Surely, this swampland was not their destination. They crossed yet another river, where dark men in dugouts waved at them. Trevor waved back and they approached a hay-coloured savannah steppe. Huts flew past, palm trees and dark patches of freshly ploughed fields, then the outskirts of a city came into view.

"It looks like we are in the city of Kem-Oun," Azurias Maya said, stretching himself. "This is the Black Land."

Over the past few years, this new city had spread rapidly in all directions. More and more swampland was drained and canals were built. The former fishing village was now a spanking new city. Kem-Oun had a respectable harbor. The embankment formed a half-circle and was still under construction, but ships from Gubla and Retjenu were already anchored in the harbor. There were also gleaming amphitheatres and parks around the citadel.

"We will only stay for a short while," the maiden said and prepared for the landing.

The vimaan set down on a patch of lawn between the citadel and the prytaneum with its eternal flame. The jungle still blocked the view from the citadel to the Blue Sea, but it gave the city a tropical feel.

The Lady of Kem-Oun greeted them personally together with the usual ritual. Tafawana had sent word - or rather thought - of their impending arrival. As soon as the welcoming song had ended, they were shown to their quarters, while Nubi and Tepi took off to thoroughly explore the citadel grounds.

"Why on earth did we come here and not straight on to Ush-bantoun?" Chryséis asked impatiently.

"How are we supposed to know?" Trevor said. "Maybe there's still something wrong with the vimaan. Tafawana disappeared so quickly that we couldn't ask her. All we can do is wait."

They shared a large room again and wasted no time. The log had to be updated and Trevor showed the girls the picture of the stone circle he had taken above the heath.

Later, Tafawana told them that, there was indeed something else they needed for the vimaan that had not been found in the village of Urka. She also told them that she had word from Hyela. "Enforcements are arriving daily to assist the Oinotrian warlords, but a war takes its time."

"For sure," Trevor said. "Honourable maiden, would you know how long we have to stay here?"

"Until the vimaan is ready," she had answered simply. "Then we'll continue to Ush-bantoun."

After learning of their ailments, the Lady of Kem-Oun insisted that Katherine and Azurias Maya should see the medics downtown at the new 'House of Life'. Meanwhile, Chryséis and

Trevor went on a tour of the city, leaving the dogs behind at the citadel. The medics told Azurias Maya that the injuries to his head needed to be treated in order to heal properly and that treatment was to begin at once.

So the famous Algiran astronomer moved into a blue-green room with a wonderfully soothing view of the inner gardens. Depending on the medic's diagnosis, the colour, scents and melodies in such rooms were adjusted to each of their patients.

"Please wait here in the hall for your medic," a friendly woman said to Katherine.

She attended to a young mother and her squalling baby first. The baby was not happy at all.

Since their arrival in Kem-Oun, Katherine felt much better. She waited on a comfortable bench and watched the fire in a metal bowl in the centre of the hall. The dark blue floor was polished to a high shine and inlaid golden stars reflected the fire.

Outside on the lawn, birds pecking greedily at crumbs and across the burgundy lawn was the 'House of Knowledge', the library of Kem-Oun, half-hidden by a tall water feature.

The baby's crying stopped and soon the smiling mother reappeared from the treatment room. As she left, the round têrakhon entrance slid open and a fisherman was brought in. He was obviously in a lot of pain. A small swordfish had stuck its head through the net as it was hauled aboard and impaled itself in the man's leg.

Oh boy, Katherine thought, and felt a bit nauseous at the sight of it. It was an emergency and meant that she had to wait even longer. The medics were expecting the man and got to work immediately. Katherine was called to another room, shortly after.

"Kathín of Oxfol, your body does not agree with the pollen of the herb sylphium. You arrived from the 'Pastures of Heaven'. Were you in contact with this rare herb?" The medic asked.

"Yes, there were fields of sylphium all around."

The medic put the diagnostic device away and took something off a longish table under the window to begin the treatment. There were a number of rods that emitted healing light and sound energy arranged on the table.

While Katherine was at the 'House of Life', Trevor and Chryséis had gone sight-seeing in downtown Kem-Oun and the harbour. Now they waited for their friend in the entrance hall. They didn't have to wait long.

"Guess what…" Katherine said as they left the building through the round têrakhon entrance. "I'm allergic to sylphium."

Chryséis and Trevor looked puzzled. "What's that?"

"Remember? The yellow flowers we saw in the fields around Urka? They showed me a picture of the flower and it was definitely the same plant."

Katherine told them excitedly about the treatment. "She used some rods. Really cool. I have to come back again later. The medic is preparing some potion I have to take and she said the allergy will not return."

"Amazing." Trevor was impressed. "As easy as that?"

"Apparently," Katherine said. "If we could find out how those rods work, we could make a fortune back home."

"Sure. As if anyone would take us seriously."

"We could wait until we are grown up and then get a patent. At least I think that's how it works," Chryséis said. "All right, let's get onto our library project then." She changed the subject and pointed with her chin to the beautiful white building across the square.

"Actually I'd like to search for info on sylphium as well," Katherine said.

"Sure, why not."

The paving on the square was new and shiny. Everything seemed to be new in this town. They walked across the lawn to the 'House of Knowledge' and discussed what had happened in Urka and that Egypt was not at all what they had expected.

"It kind of makes sense that people aren't dressed in loincloths and have a bob-haircut, but nothing so far reminds me of Egypt," Trevor said.

"I know. Women are wearing their hair tied back, except for two thin braids in front of the ears. I mean, what's that all about? Are they Vikings?" Katherine tried not to stare at the people around them. "Then look at these pointy red caps."

Men sported trimmed beards and long hair, tied to the back. The footwear was also interesting. Upturned shoe tips and lace-ups were all the rage in Kem-Oun and women wore the same loop-shaped heels and chunky soles made from têrakhon, they had seen in Hyela.

"Just their clothes seem to be made of fine linen and silk, similar to the Alesian suits. So at least we're fitting in around here."

"Did you see that half the people we passed are wearing a 'Horus Eye' around their necks? Wonder what that means," Trevor said.

"Probably some sort of charm," Katherine surmised. "Babies and small children have a large blue bead tied around their wrists. Didn't the Berberi also wear something like that?"

"I think so," Trevor answered.

They arrived at the limestone building and studied the front entrance. A black diorite statue of, the cobra goddess' Meret Seger was placed on one side and a white marble statue of Djehuti, who had brought the art of writing to Ta Mery, on the other side.

"Meret Seger, she who loves silence," Chryséis read aloud. "And the god Djehuti - that's Thoth - he who loves books."

"Okay, interesting," Trevor said. "The stone is so smooth. Good work."

"Why is there no cat-statue this time?" Chryséis wondered. "Let me take a quick picture of this."

They entered the building. As the children were familiar with the way these libraries worked, they went straight to one of the viewing tables.

The surface was also covered in a thin web of gold. Katherine walked up to the librarian, who looked just like the librarian in Felsina, and confidently asked for a book on the plant called sylphium.

The librarian returned with a heavy book from the 'Plantlore Section' and put it carefully onto the golden web of their chosen viewing table.

"The 'Plantlore Section' contains scrolls, clay tablets and thick tomes on every conceivable type of known plant," he said, "but I believe that this work is best."

They opened the book and studied the paintings and writing on the thin pages. They didn't understand much of the formal text, although there were pictures, showing the preparation of potions, but the librarian helped them to find the painting of a sylphium plant.

"I see that you read the book with your eyes only. If you want to find out the nature of the sylphium plant's properties, you need to understand the essence of the plant," The librarian moved the Ze-phir in its cradle right above the painted sylphium flower. He looked through the amazing crystal lens and smiled.

"What exactly is the essence of a plant?" Katherine asked.

"It takes our medics long years of study before they can fully understand the essence of plants. You can have a look at the book through the Ze-phir crystal and find out for yourselves."

This librarian was much nicer than the other one. He didn't seem to mind helping the foreign children.

Katherine was the first one to look through the lens. A throbbing note of faint music rose from the page. The music increased and the plant itself seemed to rise from the page, dancing up in waving movements. A pale green tendril at first, then the whole image unfolded and emerged through the crystal. There was a faint blue vapour around the picture. Hardly noticeable and Katherine felt drawn into the painting. The plant continued to move and wave to the music.

"That's amazing!" She marvelled.

"It is the growth-music of the plant," The librarian explained patiently.

The music grew in intensity and even the thin golden net on the table began to throb and interweave.

"Unbelievable!" Katherine cried.

"Come on, we also want to have a look!" Trevor said.

"Just now."

The moving image of the sylphium plant began to shoot out more tendrils in a brilliant green colour. The shoots put out folded buds. Buds unfurled into leaf-shapes. Roots were spreading, sun-nourishment pressed into the eager plant and…there was sun-music, air-music, water-music, earth-music mingling into a glorious symphony of melodies… pollen became airborne.

Then there was a sudden shrill whistling sound and Katherine went pale. Chryséis didn't like what she saw.

"Don't have another allergic reaction, please."

"Okay, you can have a turn now." Katherine sneezed, but recovered quickly. Chryséis and Trevor stared together at the book page.

"Wow, how can all of that be on one page?"

"But that's how all books are written." The librarian sounded astonished. He took the polished crystal out of its cradle and put the Ze-phir down next to the book. The painting was as flat and static now as it had been before and colour returned to Katherine's cheeks.

"Feeling better?" Trevor asked.

"Hmm? Oh yeah, I'm …better. Wasn't that just an awful sound, guys?"

"It was just a little shrill…" Trevor started, but Chryséis nudged him. All they needed was for Katherine to start sneezing again!

"Ehem, yeah. Seems like we found the reason why you react to this plant with an allergy… must have been the pollen sound."

"And that's how you read the plant book properly," The librarian said in an encouraging voice, shooting a quick glance in Katherine's direction.

The dark-haired girl had reacted strongly to the plant music, but he had seen this reaction before. He tried not to pay attention to the strange language these children suddenly spoke so impolitely and put the Ze-phir crystal back in its fitting.

"Is there a metal foil library in this 'House of Life'?" Chryséis wanted to know. She was dying to study the intriguing thin metal foils they had come across before.

"The metal foils?" the librarian frowned. Interesting that the children, who were so ignorant about plant books should know about metal foil libraries.

"The 'Room of Repeated Vision' is overseen by Seshat, the goddess of writing and record keeping. The metal records are very old and not open to the public," he explained. "However, I can tell you about them..."

And so he told them that, after the Dark Age, nobody remembered where to find these secret records. They had been stored in the Koh Kaf Mountains and in underground passages in the Southern Continent of Pâtâla before the great cataclysm. Now there were only a handful of metal foils with the knowledge and records of many thousands of years left.

"Only scientists know how to decipher the rare scripts," the librarian concluded and excused himself. He took the book with the sylphium painting with him.

There were ancient records in secret places in some mountain caves somewhere in Hindustan and South America. What else was there to discover? They were so engrossed in what they had seen and heard that they completely forgot about the formulas for têrakhon. The reason they had come to the library for.

Another librarian ushered a group of young school children into the 'Mirage Section'. They were about to view a mirage with the title 'Deluge of Pelasgia'. The 'Deluge of Pelasgia' came in two parts and the subtitles read 'The Passage of the Golden Pillars' and 'One of the Worst Cataclysms Ever to Befall Mankind'.

"Do you want to have a look what that's all about?" Chryséis whispered.

"Sure, why not?" Trevor said. They followed the group into a large viewing room and stayed in the background.

The teacher struggled with the mirage roll and the librarian helped to place it in the wall socket.

Most of the children had seen this particular mirage before. It showed the peoples of Punt and Hesperia travelling across the broad causeway between Northern and Southern Berberia before it collapsed. The ancient clothes and hairstyles were a hoot and there was much giggling.

The ancient paved causeway had been lined left and right by enormous megaliths all the way from one continent to the other. Two massive pillars were covered all over in fine gold bouncing off the sunlight, and copper inscriptions in the ancient magic language of Râkshas Bhasa encircled the pillars.

One of the pillars told of glorious and shameful deeds of humankind over the ages. The other pillar bore scientific formulas and secrets of how materials and weaponry and such could be manufactured. It was the knowledge of the gods.

That's how the 'Passage of Golden Pillars' had received its name. The land bridge divided the cool waters of the Gadiric Sea on one side and the lowlands of Pelasgia on the other. The fabled country of Pelasgia with its green hills and sparkling lakes and streams. Farmsteads dotted the slope on the Pelasgian side and a few fishing villages huddled against the steep shoreline of the Gadiric Sea.

One could see as far as the serpent hills, called The Carnacs, way up in the province of Morbihan. Donkey carts rolled noisily along deep grooves and a motley crowd of humans walked along the broad causeway in both directions.

The children laughed at the comical antics of a moki, faced with a stubborn sheep and a baby grasping at his mother's large dangling earrings.

Then a breathtaking panorama view took in the beauty of this long-lost countryside. The Tirennian Lake in the east, into which the mighty Nila River had then emptied its waters. The valleys of Isaguri and Gurgôn even more beautiful than those of Lyonesse.

Then there was a quick look to the left, where the waves of

an ancient Sea below the fishing villages were lapping the rocks. Dolphins were jumping happily into the air and ships with sails like red fish fins took their usual routes between the islands. The faint contours of land in the west and the first mirage suddenly ended.

But the school children knew that the interesting part was about to begin. The giggling died down as the second mirage began to flicker.

The land bridge grew more distant. Now it would happen. Just now. The children grew excited and the teacher spoke calming words.

Suddenly the Gadiric Sea began to foam and the narrator described what followed in a composed voice.

"When the mother continent of Atland was forced to the bottom of the sea, the land bridge collapsed and the Gadiric Sea turned into an angry demon that rushed in to cover the fine country of Pelasgia with its torrents."

Massive waves pressed more and more forceful against the land bridge between Spain and Africa - or in prehistoric terms, between Hesperia and Berberia, first erasing the fishing villages, then ships were smashed against the rock. The land bridge ruptured.

Slowly at first, the swelling ocean waters carried debris and mud over the passage, pushing the throng of travelers and animals with it down the slope into Pelasgia. Then the waves rushed through the crumbling rock and buried the fair lowlands, its beautiful cities and green pastures.

'The waters rapidly submerged all but the peaks of the highlands. Pelasgia was no more and only the mountain tops of Kretaland, Tenero and Lukania peeked through the waves. For sheaves of years they would remain uninhabitable marshland.'

The young scholars sat with their mouths open. Some had tears in their eyes. This mirage was always so tragic.

The narrator continued. 'The Blue Sea as we know it today came was created by the sea god's design. There were not many survivors. The fruits of the golden fields were lost along with many lives and there was much hardship.'

The children gasped at the sight of massive tree trunks snapping and bodies floating on the turbid waters.

'When the angry ocean finally settled, streets and buildings were buried under layers of mud and sand, and for a long time, only the roofs of once splendid cities could still be seen in the clear waters. The islands became the dwelling places of Kabiri, the giant 'Great Dragons'.'

The mirage allowed a view into mining operations on one of these islands. Stern-looking giants and dwarfs were toiling in the rocks side by side. 'The marshlands were drained and before long, crops and livestock were thriving again.'

Some long-horned cows chewed with such a funny expression that it made the children laugh.

'Humans did not trust the sea and trekked farther inland. New farmland was ploughed and planted and soon the land was once again blessed with abundant harvests and a budding civilisation.'

One of the librarians, who happened to pass the group removed the mirage rolls of the 'Deluge of Pelasgia' after the finishing harp notes had died down. The school children left the library while their teacher reminded them not to make a noise.

"That was unbelievable," Katherine whispered. "All of that land is now under the Mediterranean Sea! And only the mountain tops are sticking out. Those are the islands!"

"I've actually watched a YouTube documentary, but it was nothing like this," Trevor said. "They looked at different theories."

"Do you want to go back to the citadel now or look at more books?" Katherine asked.

"We're already here, so might as well look at more books," Chryséis answered.

Back at the viewing tables, they studied an open scroll through the Ze-phir lens. It had something to do with measurements. The use of certain measurements had been developed to a fine art in Ta Mery.

Katherine opened a page, which showed the picture of a mouth. The writing taught that the mouth was not simply a picture, but a ro or 'mouthful'. Equal to about a modern tablespoon, a ro was used to measure spices and medicines. There were 320 ro to one heqat. One-tenth part of a heqat was called a hin, a measurement for liquids.

One hin held about half a litre of beer. All this was graphically and musically explained.

A workman measuring the side of a boat and various items for shipbuilding, drinking a hin of beer, becoming sick and taking one ro of medicine at a 'House of Life' and so on. The measuring of land or buildings was called 'stretching the cord'. The cord was 100 cubits long with knots after every cubit. One cubit corresponded to 52 meters.

"Wow, I think I'll take a picture of it," Chryséis said. "Who's supposed to remember all that?"

Trevor shook his head. "You can't see what the crystal sees."

"I can try and take a photo through the Ze-phir lens."

But it didn't work that well. They unrolled the scroll further.

There were the 'Horus Eye Fractions' of the reciprocals of the powers of two, such as a half, a quarter, an eighth down to one sixty-fourth part of a heqat or 4.5 liters.

The book mentioned that the 'Horus Eye', which was also called 'Healed Eye', deflected evil looks, even illness and was a powerful amulet-symbol. Odd that something like protection charms should be referred to in a book on measurements.

"How boring," Chryséis sighed. Trevor was taking pictures of the drawings. They could study them later.

"Well, I sort of understand this. You take the drawing of an eye apart and assign a value to each part."

"Who's ever heard of that?" Chryséis didn't like admitting that she didn't understand something.

School children pushed past their viewing table. Some of them stole a glance at the big children all by themselves.

Their giggling and talking still echoed in the hall after they'd left. Trevor stood in front of the bookshelves next to their viewing table. A whole shelf was on Al Kemi, the 'Art of Matter and Energy Reaction' as the science was called in an ancient Atlandian scroll.

A note on the front said that the scroll had been detected in a cave in the Koh Kaf Mountains and brought to Kem by a trader. Scientists had preserved the parchment and its priceless content. The date was given as the fifth year after the building of the 'House of Knowledge' in the month of Montú on the day of the hare hunt. This couldn't have been that long ago, since the city was still relatively new.

"Why isn't this in the secret section?" Trevor wondered.

"Who knows…" Chryséis said.

A man from the harbour master's office came rushing through the entrance. He carried maps and sky charts and deposited them noisily on another viewing table. The time travellers stared after him as the man stomped off without paying any attention to them, to find one of the librarians.

He had ordered a scroll that was urgently needed at the harbor office, but it was not with the lot, he had taken with him. Where was it? It was the scroll on measurements, Trevor had taken earlier!

The ill-tempered man bumped into a storyteller, who dropped the book he was carrying with a loud thump. The men were arguing with each other and the librarians joined in, trying to calm them down.

"Come on, let's get out of here, it's getting late," Trevor said.

They sneaked out, trying not to draw too much attention to themselves.

*

Meanwhile, Azurias Maya was recovering at the 'House of Life'. He had some time to think about his next course of action. It would be best if he did not let his research go to waste. Before returning to Atala, he should go to Mintaka in Ta-Neteru further up the Nila River, just as he had planned before their departure. The treatment was successful.

▶▶▶ 10 THE KNIFE ATTACK

"Maybe we should also wear an amulet like that to blend in," Katherine said. "Or one of these large blue beads."

They were sitting under a shady tree in a small park next to the library and watched a water feature.

"We won't be here that long. And anyway, I don't like necklaces." Chryséis watched roller birds fluttering around an old lady who crumbled dry bread rings on the paving in front of the 'House of Life'.

Katherine changed the subject. "This sylphium plant was scary, don't you think?"

"Hmm, not really," Chryséis said. "But how cool is it that your hay fever has something to do with the song of its pollen."

"Katherine's clearly sensitive to the sound," Trevor cut in. "Just listen to us - as if this was normal science."

"Well, here it is. We've been around so many plants since we arrived. Why am I allergic to this sylphium?"

"Who knows? Just take your medicine and avoid the plant in future," Chryséis said lazily.

The school children from the library sat on the burgundy lawn, eating a lunch snack. Two of the boys jumped up and splashed water at each other. Their teacher scolded them and they apologised to the old woman, who was feeding the birds, whose tunic had become wet.

"Oh, I think the medic is calling me. The potion must be ready." Katherine was proud of her telepathic skills and that she could receive a simple message like this one.

"Wow, that's impressive," Chryséis said. "Let's go, then."

On their way back to the citadel, they passed under a pedestrian bridge connecting two cream-white buildings.

They wanted to explore a small square with an elephant-shaped fountain farther up the road. There were a few market stalls on the square selling produce. Chryséis snapped pictures of heaps of bulbous gilora cucumbers, white serm and golden squash that were piled high in coarse baskets. Herbs and spices in open sacks smelled so good and one stand offered pyramids of fresh eggs. Large eggs with bouquets of sylphium flowers hanging above them.

Katherine carried her small bottle with the potion on a necklace like a charm, but just seeing the yellow flowers made her skin crawl. She hurried past the produce market to a storyteller, who sat on a colourful carpet. An audience of mainly housewives waited patiently for him to begin a well-known story of the birth of planet Earth.

The grey-haired man picked importantly at his wide sleeves, which amused the crowd.

"That' gonna take a while," Chryséis sighed.

She wasn't sure if she wanted to stay and listen. They had already seen and heard so much today, but the crowd pushed them forward, closer to the house wall. There was no getting away from the story now and the rawi began to speak.

"My children, as you all know Wr-alda created the stars out of clouds of dust, which he hurled into space." The rawi's hands described tornado-like motions. "That's why the basic movement of the world is the whirlwind. The vital force of the Earth is water and we are blessed with water in Ta Mery."

People murmured and nodded. The rawi continued after waving his long bulky sleeves out of the way.

"Many, many sheaves of years ago - long before the First Time began..." The rawi's voice boomed and the time travellers struggled to understand what he was saying. "...and that child shall be named Earth."

His expression changed to one of surprise, as he looked at the palm of his right hand. "The child called Earth was as fiery as its parent."

"What is he talking about?" Katherine whispered.

"Not too sure. Some sort of genesis story, I think," Trevor said. The rawi paused and lowered his eyes. A murmur went through the crowd. Had the old man fallen asleep?

He suddenly looked up again and his hands flew through the air. "Then, as the moments passed, which would be a thousand, thousand cycles of arc in Earth's time to our understanding my children, the Overlords watched the heavenly child cool down. And as it cooled, the overlord Ptah breathed upon it."

Another brief pause followed for effect.

"The breath of Ptah sent life vapours to wrap the child. A great water formed on the face of Earth. Solid rock and minerals formed. Then the mighty Ptah heard the voice of Holy Wr-alda say: 'Plant in the cooled great waters and upon the rocks the life seed of plants, which grow in heavenly fields.' So Ptah came down with his bowl of plant seed from heavenly fields and scattered the seeds on the warm oceans, just as the sower scatters wheat on the newly-turned earth."

The storyteller kept making movements with his hand.

His hands stroked the smooth imaginary surface.

"This is taking awfully long," Katherine said.

"I know, but we can't leave yet," Trevor answered.

"Sshh," somebody hissed from behind.

"... so Ptah touched the source of life with his finger, and drew it in his own likeness." The rawi's finger moved through the air, writing. The crowd murmured and nodded. Everyone knew that. "... to you is given the wisdom above and the spirits of your companions of the lesser life. You are to show the path of truth to all those still in the half-light of earthly sleep.'" The rawi paused one last time for effect. Everyone held their breath. "And thus it came to pass."

It was the end of the story.

Adults and children clapped noisily and praised the storyteller's skill. Sesame-covered bread rings and tender were flung onto the colourful carpet. The rawi had done a good job.

At last, the children managed to get out of the crowd and

hurried up a steep road.

"Can you believe it? More gods! I've never heard of a God called Wr-alda before," Trevor said. "But Ptah is an ancient Egyptian god as far as I know."

"Well, you live and learn, Trev." Chryséis avoided a puddle.

There was no doubt about it that even in Ta Mery it rained a lot. Modern Egyptians had to protect themselves against the sun and the people of ancient Ta Mery wore heavy raincoats.

The time travellers had brought their rain jackets and sneakers, which earned them sideways looks. Luckily, Kem-Oun was a new town, where many cultures mingled.

Quite by chance, they passed a cobbler's shop, tucked away in a corner on the steep road and purchased new pairs of sandals. The old ones from Cydonia were completely worn. They had carried the time travellers through many countries and even survived a shipwreck.

Some of the shoes on the narrow shelves had upturned tips and bulky hollow heels, but they preferred the simpler sandals.

Then, when it came to payment, there was some confusion. The cobbler liked Katherine's rain jacket and tried to bargain for it, then his gaze fell on Trevor's pocket knife that hung from his belt.

In the end, he settled for the exotic Alesian tender the boy took from a finely worked saurian-leather purse.

"What do we have here?" Somebody said behind them.

The children turned around and saw a not-too-clean man cleaning his dirty fingernails with a knife. His head was covered by a hood, but he was obviously bald.

"Leave them be, Tuyo. They are just children," The shoemaker said.

"Oh, but look at all that tender they are carrying. I'm sure; they don't need all of that!" The dirty man mocked and the shoemaker shrugged his shoulders.

The three friends stood frozen at first, wondering what was

going on, but eventually, Chryséis spoke up. "What do you need our tender for?" She asked. "If you can make your own?"

"Hoho, we have a feisty one here, don't we? I'm not very good at making tender, so I'll need yours." He sighed in an over-the-top manner.

"You are just lazy then?" Trevor stated.

He tried to remember the self-defense moves, Gwendola had taught them after the Firbolg attack in Prydhain. Trevor was determined not to let this man harm them or take their tender away, but it didn't come to that.

A red vimaan moved toward them and down onto the cobbled road. Suddenly, the dirty man vanished up a narrow staircase on the other side of the road and Tafawana stepped out of the vimaan.

"Tafawana!" Chryséis had never been so glad to see her.

"There you are, athenai, I was looking for you all over. The medics at the 'House of Life' told me, you had already left."

"How did you find us?" Katherine asked the maiden, still a bit upset by the attempted mugging.

"Well, I followed your thoughts, of course."

"Of course, you did," Trevor said. "Thank you so much for picking us up, honourable maiden."

The shoemaker slunk back into his tiny shop and watched them through a crack in the door. He could only hope that the children didn't blame him for the incident with the mugger.

It was not a good idea to be seen as an accomplice to criminals. The punishment for such incidents were harsh and some people had already disappeared without a trace. He had better watch out.

The Lady of the Citadel did not tolerate any sort of crime in her new colonial city.

Chryséis and Trevor sat on the spacious citadel veranda at a safe distance from crocodile-infested lagoons. In the distance, above the jungle, they saw the bluish ribbon of the River Nile, but what caught their attention was a group of bathing children in the lagoon not far from the citadel.

"Wow, look at that. Those kids don't seem afraid at all," Trevor marvelled.

"Maybe, they are somehow protected?" Chryséis wondered.

"Yes, maybe, but how?"

"Maybe they have an agreement with the crocodiles." Chryséis shrugged and leaned back in her chair.

A mossy, old barge house rotted away on the edge of the water and crocodiles on a sandbar were basking in the sun. The reptiles didn't seem to take much notice of the youngsters. They were more interested in small therasaurus that circled the waters on the lookout for nesting birds and fish.

The flying dinosaurs screeched wildly whenever a crocodile snapped at them. The sheer number of the reptiles quashed any desire the time travellers might have to explore the marshes.

The city was on the shores of the mighty Nila River and most of the delta was covered in jungle. A shy people lived in the trees around the brackish marshes. They moved around in canoes, made from tree trunks, carved in the front like crocodile heads. The marsh people believed that the crocodiles would not attack the canoes if they looked like their reptile kin.

The marsh people must be doing something right,"

Trevor said. "Or they would all have been eaten by now."

They had almost forgotten about the thief, who had tried to steal their tender a couple of days ago. Now everything was geared towards leaving this city behind.

Although the vimaan had been properly fixed and Azurias Maya had come back from the 'House of Life' much healthier, Tafawana was still occupied with some errand or other.

They would be leaving for Ush-bantoun tomorrow, but Azurias Maya had other plans.

"It's clear that the Nila River must be the Nile, but there are so many cities, Hal-Khón, Naukratis and Ush-bantoun.... and none of them have major ports, except for Kem-Oun. Maybe we should just stay here then," Trevor said.

Chryséis sighed. "But hey, we are in Egypt and we'll see the Nile and we'll travel again, see new things..."

"I'd much rather go home now."

"Don't be such a bore, Trev," Chryséis said and leaned back in her chair. "We are in Egypt." Apparently, her attitude had changed.

What they knew about the river Nile, they had seen on the Adventure Channel or read in books. At the beginning of summer, a constant trickle of meltwater from glaziers dripped from the hills onto moss and ferns collected in small brooks and eventually the Nila River. Fertile mud covered the Black Land during the seasonal flooding.

Here they were told that the Gods had taught Ta-Merians how to straighten the river, how to build dykes and canals and how to use the fertile mud.

Kem-Oun itself was free of mosquitoes and other insects, thanks to laser beam technology, but the marshes were full of them.

"Nice here," Trevor observed.

"Hmm yeah," Chryséis said. She was busy updating their travel journal on the palmtop computer and didn't even look up. Trevor played with the model of an astrolabe he had found in a cupboard in the passage. Winding up the little machine until the planets started to move slowly along their metal tracks around the golden sun ball in the middle.

"I don't like leaving Tepi behind," Katherine said as she joined them on the veranda. "Azurias Maya is taking both dogs with him to Mintaka tomorrow."

"I know, but what are we supposed to do with Tepi when we have to go back home through the vortex?" Trevor asked her.

"I know, but it's still sad."

They would miss Tepi terribly, especially Katherine. But a dog chooses where it wants to be and Tepi had chosen her new companion Nubi and Azurias Maya.

Tafawana now also joined them on the terrace and sat down on a type of deck chair.

"We will be leaving this handsome new city of Kem-Oun early tomorrow morning," she announced. "I have every intention of arriving in time for the 'Festival of Sokhar' in Ush-bantoun."

She had relieved the driver of his duties and he was already on his way to Felsina with five passengers aboard, headed for the 'Pastures of Heaven', as well as a crate of Kemnite delicacies for king Takelot. A merchant had agreed to transport the maiden and the Alesian children to Ush-bantoun in his rather modern vimaan.

The following morning, when it was time to leave, the Lady bade them farewell in the citadel gardens. Tepi was nowhere to be seen and it was probably better that way.

Katherine wiped a tear from her eye, but she knew they would have to say goodbye to their loyal dog sooner or later.

Tafawana was in high spirits. She would enjoy a gorgeous festival at the warlord Rissa's specific command before returning to Hyela. Alone to see the mighty blue Nila River from above was worth the journey south.

She had been told to hand the children over to the queen in Ush-bantoun and then they would no longer be her responsibility.

After a short, pleasant trip, they landed in the main court within the citadel grounds of Ush-bantoun. The vimaan stayed only long enough to drop off the four passengers then the trader went on to his own quarters.

The city in the western Nile Delta had no harbour to speak of. Merchant ships negotiated the Nila River upstream towards the Red Land and ships laden with the mineral riches of the south passed Ush-bantoun downstream.

There were lots of bridges over canals and peculiar cone-shaped towers in the middle of town. The large cones were Ush-bantoun's landmarks, although they could also be found elsewhere. The annual Festival of Sokhar' was a big event in this provincial town and Ta Merians were known for their love of boisterous festivities. A multitude of tents had already been erected on the grassy riverbanks to house the visitors streaming into the city.

A court official, called the Wzir, met them in the citadel courtyard and invited the three children and Tafawana to stay at the Per-aa or 'Great House' of Ush-bantoun instead of the citadel.

They were taken to the royal precinct, but Tafawana still complained that it was unusual for the Lady of the citadel not to welcome the maiden from Hyela and her young Alesian guests.

"A contagious disease has forced the honourable Lady into confinement within the citadel precinct. The queen has therefore taken over the poor Lady's duties," the Wzir explained.

"What contagious disease?" Tafawana asked him.

"It is not yet known, honourable maiden."

"Hmm if you say so, athenai," Tafawana grumbled.

"Indeed, I will hand your paizas to her majesty. Please

follow me this way."

He led the way through tiled passages into the bowels of the palace to the impressive guest quarters. There were four beds on wooden lion's legs in the large room, covered by brightly coloured blankets.

Tafawana was rather keen to see the 'Festival of Sokhar' and soon said goodbye to the three outlandish children.

"We will no doubt see each other at lunch time," she said and was out the door, before the children had a chance to decide that they wanted to come along.

Tafawana decided that it would be good manners to stop by the towers, where the Lady and her maidens lived to inquire about their health. She headed through the gate towards the large pink citadel across the paved road. The maiden looked back and waved, but the time travellers should not see her again.

"We are in Egypt. In a real Egyptian palace!" Katherine marvelled.

"Come, let's check out the bathroom," Chryséis went straight over to the sliding doors and had a good look around. The round bathroom was decorated in pale-green ceramic tiles. The walls above the tiles were painted with reeds, frogs and fish. Two steps led up to the large oval alabaster bathtub let into the raised platform and when one turned on a golden lever, warm water spurted from the mouth of an alabaster frog.

"I can't wait to take a bath," Katherine said.

Just behind the tub were three long têrakhon windows and a pile of folded linen towels was stacked on a narrow shelf next to a table with green glass jars filled with scented soaps and oils. Of course, they had to try everything.

Nautilus shells were mounted on the wall next to the sliding door and in between the three long windows. The toilet was a small area, tiled with alabaster in one of the corners of the bathroom. They went back into the bedroom.

Trevor and Chryséis had already chosen their bedsteads and were busy unpacking their sleeping bags and a few things then placed their backpacks underneath their beds.

"Not bad!" Trevor said and whistled through his teeth. "Come on, Katherine, hurry up."

Katherine was busy washing her hands and face, just to try out the amazing bathroom. "Okay, I'm coming."

"Look at that view," Chryséis marvelled.

They could see the Nile River through large windows on one side of the room. The paved courtyard just below the windows was surrounded by high walls and the main entrance was a guarded stone portal.

Long cream-coloured curtains let in a soft light and Katherine had a closer look at the wall paintings. There seemed to be a small vertical gap in one of the paintings. One of the palm fronds was actually a door handle.

Katherine pulled on it and a door opened on well-oiled hinges. "Now what do we have here?"

Behind the hidden door was a dark passage, but where did it lead?

"Do you think they keep guests under surveillance?" Trevor wondered.

"Maybe it's common to have such passageways as escape routes. You know like in medieval castles..." Katherine said.

"I'd like to go in, but I'm not sure that it's safe to risk exploring the dark space, just to see, where it leads." Chryséis tried to get used to the darkness inside the passage.

After a short discussion, the time travellers decided that it was probably safe and entered the dark passage. For a while, they couldn't see or hear anything.

Trevor thought he had felt a wooden panel once on the wall, but he didn't want to speak, in case they'd be discovered. The passage curved slightly to the right and they saw was a crack of light just ahead. The children walked faster, glad to see something else than just darkness. Did the passage lead somehow outside?

But it didn't. They stood in front of a door and heard voices. One female voice was rather impatient and spoke in a dialect they didn't understand very well. Chryséis opened the door just enough so they could see what was going on the other side. The first thing they saw was that furniture and walls were covered in shiny gold.

By the looks of it, the impatient voice belonged to the wife of the king. She wore a dress full of jewels. Her hair was blonde and she had a freckled, stubby nose. A small golden circlet completed her hairdo, but somehow, the woman looked very modern to them.

The queen sat in front of a decorated dressing table in what appeared to be her bedroom and gazed into a polished metal mirror and her blue eyes. Since the woman didn't say anything further, they had seen enough and retreated as quietly as possible, leaving the door a little ajar so that they would have some light to see in the dark passage.

Suddenly, Katherine pushed her hand against her mouth. There was another door ahead and it was now half-open. Inside the room was an alchemist's laboratory or something that looked like an alchemist's laboratory.

A tall, thin man in a black cape stood with his back toward the door. He handled the equipment and didn't seem to notice that the door stood open. They had seen such a black cape and such encrusted hair before, but this could not possibly be the High Priest of Shirak. This man was not a giant!

It had to be another evil sorcerer.

They didn't know that they were looking at the laboratory of the once-powerful sorcerer of Kem, who had been locked up in the Gogmagog Mountains by three of the most powerful Ladies of the 'Alesian Epoch'.

Chryséis motioned hectically for them to walk on, trying not to make a noise. She wanted them to get out of the passage and back to their tower room, but before they could move, the sorcerer turned halfway around.

The children froze.

They could see that he had a handsome face, not at all like the other sorcerers they had seen so far, but his earlobe was injured as if something had eaten a piece of it.

Another man walked toward him. He looked younger than the sorcerer but was rather ugly. With his small face and big nose, he looked like a bird. The younger man lowered his shaven head covered with a black skullcap as he poured a bright green liquid from a bulbous bottle into another vessel. They noticed his dirty fingernails and there was even some dirt on his arm.

Katherine, Trevor and Chryséis squeezed as quietly as possible past the door along the opposite wall, trying not to breathe. As soon as they had reached their room, Katherine closed the passage door carefully and began to breathe again.

"Oh, my goodness. That was so weird!" She cried.

"Sshh! Don't make such a noise," Trevor warned her.

"I just knew something was wrong with this place. I wonder what they need a sorcerer for around here," Katherine said.

"Do you think he knows who we are?" Chryséis was still whispering.

"He must be one of those dark magicians, who keep trying to get hold of the speaking stones. Did you see his hair?" Katherine whispered back.

"Well yes, but he's not a giant."

"Neither were two of the other sorcerers in Prydhain."

"Do you think he wants to take revenge on us...?" Chryséis asked.

"I've no idea... but it's not good. Not good at all." Trevor shook his head. "Chris, can't you figure him out? You do that telepathy thing best of all of us."

"Listen, I'm not that good. And he might get a whiff of it when we try to suss him out."

"Maybe he doesn't know who we are and just does his normal thing," Trevor suggested.

"His normal thing?" Katherine asked. "If he's just a medic, we worry about nothing,"

"Medics with blood-encrusted hair and dirty fingernails? No, this guy and his little helper are no medics."

"When is this audience with the queen?" Trevor suddenly asked.

"No idea, but we must be careful that we don't look suspicious," Katherine said. "They'll probably call us."

"We could use the bathroom one by one while the others stand watch," Chryséis said. "But I really have to go."

"Okay, not a bad idea," Katherine agreed. "But I'm first."

At noon, the Wzir appeared and told them that it was court day in Ush-bantoun in the province of Kem and King Osorkon was busy hearing cases together with the citadel judge.

"He will welcome you later. His wife Mé-lis-ah, however, will receive you now in the audience room here at the Per-aa."

The Wzir then asked them to follow him again through complex passages that were well-lit.

There were guards everywhere, but they looked straight ahead and didn't move.

Despite all the luxury around them, the children didn't feel as comfortable in the Great House as they had in all the citadels before. The palace was quite large, but almost nobody else was around.

Pink marble from the Blue Sea island of Keftiu covered walls and ceilings and plastered walls were painted. They walked past stone sculptures that seemed to follow them with their stony eyes.

Their sandals padded softly on the polished stone floors, but the slightest sound rang off the gleaming marble walls. They turned yet another corner and walked down a short flight of stairs. Wherever they were going, it was high up now and far from the main entrance. Eventually, the Wzir stopped, opened a heavy, carved door and waved them inside, then he turned around and left without saying another word.

"Strange," Katherine murmured.

The audience room shone with gold and there was even a golden throne on a dais at the far end of the room.

"Not bad, eh?" Chryséis looked around.

"Bit overdone with all that gold," Trevor said.

"We are in a palace in Egypt." Katherine pronounced the words slowly as if she was explaining it to toddlers.

"Okay then," Chryséis said. "Here we are. And where is the queen?"

"I don't know," Trevor answered. "But as long as we don't have to meet this sorcerer again, I'm happy." But they did meet him. Over lunch, after a brief ceremonious audience with the blonde queen they had seen earlier from the passage.

They also met his apprentice Totolin of Ereb . Totolin meant 'little turkey'. It was an apt name for the young man, who stood behind his master's cushion throughout the meal, awaiting orders to fetch this and carry that.

His little head was perched on a scrawny neck and he constantly nodded in amazement at the sorcerer's words. The tight skull cap turned out to be short black hair that covered his head. Totolin had seen much black magic during his apprenticeship and learned to be careful of his master's dark moods. Apart from that, he felt that the sorcerer's magic powers gave him also a great deal of importance.

The king was also present at the lunch table, so the court day must have ended. He was kindly, smiled at the children and welcomed them to court.

The time travelers learned that the sorcerer came from Ereb, the 'Land of Darkness' to the north of the Blue Sea. He was allegedly skilled in telling the future by studying the fresh liver of a mountain goat and if needed, his apprentice quickly fetched clay models of livers with mysterious lines and writing on them.

Such practices were frowned upon in civilized countries, but the children weren't sure that they understood everything the king told them.

The new Magi had taken over from the old Sorcerer of Kem at the court of king Osorkon after the other Magi had disappeared under mysterious circumstances in Prydhain.

The children knew, of course, what had happened to him.

What the king didn't tell them was that the new sorcerer

was not very popular with the people of Ush-bantoun, but the queen liked him and so he had quickly become queen Mé-lis-ah's trusted advisor. The swishing of his black coat was never far away. He oversaw the queen's 'crickets', a number of spies who were dispatched all over town.

From time to time, Totolin began to bounce forth and back from heel to toe. It was actually quite comical to watch, but the children tried not to smile or even laugh.

Platters and bowls with omelettes, spinach and chickpeas, sliced cucumbers and olives and many other Ta-Merian delicacies were served.

King Osorkon welcomed another guest, a merchant called Manassi of Naharin. He had been forced to land in Ush-bantoun a couple of days ago because his cargo of garum fish sauce had moved to one side of the vimaan that had made further flight too dangerous.

King Osorkon joked that Manassi had flown the vimaan too fast, which the merchant strongly denied. He hoped to be leaving the following day.

"Then you will have to tie down your fish sauce containers properly so that it won't rain fish sauce in the Mâ-Rock Mountains," the king chuckled.

"For sure your Highness. And has there ever been a more pleasant wait than in this beautiful spot in the Black Land?" The merchant said smoothly and poured a little fish sauce from a small crystal bottle on his omelette.

Mé-lis-ah's eyes followed his movements closely.

"Where is the maiden Tafawana, who came with us to Ush-bantoun?" Trevor asked the king. "Wasn't she supposed to be here for lunch?"

"Oh, she preferred to eat with the Lady and her maidens…she had to quarantine… the sickness…you understand…" Mé-lis-ah said in a careless tone. This was news to the three friends, but they didn't question her answer.

A few fat flies hovered over the food bowls and a servant was called to fan the table with a large device mounted to the ceiling. The queen cut in when her husband was talking more often now, and it seemed that the wine had something to do with it that the children were not permitted to drink.

The meal dragged on into the early evening and they didn't get a chance to speak to each other until bedtime. They thanked the king and his wife for their hospitality and were led back around the palace to their quarters.

"Man, I'm ready to pop," Trevor moaned and let himself fall onto his bed.

"Poor old Ossi," Katherine said and meant king Osorkon. "He didn't seem very much in charge in his own palace."

"Why does he have to be such a wuss? The queen and her sorcerer practically run the show," Trevor said.

"What's the story with Tafawana? I'm sure, she said she'd be back for dinner," Chryséis wondered.

"Yes, that is strange. I mean, why should she eat with all those sick people at the citadel if she could eat here?"

"No idea," Katherine said.

They knew they had to be on their toes if the queen was friends with a sorcerer... but there were still Tafawana and the Lady of Ush-bantoun with all her maidens to protect them. Sick or not.

"She wanted to take us to see the 'Festival of Sokhar' tomorrow," Trevor mentioned. "I wonder if she'll be back by then."

That night, Chryséis didn't sleep very well.

Oh, there it was again. The door to the door to her room at home in Etheridgeville. The familiar smell of beeswax polish and the pictures on the wall. Everything was the way it had always looked, and that's how it should be. So warm, so comforting. At home.

Chryséis saw the room clearly before her inner eye. She got up and walked straight towards the concealed door of the secret passage and thought it was her own bedroom door at home. Shortly after, Trevor and Katherine awoke from a commotion in the room.

They sat up, rubbing their eyes, and saw how Chryséis walked back into the room and straight towards her bed.

They watched in horror how the secret door flew open and Chryséis was rudely pushed forward by Totolin.

She had sleep-walked right into the alchemist's laboratory and Totolin, who slept on a mat in front of the sorcerer's bedchamber, had followed her back to the guest chamber. The girl fell onto her bed and was all confused.

"Who told you to spy on the queen?" The sorcerer's assistant hissed, eyes flashing. He tried to keep his voice down to not alarm the guards outside.

Totolin bounced up and down. "Out with it! Who told you?"

The children looked at each other in obvious surprise. Spies? What? "Chryséis has a sleep-walking problem," Katherine answered and yawned.

"I see…" Totolin realized that he had made a mistake and they were mere children after all. He gave an uneasy cackle. "We shall not speak to the queen about this incident. It would upset her terribly."

"Ahem, yes alright," Trevor croaked and Chryséis rubbed her eyes not quite awake yet.

"Very well then. Let's get all back to sleep and forget about the incident."

They heard how the door to the secret passage was locked from the outside and Totolin's steps moved away fast.

"Are you okay, Chris?" Trevor asked in a hushed voice. "That was a close shave..." He couldn't even remember what he'd been dreaming about. Just that he was standing outside in the moonlight…and then…then…no, now it was gone!

Chryséis answered with an extended yawn.

"Oh Chris, you sleep-walked through the secret passage and into the lab. That's very dangerous," Katherine cried. "Oh, why didn't we lock the door…?"

Chryséis just turned around in her bed and soon, all three of them were fast asleep again.

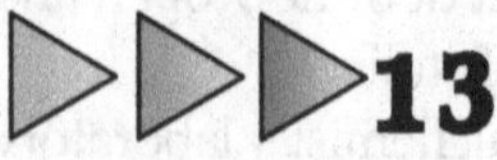 **13**   # QUEEN MÉ-LIS-AH

The following morning, they had all but forgotten about the late-night incident and it seemed like a distant dream. Apparently, the Magi hadn't mentioned anything about Chryséis' sleep-walking to the queen, because nothing was mentioned.

And it was for the best.

The queen had retired to a small garden at the back of the Per-aa with her entourage for the morning meal and the children had been told to join them. There was no rain – which was perfect for spending some time outdoors. There was plenty of space to play on the lawn and Trevor brought the orange Frisbee with him he still carried around in his backpack. After all that travelling in vimaans, he felt like running around a bit.

"Your Highness, may we play an outdoor game?" he asked the queen politely after the breakfast.

A flicker of recognition seemed to flicker across the queen's face when she saw the orange plastic disk. But that was quite impossible. Where could she have seen a Frisbee before?

But Trevor wasn't wrong, the queen had seen a Frisbee before. Just like the one Trevor had brought along. In fact, she had seen many. the queen a somewhat direct question.

"Honourable queen Mé-lis-ah, do you have throwing disks in Kem?" Trevor asked. "It seems that you are familiar with such Alesian playthings."

The queen looked astonished at his boldness and set her mouth in a thin line. Then after what seemed a very long minute, she had overcome her shock. Queen Mé-lis-ah rose abruptly from her cushioned seat and said: "There is something I forgot in the audience room that I wanted to show to our new guests. Enjoy yourselves until we return." She gave her entourage a forced smile.

Her chamber ladies didn't dare show their relief, but the musicians began to play a jolly tune.

As they reached the audience room, the queen turned around to face the children. "Athenai, where did you come from… I mean before Alesia?"

"Whatever do you mean, your Majesty?" Trevor asked her as they entered the room.

"You know exactly what I mean!" The queen snapped and her eyes flashed.

They looked at each other in surprise as they entered the room. What did she know? Was she also a time traveller? The Lady of Cydonia had warned them to hide the fact that they came from the future. Just that this woman seemed to already know and apparently, she didn't like it one bit.

What were they supposed to do now?

Katherine decided to broach the subject carefully.

"Is it possible that your Highness might know where we are from or has perhaps been there herself?"

The queen's expression changed. She looked around. Two guards stood by the carved door inside the audience room, waiting for her instructions. Otherwise, nobody else seemed to be around.

"Leave us at once!" Queen Mé-lis-ah ordered the two men.

The guards positioned themselves outside and the queen closed the heavy door behind her.

The children realised that they must have met another time traveller just like the Lady of Cydonia, but this woman seemed upset about it. Her reaction couldn't have been more different to the Lady of Cydonia's.

"Let's just say that it can't be this time."

"Have you travelled through time and space... your Highness?" Trevor asked. "Were you..."

But Mé-lis-ah interrupted him. "Oh, very well if you must know..." the queen said testily in perfect English with an undefinable accent.

She proceeded to tell them how she had come to Kem from her time in the future. It was an almost truthful account. Almost.

Melissa El Essy was the daughter of an American-Arabic diplomat father and a French mother. Her mother had been a secretary at the French embassy in the capital of Madagascar, in the late nineteen fifties. She'd fallen in love with a handsome diplomat and they got married. Melissa and her sister grew up in many cities around the world but called Cairo their home.

In 1976, at the age of seventeen, Melissa befriended a young man in the park down the road. He seemed a bit lost and spoke Arabic with an awful accent.

This young man told her that he came from a city called Ush-bantoun, district of Cuma, in the land of Kem. Melissa had never heard of such a place.

His father Bok-en-Raf, was king of Ush-bantoun. Although Melissa had never heard of such a place, his polite old-fashioned manner had moved her heart.

She laughed bitterly. "He had the deepest blue eyes I had ever seen. Osorkon had come to Cairo as a student. He was not specific about his subjects - something to do with engineering. Or so I thought at the time," Melissa told them. "I was bored at home. My mother was planning all these parties to introduce me to society. We often met in the park or at one of the liberal coffee shops. We fell in love and eventually he told me the truth. That he wanted to take me back in time as his bride. This was true destiny. How exciting. A bit odd perhaps, but I didn't question him. He was so different to the other boys I knew."

All they cared about were pop bands and sports.

Melissa also liked the Bay City Rollers and Suzy Quattro, but she was romantic.

Osorkon flattered the teenager that was the most beautiful creature he had ever seen.

"He was convinced that Mé-lis-ah, as he came to call her, would elevate the bloodline of his noble family. Their offspring would become the most powerful kings of Kem, nay all of Ta Mery. He promised me wealth beyond my dreams if I became his wife. Of course, I consented. Then one day, Osorkon and I went hiking and suddenly, we were inside a whirlwind."

That's how she remembered their trip through space and time.

"Then I found myself in this wonderful palace and I became the queen of prehistoric Ush-bantoun. My name changed to Mé-lis-ah Nûr-ah-Osorkon - Queen of Ush-bantoun, the light of Osorkon. Or Queen Mé-lis-ah for short."

When it became clear that she would not return home, Melissa had grieved for her family and carefree lifestyle. But after a while, she began to enjoy the luxury Osorkon was able to offer her. He adored Melissa's beauty and haughty bearing at first then her sweet, wide-eyed nature had become tainted with mood swings. The king missed the sweet, beautiful girl who had arrived with him from the twirling ether of time.

"The pear-shaped instrument that had taken Osorkon into the future and back has been in his family's possession for generations. It's now back in a têrakhon box under an electromagnetic shield in a secret locked room."

The Magi of Kem, tutor to the young prince had told Osorkon that the magical object had been taken before the Dark Age from a citadel in the east many sheaves of years ago. That it belonged to the Gods. There was also a short staff, shaped like a hockey stick. It was supposed to have magical powers over life and death, but the knowledge of how to use it had been lost a long time ago.

"The Magi could read the instructions, that's how Osorkon time-travelled and came back with me. Nobody noticed that he had been gone, except for the Magi. That's all I know. When I saw you taking out the Frisbee, I knew you couldn't possibly be from this time."

"Why couldn't you just travel back and visit your family?" Katherine asked.

"My husband forbade it and then the Magi disappeared. He was the only one who could read the instructions."

"Right. Wow, that's some story," Chryséis said.

"Are you saying that I'm lying?" Melissa snapped.

She didn't tell them that her husband took her to the 'House of Life' for a cure of her temper, but no remedy helped for long. Then Osorkon decided to ignore his wife's antics. After all, she was a rare treasure. A calming potion was administered when necessary. To Osorkon's regret, their marriage had remained childless.

As so often, Melissa had now developed a splitting headache and told the children peskily to leave her presence at once.

"What a story!" Katherine said under her breath as they closed the heavy door behind them. "And did you hear that the time travel device is also pear-shaped like ours?"

14 A SPY AT THE INN

Alas, they hadn't seen the last of the queen's bad temper – or the new sorcerer of Ush-bantoun.

Out of nowhere, he appeared in front of them as they stepped out of audience room and seemed to be alone for once.

"So, it is you," he said smugly and moved in like a predator on the prowl. The children jumped in surprise. Was this about Chryséis' sleepwalking adventure? Their experiences with sorcerers had proved unpleasant so far, to say the least.

"Whatever do you mean, Sir Magi?" Trevor tried to sound innocent.

"We had the pleasure of meeting yesterday at the king's lunch table, didn't we?"

But the sorcerer wasn't easily distracted. "It was you who summoned the power of three Ladies to vanquish my brethren of the 'Left Path'. Wasn't it?! Now they languish in the Gogmagog Mountains."

He had come right out with it.

"Well, we didn't exactly..." Katherine began, but Chryséis elbowed her in the ribs and Katherine fell silent.

"Oh but my dear children, you quite misunderstand my intentions. I am on your side." The sorcerer said in a silky-smooth voice and moved closer.

"You are?" Trevor moved two steps back.

"But of course." The Magi flashed his false smile again.

"See if it hadn't been for you, I would not have become the advisor of Queen Mé-lis-ah ..." His lips barely moved as he spoke. "This is a very good thing for me."

The time travellers understood. This unpleasant fellow had eyeballed the powerful position and was pleased to be rid of the competition. So much for dark brotherhood.

"That's nice of you, sir. But we had no part in this…"

"Is that so?" The sorcerer looked surprised.

"Indeed, sir," Trevor said firmly.

"Let me know if there is anything you need. Anything at all, athenai. A little blood-letting might relax you…"

"Sure. Thank you, sir." The children tried to hide their discomfort. "We'll get back to you on that."

"Good, good." With that, the sorcerer bowed and oozed his way toward the other end of the corridor.

"At last!" Chryséis said relieved.

"His facial muscles must be paralysed by now. All this grinning…" Trevor said. "I don't trust that guy one bit."

"…if you need anything, anything at all…" Chryséis repeated mockingly. "Yeah right, we'd ask him for sure."

"What should we do now? He knows who we are," Katherine said. "I say we make a beeline out of here."

"Do you think they will let us go?" Trevor asked

"What do you mean let us go? We'll just say thanks very much for your hospitality, gotta go," Chryséis insisted.

"I have a feeling it won't be that easy," Katherine moaned. "They are not easy-going people. Melissa seems mad and that doesn't help."

"Tafawana will help us. And the Lady of Ush-bantoun," Trevor answered. "Let's calm down. We can walk into town. We shouldn't talk about this around here." The girls agreed and they left the Per-aa.

They met the merchant Manassi again in the palace courtyard and he promptly offered to accompany them into town. He had to take care of more business there. Since he was a merry type of guy, he had already made friends here and there.

After talking to the queen and her evil advisor, the children were thankful to be around somebody, who seemed normal. Manassi was planning to visit an inn on the large square. They passed a rawi, who told a group of children some exciting stories about the gods. He sat on a brightly coloured blanket with a whirligig pattern. The children were engrossed by the story of how the goddess Iset and her husband had abolished cannibalism in the country.

"Would you like to listen to the rawi?" Manassi asked.

"No, I think we've heard enough stories for a while," Chryséis answered.

"Oh, but there will be much storytelling during the festival. You must hear at least some of the stories."

"I think we definitely will - later."

They walked onto the largest central town square between cream-coloured buildings. Some of the buildings were terraced like the Atalian library. They hadn't seen this style since Atala, but there were no proper pyramids. The square teemed with activity. Women were dressed in brightly patterned clothes, long embroidered tunics and black skirts. Others were wrapped in colourful lengths of cloth, draped like Indian saris.

Apparently, facial tattoos were quite the fashion even here. Less permanent dark-red henna tattoos that were applied by barbers' assistants in front of their shops. There were also a few stalls, selling odds and ends.

"There will be many stalls all over town soon," Manassi said and pointed to the south. "Booths are set up along the great plaza and certain areas are assigned to performing artists."

"I can't wait to see that," Katherine said happily.

They entered a 'public house', called the 'Wild Boar'. The inn was panelled in dark wood and cosy, but not exactly quiet. A group of beer-swilling men chatted noisily in a corner, their wooden beakers brimming with frothing sorghum beer.

A harp player strummed his instrument listlessly in another corner of the inn and sang a little tune. Nobody listened to him. Two women in bright pink and green saris ordered savoury pies for their children.

On the dark counter, traditional snacks were displayed: bowls with large tender olives and a dukkah mix, roasted vegetables, dried dates and fresh figs, all pink inside. Stacks of oval flatbread was next to green flasks with olive oil and the ever-popular fish sauce garum.

The leavened flatbread was dipped into olive oil then eaten with olives and dukkah. Dukkah was a mix of roasted nuts, sesame seeds, spices and salt, all ground together. The children had learned that at Bibi Gul's house. A choice of dishes was on the menu, drawn on the walls.

"That's my fish-sauce," Manassi said proudly.

On the menu was yoghurt with chopped up cucumber pieces and garlic, fried crumbed balls made of mashed chickpeas, pies and roasted lamb seasoned with lemon and rosemary. Trevor had the camera in his shirt pocket and took a picture of it.

Ta-Merians were fond of barley beer and an alcoholic drink brewed with juniper berries. Not that they were good at holding their drink. If their inner rabbit was set loose by too much alcohol, it performed silly antics. During the festival, this apparently happened quite a lot.

If one didn't favour 'water of life', guests could also choose between sweet and sour yoghurt drinks, cucumber water, and chai. A tea flavoured with cinnamon sticks and cardamom pods.

"One hin of your good bouza beer! And three hins of cooled cucumber water," Manassi ordered. He felt generous today.

Not far from their table, a 'cricket', took note of the ordered beverages. As a cover, he acted a little drunk while he spied on the palace guests. They didn't notice the spy and simply enjoyed their drinks.

At the table next to them, three men were busy at playing a board game with beans for counters.

The innkeeper Hapu Pa Geb-Iset was obviously a good friend of the merchant and joined them at the table. They were introduced to him and he apologised for the poor fare in his modest establishment.

To the children's surprise, the men started talking in hushed voices about the king of Ush-bantoun his queen Mé-lis-ah, his strange outlandish wife.

"I have it on good authority that a pretty dame smiled just a bit too much at a reception in honour of the king's birth feast. Some say, the king did have plans to take a second wife at the time," the innkeeper gossiped.

"Yes, and?" Katherine wanted to hear the whole story.

The innkeeper was surprised at the forwardness of Alesian children, but he loved to tell a good story and continued. "The following day the queen wore a necklace of human teeth around her neck. The pretty lady was not so pretty after that." There was a stunned pause.

"That's so cruel," Trevor said in disbelief. "Are you sure this really happened? Mé-lis-ah seems so civilised to me."

"Ah, civilised." The innkeeper rolled the word on his tongue. "On her better days, she may be …civilized, but on her days of insanity…you better be far away." Melissa was that insane?!

"Oh dear," Katherine said. "Instead of an ally, we've met Lady Macbeth." That was bad luck, indeed.

"Lady of Mek-bès? Who may that be? Is she the Lady of an Alesian citadel?"

"No, never mind…" Katherine said. "Lady Macbeth was just another Mé-lis-ah, I suppose…in a…a play." Katherine couldn't think of a better explanation. How did one explain a play by Shakespeare to an Egyptian innkeeper from 12,000 years ago?

Hapu scanned the inn discreetly. The queen's 'crickets' were never far away and he wanted to be sure that it was safe to speak. Mé-lis-ah Nûr-ah-Osorkon ah Per-aa Ush-bantoun, the light of the king Osorkon of the 'Great House' of Ush-bantoun, was sensitive to rumours.

"You'd be surprised…" Chryséis began. She wanted to

say something about modern days, but Hapu didn't listen.

"The poor Lady of Ush-bantoun," the innkeeper muttered.

"Why what's wrong with her? Is she getting worse?" Manassi asked.

"Rumour has it that she languishes with her maidens in the ivory tower. Queen Mé-lis-ah has taken over the citadel and doesn't want any citadel staff around…" Hapu almost whispered now.

A servitor who arrived with the food interrupted their conversation. Hapu had ordered a few dishes on the house for his friend Manassi and the children and helped to place them on the table.

"Is this what I think it is?" Chryséis whispered to Katherine and pointed to a fried insect.

Katherine couldn't answer her. The innkeeper urged his guests good-naturedly to taste a delicacy and Manassi tucked into the spicy dish with relish. It was fried cow-eyeballs. Chryséis gingerly picked an eyeball up and pushed it against her mouth. That seemed sufficient to make their host happy. Katherine tried not to look too closely and did the same. They let the eyeballs fall to the ground and made chewing movements.

"Mmm, yummy," Katherine said and nodded.

Hapu was called to the front by a group of customers and Manassi accompanied his friend to the counter to get more olives. It was getting a bit dark inside the inn and soon rain began to drum against the windows.

"Melissa sounds like a nut case," Chryséis said. "I say, we clear out of the palace," Trevor whispered. "I don't care if Melissa is from the future. It's getting a bit dicey."

"We should find out, what happened to the Lady of Ush-bantoun." Chryséis said and bit into a rather large olive. "Maybe she needs out help."

"You're right. Melissa's stories sound phony. We must find the Lady and speak to her." Trevor picked up some of the eggplant salad from a blue glazed bowl with a piece of bread.

"How are we supposed to help the Lady if she is in trouble? We don't even have our paizas anymore."

"You're right, Katie." Chryséis thought for a moment. "And if we rush things, Melissa might become suspicious."

Hapu and Manassi came back with more bowls.

"We should go back to the palace, soon," Trevor said quickly when they arrived at the table.

But, the cheerful merchant and his friend had other plans. Hapu insisted on showing the children from Cydonia the festive town. "No, no, no. It's no inconvenience at all!" He said. "We can go right now. It's the best town in all of Ta Mery," he bragged. He gave sharp instructions to his staff and clapped the serving boy behind the ear for not listening and soon they stepped out onto the wet pavement of the town square. Hapu started to walk ahead, greeting townspeople as they went down the square.

"Okay then, better than hanging around the palace with crazy Melissa, I guess," Katherine whispered.

"Look at the prytaneum over there," Trevor said. He pointed at a building to their left, but Manassi and Hapu took them to the right side of the square and into an alley.

The two men were chatting away, so the time travellers switched to English. The alley led down to the Nila River, or rather a channel of the mighty river. They went up a broad flight of stairs and continued the tour on a promenade with an excellent view of the city.

"Look at all those white cone-towers, but it feels strange that there are no pyramids around," Katherine said.

"That's because it's way too early for pyramids," Trevor said and scanned the city for the odd-looking towers.

"I know that," Katherine answered slightly irritated.

Two such towers were right ahead of them. At the base grew colourful azalea shrubs and bright red hibiscus and right on top of the cones, fluttered flags with the image of a yellow winged sun on dark blue background. Spiralling staircases on the outside of the towers led right up to the top. They had seen their first tall cone-shaped structures in Cydonia, but this was Egypt.

"I wonder what they are," Chryséis said. "Graves of kings or storage silos… or flat buildings maybe…"

Trevor took a picture of the city and the cones. Little birds flew up as they walked past a park. They pecked at a piece of bread somebody had dropped carelessly on the pavement. From here, one could see tents on the meadows around the city.

They passed two or three tent that looked like yurts.

"Country folk, who make camp in the park, which isn't exactly allowed", Hapu said. He led the way past an archery school right by the park.

A temple to the goddess Iset stood lonely on the grassy riverbank, not far from a bridge and the southern gate. Hapu stopped a few times to explain the sights, but Ush-bantoun wasn't that big and they soon walked back to the inn of the "Wild Boar" after having seen the prytaneum, library and courthouse.

More stalls had been set up on the central square. Statues and pillars along the shaded porch in front of the courthouse were decorated with branches and ribbons. The royal household would be seated up there on the morning of the 'Festival of Sokhar'.

An old man with a turban on his grey head sat on a large round blanket with a colourful whirligig pattern. An audience of about ten dawdling workmen and shopping housewives were standing around the blanket.

The rawi was in the progress of telling the story about the incomparably beautiful 'Neomah and the Stolen Shoe'. He had already told a captivating, romantic story of the desert prince Antar and a stanza from the 'Thelik Tephan', or 'Breath of Life' book. Hapu and Manassi couldn't resist a good story and stopped to listen, while the children walked around and had a good look at the neighbouring stalls being set up.

When they returned, the rawi ended his story with the words "…and that is why women should best keep their shoes covered with dresses or blankets. A bird might carry their shoe to a man they don't want to marry."

Manassi and the children thanked the innkeeper for the food and the sight-seeing tour. It was getting late and they should go and have supper at the palace as planned.

Manassi took a shortcut and soon they were standing in front of the palace gates. Boxes of saurian hide were being unloaded from a large moki at the front entrance. A box with white pearls from Dilmun, as large as cherries, were destined for the king's wife. She loved jewellery and her husband sent far and wide to find the choicest pieces.

The children thanked Manassi and went up to their room. They didn't know that the 'cricket' from the inn had already reported to the queen.

A guard intercepted the guests and promptly showed them into a green and golden room. Mé-lis-ah Nûr-ah-Osorkon was already waiting.

Trevor ducked just in time, as a mirror of polished metal flew past his head and hit the wall behind him with an ugly thud. The children stared at the time-travelling queen in shock.

"Useless. Get out of my sight if you know what's good for you," Mé-lis-ah screeched. A servant girl began to cry and ran past the children.

When the queen saw her young guests, she changed her voice to a honey-sweet purr. "Oh, here you are, darlings. At last."

Then she saw servants hovering frightened in a corner of the room and her tone became harsh again. "These servants are so useless… Go now you useless…fleas."

She yelled something rude in Ta-Merian and the servants fled helter-skelter out of the room. The three children would have liked to do the same.

"Ah, there we go. Now we can talk." There was the honey-sweet voice again. Hapu, the innkeeper had said that Melissa was insane. Perhaps he had been right…

The blonde woman in her jewel-encrusted dress didn't seem to think that there was anything wrong with her behaviour.

"I hear you spoke to Manassi and the innkeeper at the 'public house'. What a place to take children. You mustn't believe the lies people tell you about me," she said abruptly.

The children stared at her. The story about her 'crickets' was also the truth then. There must have been a spy at the 'Wild Boar'. Great.

"What lies, Melissa? About you? We only talked about Ta Mery and Ush-bantoun and traditions… and went sight-seeing," Katherine said with an innocent look.

Her eyes could have melted an iceberg, but Melissa didn't buy it and her reaction took them off guard. "That would be queen Mé-lis-ah to you. And did you think I wouldn't find out about it if you blabbed behind my back?" Melissa snapped at her coldly.

Melissa's friendly mask began to crumble. She checked herself with difficulty, remembering the reason, why she kept the children around.

"Our honourable Lady of Ush-bantoun seems a little better today. Perhaps she'll be ready to see you in a few days - and the maiden you came with." The queen had obviously forgotten Tafawana's name and her smile sat a little crooked on her face. *Sure we will see her*, the children thought and smiled carefully back. Even sooner than you think.

Well, I will get the truth out of you sooner or later, Queen Mé-lis-ah thought maliciously then cried happily. "It's time for dinner. Aren't you famished? You ate at the inn an eternity ago."

"There is plenty of space for more delicious food," Trevor flattered her.

"There better be." The smile disappeared from her face.

*

During dinner, the children were rather quiet. You never knew what set the madwoman off. But Melissa didn't say anything more about their excursion to the inn this afternoon and chatted with the Magi next to her. The spread on the table was irresistible.

Stuffed figs, grilled line fish and pieces of a large well-tasting fowl with some sort of herby crust. The children ate as much as they could, and then asked permission to leave the table, claiming to feel tired.

Back in the safety of their room, they began to make plans. It was obvious that Melissa didn't mean well.

"How did she know we were at the 'Wild Boar' with Manassi?" Katherine sighed and threw herself on her bed.

"There is always the Internet of the mind."

"You think she has somebody follow us, who sends her telepathic reports?" Katherine asked.

"It's possible," Trevor said.

"Who do you think was the spy?"

"Probably not just one, but a few. I saw this guy from the palace sitting at a table in the corner. He looked a bit drunk and wasn't close enough to hear what we were saying."

"Unless this 'cricket' has supersonic hearing," Chryséis said.

"I think we can't trust anyone, who works for Melissa," Trevor said. "Especially not that slime ball of a sorcerer."

"I say, we have to get out of this Per-aa as soon as possible. Maybe we can walk to the next town. It's better than watching her go off her rocker again," Katherine said.

"If we run now, they might catch us and then we're in a worse position. We should try to keep her happy for a while. Remember that she was interested in our time travel? We could dangle that carrot. There is something she wants."

"She's cray-cray, so who knows. The mirror throwing and all that stuff was off the wall. We should find Tafawana. She has to be here somewhere. Then we decide what to do," Chryséis said and the others agreed with.

But the time travellers were in for a nasty surprise.

▷▷▷**15** THE FESTIVAL OF SOKHAR

Katherine woke up early and couldn't go back to sleep. She stood by the windows in the bathroom, looking out onto the river. The Nile was right there, outside the palace walls. Fantastic.

A misty veil still lay over the water surface when a flock of red heron soared into the air from one of the trees by the shore.

"What a beautiful place," she murmured dreamily. "All these broad trees and palms covered in red and white birds."

The rooftops of Ush-bantoun peeped through the tree-tops and white conical towers were mirrored in the slowly moving waters. Boats were slowly rowed upstream. As the sun rose, the mist dissolved and the boats disappeared from view behind palm trees and ferns on the riverbanks. She remembered the story of the little boat in one of the books they had viewed through the crystal and Katherine began to hum the melody.

A voice abruptly interrupted her reverie. "Come on Katie, get ready."

Katherine hadn't noticed Chryséis come into the bathroom. "I could watch this forever," she said and began to wash her face.

"We don't want to grow old around Melissa," Chryséis grumbled. "So be careful when you say 'forever'."

"Gosh, you're in a bad mood today."

"Yeah, small surprise. At least, I didn't sleep-walk again last night, or I think I didn't."

"No, I don't think you did."

Despite everything that had happened yesterday, they would be going to a real ancient Egyptian festival! Well, sort of. Then, they had to find a way to contact the Lady of Ush-bantoun and leave this place as soon as possible.

But Melissa had other ideas. They were soon summoned by the queen and Melissa didn't lose much time with pleasantries.

"Morning," she said. "You come with me." She pointed to the children. "And you stay here." The guards lowered their heads and stayed behind.

Melissa took them up and down a few flights of stairs then stopped in front of an embroidered screen under heavy guard. No one was allowed behind the screen, except her, and the small empty room was quite dusty inside. Melissa opened an old scratched door with a strange-looking key.

What was the woman up to? They didn't want to set her off with questions, but why did she want them to come with her to see a secret room?

Soon they had the answer. It was the time-travel apparatus, Osorkon had used to bring his bride back from the future. It was kept here on a table under what looked like a see-through cheese cover.

The children gawked at an object that was much larger than their own TPF. It had the shape of a small turtle with short wings – not that of a pear. The stone was of a dark pinkish colour. Another object that looked like a hockey stick, just as Melissa had described it was right next to it. This thing could have been anything. The têrakhon cheese cover had to be protected by an invisible electromagnetic shield.

Melissa told the children that after she had travelled into the past, she had found herself inside a têrakhon booth. "I felt nauseous and lost consciousness. When I woke up again, I was in a room, decorated with carved furniture that was inlaid with ivory and gold. Servants were waiting on me at the foot of a large soft bed, draped in veils. I was treated like a queen..."

"You must have travelled through a vortex," Trevor said. "We know what that feels like."

Was this going to take long? They wanted to go and see the festival.

"You understand nothing of how I feel," Melissa flew at him. "You have the freedom to travel back to your own time whenever you feel like it. I, on the other hand, I am a prisoner."

It was true that Osorkon, the king of Ush-bantoun, refused to make the time-travel device available to his moody wife.

"The electromagnetic shield is too strong to get through," Melissa complained. "I've tried, but he just won't let me go."

"So what can we do about it?" Katherine asked.

"Give me your time-travel device and you shall be richly rewarded. Anything you want. Gold, land, diamonds, servants... anything. but I must have your device." Melissa was desperate and dead-serious.

The three friends gave each other a puzzled look. To give up their TPF? Melissa didn't know that they had three of them. Trevor thought of a way out of this impossible situation.

"Melissa..." His throat felt dry. "Can we please think about this? It comes as a surprise. We had no idea how much you were suffering..."

"Six years. Six long years I have spent in prehistory."

"That's a long time," Chryséis said carefully.

"Yes, a very long time... but of course, you may think about it. Go and enjoy the festival. We'll talk later."

The children felt numb as they left the audience room and were led directly into the yard. They all knew what their answer had to be. Melissa hadn't actually asked them. She had demanded the time portal finder.

"Great, now what are we going to do?"

"Katie, I don't know. We should have taken the TPFs with us, but they won't let us go back to our room now."

The guard was not smiling and just kept showing them the way through the courtyard to the gate.

"Should we contact the Lady of Cydonia?" Trevor asked and began to walk.

"What if Melissa or the sorcerer pick that up. We have to be really careful now," Katherine said. "The Lady of Cydonia is too far away to do something fast."

They had more than one device, but they still needed to be tested. Plus, they couldn't just give Melissa a time portal finder. It couldn't be programmed exactly to the point in time when she had left Cairo in the seventies.

"If it's Melissa, who appears in Carter Valley instead of us, it can cause a weird situation."

In any case, they needed some help here! This whole thing with Melissa was getting out of hand. They had to go and find Tafawana!

*

The children couldn't walk straight across the road to the citadel for fear of being apprehended by guard, who was still behind them, so they first went into town and hoped to disappear in the crowd. The town centre was bustling with activity, because everybody prepared for the festivities.

Sokhar was a Ta-Merian god of agriculture, the patron of craftsmen and protector of goldsmiths. The 'Festival of Sokhar' was in the god's honour and held every year after the first harvest. People came together from the Puntian continent to Ush-bantoun to celebrate this event.

The children hadn't seen Manassi at the palace. He had probably already left to speak to the travelling vendors on the town square. There were so many people in the streets that they had managed to lose their guard, who had followed them at a distance on the way into the city.

"If we had our stuff, we could just do a runner now," Katherine said.

"But we don't, so we'll do the festival for now and then do the runner." Trevor was amazed by all the stalls and booths that had sprung up overnight along the avenues of Ush-bantoun.

Colourful banners in red and green hung everywhere and the once peaceful town centre was pulsating with visitors. The banners hung on wooden poles between bronze statues and were painted with hieroglyphs. *Long live King Osorkon! Sokhar is proud of the Kings of Ta Mery!*

*

Back at the Per-aa it was time for an audience.

Melissa sat in her gold leaf-covered throne and had developed a headache. She had already seen two messengers and was growing tired of everybody's problems, while her husband was engaged in formalities connected to the festival.

The Magi stood stolidly next to her chair and whispered in her ear.

"A message for you my queen. It is of a certain importance."

He made a sign towards the doorway.

"Out! Everybody out! Enough for today," Melissa yelled and the room was cleared in no time.

The men guarding the door held the two wings wide-open and one of the Lady of Ush-bantoun's messengers entered the room.

He wore a long green tunic with the blazon of Ush-bantoun was embroidered on the back. He was one of the very few in the Lady's employ that Melissa found useful.

"Honourable... ehem... Queen Mé-lis-ah, Light of Osorkon..." protocol demanded that he address her by her full title. Strictly speaking, Osorkon and his wife were neither king nor queen, but Mé-lis-ah's ill-tempered behaviour was well-known and the messenger decided to

142

humour her.

She extended her bejewelled hand to the messenger, but the poor man looked quite embarrassed. What was he supposed to do with the queen's hand? This was not customary. Eventually, he extended his hand deftly in the same way and withdrew two paces.

Melissa sneered at his ignorance. "Fool," she hissed barely audible.

She battled to control her contempt for these prehistoric dolt. Soon she would once again be free to come and go as she pleased. The thought lifted her mood and she managed a pearly-white smile for the sweating messenger. He took heart and spoke.

"Your Highness, slave traders are reported to roam our beautiful land. Two children, one in Innu and one in Ush-bantoun have gone missing quite suddenly since yesterday. Then two brothers from the south…"

"Ah, slave traders…" the queen relished the word. She suddenly had a brilliant idea. "Good!"

"But your Highness, the 'House of Truth' must investigate at once. The families are in distress. We mustn't lose any time…"

The messenger grew nervous, nearly tripping on the hem of his green robe. What was she waiting for? He composed himself quickly and straightened his tunic. "The Lady would do so herself, however…"

"Ah, balderdash!" Melissa said impatiently "What a din about a few useless children…" she caught herself with an elegant gesture, remembering her status. "You may go now. I will make my decision later. Now, I must get ready for the formal festivities." She ended the audience.

When the confused messenger left the room, Melissa turned to her advisor with a malicious smile.

"Find me those slave traders," she commanded. "I have a proposal for them they can't refuse."

*

Back at the main square in town, the time travellers threw themselves into the crowd around the many shops and booths. Two stalls offered engraved and painted ostrich eggs from Yam, where Azurias Maya had spent his time. Yam was also the home of the Nyam Nyam pygmies, often employed as jesters at Ta Merian courts.

Unfortunately, there were no jesters left in Ush-bantoun as they had either perished or had fled. Katherine picked up one of the painted eggs. Some of them were definitely too big to come even from an ostrich.

They strolled towards the prytaneum, where a fierce-looking shaman from the land of Zinj interpreted messages from a fake 'speaking stone' to entertain his spectators.

The shaman claimed that he - and he alone - was able to understand the black stone's silent answers to questions by the audience. This speaking stone was allegedly able to telepathically communicate.

The children grinned. Of course, this man was a charlatan.

At the next stall, a dark-skinned woman, who wore a large disc-shaped hat, offered love letters made from strings of beads. She threaded the beads according to the customer's wishes.

Black beads – marriage was intended. Green beads signalled an unmarried status, white beads that the lover was wanted back.

Next to the bead-letter shop, sought-after Mashru fabrics from Dwarka were laid out on a table. Then there were spices and herbs in sacks and têrakhon containers. Incense, salt, garum and exotic foodstuffs. Mother of pearl earrings and necklaces from the coastal region next to golden tiaras and rings from the East. They were supposedly crafted in the way ancient goddesses had preferred them.

Woven pots, calabashes and amphorae made from blue clay with handles in the shape of lotus flowers, fine deer leather bags from Prydhain and embroidered shoes from

Atala were also on offer. Somebody proffered golden apples from Hisbernia, but the time travellers wondered whether they were actually the real thing.

This was a real oriental bazaar!

A bard cheered the feast with a song to the clangs of his kithara and a blond boy next to him held up large flip cards while his younger brother worked the cymbals in rhythm to the melody. The painted cards showed a story and the boy had to hold up the matching cards to the song.

Some people were waiting in a queue to hear their future from a mysterious Puntian man, dressed in hides and hung with many necklaces.

The time travellers picked their way around the queue and walked toward a row of booths on the other side of the plaza. A speech was to be held by the ruler of Ushbantoun later on the porch of the 'House of Truth.

The broad stairs in front of the building were already cordoned off and just as Chryséis was about to purchase three dozen transparent beads, a piercing trumpet signal was sounded. The king and queen were arriving.

Dull drum rolls rumbled in the background and the crowd murmured in adoration as it gathered around the 'House of Truth'.

The children found a place near the back of the crowd when trumpeters called to silence. The rumbling stopped instantly and the happy noise of the festival died down.

A procession started by the prytaneum that led across the square. The Wzir, dressed in regal costume, walked ahead stomping a painted staff on the ground. Behind the Wzir, the other officials filed toward the 'House of Truth'. Royal dignitaries resplendent in furry uniforms followed. Each of them wore an ornament through their pierced noses.

The officials were lining up around the two thrones on the wide porch to the boom of a drum. Then the king walked towards the porch, holding the hand of his wife.

The crowd cheered as Osorkon and his queen walked past, fanned by servants. Melissa wore a golden dress and dripped with jewels, a spotted doe's fur around her shoulders as a sign of her status. A spotted fallow deer hide was reserved only for the king himself.

King Osorkon, chieftain of the Cuma people, relished the public attention. Still a handsome man, the king was; with brown hair and hazel eyes. His subjects thought he was very impressive, despite the small paunch he had grown from drinking too much barley beer.

The couple walked up the stairs and positioned themselves in front of the thrones.

As he stood before his subjects in a simple white tunic, a spotted deer hide around his shoulders, the king was cheered as the representative of the god Sokhar. He seemed to wait. Where was the good Lady of Ush-bantoun? She should have attended the ceremony with all her maidens, as the custom demanded. Instead, his wife the queen sang a song to her god-like husband, who then wrapped his arms around her.

Why was the honourable Lady not in the procession?

A murmur rose in the crowd, while the Wzir gave the usual introduction. "On this auspicious day in the first month of summer, day eighteen in the thirty-seventh year of the appearance of King Osorkon, Son of Bok-en-Raf I, son of king Sutekh, son of king Pentaware…" The Wzir went on to recite the ancestry of six generations.

"…Ruler of the Nome of Kem with Per-aa residence in the prosperous city of Ush-bantoun and his queen Mé-lis-ah, mose Magdi el Essy Pa Cairo, Mery-en-Neith…" which meant as much as queen Mé-lis-ah, 'born of Magdi el Essy from Cairo, beloved of the goddess Neith – the first exalted queen regnant of Ta Mery, the 'Beloved Land'-… these were apparently Melissa's official titles.

The voice of the Wzir droned on and Katherine and Trevor began to feel sleepy as did many in the crowd.

"...on this the seventh occasion of the Festival during the reign of our blessed ruler Osorkon in honour of Sokhar, revered god of agriculture and..." When the Wzir ended his introduction, Osorkon began his speech after much pompous stomping of staffs and booming of drums.

The time travellers were again wide-awake. Osorkon spoke about ordinary pebbles being out of place among precious stones. Blue stone must not be mixed with ordinary gravel, which litters dry riverbeds. He meant of course, that nobles couldn't mix with the ordinary folk. Of course, the time travellers didn't understand this allegory.

Chryséis wondered, but what did all this stone talk have to do with addressing the folk at a festival? Perhaps it was some kind of tradition. The murmur in the crowd rose and ebbed. The Lady of the citadel represented the Earthmother and should have spoken to them.

Many were upset.

Children threw handfuls of flowers and the people of Ush-bantoun did their best to ignore their outlandish queen's reputedly unpleasant character. It was not their place to criticise those close to the gods.

"There is no star brighter and warmer during the day than the sun. Likewise, no festival is grander than the 'Festival of Sokhar'. Let the festival begin," the king opened the festivities at last.

Dark-skinned Little People filed down the central plaza. They led strange-looking animals around, native to their homeland. Reptilians by the looks of it, with their green and brown-dotted backs. These Dwendis had painted their faces and almost resembled reptilians themselves.

A group of jugglers followed. Two moving pyramids of three, the top men throwing objects at each other at lightning speed attracted much attention.

"Wow, they're good. They haven't dropped a thing," Trevor said.

A woman next to him looked at the children out of the

corner of her eyes. What kind of language was that? Perhaps it was something to report to the Magi...

A young man grabbed Katherine laughingly from behind - and fell victim to a well-placed karate chop. Puzzled by the glaring look in her eyes he apologized, obviously having made a mistake. Two Ta Merian girls stared at Katherine. Wasn't she pleased with the attention the young man had given her on this joyous occasion?

"What are you looking at?" Katherine snapped at them hotly. She suspected the young man wanted to steal her moon bag, just like the mugger in Kem-Oun.

"It's just merriment..." one of the girls said.

"Oh no - it's not! Go and be merry somewhere else."

A blue bird on the foot of a statue next to Trevor cocked its head and looked at them. Trevor and Chryséis ushered Katherine away. The last thing they needed was a crowd pitted against them.

The plaza was swarming with performing artists, musicians and spectators. What a din! Nobody followed them or was even looking at the children as they walked into one of the side streets.

'Susinku the Sand Reader,
Giant in stature,
Giant in accuracy'.

The sign leaned against the thick wall of a yurt. Katherine was curious. "A sand reader? As in reading the sand?"

"Probably something to do with tea leaves in a cup..." Trevor said. "Why do people in these times need fortune-tellers anyway? I thought they can read minds and all."

"That's not exactly the same as seeing into the future now, is it?" Katherine said. "In any case, the Lady of Cydonia said that many people can only read general moods and stuff, not actually read thoughts."

"Do you want to have a closer look?" Chryséis turned towards the tent's entrance. "Oh look, she's got a customer."

It was a matron in a pale pink sari. Susinku, the giant

sand reader, promptly lowered the blanket in front of the entrance.

The children peeped through a gap in the felt cover. Golden rings jingled on the customer's ears and arms. The matron was told to put her hands into a flat metal bowl with fine white sand. She touched the sand and ran it through her fingers. Then she laid her bejewelled hands flat on the sand for a while and lifted them quickly, shaking off the excess sand.

The giant Susinku had a mysterious look on her face and bent down to examine the sand. The customer was nodding now and then. Finally, Susinku was paid with a couple of small green feathers and the customer left the yurt. As she went back inside the tent, the gaze of the giantess fell on Trevor. He would make a good roast that one, she thought. Then she saw Chryséis. Pity the girl was an albino. Quite pretty otherwise, tender meat no doubt. She knew that cannibalism had been prohibited since the time of Osiris and that punishment was meted out to those who reverted to the old ways, but old habits die hard.

Chryséis felt uneasy under the woman's stare and urged her friends to walk on. They left the city centre and walked down a narrow alley. At the southern end of the alley, they found themselves on a green embankment along the great Nila River.

Men in white linen had gathered to show off their strength in various sports. Wrestling each other and competing in running, throwing tree trunks and lifting stones. Most of the contestants were rather large, giants almost and obviously rather strong.

The children watched in amazement and decided that it was far too early to return to the palace.

▶▶▶ 16   THE MAGICAL AMULETS

Meanwhile, the Lady of Ush-bantoun sat sadly in her tower, shielded against thought transfer and any contact with the outer world. Palace guards were positioned to keep people out and nobody was allowed to leave. Yet, here was no sign of illness at the citadel.

Only a few luxuries were allowed in the rooms the Lady of Ush-bantoun was forced to occupy with her maidens.

Tafawana of Hyela was quite beside herself. The tower had become her prison, too when she tried to visit the Lady the day before.

Other maidens and citadel staff had already disappeared while trying to escape or contact other Ladies in the realm. Loyal staff occupied the cone-shaped buildings that surrounded the citadel. They were waiting for better times to come, but others had moved into the palace and now served a different kind of mistress.

The Lady of Ush-bantoun rose from her chair. "Are you sure about this, Mingio?" she addressed her most trusted maiden.

"Lady, I am assured…" Mingio began.

"Yes… then we have to act quickly, friend. Those poor children. Travelling through time, then ending up shipwrecked… and now Mé-lis-ah and the sorcerer are trying to use them for their own selfish ends. We have to warn them. It is too dangerous for them at the palace."

"Ush-bantoun has become a dangerous place, honourable Lady. The queen's 'crickets' are making sure of it. Osorkon is bewitched by Mé-lis-ah's charms or potions. He won't listen to any advisors – and, in any case, it has become a game of life and death to advise the chieftain," a senior maiden lamented.

"I know, I know," the Lady said. "And it breaks my heart that it had to come to this. I should have known the moment I found out about Mé-lis-ah's little secret. But it is too late now. Arrange for little Pepi to carry a message to the children while they are in town. We have to try, at least."

"Many receive presents in the streets during the 'Festival of Sokhar', Lady. Pepi will do his best," the maiden Mingio assured her.

"He must take care not to arouse any suspicions. Mé-lis-ah's spies lurk in every corner," the Lady sighed.

"Oh, I so wish we could send a message to the Lady of Innu to help us in our plight..." Mingio said.

"Little Pepi is a bright boy, Lady. He will know what to do. The Earthmother be thanked that he escaped the Per-aa."

"He must be careful. We wouldn't want to lose him as well."

*

By now, a group of giants from Keftiu entertained the excited crowd on the grassy embankment by the river Nile.

They built human pyramids and as soon as a young child balanced on top of the last tier, the tower tumbled down into a laughing jumble of arms and legs.

Another giant from the island of Kibris performed magic tricks.

His head was covered in a purple turban and his robe had been embroidered with gleaming magic symbols. It was an entertaining performance. The bangles of a woman disappeared from the magician's hands and just as the feisty woman about to curse him, the bangles reappeared. On the bald head of an unsuspecting spectator. The crowd applauded eagerly.

"How did he do that? That was awesome!" Chryséis said as she clapped.

"Must be some trick to confuse the eye. Did you see

David Blaine on TV? These Magicians are really fast."

"It must be a trick, Trev." Katherine was not easily impressed.

"Yeah, but a good one."

The palace guard, who had orders to follow the children, had found them again in the crowd through sheer luck and He kept a close eye on them. The children were too captivated by the spectacle around them to notice.

A tiny hunchback with a fearsome mask now mimed the hulking magician's movements to the amusement of the audience. The giant growled in playful scorn and everyone howled with laughter.

The children moved along with the throng of people, gawking impolitely at some exotic-looking visitors with thick nose rings.

An old woman, who gave away amulets at the street corner, closed in on the three children. Unbeknown to the time travellers, she was a servant of the sorcerer at the Ush-bantoun palace.

Three identical amulets, she had drawn from her long apron, suddenly dangled on her arm. As she attempted to hang an amulet around Katherine's neck, the girl instinctively moved away from her.

The hag gave the children her best approving smirk.

"What charming modesty!" she cried. "So rare in young people these days."

She managed to pull the other two amulets over Trevor's and Chryséis' heads, and clapped her wrinkled hands with delight. "For good luck. For good luck, athenai."

What a shame that the foreign girl was an albino, she thought, staring at Chryséis' light blond braids and light complexion. Not even the queen was that fair. Chryséis squirmed under the old woman's stare.

"You, my blossom are a lucky girl," she cackled. "A prince, important and handsome will desire you soon to be his wife," she flattered her.

"In your dreams," Chryséis said and walked away.

The palace guard nodded at the old woman, indicating that she should leave now. Her job was done. He took a minute to watch pygmy dancing girls from Yam. Then the guard, who had orders not to leave the three children out of his sight, turned around for just a moment at one of the food stalls to buy rolled bread with olives and cheese and stuffed aubergines.

At that moment, a boy, barely ten years old, approached the three children. A few amulets were hanging over his arm and he offered them to the time travellers with over-the-top gestures.

"My goodness, these people are obsessed with amulets," Trevor groaned and shook his head.

"Shelanti friend Trevór," the young boy said. He had been carefully instructed by the maiden Mingio what to say. "We don't have much time. Listen carefully. The Lady of Ush-bantoun is imprisoned with all her maidens and... Tafawana. Mirá athenai, these amulets the old woman gave you are tracking devices..."

Trevor was stunned. How did the boy know his name? The Lady was imprisoned? There were tracking devices?

The boy held up his hand to stop him from saying anything and kept looking in the guard's direction. The guard was busy purchasing food. A fire blower, who performed to the clang of massive cymbals, distracted the guard even more.

"No time for questions, athenai," the boy said simply. "My name is Pepi, the Lady of Ush-bantoun sends me. You are in grave danger. Take off these amulets and put these ones on."

"What if it is a trick?" Katherine cautioned Trevor.

"I don't think so," he answered. "The boy's convincing."

"It is important," Pepi said and wondered about the strange language the children spoke to each other.

They handed over their old 'Healed Eye' amulets

without protest. Pepi took the tracking devices and hung the new amulets around the children's necks. They looked exactly like the old ones. Pepi looked around to make sure they weren't watched then he quickly pressed a folded piece of parchment into Trevor's hand.

"A message from... the Lady. Don't tell anyone." He put his finger to his mouth "Find my sister Nedjem at the palace. She will explain to you."

The boy melted into the crowd, ogling the tiny dancing girls from Yam. He charmed three of the spectators into accepting the amulets he had taken from the children. Then he was gone.

"Why did we trust him?" Katherine wondered.

"Because he knows who we are and we didn't trust that old woman," Chryséis said, "or Melissa or her sorcerer..."

"I have a creepy feeling about Melissa. Just think about her time travel story and all. If it's true what the boy said then the maidens and the Lady are all her prisoners in the tower."

"Remember that Melissa told us that Tafawana had to be quarantined, because she visited the Lady of the Citadel? Now we know that they are all kept prisoners in the citadel tower," Trevor said.

"Okay, maybe we've seen enough of the festival and should go back," Chryséis said. "We better do something."

When the guard turned around, eating his tasty bread roll, he saw that the children were still wearing their amulets. The next moment they were gone, no doubt viewing the next performance. He was not too worried, because he could follow them anywhere. Or so he thought.

Meanwhile, they threaded their way through the crowd and briefly saw Pepi again. He smiled at spectators and put his remaining amulets around their necks. A few other children did the same thing with common lucky charms.

Pepi looked at the time travellers and winked at them.

# 17 THIEVES AT THE PALACE

They returned to the palace just as it started to rain and hoped that they wouldn't have to face Melissa. But as they were walking up the stairs, they were intercepted by one of the queen's scurrying servants.

"Great," Katherine moaned. "Bad luck."

They had no choice but to follow the young man to the queen's chambers, where Melissa sat at a small table, busy with her jewellery box. She took out one extraordinary piece after the other, only to put it back into the box. There was no one else in the room and the children waited.

"Oh, how I miss shopping at department stores…" she said at last.

Was she having one of her mad moments?

"But… you have so much more here." Chryséis tried to flatter her, "I mean look at this place. The clothes and all these wonderful things…"

"Yeah I know," Melissa said self-importantly. She spoke to her mirror rather than her guests. "You wouldn't have lipstick with you?"

"Ehm no - I'm only eleven," Chryséis said.

"Ah, well. Come sit next to me, little sisters," Melissa cooed. "I want to show you my pretty things."

Katherine and Chryséis began to walk toward the table.

"Not you," Melissa said roughly to Katherine.

Katherine froze. What was the problem now?

"How could you be my sister with your olive skin and dark hair? The little blonde one looks just like me."

This was too much for Chryséis. How dare this woman

insult her best friend? By what stretch of the imagination was it okay to say something this stupid? Little sister... my foot!

She gave the queen a piece of her mind. Melissa grew pale around her nostrils, staring at her furious young guest. She had hoped for a more pleasant visit and that she would succeed in dividing the children.

Katherine and Trevor stared at her. This was not good, not good at all! *Chris, shut up,* Trevor concentrated very hard on the girl and hoped that his telepathic ability was enough. *Melissa is not Holly Benson.*

Chryséis got the message and stopped in her tracks.

Melissa struggled to compose herself. "How dare you! Insolent! I think it is better if you all go to your room now. There will be punishment of course... You are not to leave your room until... until you are summoned to dinner. Then we will see..." Her tone was threatening.

She grew tired of her own game – it was no longer fun. These brats were no longer of use to her in any case. Her plan had been set in motion.

"Nice going, Chris," Trevor mumbled as soon as they were back in their quarters.

The rain had cleared up and a faint moon sickle surrounded by a pale halo peeped from behind floating clouds. The sunlight was already fading into dusk and the guards lit the oil lamps along the walls before leaving the room.

"Thanks for standing up to her, Chris, but you shouldn't let her tick you off like that," Katherine said.

"What? Do you think she should talk to us that way?" Chryséis asked hotly.

"No," Trevor answered. "But... wait a minute... where is my backpack?"

His hands were tapping the floor under his bed.

"Mine is also gone," Katherine cried and looked for hers as well.

Their room had been broken into and almost all their things were missing! Only the sleeping bags on their beds were left where they had been and the toothbrushes were still in the bathroom.

"So while we were enjoying ourselves at the festival, Melissa stole our stuff. I can't believe it!" Chryséis flared up again. "How could we be so naïve and think that she was an honest person?"

"I'm sure it was this weasel of a magician… or his slimy sidekick…" Trevor stomped back and forth between the bathroom door and the beds like a tiger in its cage.

Chryséis just wanted to storm through the secret passage and confront Melissa again. Obviously, this was not a good idea and, in any case, the passage door was locked and she yelled in frustration.

"Chris, will you stop shouting this moment!" Katherine was about to lose her cool with her best friend. "What if the guards hear us and run in?"

"Our time-portal finders! Our palmtop, clothes, just… everything… oh no, the palmtop is also gone!" Chryséis wanted to cry, but she bit her lower lip and swallowed hard. It almost worked. One little tear escaped.

"I just want to go home, she sobbed. "I hate this stupid place!" Her anger had blown itself out.

"Get a grip, Chris. You are not helping," Trevor said. He was also upset, but they had to find a way to get their things back and get out of this place. The sooner the better.

"Why did she do that?" Katherine wondered.

"Melissa is after our time-portal finders, of course." Trevor clenched and unclenched his fists. "She must have decided to do some shopping in our room."

"How are we going to get back home without our TPFs?" Chryséis seemed to calm down now, but Katherine got upset.

"They will never let us go. We'll never get out of here. We should have gone back to the future. In Cydonia…"

"What are you talking about, Katie?" Trevor said. "We've come sooo far! We've travelled through time and survived a war with evil giants, a sea monster attack, the shipwreck…

remember? Of course, we'll get out of here. We just have to find a way. We have our VICs."

"Yes, that's true," Chryséis said. They were still wearing the headbands. They also had been wearing their moon bags with all sorts of useful stuff.

"Melissa could already be on her way to Carter Valley with her creepy sorcerer..." Katherine said.

Trevor's face lit up. "At least, she doesn't know how to use our TPFs."

"She'll figure it out. Even if she's from the seventies, she'll know how to press a button," Chryséis said meekly.

"Yes, but the question is, which one to press. There is a chance that she took only one device. There were three. She won't need all three of them to travel back to the future."

We could sneak out of the room invisibly - and search the palace," Katherine suggested much calmer now.

"And where would you start looking? I say we try to make it to the next citadel and ask for help," Chryséis said.

"And how do we get past the guards? They must be on high alert by now and they might detect even invisible people at the gate."

"I doubt it, but we could send a telepathic message," Katherine suggested.

"I think the building might be shielded by now. Or worse, they could pick up the thought transfer, and who knows what Melissa will do to us then." Trevor sat down on his bed. That wasn't easy at all, but at least they were trying to find a solution now.

"No, it's better to try and get out of here on our own," Chryséis decided. "Then we can contact the Lady of Cydonia again. She will know what to do." The old Chryséis was almost back.

"Why didn't we do that already?" Trevor said. "We should never have trusted Melissa even one bit with our stuff!"

"Oh dear, I'm too young for this," Katherine moaned. "It's just too much!"

"Honey, you are also too young to time-travel." Chryséis tightened the strap of the sleeping bag. "So deal with it."

"That's a different thing altogether." Katherine pushed her lower lip out.

"No, it isn't!" Chryséis insisted.

"And who was throwing a tantrum just now?" Katherine asked.

"I don't know what you're talking about..."

"Oh, stop it already, you two! I can't think while you squabble." Trevor had the feeling that he had forgotten something. "We'll have to contact the Lady. The boy at the market said something... wait."

Trevor had almost forgotten the folded message Pepi had given him at the festival. He searched in his trouser pocket. "Of course, that's it! The boy said that it's a message from the Lady of Ush-bantoun."

"Go on, open the message!" Katherine cried.

Trevor unfolded the piece of parchment and - looked puzzled. There were characters or rather pictures on it like hieroglyphics, but the time travellers had no idea what they meant.

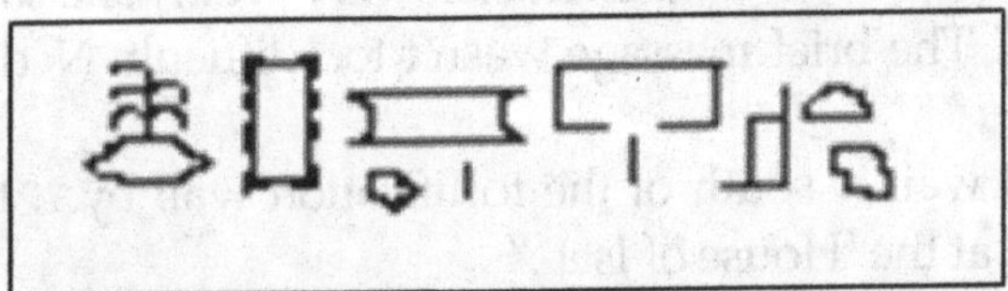

"Excellent. We can't read the message. What now?"

"I think I know what to do," Katherine said. "Pepi said that he has a sister at the palace. What was her name? Nedjem or something like that. He said she would be able to explain."

"Then let's find this Nedjes. Then we can go to the citadel and speak to the Lady of Ush-bantoun - and Tafawana is also there." Trevor shrugged.

"How do you want to do that? We can't even get out of this room."

They thought for a moment and soon came up with a good plan. Katherine opened the heavy door to their room and asked the guard sweetly, "pray good guard, see to it that the girl Nedjem is sent to us to help with my bath."

The guard seemed happy to help. The queen could be harsh with people sometimes, and these were mere children. He didn't notice that an invisible child sneaked barefoot past him. Trevor stole upstairs and in the direction of the queen's bed chamber. So far so good.

There was just one snag: unfortunately, the guard had misunderstood Katherine's request. Instead of the girl Nedjem, he summoned a woman by the name of Nedjes.

Soon a short black-haired woman, who could have passed for a Dwendi, shyly opened the door. Since they had never met Pepi's sister eye to eye, the children didn't know any better.

Nedjes was a laundry woman and knew just a little about the youngsters, but not enough to notice that one of the children was missing.

She was surprised when the girls gave her greetings from her younger brother and then asked her to tell them what the note said. She only had a brother, who was older than her.

"I don't know how to read characters very well," she said, "but I can try." The brief message wasn't too difficult. Nedjes read haltingly.

"Come and wait… south of the fortification wall by… the waterway at… at the 'House of Iset'."

"Are you sure, that's what the message says?"

"Yes, it is all there. I'm sure of it," the laundry woman said firmly.

The girls just looked at each other in silence and thanked Nedjes. They asked her to show them how to run the bath, so that the guard wouldn't get suspicious. Then Nedjes left the tower room, nodding importantly to the guard, while Trevor managed to push past the servant woman and back into the room in the nick of time before the heavy door closed behind him.

"And?" He asked and became visible again.

"Well, she said that the note says: Come and wait, south of the fortification wall by the waterway at the 'House of Iset'," Katherine answered.

"How are we supposed to know where that is?"

"We'll find out somehow. What did you see, Trev?"

The news wasn't good. "No trace of our backpacks anywhere, not even in the audience room."

"Great. I wonder what they did with them." Chryséis checked her watch. Time was flying!

"If we want to get out of here before dinner, we better get going!" Trevor said. "Step 3."

He used his Swiss army knife that he always had in his moon bag, to rip one of the thick linen sheets into broad strips while a small waterfall ran noisily from the broad frog tap in the bathroom. They knotted the strips together to form a long rope.

"I'm hungry," Chryséis complained.

"Come on, not now!" Katherine was irritated. "I have some beef jerky in my moon bag. We can eat it later."

Trevor felt his breast pocket – but the digital camera was in his backpack! He closed the button and tightened the last knot. Then the children rolled up their sleeping bags and strapped them to their backs.

They tested the invisibility devices and stuffed the little they had and a couple of soaps from the bathroom into the moon bags. The saurian hide purse from the Lady of Cydonia was still around Katherine's waist with most of their tender inside. They had only bought some stuffed aubergines at the festival today. It was all they'd had to eat since this morning.

"Ready?" Chryséis asked.

"Ready!"

Trevor was first. He climbed down the makeshift rope and let himself fall softly on his sleeping bag. Then it was Katherine's turn and finally, Chryséis let herself down the rope. They paused for a moment in the courtyard and listened. Everything was quiet.

"I forgot the amulet on the table!" Chryséis slapped her

forehead. Trevor mumbled something rather unkind under his breath and Katherine rolled her eyes.

"No need to be rude. We can't go without the amulet," Chryséis insisted.

"What do you want to do, climb up again?" Trevor asked sarcastically. "You always forget something."

"Yes… sorry."

"We are running out of time, Chris," Katherine said nervously. "We have to get going."

"There has to be enough time. Stop talking and help me up," she ordered her friends. Trevor folded his hands to make a step and Katherine pushed from below.

Chryséis pulled herself up over the marble ledge of the window sill with surprising strength and grabbed the amulet. It was still on the table under the window. With the amulet securely around her neck, she abseiled down again. Chryséis fell softly on her rolled up sleeping bag. Small bats swished past her, chasing each other in the pink twilight.

It was still quiet in the palace. Maybe a bit too quiet.

They heard agitated voices coming from the room, where Chryséis had fetched the amulet just minutes ago.

The three friends looked at each other for a brief moment. Then they disappeared one by one – and just in time!

Somebody had discovered the knotted-sheet rope tied to one of the red pillars and pulled it back inside.

"Ungrateful!" Melissa ranted. "They will pay for this… unworthy fleas. They won't get far! Guards!"

Her voice grew fainter as the three friends sprinted through the palace gates. They walked on without looking back. Guards would be on their heels any moment now.

*

Far away, across the Atlantean Sea in the city of Cydonia, their friend the Lady of the citadel tried to contact the young time travellers telepathically once again, but no matter how hard she tried, there was no answer.

 **18**   **THE TRAP BY THE RIVER**

"Okay let's go to the river and find this 'House of Iset',"
Trevor whispered.

"I have an idea where that could be. Stay close to the
walls and let's take each other's hand...," Chryséis' ghostly
voice gasped out of breath.

"Yes, commander..."

"Ha, very funny Trevor. Come on, let's go!"

Around them, the city of Ush-bantoun was calm and
peaceful. A pale moon disappeared behind veils of clouds
only to reappear again. Katherine jumped at every little noise,
but the guards didn't come after them. Without the amulets,
the hag had given them at the festival, they couldn't locate the
children. The new amulets protected them from discovery.

They crept along the house walls in narrow roads as fast as
they could, then walked across the large town square. Once they
heard the footsteps of guards and the invisible children pressed
themselves quickly against a house wall. Clack, clack, clack.

Three guards turned a corner and Chryséis winced as
Katherine pressed her hand hard. The guards pushed a very
drunk giant out of the way, who staggered up some steps
from a drinking house onto the town square.

They heard the giant shout something in a strange language,
but the palace guards ignored him. Then the steps departed in
the direction of the Per-aa and the square lay again deserted in
the dark, still strewn with leftovers from the festival.

The festival had traditionally ended with the setting of the
sun. Many stalls and booths had already been taken down.
Trevor wanted to pick up a glittering stone in a heap of
rubbish, but Chryséis felt the downward pull and hissed,

"Leave it alone, Trev."

The inn of the 'Wild Boar' was closed for the night.

"Which street did Manassi and Hapu take to get to the riverbank?" Chryséis asked very softly. "I'm sure that there was the temple of Iset somewhere."

Katherine saw a large sign, nailed against a house wall, pointing to the riverbank.

"Look, over there," she said and pointed to the sign.

"Where? Chris, you're invisible…"

"Oh sorry, I forgot." Chryséis pressed the button on her aliceband and pointed again to the sign.

"Okay, I see it," Trevor whispered.

Chryséis switched her VIC back on, but she had been visible long enough for the drunken giant to stare at her. When the girl disappeared again he shook his head and promised himself to drink less of the good bouza beer.

"Phew, that was close!" Chryséis whispered and pulled the others forward.

"Be careful, that hurt!" Katherine hissed.

A waterway flowed under a long bridge to the right and there were a few buildings on the other side of the bridge.

"See that canal over there? Maybe that's where the temple is," Trevor suggested.

"Where?" Katherine asked.

"To the right."

The children searched the riverbank. Many of the festival visitors already slept in their yurts or sat around fires, singing and drinking bouza.

Suddenly, a young boy stood in front of the time travellers as if he could see them. He held up his hand and said, "stop, young travellers. I will take you to the 'House of Iset'." A thin veil moved away from the moon and they recognized the boy. It was Pepi. Mingio had asked Pepi to look out for the children. Something had told her that they would come tonight.

When Pepi heard noises and children whispering, he had stepped courageously forward. He couldn't see anything and if it wasn't the children, he would run away quickly. This wasn't necessary, because the children appeared one by one in front of him.

"Shelanti, athenai," he said, his voice quivering only slightly. "You read the note then and found the way?"

"Your sister at the palace explained it to us. We told her that you sent greetings," Katherine said.

"The Earthmother be thanked for Nedjem," the boy sighed.

"No, not Nedjem. We spoke to Nedjes…" Chryséis realized that they had made a mistake. A big one.

Of course, the Dwendi woman was not Pepi's sister! How could they have been so stupid?!

Pepi didn't know what to say, but he looked troubled as he led them to the 'House of Iset' and waved them inside a small thatched hut not far from the temple. The simple wooden door opened with a wobble. It was dark inside the hut. They couldn't believe their eyes when a real maiden appeared in the doorway. The first citadel official they had seen since arriving in Ush-bantoun.

"Shelanti athenai, my name is Mingio." Her hands flew to her heart and lips in the familiar greeting and the children responded in the same way.

"The Lady of Ush-bantoun and all those loyal to her are in great danger. We need your help…" then her gaze fell on the sleeping bags strapped to the children's backs and the moon bags.

"I see that you have already decided to leave town. A wise decision…" Pepi interrupted the senior maiden and told her quickly what had happened at the palace. Mingio looked alarmed.

"We have to leave immediately. The guards will be here any moment. Nedjes is the sorcerer's servant."

She fetched something from the hut then waved to the children to follow her into the dark shadows of a tall juniper hedge. She gestured for them to be still and listened intently. The strumming of a kithara came from the tents, then laughing and happy singing.

The moon stood now brightly against the deep-blue sky and thin clouds closed in on the yellow disk.

In the shadows, the maiden Mingio handed some biscuits and a bottle with drinking water to Katherine as well as two pieces of folded parchment and said, "Listen carefully, athenai. Cross the bridge over this waterway." She pointed to the city wall.

"Leave through the gate. There will be no guards now. Keep to the right where the road forks. That's the road to Innu. Stay in the cover of the trees and look out for wild animals and especially humans."

She saw their horrified faces. "Never give up hope…" she said gently, "you never know what awaits you around the next turn."

That didn't sound very reassuring.

"The one parchment is a letter of passage, should it be required. Show the other document to nobody. It is a message only for the eyes of the Lady of Innu. Keep your amulets on you and never take them off."

Katherine put the documents into her already bulging moon bag and struggled to close it again.

Mingio looked around and spoke urgently. "Find your way to Innu and avoid settlements. The Earthmother and the Bird God be with you. Leave now at once."

No explanation how and where they were supposed to find this Lady of Innu, so they would have to figure it out by themselves. Mingio took Pepi's hand, turned around and walked as fast as maidenly possible in the opposite direction. They soon disappeared into the quiet shadows of cone-shaped towers.

The children switched their VICs on and hurried toward the bridge. Mingio had been right: there were no guards. They passed through the open gate and had barely reached the top of the bridge when they were startled by a loud bang and flash behind them. The children spun around and saw the little hut where they had just been go up in flames. Nedjes, one of the Magi's many 'crickets', had reported the hieroglyphic message and Melissa had reacted quickly and deadly.

The three friends hurried across the bridge, far away from the lamenting and shouting that came from the yurts and far from the crackling fire.

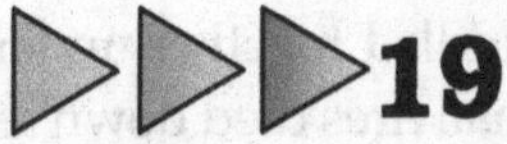**19**   SLAVE TRADERS

Apart from a group of Dwergar, who spent the night in tents by the side of the road outside the city gate, they didn't come across anyone for a while. Not that it mattered, because they were still invisible.

The time travellers walked on and on through the night, just as the maiden Mingio had told them to do.

"Gosh, I'm tired. I wish I could sleep in that nice, soft bed at the palace," Katherine sighed.

"Sure if the big soft bed is more important than your freedom then let's turn around and go back to the palace," Trevor said.

"I didn't mean it that way…"

Trevor stopped abruptly and pulled the others gently forward. "There's a large group of people down by the riverbank."

"I wonder what they are doing there," Chryséis yawned.

There were no shrubs or bulrushes to obstruct the view of the slow flowing river, but it was dark and difficult to tell if those people were friendly or not. A few mokis were lying on the ground, tied to strong tree branches, and lowed softly in their sleep.

"It could be a large caravan. Do you want to check it out?"

"No," Chryséis said. "Maybe later."

"We need to rest anyway," Katherine said. "Let's have some water and beef jerky."

The children sat down under a tree and rested, still invisible. Mingio had warned them against contact with strangers, but it felt safer to be close to other human beings.

Perhaps they would find some scraps of food later when the caravan moved on or they could follow them.

They dozed for a while leaning against each other, unable to fall asleep. The group by the river huddled together under the broad crown of a fallen tree. Their small fires died down as the moonlit night sky began to fade into a grey early morning. The time travellers could see better now what was going on down by the riverbank… and couldn't believe their eyes!

The people, they had thought were merchants, turned out to be a group of captives, bound together with twines. Men and women and children and most of them sat there with drooping shoulders and sad faces. Guards walked around and handed out water.

The children knew that the trade with human life was as despised in the civilized Known World as it was in the future.

"Gee," Chryséis said softly. "Poor people."

The slave traders had been busy throughout the realm and waited by the river for the delivery of merchandise that the queen of Ush-bantoun had promised them. Three children, fine strong specimen, destined for Ta Shemau, a country in the Red Land.

Ta Shemau was in the south if you followed the course of the Nila River. Not very fertile, but rich in ore, so mining was its main trade. A grave illness had decimated the population five seasons ago. Before the disaster, two righteous Ladies had disappeared from their citadels and rogue warlords were blamed. What they needed were workers to mine the ore. The 'Council of Nations' of the Known World' was concerned and needed to intervene soon.

Slave-trade was forbidden in the Known World, where freedom, justice and wisdom were still prized high. For now, the few slave traders felt safe in their business with Ta Shemau, protected by a hostile stretch of desert, it presented an ideal hiding place from the laws of the civilized world.

The sun rose higher in the sky.

"Do you see what I'm seeing?" Chryséis asked.

A familiar figure wrapped in a dark cloak arrived. The slave traders and the magician began to speak to each other.

"Melissa's bosom-buddy!" Katherine gasped. "And look who's also here." Totolin, who stood a few steps behind his master chuckled, then started to cough into his grubby hand.

"… this was not the plan... we lost time…"

The three friends eaves-dropped on their muffled conversation.

"There will be no children from Ush-bantoun tonight, Khopri. Our plan went cock-eyed. The children have disappeared and their things were stolen. The queen regrets. Go and find some other specimens. You should have no difficulty with that…"

The leader of the slave traders didn't like this very much. The gold that the queen of little Ush-bantoun had offered him would not be paid now.

Neither would the good land and the priceless device she had promised for a successful transfer. Good black earth in the new territories of Kem... he had planned to settle there.

Chryséis motioned to Katherine and Trevor that they should make a wide berth around the group. They were making their way quietly away from the campsite when there was a commotion. Where was the girl, they had abducted from their parents' yard yesterday?

The slave traders counted the individuals. Then began to search everywhere, uttering curses as they climbed the elevation that led up to the road. They inspected the spaces between the rocks and trees. Nothing.

The search party moved in on the children and two hound dogs sniffed and barked at them. Invisible or not, the dogs could sense them. It became clear to the children that they had to run or risk discovery.

Excited voices came closer and Trevor began to run towards a jumble of rocks, pulling the girls with him. They were desperately looking for cover on the far side of the rocks, holding onto each other's sleeping bag straps all the time. A narrow opening next to the exposed roots of a great tree was just big enough to slide through!

"In here!" He yelled.

They crawled into a concealed opening in the ground and fell onto a pile of soft forest soil. The light inside was dim and they tried to lie still for a while.

"I'm scared to go any further. Let's wait here until they go away."

"Katie, it's better to move deeper inside. What if the dogs can sense us so close to the opening? Or jump in?"

"Trevor is right," Chryséis whispered. "We should hide deeper inside. Let's switch off the invisibility capes. It's better if we can see each other."

"What if there are wild animals in here? I wish I still had my pepper spray with me…" Katherine wailed. But then she also pressed the button on her aliceband.

"Not so loud! Do you want to be snatched by the slave traders?"

"Of course not…"

"Well then, come already!"

As they moved away from the opening, they came across a wall of neatly dressed stone blocks that formed the side of their low cave. Could it be an underground building? The sandy soil trickled through cracks above onto the wall. The voices outside grew louder and shadows passed the opening.

"I'm afraid we don't have much time …" Chryséis said.

"Try not to think too hard. The sorcerer might pick up on our thoughts." Trevor war already looking for a way to escape deeper into the cave.

"Maybe the amulets are still shielding us," Katherine said.

"You're right."

Their eyes got used to the darkness. Further down, the remarkable wall was almost hidden by gravel and sand. Roots of forest plants were hanging down into the cavity. They heard dogs barking and hacking voices zoomed in around them. The children crawled further down. Luckily, the slave traders hadn't discovered the gap yet.

Trevor slid down a gravelly slope, taking care not to make too much of a noise. Chryséis followed and then Katherine. The sand was littered with rocks and coloured shards of earthenware, then the ground became smooth rock and was completely level.

They were standing on a massive stone lintel across two square pillars. "It probably supports the ceiling," Katherine said.

"Amazing," Trevor marvelled.

The astonishing wall was much taller than it had looked before. The children groped their way along the wall past boulders into darkness. It was fortunate that they didn't see the scorpion with its young clinging to its back that crawled back under a pile of rubble.

"I don't think, they found the opening," Katherine said relieved and fasted the strap of her backpack.

"Or maybe they found the runaway slave girl they've been looking for." Trevor balanced over the lintel and down another pile of rubble.

A beam of light cut through the dim light. Chryséis had pressed her torchlight button by accident.

"Gee, you could have warned us, Chris!" Trevor said and rubbed his eyes.

"Sorry, mistake..." Chryséis mumbled.

"Might as well leave it on, so we can see something," Katherine said.

There was an open door frame just ahead and faint light on the other side. Maybe this was a way out.

Trevor clambered over a smaller pile of rubble. Water trickled down the strange wall in several places.

"Do you think we are close to the Nile?" He asked.

"Could be."

Trevor climbed up the rubble and stood inside the broad stone door frame. He was looking into a large hall.

The high ceiling had fallen in places and sunlight hit the floor in long dusty streaks. More stone lintels held up the roof or what was left of it.

There was enough light to see where they were going and Chryséis switched off her torchlight. The children jumped off the threshold and onto the dirty paving stones inside. They had all but forgotten about the slave traders outside.

"This place is awesome!"

The children carefully stepped around stone rafters that had tumbled to the ground. The floor in the middle of the hall was quite a bit lower. It looked like a large swimming pool with steps leading into a shallow remnant of water. The dirty water was smelly and cluttered with debris.

"Do you see those cubicles over there?" Trevor asked and pointed to a row of smaller 'cabins' along the swimming pool.

"They look like change rooms. Actually, this place looks a lot like an indoor swimming pool for giants," Chryséis said. "Do you think that giants lived here?"

"Possibly. Remember that the Children of the Moon had a high civilisation before the Dark Age?" Trevor said.

"I wish we could take a picture of this," Katherine said, "but there's probably not enough light in here."

"I don't care where we are. As long as we get out of here safely," Trevor said and looked up at the ceiling. "That's too high to escape."

"I hope these stupid slave traders didn't get the girl. Where do you think the girl they were looking for has disappeared to?" Katherine asked.

"I'm sure she can look after herself." Chryséis wasn't very sympathetic right now. They had their own problems to deal with. "We can't save every prehistoric slave, Katie."

They tried not to fall over the debris around the 'swimming pool' as they made their way to the other side.

"I'm really hungry," Katherine complained and stumbled over a stone. "Ouch!"

"Really? You are hungry again?"

"Yes, Trevor, sorry, but I'm only human."

"Well okay then. Let's have a bite to eat. Maybe in one of

the cabins. I think it's safer there." Judging by the dimming light it must be afternoon.

"We have some beef jerky left and Mingio's wheat biscuits," Katherine announced. "Bugger that most of our emergency food was stolen."

"At least we still have our sleeping bags," Trevor said.

"Yeah, at least."

"We'll have to figure out how to get our stuff back," Chryséis said, "but first things first. Who wants a wheat biscuit?"

They ate and drank water from the bottle Mingio had given them and listened out for voices or footsteps. But nobody had followed them into the cave. Or so they thought.

"Do you think that guardian angels come with you when you travel through time?" Katherine asked.

"Here we are trying to get out of this place and find our way to Innu... and somehow and search for our stolen things ... and you worry about angels?" Chryséis grumbled.

Trevor was snoozing and snored slightly.

"I always feel like something is protecting..."

"Really Katherine, things are already complicated enough even without guardian angels," Chryséis moaned. "Okay if it makes you feel 'more protected', I think your guardian angel probably came with you to the past. Happy?" Chryséis said mockingly.

"Thanks so much, Chris... I'm more talking about this thing..."

Chryséis knitted her brow.

"Trevor... Trevor, wake up." She shook Trevor's shoulder. "We have to move." A poisonous button spider crawled into his sleeping bag where it was so nice and warm and was crushed when he turned around with a thump. The girls were packing their things.

"What?" Trevor asked sleepily.

"We have to get out of here, Trev." Katherine abruptly stopped and listened. "Are there large birds in here?"

"Large Birds? Why? I don't think so."

"Because of this…" Katherine picked up a soft white feather. It was rather large and – very clean.

"How did that get in here?" The children listened for a tense moment, but there were no bird-like noises at all.

"If that doesn't come from a bird then what?" Chryséis wondered. "Are there dangerous dinosaurs around that don't make a noise and wait to attack us?" They had come across dinosaurs with feathers before. The children were looking around, but they didn't detect a trace of dinosaurs.

"I don't want to find out. We better take the same route back. Slowly and quietly. At least we know that we'll get out."

"What if the slave traders and their dogs are still there, just waiting for us to show ourselves?"

"Hmm, but we could lose our way badly if we go deeper inside the cave. Even if there are no dinosaurs, what if we hit a dead end or kick stones lose and get buried under rubble… or starve to death?"

"Okay, let's first get out of this cubicle. I can't think in here," Chryséis said and stood up.

She got a mighty fright when she heard a crunching step next to her. A hand stifled her cry before she could make another noise and a cold knife touched her throat. Katherine and Trevor jumped up.

A young man was holding the knife against their friend's throat and they saw a young woman in a blue dress peeping from behind a pile of rocks. Their minds were racing. These were definitely not the slave traders they had escaped from!

"What is this? Who are you people?" Trevor demanded to know.

Seeing that he was dealing with children, the young man with the knife pulled his blade back. He patted Chryséis awkwardly on the back. She let out a moan and stumbled a little forward.

"Who are we? Who are you?!" The young man wanted to know. He wore a quiver slung across his shoulder. The feather they had found earlier had obviously been attached to one of the arrows in his quiver.

"Why should we tell you when you threaten to kill our friend?" Trevor answered with a question. "Come here Chryséis…" Chryséis nearly fell over a stone and Katherine caught her shaking friend.

"Apologies, athenai. We did not see that you were children. We were unforgivably rude," the young woman said well-mannered. She came forward, holding her ears between forefinger and thumb. A sign of remorse.

"That's one way to put it!" Katherine said.

"We thought you belong to the slave traders and their henchmen. My name is Rhodopis of Innu," girl said. "We ran away at dawn. They were searching for me. This is Charaxus, my betrothed." She looked tenderly at the young man with the knife.

"Charmed. We are Trevor, Chryséis and Katherine."

"Please to make your acquaintance," Rhodopis said. "We found shelter in this, this... cave. Just like you, it seems."

"We heard the slave traders speak only about a girl that had run away. We overheard it from the top of the slope and suddenly they were also chasing us."

"When Rhodopis was taken by those scoundrels, I followed them and waited for a chance to free my beloved."

"Hmm not a bad plan," Trevor said. "So, you two got away."

"It seems so. Where are you from? Did the slave traders take you also?" Charaxus asked.

"No, we… we come from Ush-bantoun and are on our way to Innu to... to meet our parents..." Chryséis answered.

"...the slave traders began chasing after us and that's how we ended up in this caved-in building." Trevor finished the story.

"Do you have food with you?" Katherine asked Rhodopis. "I'm still hungry."

"I have some bread rolls in my knapsack and walnuts," Charaxus answered. Glad that he could make up for the mistake he had made earlier, he gave the grateful children some of his provisions.

"How do we get out of here?" Katherine asked.

"I'm a merchant's apprentice," Charaxus told them. "I know of ancient underground passages in the area that the merchants sometimes use in heavy weather." It would be safer for them to move in those passages for a while to stay out of sight.

"Brilliant plan," Trevor admitted. "I just hope we find our way to Innu."

"It won't be a problem. The exit is on the river bank. We'll take a boat from there."

Charaxus soon found the entrance to the subterranean passage he remembered and led the way. The dark passage was damp and mouldy, but they bravely made their way forward. There were no candles or torches on the walls, but Chryséis switched on her torchlight.

"That is a very handy tool, athenai," Rhodopis said approvingly.

"Thank you, Rhodopis. It comes in handy."

To Katherine's horror, something slithered past and sniffed at her feet once or twice. It didn't take long before they walked through a hidden door behind two massive oak trees.

"We must cross the river to get to Innu," Charaxus said. "That's a ways up the river."

"As long as we don't run into the slave traders," Chryséis warned.

In front of them, the mighty river wound its way in a broad glittering band from south to north.

They rested by some hazelnut bushes on the grassy slope, shielded by bulrushes and watched sleek boats with large staring eyes painted on the hull, float up and down the river.

Rhodopis showed the children how to crack hazelnuts with stones and they ate as many as they could. Katherine tried to stuff hazelnuts into her bulging moon bag, so they would have a snack later, but there wasn't much space left and the seams threatened to pop.

Rhodopis decided to make a shoulder bag for her from the tall rushes. She worked fast, singing a little song and handed

Katherine the finished bag. Then she made another one for herself and filled it with nuts and some sweet fruit she picked from a nearby tree.

Katherine did the same while Trevor cut twigs off the fruit tree to make new toothbrushes.

Charaxus explained that they had to cross the river soon if they wanted to make it to the city of Innu before sunset.

"If my memory serves me right, a boat big enough to transport a vat of wine should be moored close by."

They didn't have to search long. In between the rushes, a small boat was fastened to a sturdy branch at the water's edge. There was just enough space for the five of them.

Charaxus paddled the boat through a narrow space in the bulrushes and then across the river.

Luckily, most of the boats had anchored along the waterway for a couple of hours to wait out the heat of the day. To the children's surprise, odd-looking river dolphins appeared around their little vessel and soon they felt as if the boat was being steered for them.

It slowed down and began to move almost on its own against the current toward the opposite riverbank.

The little boat reached the other side of the Nila River in calm waters, far from a crocodile that was sunning itself on the riverbank. The vessel lodged itself into a shallow spot and they climbed up the steep bank after tying the boat to a rock. The young man helped them onto dry land, but Chryséis was still wary of the knife and hopped onto dry land by herself.

From the riverbank, a picture of shining lakes and a city with shiny buildings and farmland presented itself.

Yellow and turquoise flags fluttered above the city. This was Innu, the sprawling 'City of the Sun'. They were close to their goal and Charaxus and Rhodopis promised to show them the way to the citadel. The time travellers forgot their trouble for a while.

A very short while.

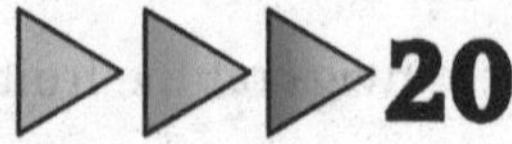
20   CITY OF THE SUN

"This must be the forerunner to Cairo," Trevor said all excited, "but it doesn't look anything like Cairo in Egypt."

Of course, Rhodopis and Charaxus had no idea what he was talking about, especially not in this strange language.

But the time travellers were just too happy to be in a civilised place to notice. There were people working in the fields and vimaans were moving above the streets and farmsteads. What a relief.

Many of the fields shone in a deep yellow colour.

"Oh dear, I hope that's not sylphium!" Katherine said and touched the little bottle around her neck.

"No, athenai, those are sunflowers," Charaxus said. Amazing - thousands of sunflowers that stretched their necks toward the sun.

They walked down onto a paved road and Charaxus, who knew the area well, lead the way into town. The farmers in the fields greeted the five young people in a friendly manner as they walked past, before turning their attention to weeding and loosening the soil again.

Next to the road was a rock formation, where spring water trickled over the rocks, green with dewy moss. It formed a little brook below the rocks and flowed into the valley along the road. Chryséis joined a group of smiling girls by the brook, and filled their water bottles with the clear liquid. She touched a fragrant leaf off a dusty shrub next to the spring, rubbed the leaf between her fingers and smelled it.

"Mhm, it's sage," she said and picked a few of the leaves.

Katherine took a leaf and smelled it. "You're right,

that's sage."

Chryséis put the leaves into the grass pouch that Rhodopis had made for her, just as a farmer stopped his vimaan, adorned with the winged sun disk of Innu, and offered to take them into the city.

"Thank you athenai, that is kind of you," Rhodopis said and they scrambled into the vimaan.

The vimaan reached the 'City of the Sun' rather quickly and the time travellers had to constantly remind themselves that they were in Egypt.

A long time before the first dynasties of the pharaohs rose to power. Now, there were no pharaohs here, no pyramids yet and probably no mummies, either.

They passed through the city gate, guarded by two large obelisks, topped with 'Birds of Fire'. Every statue they saw was covered in shimmering gold, silver or orichalcum, and strange symbols and shapes could be seen everywhere.

"Where to, athenai?" The farmer asked as they reached the central square.

"We have to go to the citadel," Charaxus answered and the vimaan took a sharp turn to the right.

They passed the famous 'House of Knowledge', the most ancient of all the libraries in the Known World. Many came here to study the rarest of documents in vellum, parchment, bark paper or clay tablets. A long time ago, 'Followers of the Bird God' had also brought scientific scriptures with them from the countries of Su Mâr and Airyana Vaëgo.

They were now close to the citadel on a flat hill in the suburbs.

"That's the 'School of White Magic'," Rhodopis said proudly and pointed to a large building that almost disappeared behind a Kabiri temple. "It's run by the priesthood of the 'Right Path'. They advise the Lady of Innu in important matters and even the 'Council of

Nations' in Algiras."

Rhodopis was visibly proud of her hometown. The vimaan moved around the temple and soon landed in front of the citadel gate. A long line of tall palms led up to the white buildings on the flat hill. They all clambered out of the vimaan thanked the farmer for his help. He nodded with a smile and took off immediately to make his way to the marketplace.

They showed the citadel guards the letter the maiden Mingio had given them and were taken to the Lady of Innu. The Lady was quite young and rather smart. She read the Lady of Ush-bantoun's letter and asked the children a few questions.

There was no doubt in her mind that King Osorkon and Queen Mé-lis-ah had broken the law in the most unspeakable way.

A Court of Justice on Atala dealt with such matters and would determine the perpetrators' fate, but in the meantime, she set a rescue plan in motion.

Charaxus and Rhodopis told her about the slave traders and the Lady referred the matter to the 'House of Truth'. Afterwards, the young couple said goodbye as soon as all formalities had been dealt with. They couldn't wait to go home and a vimaan was already waiting in the courtyard. The children grew tired and hungry and the Lady of the citadel didn't have to read their minds to guess as much.

"Food has been prepared in your chamber. I advise you to rest now," the Lady said and continued rather formally. "On behalf of all righteous rulers in Ta Mery I wish to apologise for the abominable treatment you received in the 'Black Land'. The Lady of Cydonia has informed me that she is relieved to hear of your wellbeing. You must be very special to her. She sends her greetings and good wishes. We shall continue our conversation in the morning."

The children were glad that their friend, the Lady of Cydonia, had not forgotten them. At last, they felt safe in this city.

True to her word, the Lady of Innu received the children in the morning.

"The Lady of Cydonia told me that you are indeed time travellers. Extraordinary." She looked somewhat surprised.

"Yes, honourable Lady. We want to return home to the future soon, but our travel devices have been stolen together with our luggage at the palace in Ush-bantoun."

"I see. We will look for your belongings once we gain access to the Per-aa, athenai, and we will do our best to find the thieves - and your devices. In the meantime, please accept our hospitality here in Innu," the Lady said formally and fastened a loose dark braid back into place.

"Thank you so much, we gladly accept." Katherine made a little bow.

"The good Lady of Cydonia has advised me to show you the 'School of Magic' while you reside in our city."

"Oh, that sounds exciting!" Chryséis said.

"She believes that you'd benefit greatly to learn more about our white magic, considering that you have achieved a certain degree of white magic yourselves."

"Thank you, honourable Lady. We would love to do that."

The lady lifted her hand and a tall dignified man stepped forward. He was tanned and had laugh lines around his eyes.

"I'd like you to meet the High Priest Kha-Tefenet. He is the principal of our famous 'School of Magic' and will now take you there with him."

They followed the man through a delightful rose garden, past water features and through a small gate into the school grounds behind the citadel. On the way, they passed an ancient-looking obelisk. Kha-Tefenet noticed their gaze at the firebird balancing on top the column.

"The 'Followers of the Bird God' erected this Southern Pillar, the Iwnu Shema, when they arrived in Ta Mery sheaves of years ago. It is a very famous monument," he explained.

Laughing students in white tunics were on some kind of errand for their teacher and grew all-polite when they saw the senior priest. Hands flew to their mouths and hearts and Kha-Tefenet had a few words with them. The students ogled the three newcomers curiously.

"Welcome, athenai from Cydonia," they said and walked on.

Kha-Tefenet and the children crossed the paved courtyard and he led the way up a wide staircase. From here, they could see a number of vimaans floating along the main road beyond the citadel building. To the left of the inner courtyard stood a large golden scale, mounted on a marble pedestal. A large scarlet feather lay in the balance.

"We aspire to a state of Maet: harmony, balance and peace of mind based on understanding," the priest explained as they climbed the stairs next to the scale. "Only with understanding comes acceptance."

"Right," Trevor replied. "I guess we are not very balanced right now."

The priest nodded his head and they walked through massive wooden doors. They were guarded by two stone sphinxes.

"This is the sanctuary of Astrea, the goddess of justice. To the right you can see the Initiation Centre."

"At last something typically Egyptian apart from the obelisk," Trevor whispered and they studied the simple hall.

He explained to them that in case of a war-like altercation, the victorious party would adopt the traits of the besieged. This was one of the reasons why some acolytes were sent out into the Known World as missionaries to provide guidance and use science or white magic to keep things in balance. After their last exam, they were initiated as 'Brethren of the Right Path' in this hall and received the title of Hanôk or 'Wise One'.

The school principal showed them the ceiling. It was

painted with star signs and all sorts of symbols. Chryséis pointed to a large lizard.

"This is the Crocodile-God called Sobek," Kha-Tefenet answered. "And do you see the woman with her dog over here? The goddess Sopdet, heralds the New Year. The thirty-five bright stars over there are called the Ikhemsu. They determine the correct measurement of time."

The time travellers had never heard of any of them.

Over there is Mount Meru on the far northern edge of the Known World. Now buried under eternal ice and surrounded by an ever-frozen Ocean."

The picture of a swirling sun was right on top of the stars. Kha-Tefenet called it At-al-as, the 'sun at its most high'.

"That sounds almost like the capital of Atland," Katherine said.

"And you may be right, child," the principal answered and walked on.

"Damn that we don't have the camera with us," Trevor said softly. "I'll never remember all of that."

They left the hall and descended another flight of stairs and Kha-Tefenet took them along a garden path to another school building. Rows of life-like statues on either side of the footpath reminded Katherine of the army of warriors that had been unearthed in China. Each face had a different expression. Of course, he must have read her mind.

"Sculptures of all the kings and queens from before the Dark Age," Kha-Tefenet told them.

"Really? They must be very old, then!" Chryséis said.

"Yes child, they are very ancient, indeed."

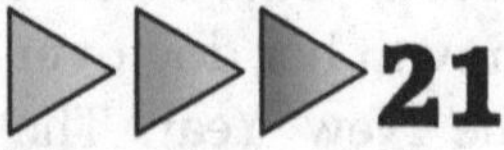 **21**   **A SCHOOL OF MAGIC**

They entered a building with a golden sun painted over the broad doorway. A 'Healed Eye' and a snake on either side. The building housed the 'Lotus Flower Seminary', where introductory classes were held at the 'School of White Magic'.

"...after honouring the month of 'Desire for Rain'. The 17th day of the month Athyr, the date when the overflowing of the Nila River has ceased. The second month after the autumnal equinox..."

They heard a pupil recite in the first classroom to the left as they walked along the corridor. The building was light and airy. There were roofed-in corridors and a small central garden with fountains.

In another classroom, pupils concentrated on practicing the first steps in the correct use of a narthex wand. Simple spells would come later.

Outside the classrooms were shelves with orderly rows of rush sandals and a shepherd's staff leaning against the wall.

They saw about a dozen fifth-graders sitting on rush mats listen intently to the deep voice of their teacher through another open door.

"Remember, that the words must flow from your quill like a river by moonlight," he reminded them. The pupils practised the art of calligraphy on sheets of thin bark paper.

Pupils were dressed in white and teachers wore dark blue tunics with the turquoise stripe of all citadel staff.

The subjects taught at the first level of the 'School of

White Magic' were often more academic and boring than those of the rather more practical second and third schools.

Kha-Nefet walked across the little garden in the middle and the children followed him. A group of older pupils practised a song next to the fountain.

"The theme song of the Bird Festival," Kha-Nefet said. The musicians wore tunics with silver cords. They played on harps and reed pipes, small terracotta drums, double flutes and kitharas.

"...ever swifter you climb on the wings of the wind.

Your plumage as bright as the raiment of the Bird God.

Like him, your abode is both on heaven and on earth..."

The last note faded and there was a change in tune. They began the bird choir, merging into a crescendo of bird voices. The small school garden came alive with nightingales and mockingbirds, warblers and the hoot of owls. The three time travellers stared at the little orchestra.

"Priest Kha-Tefenet," Katherine said. "Do sorcerers also attend this school? We have met some bad ones recently..."

"No," the priest said simply, shaking his head. "Not this kind of magicians. Adepts of black magic serve not humanity but themselves and their worthless followers."

With a gesture of his right hand, he invited them to walk on. "Students of the third and last 'School of White Magic' are instructed in 'Ashtar Vidya', the highest magical powers. For the good of all. This is quite different to the selfish endeavours of sorcerers of the 'Left Path'. However, certain disciples or even priests with weak characters, have at times lost their way..."

"Really?" Trevor said.

"Initiates have their right ear pierced with an earring in the shape of a key. If a priest or priestess commits a crime, the public brings them to the nearest citadel. If they were found guilty, a senior priest pulled the earring out. This left the earlobe split in two. 'Split-Ears' are rare and the people of Ta Mery avoids them'. Most have to leave the country or live in remote places, but some brethren of the 'Left Path' know how to hide such split ears or disguise themselves."

The children remembered that the Magi at the Great House of Us-bantoun had had such a split ear.

"And why are there so many giants on the left path?" Chryséis asked.

"Giants were knowledgeable in the ways of the Gods and very talented. Unfortunately, many use their abilities for sinister purposes," Kha-Tefenet said. He seemed to listen to a silent voice now, nodding.

"I'm pleased to say that the chieftain of Ush-bantoun and his wife have been taken into custody. Their sorcerer was located and found to be with slave traders," the school director announced. He had obviously received a telepathic message from the 'House of Truth'.

"Those special devices as described by you," he also told them, "have not been found in Ush-bantoun. The queen pretends not to know anything about them or your belongings. In fact, she said that the children must have taken them when they ran away. Her own device is also missing."

"Oh no, where is she hiding them?" Katherine cried. "We need them back. And our other stuff as well!"

"If Melissa doesn't have them, then the Magi must have them," Chryséis said with tears in her eyes.

"Do not worry yourselves," Kha-Tefenet assured them. "They will be found. We are all born with a rabbit leading us here and there. We follow where the inner rabbit leads us."

"The rabbit?" Trevor asked.

"It means that we must learn about Maet - inner harmony - and accept our fate no matter where it leads us," the priest explained patiently.

"Right, a rabbit," Trevor mumbled somewhat confused.

They had reached the opposite side of the garden. Kha-Tefenet immediately spotted one of the senior disciples of the third school, by the name of Djehuti. He had come to the 'School of White Magic' as a young boy and sometimes helped out with teaching younger pupils. Djehuti had been busy with disciples practicing the seven laws of noble energy when Kha-Tefenet arrived with the children and proper greetings were exchanged.

"Forgive me, young friends," Kha-Tefenet apologised. "I must leave you now and Djehuti will look after you. The council is in need of my presence. There are urgent matters to attend to."

He handed the visitors over to Djehuti and walked away. Then a deep gong sounded.

"Ah, it is time for the mid-morning break," Djehuti said. "I heard that you have been to my homeland, the 'Pastures of Heaven'?"

"Yes, well we stayed in a village called Urka for a couple of days." Katherine wondered what else he knew everything about them. Perhaps even about their time-travelling.

"Ishpateh, prusht taza?" Chryséis used a phrase Bibi Gul had taught them. Greetings, how are you?

Djehuti had to laugh. "Ishpateh baba! Ishpateh baya! Prusht taza?" Greetings sister, greetings brother. How are you? "That's very good, athenai. You remember our language."

"Only a little," Chryséis said. "In fact, that's all I remember."

Their sandals scratched over the polished marble floors and they chatted a bit about the village of Urka, bee-keeping and the falcon queens, while Djehuti led the way outside. "Did Bibi Gul also show you the bats? I remember that there are quite a few caves around that area."

"Yes, she did. Eagles swooped down from the top of the hill and caught them as they flew out," Trevor said excitedly.

"That sounds about right," Djehuti said.

Pupils of the different schools streamed into the courtyard and into the gardens, laughing and chatting like normal school kids.

"It's just like Pemberton, don't you think?" Chryséis whispered. "The gardens and the games they play."

"But, we don't have boats like that," Trevor said.

Some of the school children rowed small boats on a narrow stream that ran into a lake close to the citadel. Others strolled along the footpaths between flowerbeds and the riverbank.

"Look over there!" Katherine pointed to a group of younger students, who practised with their narthex wands on an alabaster vase the basic principles of transformation. The vase turned into a tiny vimaan, then a scroll and back into the vase.

Another group inspected their 'Moving Stones' that had been confined to a spot in the rock garden with a simple spell and swish of the narthex wand. The day before the large pebbles had been moved to different locations on the school grounds, but by now, most of the 'Moving Stones' had found their way back to their original place in the rock garden.

Two children were playing with frogs on water lily-leaves in a small pond. One girl remained at a safe distance.

"I don't like frogs," she complained. "They are so cold and slimy and scare me with their jumping."

Katherine giggled. She had to think of the prank they had played on Holly Benson back at Pemberton.

"Well come along for a game of Pigsnout then," her friend said. She turned to the time travellers. "You are welcome to join us, foreign athenai," she invited them.

She didn't have to ask Trevor twice. He couldn't go and play Pigsnout soon enough. Katherine and Chryséis trailed listlessly after them to the sports field with its six Pigsnout courts, but then they also had fun with the game and Katherine even scored a goal from the second circle.

"Would you like to join me in class, young friends?" Djehuti asked them casually as they sat still panting next to him on the lawn. He had been reading in a scroll while keeping an eye on the children.

"That would be very nice," Katherine said and bound her hair into a ponytail.

Although she was much fitter now than at the start of their journey through the vortex, a game of Pigsnout still tired her out. She adjusted the amulet she wore underneath her tunic and wondered when they would hear more about the thieves, who had stolen their belongings. Perhaps the 'House of Truth' had already found them…

"Not yet, athenai. You must be patient," the young scholar said.

Of course, he had read Katherine's thoughts.

The deep gong sounded again and free-play ended.

In Djehuti's class, they tried to copy a still life of a fruit bowl on a low table. Some of the youngsters hardly older than the three time travellers stuck their tongues between their teeth in deep concentration. A single boy busied himself with woodcarving close to the window. Under the knife of the budding temple sculptor, a bird come to life out of a block of wood.

"That's what I would like to do," Trevor said.

Then a priestess walked in to relieve Djehuti. She quoted from the book of Thelik Tephan, the 'Breath of Life' while the pupils kept working away. Time flew and before they knew it, the familiar gong called the students and teachers to lunch.

Carved tables and benches were lined up in a hall. Another dining room next to the third school building was reserved for senior priests and initiates. On the way to the dining hall, Djehuti showed them an inner sanctum. Inside was the essence of all knowledge. It was a disappointingly small cubicle with drawn dark, heavy curtains.

"This is meant for students, who are ready for the way to the truth and higher understanding," the young man explained.

Trevor and Chryséis were intrigued and decided to

sneak out during lunch to get a good look at this mysterious cabin. Perhaps it was an oracle of some sort, and they would find an answer to their burning question where their backpacks and TPFs were. Katherine was worried that some important school rule might be broken and decided to stay behind.

"Are there still no news about the thieves?" Trevor asked Djehuti, who had joined them.

"I'm afraid not," the young teacher said.

The meal was simple but tasty. After a while, Chryséis and Trevor sneaked out. There were no guards or priests around and the pupils ignored them. Good. They slid through the dark curtains and found themselves facing a mirror! A large mirror with Akkadian writing in gold on the broad frame. 'Jinåsuh svayahám. Know Thyself.'

"That's the essence of all their knowledge?" Chryséis was disappointed. "It's just a mirror! Do you think it's a joke?"

"They don't strike me as the joking kind. Know yourself... hmm. At least now we know what's inside here."

"If they can't think of anything better than a mirror, they can't be very good priests. And they say they have the magical teachings from the Gods and..."

Trevor interrupted her. "They have no reason to make something like that up."

Chryséis thought for a moment. "Fair enough, but I'm still not convinced..."

"Come now. We have to go back to the dining hall. Who knows what they'll do if they see us out here."

Outside the heavy curtain, a priest moved swiftly behind a pillar and walked down the passageway. It was Kha-Tefenet. He smiled to himself as he returned to the second floor and the conference with his peers. Djehuti had done well. The children would understand the meaning of the mirror in time.

Lunch was followed by a period of rest. The pupils were allowed to spend the afternoon in the gardens or in their rooms. Resting the mind was as important as it was to learn.

Most of them played sports or practised spells.

When Djehuti took the visitors back upstairs, a mirage flickered at one end of a classroom to the second floor. The frosted têrakhon ceiling let in a soft light. The walls were painted with frescoes and white tulip-like flowers grew in tall pots. They cleaned the air and were replaced when they turned purple. There were books on shelves along the walls. They had a school library in the passages?!

They sat down on pale-green chairs and Djehuti excused himself after a while. Katherine and Trevor looked at the books of the small library while Chryséis dozed in her chair. The time travellers were grateful for the brief rest. Only a couple of days ago, they had escaped from an evil queen, magicians and slave traders.

In the late afternoon, Djehuti accompanied the time travellers back to the citadel. Faint tunes carried across from the amphitheatre. Last-year students practised the valediction song.

"…The sun paints dappled shades below.

The wind is rustling the leaves,

Your roots are a strong anchor,

yet many sails might carry you away …"

A few brown birds with forked tails flew up in a fragrant Frangipani tree, scolding the children and Djehuti as they walked past.

A faint mist began to rise, muting the colourful Ta-Merian sunset, but it still reminded the time travellers of Egypt.

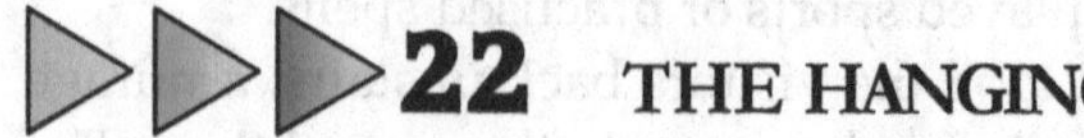

22 THE HANGING GARDENS

By the time they arrived back at the citadel, the slave traders had also been apprehended and turned over to the 'Council of Nations' on Atala.

"Some of the crickets are still at large, but things in the Black Land are returning to normal. The Lady and all of her staff have been rescued and taken over governmental affairs. Only one perpetrator has escaped: Totolin, the sorcerer's assistant," the Lady of the citadel told them.

"Well, at least something. That's good news," Katherine said with relief.

"Very good news. Alas, your stolen belongings have still not been found. I believe that if Mé-lis-ah or one of her servants had stolen your time-travel devices, we would have found them in the Per-aa by now."

"Maybe she is hiding them somewhere else," Trevor suggested.

"Although this is possible, no such thing has been reported." The Lady smiled, and the children shook sadly their heads.

"However, three men hurriedly left Ush-bantoun two days ago with a small moki caravan. They are friends of the Magi, we are told. They could very well be the thieves!"

She poured pomegranate juice for her young visitors into crystal glasses and continued speaking.

"According to the report we received, they are returning to Attock beyond the country of Magnesia and are thought to be bound for the city of Rostau next. We will try to track them. So there is hope, children from the future."

The Lady smiled again. "There was something else... the

Lady of Cydonia is not happy that she is unable to attend to your problem personally or even communicate with you..."

Of course! They were still wearing the protective amulets that Pepi had given them at the Festival of Sokhar. They seemed to shield them against all sorts of thought transfer. Perhaps it was time to take them off.

"... she will, however, dispatch a trusted maiden, by the name of Oruwen, to help you find your stolen belongings."

"She would really do that?" Katherine asked and smiled now as well.

"Indeed, she would. I am told that you know the maiden Oruwen," the Lady said.

"Yes, we met her back in Cydonia," Trevor said.

Chryséis was enormously relieved. They wouldn't be forever lost in prehistory, after all! The Lady of Cydonia was helping them to get back home.

"But how are we supposed to find the thieves? They could be anywhere by now." Trevor wasn't convinced that things would go smoothly, even if Oruwen was coming to help.

"Don't talk nonsense, Trev. We will find them one way or the other. We don't have a choice. If we use one of the time-travel devices from this time, we'll never get back to exactly the same moment, we left, but we'll get home somehow," Katherine said firmly.

"Then it's best if we find our devices," Trevor replied.

"That is true, young friend. That's why I'm giving you this device..." She showed them a little black box. "...that will help you locate electromagnetic frequencies of objects from the future the Lady of Cydonia gave us. You may see it as a thank-you gift for your braveness in saving the Lady of Ush-bantoun and all good people there. New paizas have also been issued. You will now be able to move freely around Ta Mery."

"Do our things have a different frequency?" Chryséis asked her, but the Lady was distracted by a telepathic message.

"I just heard that the maiden Oruwen will be teleported to Rostau tomorrow, so no precious time is lost. You will be taken to Rostau by vimaan at once."

"Thank you, Honourable Lady," the children replied politely.

"It was a pleasure. Go with the protection of the Earthmother and the Bird God."

And so the time travellers left the City of the Sun in the company of a guard from the 'House of Truth'. They had packed the amulets away and already made contact with the lady of Cydonia, who wished them good luck. On their way to Rostau, the detection device had already sounded the alarm. The guard investigated the ground below them, but it turned out to be a false alarm and only a novel agricultural device and a medical instrument, the astonished inventor was working on, were found.

"Great," Chryséis said all disappointed. "If it carries on like that, the search is just a matter of years."

Later, they searched the cobbled streets of Rostau with their guard in the hope of finding the thieves before Oruwen arrived. The town was built on the high plateau and at first glance, Rostau appeared to be a vast terraced garden with red, pink and white roses that blossomed on terraces along all major buildings.

"Wow, I've never seen anything like this," Katherine marvelled.

"It is indeed an extraordinary town, athenai," the guard said. "In Ta Mery, we are very proud of the Hanging Gardens in Rostau."

Flowers and shrubs seemed to thrive in every available space. There were also palms with leaves like outstretched fingers and azalea bushes in many colours. Rostau was cooler than Innu had been and it rained more often, but when the sun broke through the clouds the city presented itself in swathes of colour.

However, no moki caravan was to be seen anywhere.

While their guard asked questions in a nearby shop, the three friends watched mosaic makers in a courtyard next-door. A master craftsman worked on a floor picture, showing the face of a young man that changed into that of an old man's when one looked at it from the opposite side.

The walls of the courtyard were painted with scenes of a detailed summer garden and Trevor reached for his digital camera. Of course, it wasn't there and he dropped his hand with a sigh. At the citadel, they learned that the Naia Festival, which took place only every five years, was about to start. Musicians, poets and dance groups entertained the crowds in every corner of the town. As a crowning finale, a poetry contest attracted many visitors to the great roofed-in amphitheatre of Do'oni to the west of Rostau. It was a sacred place in the hills where the premier bards from all over were celebrated. Many came from Lyonesse, Magnesia and even Twiskland to attend. All of that meant many, many people.

"Great, how are we going to find those thieves now?" Trevor growled when they were alone in their quarters. "Remember how busy the festival in Ush-bantoun was? Now just add a whole lot of clanging and singing into the mix. Darn, do they have nothing better to do than celebrating festivals all the time?"

He took the satchels they had received from the Lady of Innu as replacement for their stolen backpacks and threw them on his bed.

"Calm down," Katherine said. "Oruwen will be here any minute. Then we can make a plan."

They didn't have to wait long. As soon as Oruwen arrived, she took the children under her wings and their guard returned with the vimaan to Innu. The maiden was as grumpy as she had been in Cydonia and not exactly focused on the search.

"No matter what the Lady says," she grumbled. "I will not leave this wonderful town without seeing Horakhti, the Great Lion."

"They have a zoo here?" Katherine asked.

"Not a zoo-animal, athenai. A very big statue, hewn from the bedrock of the plateau."

"Why is this Great Lion so important? We have to find the thieves, who took our stuff, and our... devices," Trevor protested. "What if the caravan has already left town? Then we have to go after them quickly!"

"And we will, young friend. But the Great Lion is very, very old and rumoured to have been created by the Gods and therefore brings luck. I cannot possibly leave without seeing the statue."

"These maidens don't get out much, do they?" Katherine whispered.

But the maiden couldn't be swayed, and that's how they ended up visiting the largest park in Rostau to see Horakhti, the Great Lion.

Vendors along the streets sold melt-in-the-mouth sweets made from the famous Rostauri rosewater and Oruwen couldn't resist the temptation.

Rosewater was also used in cosmetics and much in demand in other parts of the country. In fact, Rostau meant 'rose dew' and was, according to Katherine, a very apt name for this town.

On the eastern side, the park bordered on some very large buildings, which could be seen in the distance. But their function was unclear to the three children.

Large white, bulging vases flanked the Southern entrance. There were fountains all over the park and if the children thought that there were many flowers in town, they hadn't seen anything yet as they walked along the footpaths.

"Did you see that?" Chryséis whispered to Katherine.

"See what?"

"I think I saw fairies around the flowers."

"Really?" Katherine said. "Trevor, have you seen any fairies."

"Not yet."

The children knew all about fairies. In Prydhain, they had even been saved by them when they had lost their way in the Fûna Mountains.

And indeed, daêvas, fairies tending to plants, were busily fluttering between the flowers. Some fairies swept yellow pollen inside large blue flowers while others picked aphids off leaves or dropped wilted flowers on neat piles.

The maiden took large steps and didn't give a hoot about the little creatures. A mockingbird sang by a small lake and colourful peacocks strutted their stuff on the burgundy lawns, but Oruwen was on a mission.

She wanted to see the lion and walk back to the citadel as quickly as possible, and the children tried to keep up with her.

Large trees surrounded the statue, but the lion was taller than the tallest trees and somehow seemed out of proportion in this lovely sprawling park.

Horakhti was a huge limestone lion, painted red all over. Despite the paint, it looked old and weathered. A stone tablet between the massive paws explained the statue's astronomical significance among the river of stars.

"Cool," Chryséis said. "That's really cool!"

The three friends exchanged uncertain glances. Was this…? But that couldn't be!

"Is that the Sphinx of Giza?" Katherine asked. "Well, I never!" That lion sculpture was certainly big enough, but it was a lion, not a sphinx!

"Come on, that can't be," Trevor said. "And where are the pyramids of Giza? Don't they belong together?"

"Don't be silly, there were no pyramids here 12,000 years ago," Chryséis hissed.

"If this is really the Sphinx of Giza, then tell me, why there are no pyramids?" He insisted.

Chryséis just rolled her eyes. "How am I supposed to know that?"

After a minute staring at the sculpture in awe, Oruwen took the path around the statue or rather the moat that surrounded it and didn't hear what the children were saying. She admired this statue as if it was the most important thing on earth.

Again, they tried to keep up with Oruwen and finally, the maiden said, "We have to go back now, athenai. It's getting late."

The children sighed and followed the determined maiden.

On the way out, they passed the statue of a young woman and a dog with a long snout and pointy ears. Upuaut, the dog, lay with its front paws outstretched, like the humungous lion, and was painted black. It looked not unlike Nubi, Azurias

Maya's dog. The stern young stone woman was dressed in an elegant, folded limestone toga.

It was written on a stone tablet that the black dog Upuaut and the stone virgin watched over what remained of the creation of the departed gods. The lion, on the other hand, was charged with watching over the skies and to alert the virgin of the return of the gods from their starry abode. They didn't have time to read all of the text on the tablet.

Katherine felt a stab of sadness. She wondered how Tepi was doing right now. Was she happy and well looked-after?

Soon, they were on their way back to the citadel. Trevor couldn't take it any longer and blurted out a question that's been bugging him. "Honourable maiden, why are there no pyramids in Ta Mery?"

Chryséis rolled her eyes. "Really?"

"She probably doesn't even know what you are talking about," Katherine whispered angrily.

Oruwen looked surprised at such an obvious question. School children of the Known World knew all about these things, but of course, these children were different.

She sighed and answered to her best knowledge. "There were pyramids once. Not here, but on the banks of the Nila River. Then, the river changed its course, and before soon the beautiful blue and white pyramids that had adorned the banks of the mighty river had completely disappeared in the mud."

The children couldn't believe their ears. "There were blue and white pyramids by the river?" Trevor asked. "And they sank into the mud?"

"But of course they have, young friends." Oruwen tried to be patient. "It is common knowledge that the god Osiris corrected the uncontrolled overflowing of the blue Nila River and alas, that's what happened. The pyramids have never been rebuilt in Ta Mery."

Not been rebuilt? Why not? Were there plans to rebuild them? The questions pelted the surprised maiden like dropping acorns in autumn.

"No one can remember the proper art of building such pyramids. Apart perhaps from the Kabiri, but much ancient knowledge has been lost in time. The Dark Age…"

There were so many things the children wanted to ask, but Oruwen urged them to walk on. She received a telepathic message from the Lady of the citadel that a seer had offered his services to find the stolen things of the visiting children, and she told the time travellers about it.

They expected an old man with long, white hair and a beard and were surprised to find a young man with a ready smile; clean- shaven with his hair cut short.

He motioned for them to sit down and listened to Oruwen's gushed explanations. He was not surprised at the nature of the stolen items, being a seer and all.

Apparently, normal telepathic abilities weren't enough to find the thieves. At the maiden's request, he held the children's hands for a moment and told them that their things had been taken by thieves in Ush-bantoun at the command of the Magi – an evil man, no doubt - who acted on behalf of an unworthy queen.

"Ah, yes. I see that the two thieves made a deal with the sorcerer. They work for slave traders and were instructed to take the devices to a safe place in the east… after very special children escaped from their grasp. You were lucky, athenai."

"I'll say," Katherine said.

"But why don't they just take the devices and sell them or something. How can the sorcerer be sure that they will hold up their end of the bargain now?"

The seer pondered this for a moment. "The thieves were obliged to follow his telepathic instructions. They know what a sorcerer can do to them if they disobey," he said. "They have left Rostau and are on their way east. By the looks of it, the king of Attock has agreed to keep the devices in storage for the sorcerer and the queen of Ush-bantoun. There seems to be a plan to break them out of prison in Innu, soon."

"That will not be so easy," Oruwen said with contempt. "They don't even care about the king, it seems."

"I believe that the sorcerer's assistant has not been caught yet. He will use his powers to help his master."

"We just have to hurry up and find them now," Trevor said impatiently. "Can we use the device finder?"

"Yes, if we are in the vicinity of the devices. But the country of Attock is in the east and far from here. As a disguise, they are travelling on foot with two mokis, headed for Magnesia. Wait, they have lost some of the items along the way without noticing it."

He described the location as a gorge in the land of Libyaion, the Gorge of Kerinkuyu. He laughed to himself and told them that one of the mokis was tired and started kicking out in a most comical fashion.

"One of the devices you seek and a bag made of unusual material, fell into the gorge - not too deep - they can be retrieved..." He pondered for a few moments as if to say something else. "The sight is beginning to waver. That is all I can see, I'm afraid. Good luck, athenai."

The children were so excited that they shook his hand and thanked him for his help. This was a very odd thing to do by prehistoric standards, but the seer just laughed good-naturedly and took his reward from the maiden.

"You are welcome... isn't that what you say in your time?" He asked.

"Yes, it is. How did you...?" Trevor was stunned.

"He's a seer, duh!" Katherine said.

"Thank you. Shukri, athenai. Shelanti," Oruwen and the Lady of Rostau said and the seer left the citadel.

"I can't believe it," Chryséis said. "He could see all of that? We must go and find this Gorge of Kerinkuyu."

"Yes, and we will leave early in the morning," Oruwen said.

"No, we have to leave now! What if they notice that they've lost the device and go back to look for it."

"They will not do this in the dark, friend Trevór," the Lady said. "These thieves don't know that you are hot on their heels."

Trevor barely slept that night. He couldn't help thinking that they might be too late already.

23 THE LONG SHORTCUT

Before sunrise, Oruwen ordered the children resolutely to get ready. As they walked out to board the sleek citadel vimaan, they were in for a surprise. Djehuti, the young teacher from the Magical School waited for them patiently on the lawn.

"I am entering the travel phase of my training," he informed them. "It is the last step before becoming a 'Dragon of Wisdom'. Therefore, I will accompany you and be of assistance wherever I can. I am also going on a quest to find the temple of the Bird God in the Koh Kaf Mountains."

The time travellers were still sleepy and didn't quite know what to say. They just nodded and smiled. They would have a travel companion aside from Oruwen. Cool.

"Ah, young man," the maiden said. "An acolyte who has adopted the ancient name of the god Thoth. An important deity's mirror on earth. How very fitting…"

Priests often assumed the name of the deity whose traits they aspired to honour. But the children had no idea what Oruwen was talking about and it wasn't really that important.

"Super…" Trevor thought it was just cool to have a male travel companion again.

The Lady of Rostau bade them farewell and once again, they climbed into a vimaan, full of hope that they would find at least one of their time-travel devices in the Gorge of Kerinkuyu. As the vimaan gradually moved away from the citadel of Rostau, the sun moved above the horizon and a new building site in the temple district came into sight. A group of giant engineers were measuring out the outline of a temple on the cleared site. A very large site.

Children played a game of Pok-ta-pok on the cleared field below the vimaan. They had drawn makeshift lines into the dirty ground and bounced the ball off their bodies, shoulders and thighs. They played vigorously against the first two courses of a newly erected great temple wall, trying to get the ball through a ring, mounted above their heads.

The temple was built in honour of the great gods, who had lived here on the plateau before the Dark Age.

The giants didn't seem to mind the playing children. The engineers were measuring out an area with a knotted cord - a procedure called 'stretching the cord'. The time travellers had read about this in a scroll at the library in Kem-Oun.

"Still no pyramids," Chryséis sighed as they headed north.

They crossed a large lake below and took a northeasterly turn. A flock of white birds fluttered around the vimaan and settled on the lake shore. The Blue Sea was to their left as the vimaan passed town after town.

The thieves had apparently taken this route zig-zagging via the towns of Silsila, Sohag and Kena and were now heading for the seaport of Gubla. Oruwen insisted on flying low so that they could look for any items the thieves may have lost on their way east. This wasn't exactly easy, because the streets below were quite busy.

The children were anxious. What if somebody detected the time-portal finder in the gorge before they got to it?

"Is this not taking too long?" Chryséis asked. "Maybe we should skip the towns and go straight to the gorge."

"We must try to find as many of your belongings as possible," the maiden insisted. "You do not want to leave anything from the future behind, at least not more than necessary."

The children could see Oruwen's point: If they left anything behind that didn't fit into the epoch, the future might take a different turn.

"If an animal chokes on a plastic wrapper, for instance, the whole breed might die out," Chryséis said.

"That's a bit dramatic," Katherine answered.

"Maybe, but we don't know for sure, we can only assume. Let's do what we can to clean up after us."

"Alright then," Trevor mumbled.

Their search turned up a granola bar still in its wrapper that had been used as payment to an innkeeper in Silsila as well as a pair of sunglasses on the road.

"There we go," Oruwen said. "That's better."

They found the sunglasses behind a bush by the wayside. Trevor called excitedly for the driver to land immediately. Although the glasses were somewhat bent, the children were triumphant. They also found an old rush sandal, a broken flint knife and two dirty rags with a printed border of elephants that may have been carried off some washing line by the wind.

Unfortunately, the search device turned up nothing of significance, but it was interesting to see what some people had stashed in their backyards. It had taken only half a morning's time to pass through the three towns. Oruwen was rather efficient, but still no sign yet of their missing devices.

As they got closer to the Gorge of Kerinkuyu, Djehuti concentrated on operating the search device. And they didn't have to wait long. All of a sudden, the search device jumped in Djehuti's hand. He zoomed in on the exact location and... they had found the time-portal finder!

The vimaan set down softly by the side of the road, avoiding a farmer's cart drawn by two mokis, and they all jumped out. Katherine saw it first: a black distorted heap lying just below the edge of the road, stuck at the base of a dwarf palm and small cistus shrubs with their sticky branches and leaves.

She hurried toward the heap, leaned down and retrieved Chryséis' daypack. It wasn't very heavy. So there was stuff missing! They rifled through the contents, but the TPF wasn't there, nor was the palmtop computer they had used as a log book. Just some clean underwear and two t-shirts were still tightly pressed into the bottom of the daypack. It looked as if the bag had fallen out by accident, unnoticed by the thieves.

Vimaans passed on the road and people watched them curiously. Djehuti scanned the area again and walked slowly in the direction the search device indicated. The others followed him to the edge of the road. So, where was the TPF?

"It has to be here somewhere..." The maiden Oruwen said impatiently.

"Lower down perhaps," Katherine suggested and pointed toward the river at the bottom of the gorge.

"Not in the water, surely," Trevor said a little annoyed.

"Please, it can't be that low down," Katherine wailed.

Then the search-device went off again.

Trevor saw something glinting on a ledge perhaps 10 feet below. He didn't lose any time and struggled down the slope. He saw the TPF just above the ledge, and took an impatient swipe at it. But his nerves were raw and he missed it narrowly, only to set the device in motion. Just enough for it to slide further downhill.

It came to a brief halt, balancing on a tuft of grass and rolled further down, where it got stuck between the twigs of a cistus shrub. Then, it suddenly began to tumble down again. The back cover broke off and exposed the intricate technical innards. The TPF bounced off rocks and plants, until the precious time-portal finder splashed into the river below. They stared in horror. This just couldn't be true!

The rushing noise seemed to grow to unbearable levels.

"No!" Trevor screamed, angry with himself. "Oh no, no!"

Was he in a nightmare? Maybe all this wasn't happening at all and he would wake up... about now... and all would turn out fine. But it was no nightmare.

Their precious time-portal finder had vanished in the tossing waters of the river below. Trevor wanted to jump into the river after the device, but Djehuti yelled, "It is too dangerous, friend..."

Dangerous, dangerous, the gorge echoed back mocking them.

Trevor gave up his wild plan, but they had been so close. Why did this have to happen now?

He slumped down and stared at the stream not far from where he was sitting. He ignored calls from the others that urged him to return to the top of the slope. In fact, he could hear nothing but the rushing stream below.

Djehuti was already on his way down to help when Trevor pulled himself together at last. He grabbed a few things that had also fallen from Chryséis' daypack along with the TPF. Then he began to climb up the slope, crawling carefully, while clutching two toothbrushes, one tube of antiseptic cream and another with toothpaste. He saw something else that looked out of place in a cistus bush, clinging by its roots to a rocky outcrop.

It was the palmtop computer! Trevor shifted his weight to the right and away from the ledge, he stood on. Then taking it slowly this time around, he leaned forward and gently plucked the palmtop out of the bush.

There was also a small tub of Vaseline that had fallen right behind the palmtop.

"What's that, Trevor, what have you got there?" Chryséis called out to him, but the noise of the river drowned out his mumbled reply. Djehuti held out his hand and pulled Trevor over the ledge. Exhausted, he held up the palmtop. They both continued to climb, until they reached the top.

"No way! It's the palmtop," Katherine said and took the computer gently from Trevor's hand. It felt like seeing an old friend again and there was no holding back the tear that rolled down her cheek.

"Great, I hope it still works." Chryséis was practical as ever. "But we can't use it until we find at least one of the vacuum batteries."

Trevor sat down on the road and handed the palmtop over to Chryséis.

"Looks okay to me," she said. "I wonder what else is still down there or has fallen into the water. I can't even remember what I had in the backpack."

They scanned the slope and the river, but could see nothing else that seemed familiar and the detection device was quite still.

Djehuti knelt next to Trevor and put a hand on his shoulder. "Athenai, you may not understand the reason for this now, but..."

"It's all my fault that we will never return home," Trevor interrupted him. "It was so slippery... and it slid out of my hand," he tried to explain.

"Don't exaggerate," Chryséis told him.

"Not to worry about it, Trev," Katherine said, wiping the tear away. "There are two more TPFs and we just have to find them."

"Chances are we won't find them at all," Trevor moaned. "I mean, what are the odds of finding anything in this place?"

"Don't even think like that..." Chryséis shouted, "...of course we will!"

"No doubt..." Katherine said. The tears had stopped. "We can't chicken out now. We've come too far. Agreed?"

She held her hand out for a high-five first with Trevor then Chryséis. Although her friends were less enthusiastic, some hope returned.

"We must be on our way... there is still another town to search..." Oruwen urged them on and wondered about the strange ritual of hand-clapping above the head.

Djehuti said nothing else. He just got up and rubbed the dirt off his knees.

"I say we walk," Trevor said. "What if there is more of our stuff that the thieves lost around here? We could miss something and I don't want to take a chance."

It was clear that he needed action to take his mind off the broken time-portal finder. Their prehistoric friends understood. Oruwen, being the one in charge, decided that she would travel ahead to the port city of Gubla and have a good look there.

"Djehuti, you will accompany the children on foot and look for stolen belongings. We will meet again at the citadel in Gubla. It's not far from here and you should arrive there by evening. Tomorrow morning, we'll carry on together."

The maiden Oruwen left in the vimaan. It was growing smaller until it had entirely disappeared , while Djehuti and the children marched along the dusty road to Gubla.

Although Djehuti used the search device all the time, there was not even as much as a blip and after a while, the girls thought that it had been a hare-brained idea to walk all this way. A stone bridge led over the narrow gorge and around a hill. Djehuti thought would be a welcome shortcut into the next town.

"Let us walk in this direction," he suggested. "This path will get us quicker to Gubla."

The children gratefully accepted his advice. They crossed the bridge and found themselves now to the right of the hill away from the road.

Chryséis dreamily moved her hand over feathery grasses along the path. It tickled the palm of her hand. It was great to have the palmtop back. So much research had been stored on the small computer and if they wanted to hand in a great physics project, they needed every bit of it.

There was a rustle in the bushes next to the road. Chryséis looked up lazily and saw to her horror how a hissing rattlesnake stabbed its head at her ankle. She jumped aside and screamed in surprise. The rattlesnake snapped into the air. Seeing that there was no immediate danger, the reptile retreated nimbly back into the tall grass and was gone.

Djehuti, who had walked ahead with Trevor, stopped and turned around. Chryséis stared at them in shock.

"There, there was a snake… a snake," she breathed. Djehuti made sure that the snake was gone for good. Then he insisted on a short rest.

Chryséis felt uncomfortable, but Djehuti assured her that the snake would not seek them out. They drank water and ate their travel cakes. A small company of soldiers, escorts to a swift-messenger, stopped for some water and promised to look out for the thieves.

Katherine looked behind the rock she sat on and saw another granola bar wrapper stuck under the seat. The thieves had been here!

"Littering is obviously not a modern problem," Chryséis said and held up the wrapper.

At that moment, the detection device, Djehuti had put on the ground next to him, started jumping.

"That's not very reliable," Trevor grumbled. "At least we are on the right track, thanks to our shortcut."

After another hour of walking, they had only found a tattered golden earring and some rotten fruit, but soon, a shabby cottage came into sight. They could get more information here. Dirty children in rags played some game in muddy puddles in front of the cottage and a haggard-looking man was busy white-washing the front wall. An older boy helped him with this task. A garbage heap at the gate was swarming with flies, but otherwise, the place seemed reasonably clean. A woman in simple dress drew a bucket from the well and nodded in greeting.

"We will stop for a while and rest, friend," Djehuti said.

"We cannot stop for long," Trevor cautioned. "We must keep looking and reach Gubla before sundown."

The young scholar nodded and walked towards the cottage. A sign was mounted above the front door. This was a licensed inn, because underneath the painted hieroglyphics the sign read in Akkadian:

"Lodge - Feed - Quench".

A pint of bouza beer was painted underneath the text.

The man put his brush into the bucket and set the bucket on the ground and signalled a greeting. "Shelanti strangers. Do you believe in Osiris the highest of deities, the abolisher of cannibalism and slavery, the founder of civilization and symbol of the mighty sun?"

His eyes were piercing. What kind of a question was that? Was the man mad? But a quick look at Djehuti confirmed that things were in order.

It was an appropriate question in Ta Mery. "We do believe that and mean you no harm," Djehuti answered.

"Welcome then to this abode of peace. Have you travel

documents?" The man asked. He was not actually entitled to inspect such travel papers, but the innkeeper had been a citadel guard in his youth and old habits die hard. Djehuti looked at Trevor.

"Ahem, sure. Why not?" Trevor produced their paizas and handed them to the man. He ogled the clay disks. These were no ordinary children, bearing the paizas from the Lady of Innu.

The man handed the paizas back and invited them in. "Bring these good people something hearty to eat, wife, and a jug of the good ale."

"Welcome," his wife said as she walked into the house with a bucket of water. The dirty children were laughing and pointed at the strangers before turning their attention back to the puddles and a few sticks.

The innkeeper's wife served gazelle stew with white serm pods and mashed squash and the food was surprisingly tasty.

"Would you like boiled birds' eggs?" She asked.

"Thank you," Katherine answered politely. "One egg, please." The woman looked surprised. That was not very much.

Katherine stared at the little white object. The woman then dished out spoonsful of the peeled eggs to the others. At last Djehuti asked the innkeeper whether he had seen any suspicious looking men with a small moki caravan pass through.

"I remember such a caravan. Two blokes and two mokis," the man said. "I didn't pay much attention to them. They were on their way to Gubla, but it was strange that they took an off-road shortcut."

They paid for the food and set out again.

"How did you know that the man had information about the thieves?" Katherine asked.

"Athenai, I didn't know that, but I used my intuition," Djehuti answered. "And you saw for yourselves that the caravan must have come this way."

The shortcut turned out to be a path along the narrow gorge, covered with pebbles and closed in by steep rock walls.

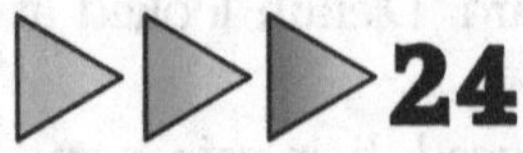 **24**   # THE FLASH FLOOD

"The stew was really good, but I'd give a kingdom for some chocolate now," Katherine said.

They had left the path further up against the rock face, when it had proved to be too difficult to navigate, and were walking over flat pebbles at the bottom of the gorge. Nobody else was to be seen here.

"Yeah or cornflakes…" Chryséis sighed.

"No, it has to be chocolate," Katherine decided, "…with yoghurt filling or with nuts and raisins."

"Oh, stop it already." Trevor was irritated. He hated chocolate. "How about just eating food, no matter what?"

"Oh boy, somebody is peeved," Chryséis said.

Djehuti paid no attention to the conversation in the children's foreign language. He had a job to do: listen intently to noises and look out for odd objects lying around, but his efforts didn't yield any results.

"We will continue in this direction. It won't be far to Gubla now," he said and walked faster.

"Don't you think it's strange that no other travellers are using this route?" Trevor asked.

*

But this was not quite true. For another unusual traveler, die obstacles on the trail along the Rockwall presented less of a problem and he was slightly ahead of Djehuti and the time travellers. His name was En-kidu from the clan of the Ipú.

He was named after the wise mother goddess with the owl head, of which a life-size statue of the goddess had once stood in En-kidu's cave far from this place. The Ipú were Sons of Nanak, the Moon, and proud of it. To the civilized folk, they were primitive Wildmen. Konks of the Wild, who preferred their own company. Like all of his kind, En-kidu was covered in reddish fur.

Civilized folk were noisy and smelled funny and had very little hair. They built their caves in large settlements with mud and dried grass and some mysterious shiny crystal. Not half as good as a good solid cave.

He had seen the caves of the hairless Ones. He loved grapes and took care not to be seen when he helped himself to a pouchful of the sweet fruit in autumn. One had to be careful, not to run into disease-carrying slave traders, though. They captured Konks like him and made them work in the quarries or copper mines in the Red Land. Two of those vermin creatures had passed him not too long ago with their two mokis and he hadn't liked their smell. En-kidu knew how to sniff them out and hide from them.

He had spent wonderful years with his wife E-nush in the lap of the clan in the spacious cave in the western foothills. Their two children, a boy and a girl grew up happy and content, playing and learning about the ways of the Sons of Nanak.

En-kidu had been a good provider and loved his wife… so beautiful with her soft reddish hair all over and her soulful dark eyes. But it pained him to think of her now.

A fortnight ago when the moon sickle had been as thin as a flint knife, life had come to a grinding halt for his clan. It had been En-kidu's turn to stay behind and guard the cave while the other males left to go hunting before sunrise.

It was always best to hunt reptilians when the air was still cool and the cold made the animals sluggish and easy to stalk. The cave had two large chambers of ochre rock that were attached to the side of a mountain.

The women and children often stayed in the second chamber to scrape animal hides or weave coarse mats and baskets.

En-kidu had loved this cave of his ancestors and it pained him that it no longer existed. He had known each red hand imprint on the cave wall by heart. The big one with two bent fingers was that of his great-grandfather. The small one next to it had belonged to his young daughter Kanah.

Then the earthquake came and his peaceful life was over in no time.

The young ones had been in the nursery. Normally a secure place, but when the rocks started falling, many of their precious children were gravely injured or even killed.

The women, who had been weaving baskets, had tried to reach the children and take them to safety. But falling rocks blocked their escape at the back of the cave. The carnage had been great.

En-kidu had been working in the front chamber, close to the entrance, sharpening flint arrowheads. He escaped with his life, but it was too late for his family.

When the other men returned from their hunt, they were greeted by a picture of destruction. They had felt only a slight tremble beyond the hills. Like the thunderous feet of giant lizards. The men joined in the wailing of the few survivors while En-kidu was digging furiously away at the back of the cave, throwing rocks onto a pile. The hunters went onto their knees and helped him free the back of the cave.

En-kidu found his daughter and young son slain by the falling rubble. It took them another afternoon before they got to the women. Two of them were still alive, but the beautiful E-nush had lain dead, her skull crushed. En-kidu had touched her lifeless arm and the reddish hair had been so soft.

En-kidu was riddled with guilt. Why had he survived? He was worthless, unable to protect the helpless clan members, as it was his duty.

That's when the experienced hunter had taken his pouch and a small figurine, made by his daughter Kanah, and left his home.

He went farther west and didn't know why – with only Father Moon for a companion. The tall, hairy Konk looked more human than the Konks of Alesia. Slender and not as heavy-set as his dome-headed cousins. He climbed nimbly over familiar rocks in the Ipú territory, until he recognized the hills no more and from there on aimlessly roamed hill and dale, not caring whether he lived or died. His shoulder had been injured by falling rocks, but it didn't hurt for a while after he'd left the clan's territory in grief.

The untreated wound had begun to swell and fester.

E-nush had been trained in plant lore and would have known what to do, but Enush was no longer with him and death seemed. He barely cared. Death would free him from the pain inside.

The small antelope he had hunted almost in passing, lay untouched in a corner of the cave above the ravine, where he'd been hiding from the slave traders. His prey needed to be prepared, but no family would benefit from a hearty meal. The grieving Wildman sat down against the rough rock wall. He cradled his injured shoulder and watched the sun slowly wander west across the sky.

*

Meanwhile, the time travellers and Djehuti hiked along the dried-up riverbed and wondered if they were still on their way to Gubla. Tufts of grass covered the pebbles now and a few bare bushes were clinging to the steep sides. After a sharp bend, they could see the skeleton of a large animal. It rested against a rock wall with only mud and stones lodged underneath the bleached white bones.

Broken branches stuck out from the large ribcage and birds hopped from bone to bone in search of juicy insects.

Djehuti decided that a rocky overhang would make a shady resting place and they made camp. He took out the roasted meat and ring-shaped travel bread, the innkeeper's wife had given him. A short break, then they would walk on and be in Gubla by nightfall. Suddenly, he held his hand up and listened. Then he was sure. "Get your things and climb up!" he yelled.

The three friends were stumped. Why up?

But there was no time for explanations. Perhaps the thieves

were nearby or dangerous animals. But the thieves were no longer near them and whatever animal was still in the ravine, tried to climb or run away.

They packed hastily. Djehuti crammed the food back into his knapsack and was already halfway up the rock face, climbing from boulder to boulder, aiming at the ledge just above him. He turned around and held his hand out to Katherine and the two other children, who stumbled up between the rocks.

Chryséis thought that from above the skeleton looked definitely like the remains of a dinosaur with a long broken tail, but then she heard a scary swishing and rumbling noise and climbed faster.

They had nearly made it. Just Chryséis was still hanging onto the ledge trying to pull herself up when the rumbling grew louder. Her hands began to chafe and Djehuti tried to drag her to safety, but she threatened to let go of the ledge.

Djehuti felt himself roughly pushed aside as a hairy hand grabbed Chryséis and pulled her onto the ledge.

The girl looked up and nearly fainted at the sight. She looked at a big hairy Konk!

Then it happened in the blink of an eye. Turbulent waters tossed down the ravine, foaming and splashing over weathered boulders like so many other flash floods before. Faster and faster the flood rushed down the ravine, carrying with it struggling animals, silt, rocks and splintering wood.

The shattered trunk of a majestic cedar collided with the rock face underneath the ledge, sending a shiver through the rock.

The dirty waters almost reached the overhang, lapping the edge and sweeping up the large skeleton, carrying its grinning skull right past them.

They moved away from the edge and sat down, panting with fright. Chryséis had a better look at the Konk, who had pulled her onto the ledge. He exuded a strong animal odour, but his facial features were rather friendly with expressive, brown eyes. They looked sad and fatherly at the same time. His forehead sloped back and his chin resembled that of a chimpanzee. His body was covered in bristly hair, but his face was almost hairless with a flat, broad nose and protruding eyebrows.

The breechcloth and leather wrap he was wearing were carefully stitched. A crude flint knife with a wooden handle was tucked into the thong that was wrapped around his midriff and a small leather pouch was hanging around his neck.

This Wildman was powerfully muscular, but he seemed friendly and signalled a shy greeting that was different from the greetings they were used to, but it was a greeting nonetheless.

"Sha-anti," he mumbled. His speech was hacked and guttural.

This morning, En-kidu had smelled the flood long before it hit the ravine. He was already using the shelter of a cave, abandoned by large cats, hngu, as they were called in Konk language. A grunt, no more, to the ear of those trained in complex languages.

En-kidu had also smelled this group of hairless people before they had come into sight. They were young ones mostly and now they were right here, looking scared.

Trevor took a deep breath and tried to communicate "Shelanti, athenai."

He saw the puzzled look in the dark eyes and realised that the Wildman didn't understand him. It could have been the thundering flood below, and they virtually yelled at each other.

"En-kidu." The Konk pronounced his name and slapped his hairy hand against his powerful chest.

To the children, it sounded like a series of swallowed consonants, but it was reassuring that his intentions seemed peaceful. He pointed up and invited them to share his shelter with him. En-kidu took care that they all made their way up safely, which took them a while.

Inside the case, Chryséis continued the introduction. "Chryséis," she said and pointed to herself.

"Krchs." En-kidu managed a smile.

He admired the girl's light hair that glowed in the sunlight.

Then it was Djehuti's turn to introduce himself. He knew a smattering of Konkese, which consisted of much gesturing and grunts. He had learned simple phrases at the School of White Magic at Innu. A glint of recognition moved across the Konk man's face. "Dju-tee," he repeated.

Next, Trevor pointed to himself. "Trevor," he mouthed slowly.

"Troro."

Trevor nodded. Now it was Katherine's turn. "Katie."

"Kee," En-kidu said and pointed to the dark-haired girl child and Katherine nodded.

She noticed the dead gazelle in the small cave and also that he held his left arm. She suspected an injury and used gestures to ask the Konk if she could have a look at it.

At first, En-kidu didn't see any reason why a hairless girl-child should want to look at his wound. Then on second thought, it was possible that the Earthmother had endowed her with special powers of healing. He sniffed at her and decided that she had a good, innocent smell. He waved for her to come and turned his upper arm so that the festering wound was exposed. Katherine gasped. The wound looked dreadful.

Without touching, she examined the shoulder.

"I don't think the bone is broken, but the flesh wound is infected." She fumbled around her moon bag for the antiseptic cream and something to cover the wound.

"Hey not bad, Mary Poppins," Chryséis said.

"Wait, I've got something." Trevor tore a piece off his tunic hem. "Here, try this."

"I have no idea if that's enough, but we must help him. He helped us, too just now."

The Wildman of the proud Ipú clan didn't mind the pain that the dressing of the wound caused, but the fabric strip stunned him. He had rarely seen anything so fine.

"Looks good to me," Chryséis said as Katherine finished up. A spark of hope returned to the heart of the powerful Konk. The kindness of these young hairless people touched him. Perhaps it was a sign from the Mother Goddess that he was meant to live after all.

*

"Aaargh!" Chryséis let out a scream that ripped through the background noise of the flowing water. The others rushed outside to see whether she had hurt herself but Chryséis seemed fine. Instead, they found staring stiffly at a snakelike head sliding onto the rock ledge. The massive head probed in their direction.

"Oh my…" Katherine felt faint. She had seen an Anaconda film once and it had been a scary film, even if there was no logic to it. But this was no movie.

Would the snake try to devour them? She searched for a rock. *There has to be a rock lying around somewhere,* Katherine thought wildly. She wanted to throw something at the snake's head and make it go away.

To everyone's surprise, En-kidu began to grunt, then yelled at the snake and marched directly towards it.

Was the Wildman going crazy? Surely the reptile would lift him off the ledge and devour him in a second.

But to everybody's astonishment, the Konk lifted his crude club and smacked the snake on the head. Just like that. En-kidu recognised the animal as being the top end of a young Diplodocus - an Uhnt in Konk language. A harmless plant-eating saurian with a large body and long neck. The head and neck slid off the edge and plopped into the water. He had only stunned the Diplodocus. The young saurian bellowed and retreated back up the ravine, shaking its head all the time.

Uhnts grazed tender leaves off the tops of trees. They could be a nuisance sometimes, these Uhnts, and curious, especially the young ones, but quite harmless. En-kidu didn't know how to tell the hairless ones about this.

The Konk trudged right back into the cave and continued to prepare the antelope for roasting. The other followed him and sat down, still in awe of what had happened. Soon, a fire flickered close to the cave mouth. He felt strangely at peace with himself, now that he had somebody to feed.

*

The flash flood receded slowly, leaving behind smelly mud and destruction. It grew dark and they had no choice but to wait for the morning to arrive.

In the glowing light of the hearth fire, Trevor had an idea. He mixed a paste with ground-up charcoal and a splotch of petroleum jelly in a shallow hole in the rock. Then he drew carefully with his index finger on the cave wall. He did his best to make his drawing a dinosaur, then a Konk. Then his friends and himself with a baseball cap, t-shirt and shorts, holding a TPF. Chryséis sat down next to Trevor.

"What are you doing there?"

"What does it look like?" he answered.

"Why are you drawing with this black stuff?"

"Because I feel like it." Trevor was too absorbed to have a conversation.

"You know that you are contaminating a prehistoric site, don't you?" Chryséis cautioned him.

"What do I care? We have left so much behind already. Time-portal finders, clothes, DNA..." He grimly inspected his pictures.

"Looks nice. Is that me?" Katherine pointed to the drawing of a girl with a long ponytail. She held her head to the side to look at the pictures.

"Yeah," Trevor said and finished his drawings.

The girls looked at each other. Chryséis screwed up her face and Katherine shrugged. They left Trevor to his creative work and sat down on the ledge outside, sharing some water from their travel supply with Djehuti.

"The cave is isolated. I say we just leave him to draw," Chryséis said.

"The cave may be isolated now, but what about in 12,000 years?" Katherine objected. "As a scientist, Trevor should know better than that."

"Look if the drawings last that long that anyone tries to

analyse them... it won't make much of a difference. It's not as if scientists pay much attention to unusual findings as it is."

"I guess you're right," Katherine said and left Trevor to his odd drawings.

Later, En-kidu gave each of them a piece of the slightly burnt meat. Trevor pecked at his food and En-kidu encouraged him to eat properly. Djehuti was already chewing on the antelope meat and seemed to enjoy it.

En-kidu crushed a large scorpion with his bare fist as it approached. The children jumped and looked uneasy. What if there were more of these creepy crawlies around?

Eventually, they spent an uncomfortable night on the cave floor, but having a strong Wildman right there felt safe somehow.

By morning, the flood had completely receded, but the pebbles in the ravine were now covered in the slippery mud.

"We will have to walk on higher ground from now on," Djehuti said. "Wildmen are remarkably resilient, but I don't want to take a chance and wade through the mud. Illness lurks in it and we are not as robust as the Wildmen..."

The Konk man had recovered from his injury practically overnight. He had taken off the bandage and there was some proud flesh, but scabs had formed under the red hair and the wound was healing.

They communicated to him that it was time to leave. En-kidu nodded, cleared the remains of the fire and the antelope bones from the cave floor and threw them into the muddy ravine. Normally he wouldn't have wasted any part of the animal, but there were no females to work the hide or relish the bone marrow. He became restless and kept scanning the ravine. The Wildman sensed CLAN.

*

En-kidu's clan members had gone looking for him. Three of them had ventured far into the land of the hairless people to find him. They needed En-kidu to help rebuild what was left of their community. So they had dared to enter unfamiliar territory.

They walked on high ground, but it didn't take them long to sense him by the ravine. A picture of devastation presented itself below where the flashflood had raged. Something told them that En-kidu was still alive and Ra-ku, the eldest of them, pointed his staff to a rock shelf and without having to speak. The three Konks walked along the top of the rock wall until they were close enough to the ledge.

Two hairless children were sitting on the ground. Two odd-looking girls. They picked leaves of a shrub and didn't hear the men approach.

Before they knew it, Chryséis and Katherine were surrounded by three tall red-haired Konk men with their spears planted on the ground.

The girls just sat there, staring at them. They didn't dare get up. Trevor, En-kidu and Djehuti had gone into the small cave to pack the leftover roast into the gazelle hide.

Compared to En-kidu, these Konks looked menacing. The men stared back at them. What were they supposed to do now?

The Wildmen didn't know how to speak to the children and stood there shyly for all their fearsome appearance. They probably had to prepare for a fight if their parents were around.

En-kidu knew what he had to do before he had even caught sight of the three clansmen. He went outside to greet his brethren and winced when friendly claps rained on his injured shoulder.

"At last we found you." Unintelligible grunts and gestures were exchanged. "We've found a new cave," they told him.

A neighbouring clan, the Neph-il had also suffered much loss of life during the earth tremor and the two groups had merged into one clan. At the next great clan gathering, they would look for suitable wives.

Djehuti and Trevor joined them as well and after some more grunting, the Wildmen shouldered the gazelle meat, said good-bye and made their way back home.

 **25**   # LOST AND FOUND

Djehuti and the children found their way and had reached the town within the hour. Gubla was a pleasant and efficient seaside town in the province of Libyaion. A breeze blew from the west and in the distance, the Blue Sea shimmered like a jewel.

The flags on the municipal buildings cracked in the wind, and sailing boats pulled on their moorings in the harbour, where large dog statues guarded the city of Gubla against evil.

On their way into town, they had seen copper mines in the Vallé Fucinaia, the valley of blacksmiths. Smoke rose from many pipes, where the metal was refined in underground furnaces.

Their story about meeting a friendly Konk, who had saved Chryséis from falling to her death during a flash flood, was received with disbelief. They ran into the maiden Oruwen just outside the town, where she was steering a vimaan to look for Djehuti and the children. The visitors had not returned in time last night and everyone at the citadel had grown worried.

"Wild Konks are surely hostile," she said. "I cannot imagine them capable of civilised thought or action. Only good for the copper mines they are." Her ranting surprised the three children. The maiden had always seemed grumpy but not narrow-minded. She was in the service of the Lady of Cydonia after all, which counted for a lot.

"Did you speak to the Lady of Cydonia while we were gone?" Katherine asked.

"Why would I want to do that? We don't need her. We'll just take this vimaan and be on our way now. I arranged it with the Lady of Gubla. No time to waste."

"Did you hear if the shipping route through the Blue Sea is safe again?"

"Oh yes, yes, sure it is. Why wouldn't it be?"

"Because of the war perhaps?" Trevor probed.

"The king has met with an untimely death, I heard. During the confrontation with the fierce Ama-zûnas and king Asol's warriors. Ships are going through the 'Passage of the Golden Pillars' in their droves."

"Then why don't we take a ship to Hyela now?" Chryséis asked longingly.

"We still have to find your things now, don't we?" The maiden answered and they had to admit that she was right.

As happy as the time travellers were about the good news about the war, it was true that they could not go home to the distant future without their time travel devices. After a short rest, they were ready to leave town.

And so, instead of boarding a ship that sailed west, the children went farther east to find their time-travel devices. Away from the Blue Sea, the 'Passage of the Golden Pillars' and even farther away from Alesia.

They couldn't quite understand why Oruwen acted the way she did, but she steered the vimaan quite well, so they let her be.

"Over there is Su Mâr," Djehuti said and pointed to a vast stretch of farming land dominated by a glowing white palace. They saw a large white stone platform between fields and trees, on which some rather large vimaans were parked in rows. They had heard about this country back in Cydonia. "And beyond Su Mâr lies Rusicada, Magnesia, Bakhtri and Soghdiana." In modern-day Asia, then.

"That's where we are headed?"

"Yes, that's where the thieves are headed and we will get them before they meet up with the king of Attock,"

Oruwen confirmed.

"Is that a statue down there? A golden one?" Chryséis asked and pointed to the ground far below the vimaan. "It's so big."

"That's the golden statue of Marduk," Djehuti explained. "The god of war. It's quite an ancient monument and a market is usually held by the statue at full moon."

"I believe it is time to take a little rest in Rusicada," Djehuti said and pointed to a rather large water reservoir and settlement on a forested hill.

"I don't think we should go to the plantation of Kharsag. That will just delay us," Oruwen objected.

"I think the detection device is reacting," Djehuti told them.

"Oh really?" The maiden said in a high voice.

"We can rest in the forest below the settlement, refresh ourselves and be on our way again. You did bring provisions, didn't you, Oruwen."

"Provisions? Of course, I brought provisions."

Djehuti sighed and waited for the maiden to land next to a little spring in a forest glade. Oruwen then produced baskets full of snacks and juice in têrakhon bottles that no one had noticed before. They settled down to a pleasant picnic while Djehuti told the children about Kharsag.

"The location was perfect for a settlement of the 'Creating Gods' and legend has it that the district of the 'Shining Ones' was built overnight," he told them. "The simple folk, who lived in the hills didn't know what to make of all this at first. Little did they understand the movements of the gods. But over time, the 'Shining Ones' managed to persuade them that they had good intentions." Djehuti helped himself to some food.

"After their initial reluctance, the natives flocked to the 'Garden of Kharsag' with its peculiar buildings and people. This is all in the past now. Nowadays, it is regarded as a great honour to live in the settlement and to learn the skills that were taught by the 'Shining Ones'. "

"So the Gods – 'The Shining Ones' brought civilisation

to them?" Trevor asked.

"I would say so. When the Gods left the plantation, the D'Ånu people took over from the 'Shining Ones' and continued the good work and teachings. The Gods had decided to establish more settlements between the rivers of Idiglat and Buranum, where they instructed the natives."

"This went on for many generations before the Gods left altogether to return to their heavenly abode. Fruit trees cover the sunny slopes. Cherry, apple, plum and pear. The Gods had brought many of the plants from faraway lands and improved them. There are said to be particularly tasty. You can have a stroll later and see if you can pick some fruit around here."

After their meal, Oruwen leaned against a tree trunk and took a nap. Since Gubla, she had become rather quiet and preferred her own company.

"Perhaps she doesn't feel well," Chryséis said.

"Yes, maybe, but this place is divine!" Katherine marvelled. "Just look at all these trees. Who comes with me to pick some fruit?"

"I'll come," Trevor said and they strolled up the hill.

They came across two rugged Utzinco men, who were on their way downhill. They were from a native tribe, who preferred not to live on the farm, but carried the goods between Kharsag and other settlements lower down. The short, hardy men carried heavy baskets with the help of leather straps slung across their foreheads. They greeted the children and were quickly on their way again.

The Utzinco were loyal to the good D'Ånu people at the plantation. They lived in primitive hovels on the hills and loved the beer that was brewed on the plantation and didn't need much for themselves.

Chryséis wiped off large black ants that had started to carry pine needles across her foot. She sat on a soft floor of moss between a tangled mass of roots. It smelled of pine needles and something else like sulphuric smoke. The copper mines were down there and the wind had changed.

It was hard to believe that this fertile region was to become the dry semi-desert of modern times. The golden statue of Marduk gleamed in the distance and the white palace of Su Mâr.

Katherine and Trevor were still looking for the fruit trees that Djehuti had told them about.

"Look, over there is an apple tree," Katherine said. The tree was close to a rough wall that must belong to the plantation. Trevor was clumsy and kicked loose a shower of small rocks.

"Be careful, Trev, it's quite steep here," Katherine warned him.

They picked an apple and tasted the tart sweetness.

"Mmh, that's really good for an apple," Trevor said.

They walked along the wall and came to a building that was part of the wall. Above the front entrance was a sign:

"Dingir   en   ge   li "
"Shining Lord of Cultivation"

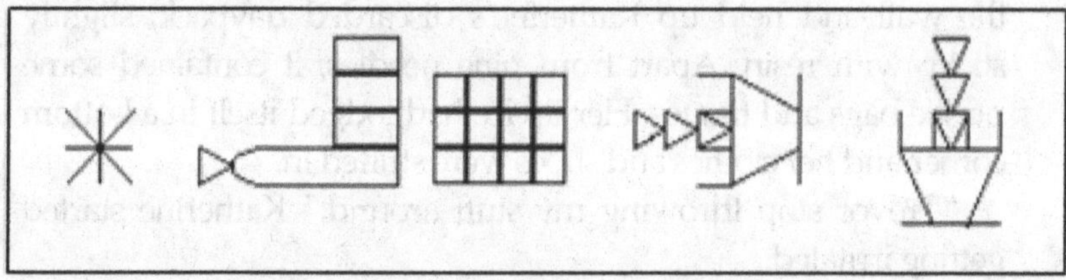

"Do you think it means farming god?" Katherine asked.

"Probably, I mean this whole plantation is about producing food for the region."

"Shalanti, " somebody said behind them and the two friends jumped. It was one of the Utzinco men. He sat down on a mossy stone and was trying to tell them something.

"Utzinco see strange men with mokis," he said. He held up

two fingers. "About that many days ago. At foot of hill."

"You saw strange men?"

The runner nodded. "Utzinco see men not good. No say greeting to runners. See take bag and throw away. Clothes. Things. Don't know…"

Obviously, he didn't know how to describe what those things were.

"Some clothes," he added, plucking at his sarong.

"Can you show us the things and clothes?" Trevor asked. He couldn't be sure, but it sounded important.

"Utzinco can show children things," the man agreed and waved for them to follow.

"I'm not running all the way down the mountain with him," Katherine protested.

"Friend Utzinco," Trevor said. "Is it far? Do you want to bring us these things?"

"No, not far. Not far. Will show athenai."

"Well if it's not far, we can go with him…"

Katherine threw her apple core into the bushes and followed the runner. And indeed, they didn't have to walk far before the Utzinco man stopped just a few meters away, scratched around the wall and held up Katherine's discarded daypack, slightly sticky with resin. Apart from pine needles, it contained some plastic bags and tissues. Her lip ice had lodged itself in a bottom corner and her clothes and shoes were stuffed in.

"Trevor stop throwing my stuff around." Katherine started getting irritated.

"The TPF is not in here!" Trevor cried. "I can't believe that they knew exactly what to look for."

"There's nothing we can do now," Katherine said. "Let's go back to the others. At least we got another daypack and some stuff we might need."

"Like what? Lip ice? What good does lip ice do if we can't go back home?"

"Hey, keep your hair on. It's not my fault!"

"Okay, okay… but we've been here way too long already."

This time it was Trevor, who was about to lose his cool.

They gave the Utzinco man some tender from their saurian leather purse and he grinned broadly. Then he zig-zagged down the hill.

They showed the others their find.

"What? This guy gave you Katherine's daypack just like that?" Chryséis couldn't believe it. "I'm sure, he went through your things and took something he liked."

"What do you want to do about it? Chase after him and tell him to give it back?" Katherine said.

"Athenai, please speak in a language everybody can understand," Oruwen scolded. She had just come back from a walk. "Djehuti, what is the matter?"

The young man told the maiden what had happened.

"This unworthy flea of a runner!" Oruwen exploded. "I will find him and he will give me the device and if I have to beat it out of him!"

The others stared at Oruwen. Even Djehuti could see what really strange behaviour this was!

"Are you feeling unwell, honourable maiden?" He asked her, looking worried. "I'm sure we can find a plant here that we can use to make you feel better."

"Pah, plants! I want the time-portal finder and I want it now. We are wasting too much time, sitting around."

"What do you suggest we do?" Trevor asked confused.

"We will pack together and get into the vimaan. Can't you sense something, Djehuti? What about your famous intuition? Tell us if the Utzincos have the device or not."

Djehuti thought for a moment. "I would say no. They don't have it, but we can still use the search device if we know where they are. Chances are that they hid it somewhere and we won't find it either way. Then we must still chase after the two thieves, who took all the devices. They will have one or two left. We know that the third one is broken."

"There is another one?" Oruwen asked with sudden interest and rubbed her hands.

"Yes, there were three of ours..." Katherine began. "Shouldn't she know that?" She whispered to Chryséis.

"We could search in Kharsag," Djehuti said.

"Oh, balderdash... we must be on our way to get the third device of theirs," Oruwen said. "Use your intuition, man."

"Very well, honourable maiden," Djehuti wasn't sure what to think, so they packed up and got into the vimaan.

When the vehicle rose up into the air, it was late morning. Djehuti steered the vimaan this time and he took the shortest route to the country of Magnesia.

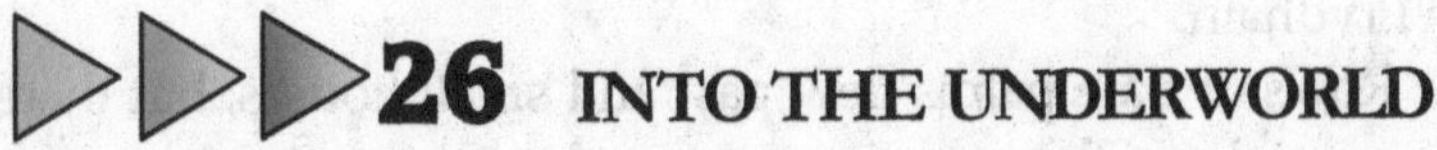26 INTO THE UNDERWORLD

Magnesia was a sparsely populated country, where the mountain region of Mysia, one of the very few places where the sacred moly flower still grew, occupied much of the interior.

"The elusive Flying People of Magnesia, the Nepeshai, live around clear mountain lakes and the Koh-Kaf Mountains to the north-east are still home to giant saurians," Djehuti said.

"Isn't the temple of the Bird God in the Koh Kaf Mountains?" Chryséis asked.

"Yes, indeed. At least that's where I will be searching for the Bird God."

"You will?" Katherine asked.

"Yes, I told you that I made it part of my mission..."

"Sure, but you will wait until we have found our devices, right?" Trevor said.

"Of course, athenai."

They flew over the remains of a large ship that lay shattered against a mountain top in Soghdiana. A grim remnant from the Dark Age when the waves of the sea had reached into the inner regions of the land.

A herd of steppe horses chased now across the plain below.

As they were about to cross over the Plain of Kaltyrion, something strange happened. The vimaan began to soar upward and, Instead of turning east, they now flew over a ridge of hills in the opposite direction.

Apparently, Djehuti couldn't steer the vimaan any longer and it felt as if the vehicle had a life of its own. The children sat anxiously, staring through the transparent cover.

"What's up with these vimaans?" Chryséis sighed.

"I don't know," Trevor said. "I sure hope it's not controlled by evil giants again." They had experienced a similar problem in Prydhain.

Rows of date palms flew past and small houses, but there was mainly endless, waving grass and grazing animals to see.

Oruwen sat quietly in the front with half-closed eyes as if the moody vimaan didn't concern her at all. Perhaps she was plagued by another headache.

When Djehuti realized just where they were heading, it was already too late. The teleporter beam brought them slowly down in front of two pyramids that were covered in highly polished stone slabs of a dark blue colour. *At least there are some pyramids in this part of the world,* Katherine thought.

Oruwen also recognised this place: the entrance to Malinkuyu. The Underworld.

There were many underground cities in Soghdiana and Magnesia, up to 15 storeys deep. Many sheaves of years ago, the 'Sons of the Gods' had tunnelled them with tools that cut through the rock like a hot knife through butter.

Above the ground in the countryside, little pointed to the existence of these near-forgotten cities. The Gods had left peculiar machinery, so food could be produced underground as well as ventilation shafts and canals.

These cities had sustained a large population during much of the cataclysms of the Dark Age, when entire communities had been sheltered in Malinkuyu. If it weren't for the occasional viewing of mirages at libraries of the Known World, the underworld would have been all but forgotten by now.

After the Dark Age, the people of Malinkuyu had moved away and established thriving settlements in the region. Some underground cities had served as hospices for the incurably sick when the knowledge to heal them had been lost. The dead were entombed in the lowest levels and when a space was full, it was simply sealed off.

That's how Malinkuyu had acquired the name

'Underworld' or the Realm of the Dead. Two other cities had even served as prisons but Malinkuyu stood now for something even more sinister. Firbolg had moved in and it was used as a strategic base of 'Those of the Left Path'.

The two blue pyramids marked the main entrance to Malinkuyu. A sign of the former presence of the Gods.

Other entrances to the 'Underworld' were unmarked. To the untrained eye, the Plain of Kaltyrion was just steppe land as far as the eye could see with tall downy grass swaying in the wind.

Djehuti knew all this, but there was no time to explain. No matter how hard he tried to get the vimaan off the ground again, it would not budge.

They waited for a while then climbed out. The maiden seemed to perk up as soon as the vimaan had set down. Recovered from her latest headache, Oruwen didn't make one of her usual feisty comments and walked confidently ahead.

"Honourable maiden, do you know this place?" Djehuti asked, but Oruwen didn't answer the young scholar.

They didn't have much of a choice but to follow her on a beaten path between the two blue pyramids. After all, she was the representative of the Lady of Cydonia, the mentor of the three children.

On the path, the long grass had been trampled by many feet and was short and lumpy. Djehuti felt his narthex wand under his tebenna. It was still there and he might need to use his powers of magic if the brethren of the 'Left Path' were around.

The time travellers felt like lost astronauts on an alien planet. Pink clouds stood starkly against a darkening sky, adding to the creepy feeling of the place. Steps led down into the ground just ahead and Oruwen walked down the steps, while the others followed her silently.

They heard voices at the bottom of the stairs and the first thing they saw was a strange creature. Then another. And a third one. The heads of reptiles.

"The heads are all sitting on the same body," Trevor said barely audible. The heads had long pointy ears, almost like those of dogs - had it not been for reptilian eyes and flicking tongues. The creature also had spikes down its back like a dragon.

"No way," Chryséis breathed. "What are we doing here?"

"Creepy!" Katherine whispered.

The heads sniffed the air and glared at the newcomers. Oruwen stayed well away from the three-headed reptilian dog and seemed afraid of the creature. Six pairs of slitted yellow eyes followed her every move.

"I'm glad that Tepi isn't here," Katherine mumbled, "She would have had a fit."

When they reached the bottom, the spiky tail whipped the wall. The sight was so impressive that they didn't notice the counter with two ugly Firbolg standing behind it. They were the gatekeepers Hormig and Piromis.

"Hey!" one of the Firbolg screeched at the five newcomers. "Mind your manners!"

They stopped in their tracks and gaped at the ugly little men.

"Oh my gosh," Chryséis said. She had wild thoughts of turning around and running up all those stairs, into the field and… just run. But where could she run to? Even if she had known how to steer a vimaan, it didn't work! Djehuti was quiet, but he stood protectively in front of the children, keeping an eye on the monster heads.

Oruwen greeted the two Firbolg with an awkward bow and they bowed in response. Djehuti's back stiffened.

"Where are you from?" Piromis demanded to know.

"Ehem, we are, we are…" Trevor began, but the maiden Oruwen interrupted him in mid-sentence.

"Shelanti, athenai," she smiled sweetly. "We come from K h a r s a g and were compelled to land. These children are from Alesia and Djehuti is a special envoy in the service of her Lady of Innu."

Djehuti showed the Firbolg the paizas. Oruwen glared at the trainee priest as Hormig took the disks and both Firbolg studied their content. It was obvious that they didn't know what they were looking at. And it didn't occur to them to ask Oruwen for her paiza. They handed the passport disks back without comment.

"The children are under special protection," Djehuti added. "There would be consequences if they should come to any harm."

The guards looked uncomfortable. So the threat of consequences carried a certain weight even with Firbolg.

"Thank you ever so much, officials," Oruwen said resolutely. "Kindly take us to your leader now."

The two Firbolg squinted at her. Their leader? What was this spinster talking about? "Not so fast, hag!" Hormig said. "State your business."

Oruwen lifted the sleeve of her left arm a little. Her travel companions couldn't see what the Firbolg were looking at.

The dwarfs gaped. "Our leader…, of course…at once," Piromis stuttered. He went inside the sturdy metal gate and disappeared for some time. The other Firbolg busied himself staring impolitely at the visitors.

"Oi, you!" He suddenly barked at Djehuti. The young priest looked up in surprise.

"Yeah, you. Is that a narthex? Give it to me. No magic allowed underground."

Despite his professions that he was a trader in magical objects, Djehuti had no choice, but to hand over his wand. They were now without defense.

When Piromis reappeared, a giant came stomping after him. The giant wore a stained tunic and untidy trousers, and his face was barely visible between bushy eyebrows and masses of dark hair. His bad teeth looked even scarier and he cleaned them with a thin bone.

He was one of the rebels from the remote Koh Kaf Mountains, who made the other mountain folk's life difficult time and again. But this one was not a powerful leader, but just a minor supervisor in the local mines.

He did his best to appear all pompous and important, as a proper leader should and the three-headed monster grew all excited when it saw the giant, whining, just like a fawning dog would have. The Kabiri threw his large toothpick in the animal's direction and the three heads fought noisily over the bone, while the giant bellowed with laughter.

"Yes, what is it you want?" He said rudely.

"Ah, good sir. I knew you wouldn't make us visitors wait for long. We were on our way to Magnesia and decided to stop over in your lovely city," the maiden said.

"Right..." the giant didn't seem to know what else to say. "Come with me."

Oruwen's companions were stunned. "What does she want here?" Chryséis whispered.

"Maybe she has a trick up her sleeve. If the thieves are in this 'underworld' and they have our devices, she is probably trying to get them back one way or the other. Maybe she just didn't know how to tell us," Trevor said.

The Kabiri hadn't even introduced himself and stomped down a steep passage. They edged their way around the counter and the three-headed reptilian dog. A massive disk-shaped stone leaned against the wall and around the corner was a large machine with spirals leading into têrakhon containers. The machine didn't look functional, but it took up a lot of space.

They reached a hall where pillars, roughly hewn out of the rock, supported the ceiling. The hall was sparsely furnished with a long table to one side and chairs of different heights and makes. A group of Firbolg stared after them.

"Interesting. At least they don't have another festival here," Trevor mumbled.

Chryséis shot him a look that could have shrivelled a Baobab tree. "I'd rather have a festival any day than be in an underground city full of Firbolg," she hissed and narrowly avoided one of the pillars.

In one section of the hall, a group of men were in the middle of a fight. Rivalling parties of slave traders didn't see eye to eye about the distribution of slaves, who huddled together in another section of the hall. Suddenly, some of the yelling men exchanged doughty blows. Then a wooden chair flew through the air and landed on the ground with a crash.

The Kabiri bellowed his mighty laugh and passed the group without interfering. He had nothing to do with the slave trade. He worked with the Firbolg in the mines, but Malinkuyu was also a place for slave traders, who stopped over.

Djehuti was horrified at the ruffians, but the Kabiri ignored him and led the way up a few stairs and through another circular doorway. Then he waved them into a smaller room, the 'guest vault' and left without another word. The room felt clammy. Grimy benches lined the walls and the unwilling guests sat down.

"Brilliant, what are we supposed to do now?" Trevor took off his backpack and plunked himself on a bench.

"Honourable maiden," Djehuti addressed Oruwen politely. "I take it that you must be planning our escape. Would you have us alert the 'Council of Nations'? Or the Lady of Innu?"

"What? Oh yes, I mean no. I have planned for us to leave this place and will do what needs to be done right away. Leave it up to me."

With this, she stood up and walked out of the clammy room. Just like that. Even Djehuti the stoic priest, couldn't hide his confusion. It was seemingly not what he had expected.

"What is she going to do?" Chryséis asked.

"We must have faith," Djehuti said trying to appear dignified. "You are not to worry. Oruwen is a senior maiden and will know what to do."

Katherine began to hum a tune from her favourite band 'Bliss Five': 'When you need me I'll be there…always and forever…'" Although it calmed her nerves, the humming irritated Trevor.

"Oh, stop it already, I can't think…" he grumbled.

Katherine stopped humming but drummed her fingers on the stone bench instead. Chryséis had no intention of waiting for the maiden to return and tell them that her hare-brained idea - whatever it was - had failed.

"What if the maiden is just trying to get away on her own?" she said. "I don't trust her. She's behaving real weird today."

"What do you think we should do then?" Trevor asked. "She might put herself in danger, and us as well."

Oruwen had been rather withdrawn and not much help at all in finding the stolen devices. Ever since Gubla, actually. Djehuti contemplated the situation and seemed to meditate.

Chryséis put her hand on Katherine's fingers to stop the drumming. Then she walked to the door and checked the passage. Nobody in sight. Just muffled sounds that came from the great hall. It was strange that no guards had been posted by the 'guest vault'. Did that mean they weren't prisoners after all?

"Djehuti," she said. "I don't want to startle you, but we have means of turning ourselves invisible. Why don't we just walk out of here?"

Finally, Djehuti answered. He didn't seem surprised that the children could turn themselves invisible. Because, so could he. He demonstrated it to the children's delight.

"Very well then," he said with a sigh. "Athenai, I shall follow the maiden and ensure that she is safe. The three of you will please confine yourselves to this room so long, and do not attempt heroic deeds on your own. We are surrounded by much evil - obeah!"

Djehuti mumbled something again that sounded like a spell and - disappeared once more.

"Now there's great technology," Katherine said. "Magic. We should try and learn this spell. Then we won't have to worry about our invisibility capes anymore."

"Hmm. Great trick, but I'd rather find a way out of this

cave, using our boring invisibility capes. I can't just sit around." Chryséis walked up and down like a tiger in its cage.

"But, Djehuti said we should wait…" Katherine said.

"I know…"

"I wonder why these ugly dwarfs - or whoever - teleported our vimaan here," Trevor said while he explored the walls of the bare room, knocking here and there. "The giant didn't exactly look like a leader to me. What do they want from us?"

Perhaps there was a hidden door somewhere. Just like the secret passage in the palace of Ush-bantoun. But there was nothing but solid rock.

"Maybe it's the time-portal finders. They have them and Oruwen is trying to negotiate. The thieves are slave traders as well and peddle all sorts of stuff."

Katherine jumped up. "You mean, they have the time-portal finders and want to sell them?"

"Maybe…" The children should soon find out how close to the truth they actually were.

*

Djehuti followed Oruwen back to the great hall. He saw a bit of white robe and a thrush sandal disappear behind a pillar and hurried after the maiden. She entered another room leading off the hall.

The slave traders were still fighting amongst themselves and made an ugly, but useful background noise. In the room, he saw how Oruwen spoke to a man. She is so courageous, he thought.

Djehuti moved closer.

There was no doubt about it. The man was a sorcerer of the 'Left Path'! An assortment of devices lay on a shelf and two of them looked rather outlandish. The children's stolen instruments? He guessed that the one to the left was intended for time travel. It wasn't much different to others he had seen. Smaller perhaps and a different colour. He should have brought the detection device with him, but that was still in the vimaan.

The larger instrument was dark-coloured and odd-shaped and a bag leaned against the wall by the sorcerer's feet.

Djehuti listened, taking care not to make a noise. But perhaps the sorcerer was able to sense his presence.

"I brought the children, sire," Oruwen said. "They will show you the correct use of the devices you acquired from the Attocki thieves."

"You have been most helpful… maiden," the sorcerer praised. "I will be very powerful indeed. Another instrument of this kind is on its way to King Acarnôn of Minnegara. He paid a fortune in slaves for it. It is his problem to find out how the magical instrument works. This one is enough for my purpose right now. We'll get the other one from Acarnôn later."

The sorcerer cackled and so did the maiden Oruwen. What an actress, Djehuti thought impressed. She made the sorcerer think that she was on his side.

"Then you must let them go, sire," she said. "They are under protection of the 'Council of the Nations'. You should not risk punishment."

The sorcerer stopped being quite so merry. "And the young acolyte from Innu?" he looked up and sniffed the air. Djehuti held his breath. Had the sorcerer sensed his presence?

"The priest does not concern me, sire. He is not a Hanôk yet and will not hamper our endeavours. I shall remain here and serve you in Malinkuyu, as promised."

The maiden is nobly sacrificing herself and wants to negotiate our release, Djehuti thought. Even at the expense of having to serve a sorcerer of the 'Left Path'. He couldn't let that happen! The good maiden did not know what dark sorcerers were capable of. A brother of the Left Path was not to be trusted.

Djehuti's plan was simple: he had to find an escape route.

He retreated as silently as possible and explored one of the passages leading away from the hall. It was a dead end. Then he tried another passage with steps here and there that led upwards. He was in luck. The passage took him above ground. Far away from the blue pyramids.

Djehuti whispered another spell and was drawn to the children's location. Oruwen had still not returned to them.

"Athenai, we must make haste. I found a way to leave this underground city. I saw your devices with an evil sorcerer."

"Djehuti, is that you?" Trevor asked. "You are invisible."

"Yes, and you should also turn yourselves invisible."

The three children grabbed their things and activated the VICs. They disappeared one by one.

"The sorcerer wants you to explain to him how they work. That is the reason why we were brought here to Malinkuyu."

"Our devices are here?"

"I saw at least one of them. The good maiden has offered to remain in the sorcerer's service in return for our release."

"But we can't let that happen…" Trevor objected.

"No athenai, we cannot. Once you are safely above ground, I shall return for the maiden and your instrument. Then we shall flee this place together."

The time travellers understood.

"Works for me," Chryséis said. There was no time for questions, so they held onto each other and followed Djehuti. They met nobody in the passages and groped their way forward, but when they reached the large circular exit, it was firmly closed. What a setback!

"We cannot get out," Trevor whispered in mild panic.

But Djehuti was prepared. He pointed invisibly at the strong-door and whispered something. Nothing happened. A narthex would have been better, but then he said the same spell in a louder voice. The huge disk creaked and moaned, then yielded, turning slowly on its own axis. When the opening was just big enough, Djehuti pushed the three children through and up the stairs into the open.

"Hide where you can," he said. "I'll come back for you."

Then he returned to the depth of the underground city.

 **27**   # THE SHAPE-SHIFTER

"Over there by the trees. Come on quick!" Trevor urged his friends. They followed him to a pile of rocks next to three haoma trees.

"We should alert the Ladies of Cydonia and Innu. About the slave traders and the Firbolg and…" Chryséis tried to catch up with Trevor and Katherine, who were walking really fast.

"We can't draw attention to ourselves now," Trevor said. "We just escaped and they'll know where we are."

Katherine panted. "Same old problem…"

They reached the rocks and hid as best they could. There were more trees and a well not far from the other side of the entrance, but from here one had a good view. Chryséis slumped onto a flat boulder and Trevor thought it better not to mention the scorpion he saw scurry under the rocks.

In the distance, green foothills piled up against the grey mountains. They were rather close to the foothills, so if they needed to run, this would be the way. They had no idea which mountains they were looking at or how to flee without the vimaan. And they couldn't contact anyone. At least that's what the time travellers thought.

"As soon as we have the TPF, we should beam out of here," Trevor said.

"We can't just leave things like that," Chryséis whispered. "We can't just time-travel back to the future without saying goodbye to anyone."

"Listen if we have to, we'll do it. You know that," Trevor whispered back in the same urgent tone. "Right now, we have to get away from here in one piece."

Chryséis was quiet for a while. "Okay then," she eventually agreed.

Katherine watched a large cockroach scuttle along the top of a rock and grabbed the insect. To her friends' horror, she stuffed the crunchy cockroach into her mouth and began to chew. Later she admitted that she still hated frog stew and cockroaches and that she had no idea, why she had felt like eating strange food. Maybe it was all the magic around.

"Are you okay, Katie?" Chryséis asked with a disgusted look on her face. "Listen if you feel hungry, we still have some other food."

Katherine ignored her. She had just felt compelled to eat the cockroach. That's all. There was sudden movement by the doorway.

"Oh look, Oruwen made it out," Katherine said, still chewing.

The maiden walked rather calmly toward a shack half-hidden under a large tree opposite them.

"What is she doing? Where is Djehuti?" Katherine wanted to jump up and run over to the maiden, but Trevor grabbed her sleeve and pulled her down. He had a feeling that something wasn't right. They hid further behind the rock piles. What was the Alesian maiden doing alone in a ramshackle hut when she should be escaping with Djehuti?

Then Oruwen reappeared from the hut.

"Wait, that's not Oruwen at all - that's Totolin!"

The children looked at each other in shock. Had the sorcerer's apprentice from Ush-bantoun shape-shifted into Oruwen? So, that's where he'd been hiding. Had Totolin killed her or was the maiden still alive?

That's why she had been behaving so strangely. It was Totolin and he was a shape-shifter!

"I knew it!" Chryséis spat the words out.

"No you didn't. None of us did," Trevor said.

"Poor Oruwen. I wonder where she is."

The maiden had seemed oddly at ease with the slave traders and now they knew why. Of course, Totolin had no plans to get them out of here. His left sleeve fell back a little and revealed a small tattoo on his inner forearm. It looked much like a snake's head with a black spider on top. That's what the two Firbolg had seen when they'd arrived and Oruwen had asked to see their 'leader'.

Totolin had also been present when the sorcerer negotiated with the slave traders by the river close to Ushbantoun. He was the connection to the Underworld!

Katherine felt cold fear creeping up her spine. "We should run away. What if we are found out and dragged back underground... and..."

"We can't just leave without Djehuti..." Trevor said. "And we don't know where to go. Djehuti said we should wait here for him. He is a magician and a good one."

"I knew something was up with her, eh, him," Chryséis hissed and her friends just rolled their eyes. "Djehuti should have known better..."

Totolin was strutting around in front of the hut, waiting for something.

"Nobody's perfect," Katherine defended Djehuti.

"Where is he? We must hide further away until he comes back," Trevor whispered. They moved swiftly. The children sneaked farther back until they were completely out of sight. Or so they thought.

Totolin had seen three shadows move away from him. *Why are those dreadful children above ground?* He'd thought they were down in the 'guest vault'. *Those little imps.* He would take them back inside now, because he had sold them to the giants in Malinkuyu.

He called the children in a sweet voice and walked up to the crouching shadows. "Ah, there you are." Totolin edged closer. "Running away all by yourself, are you?"

Chryséis looked up. "What are you doing here, Totolin?" The sorcerer's assistant was taken aback.

"You useless little ball of toad slime," Chryséis attacked him before he could answer. It was the worst thing she could think of in Akkadian.

"Oh, why so impolite, little children? We are friends, aren't we?" Totolin cocked his little head.

"Friends? My foot," Katherine glared him.

The shape-shifter didn't expect so much resistance from mere children. *Well, they won't stay resistant for long*, he thought. *Not when I am finished with them.* Trevor's hand was on the hilt of his hunting knife.

None of them noticed Djehuti, who had now also emerged from the secret passage. He held something in his hand. It was the narthex wand the Firbolg had taken from him. He had blasted the gatekeepers to get it back and then and the three-headed monster. There were two instruments in his pocket and Katherine's daypack was slung over his shoulder.

He had searched for the maiden, then decided to return to the children above ground. Now Djehuti stood in the shade by the well and couldn't believe his eyes.

In front of the children stood the infamous Totolin of Ereb. Djehuti gasped. They had been in the same class together until Totolin was expelled from Magic School in Innu. Young Djehuti had caught him performing obeah, black magic. Obeah wasn't just child's play. Totolin was already linked to 'Those of the Left Path'.

Djehuti hadn't seen him since Totolin had been expelled from the Innu School of White Magic. Now he stood there, talking to a large pile of rocks. Djehuti guessed that the children were hiding behind the boulder and there was no trace of the maiden Oruwen, unless she was with them. Hardly. Djehuti's mind worked fast.

What had the renegade magician done with her? He was a shapeshifter. It meant that Totolin had morphed into the maiden! Now, Djehuti knew just what to do.

"Maiden Oruwen, we missed you down in the 'guest

vault'," he said. Totolin looked perplexed. Did Djehuti really still see him as the Alesian maiden? Excellent!

Totolin began to act as the maiden Oruwen again.

"Ah, Djehuti, we have been waiting for you. I found a… a hidden passage. We must make haste," he said in a high voice.

Djehuti changed his tone abruptly. "What do you want with the children in our care, Totolin, Evil One?"

The sorcerer's assistant's face fell. He looked pale and swayed a little with shock. He had been found out by a brother of the 'Right Path'!

Djehuti had not been deceived. Totolin stared at the narthex the scholar was pointing at him and knew his game was up. The children appeared from behind the boulder.

"Oh, but you know I'm your friend, children..." he stammered.

Chryséis ignored his flattery. "What are we going to do with him?" She asked and Totolin's head bobbed up and down in fear.

"He will be handed to the authorities of the Known World," Djehuti said, then spoke to the crouching Totolin. "Should I turn you into a piece of wood or would you rather be a feather for a while?"

Colour rose up on the little turkey's neck. "Have mercy, Lord. Have mercy. I just did what was asked of me," he cried.

"Don't call me lord, you depraved ingrate. I trust you have not forgotten the proper ways of the Known World. In the name of Thoth, I shall not let you get away another time," Djehuti said with contempt.

Then something strange happened. The sorcerer's assistant sank to the ground in a dead faint. The children were stunned. This was unexpected. Djehuti didn't lose time and bound Totolin's hands. He lifted him up with a spell. The children stared up at the floating body.

"Wow," Chryséis said and whistled through her teeth.

"We better leave before somebody sees us," Djehuti said and walked away with Totolin in front of him. The children hurried after Djehuti and the floating Totolin. They reached the green foothills and Djehuti drew a circle around them on the ground with his narthex, turning them all invisible.

He lowered the sorcerer to the ground, before he lit a small fire and prepared tea in a small woven basket he always carried with him. He threw a few sage leaves from Katherine's pouch into the basket pot.

Only then did he tell the children that he had their time-portal finder! Djehuti placed the TPF on a rock in plain sight. They rifled through the backpack. The 'Bliss Five' CD was still inside and Katherine was over the moon to have her music back.

That's when the sorcerer's assistance woke up.

Nobody took notice of Totolin, whose hands were bound in front of him to a rock. He loosened the rope, slipped his hands out and crept awkwardly behind the rock to relieve himself. The others seemed preoccupied, so it was an ideal time to bolt. But he knew that he didn't stand a chance against Djehuti's magic if he was discovered.

He saw the instrument lying on the rock. This was the instrument the queen Mé-lis-ah had so desperately wanted. Totolin didn't like the queen. She had sometimes given him a kick against the shin when she was displeased.

This thing had to be very important. He let the rope slip down the boulder, crawled forward and groped for the device, got hold of it and grabbed the TPF hard with his right hand, pressing a few buttons in the process.

Suddenly the ground in front of him began to shimmer and moved in circles. A miracle was happening and he could hardly believe his luck.

But what was it? He gawked fearfully at Djehuti.

Totolin knew about the abode of the serpent god of obeah and this had to lead to Tiphereth, the haven of dark sorcery!

He, the unworthy servant of a great magician, received this unbelievable favour. An escape route to Tiphereth, circling like a coiling serpent!

Totolin took a faltering step forward. That's when Djehuti saw the device in Totolin's hand and the quivering vortex. "No, don't jump!" he cried out.

Chryséis dropped a wooden spoon she had been stirring with and ran towards the vortex. If she could just reach him in time… but it was too late.

"Nooo!" The children screamed at the same time.

"Haaah!" The little sorcerer disappeared with a triumphant cry. They stood in shock and watched how the churning vortex disappeared together with their TPF in Totolin's hand.

"I can't believe it," Katherine began to cry. "We can't go back home now! It was our last chance to get home."

The spot where the vortex had swallowed Totolin, was as still as before. They had been so close and now they had seen the last of Totolin and their time-portal finder!

28 BATTLE OF THE BIRDS

"I hope he ended up on top of a carnivorous dinosaur!" Trevor said. "Or inside a volcano."

"Why on earth did he jump into the vortex? Can somebody explain it to me?" Chryséis fumed. "This whole trip is jinxed, I'm telling you…"

She saw Djehuti looking at her in surprise. Chryséis spoke English. "Ehm, I mean I don't understand why he jumped." she continued in shaky Akkadian. Chryséis tried to ease back into the prehistoric language they spoke now almost as if they had never spoken anything else. But she was very upset.

"Tiphereth," Djehuti answered "The nether region, even below the Underworld. The abode of the evil serpent god. A powerful deity revered by the brotherhood of the 'Left Path'."

"This idiot of a sorcerer!" Trevor ranted, but it was no use. The time-portal finder was gone - after all the trouble they had been through to get it back from the thieves.

"Athenai, calm yourselves," Djehuti said. "There is still one more time instrument."

"Yes, but …" Trevor couldn't finish his sentence.

"Ah, young friends, you should listen to the magician teacher," a voice said. Where was it coming from?

"Have forgotten me already? And forgotten to call me when in distress?"

The voice sounded familiar.

"Who are you, show yourself!" Chryséis had enough of surprises today.

"Can't you see me? I am here. Right here."

They looked at a faint shimmering light on top the rock that Totolin had been tied to.

Right there floated – the Djin. In all his purple velvet splendour, scratching his earlobe that peeped out from under his turban.

"Oh, Djin, it's you!" Trevor shouted.

Djehuti spoke very politely to the magical being. "Honourable Djin, welcome and be thanked for your concern. Are you here to help us?"

"You should have called me, you know. It was not easy to find you out here in the wilderness. With the protection spell around you and all…"

"Sorry, we didn't think about it," Katherine said.

The Djin smiled. "I believe you are in distress and in need of help. Your despair was impossible to ignore. Let's not waste time." He looked at Katherine "Oh, what's this? I want to see no more tears."

She wiped her tears away and looked up at him.

"There, that's better. No need for tears when good old Djin is here to help. Old, indeed…ages…"

"Are you saying that there is still hope for us?" Katherine asked.

"Yes indeed, this is entirely correct, young one. First, about your amulets. The ones you received at the "Festival of Sokhar" from that little boy…"

The children wondered what the amulets had to do with anything.

"…they keep you safe but also prevent thought transfer. With anyone. The Lady of Cydonia is greatly distressed. Especially since poor maiden Oruwen was found barely conscious in a boat just outside the port of Gubla yesterday."

He held up his hand to stop unnecessary questions. "Do not remove them just yet."

Chryséis dropped her hands.

"If you cannot be detected by honourable Ladies, then certainly not by the less honourable brethren of the 'Left Path' in the Underworld. Here!"

The Djin threw a 'Healed Eye' amulet to Djehuti. He caught the necklace and put it around his neck.

"There we are," said the Djin. "Much better. I shall notify the good Lady."

"Djin, where were you when we needed you in Ushbantoun?" Trevor asked.

"Ah, yes... I believe I was not called on even then. But who do you think showed you the opening under the tree into which you escaped the slave traders' henchmen. I was not far behind when you were chased."

Of course, the children remembered. They had been hiding by the sunken swimming pool.

"Alas, I'm not allowed to go underground."

"Thank you all the same for being here now," Chryséis said. The Djin bowed slightly in acknowledgement.

"The minor sorcerer Totolin guided the vimaan to the underground city and thought that obeah was enough to get his way. He, he." He grinned and rubbed his hands together. "And now he is gone."

"The third time-travel device was given to the king of Minnegara in the country of Attock in exchange for slaves," Djehuti said. "How do we get there?"

"Yes, the king Acarnôn is a bad man." The Djin shook his head. "I'm afraid, it is to Attock you will have to go and take what is yours. But first, Djehuti has to find the temple of the Bird god. No way around it and now you have to help him."

"We have to help him?" Chryséis asked.

"Yes, athenai. You have to help someone else to restore the balance. Do what is right and the true path will appear before you."

"How long is *that* going to take?" Chryséis wanted to know.

The Djin shook his head and studied the night sky.

"How can we help Djehuti, dear Djin?" Katherine wanted to know.

"Ah, the right question. All will reveal itself."

There was a whirring sound that mixed with the laughter of the Djin. All they remembered was falling asleep.

When they awoke, the sun climbed above the mountains. They were in a mountain glade and the Djin was nowhere to be seen. He must have worked his magic to get them here, not far from the rocky shore of a highland lake.

"What are we doing here?" Trevor asked.

"I' sure, we'll find out soon," Djehuti said and took off his amulet. "We seem to be safe here, so I'll contact the Lady of Innu to ask for her help."

They didn't rest long on the lake shore. A very large black eagle came diving toward them with long, powerful flaps of its wings. The monstrous bird circled them and screeched at a blood-curdling pitch.

"Down!" Djehuti yelled. He had no time to get his narthex out in time.

The glade offered no cover nearby, so they simply huddled together and made themselves as small as possible. In an instant, the black eagle swooped down on the five travellers and grabbed Trevor by his backpack. Then he soared upwards with the boy dangling from his claws. Trevor was in shock. The air swished around his ears and he tried not to look down.

"Trevor! Trevor!" He could barely hear the faint cry as the bird soared with him into the clouds.

The thought transfer was exactly what the dark Magi of Magnesia had waited for. Being a Brother of the Left Path, he knew of the children's escape from the Underworld and being a shape-shifter, he had turned himself into a huge eagle. He would grab the other two of the troublesome children and carry them into his territory. Even Djehuti would not be safe from him.

He dropped Trevor roughly and returned to the group. Trevor had hurt his wrist in the fall and tried to hide from the large bird. When he saw the others in the glade, the eagle-sorcerer was in for a surprise. Another large bird flew straight at him. It was much bigger than the eagle and had a plumage of colourful feathers.

"It is the Simorgh Ankh, the Bird God!" Djehuti cried.

The giant black eagle took a nose-dive and tried to flee, but the powerful Simorgh Ankh chased after the large bird at great speed and the huge eagle tumbled onto the rocks below, breaking its neck.

The great colourful bird landed next to Djehuti and the girls on the swaying grass.

"What happened to Trevor?" Katherine cried.

Simorgh Ankh cocked his head. "The eagle carried a boy away in this direction," Djehuti quickly said and pointed north.

Simorgh Ankh took once again to flight and searched for the boy. After a while, the rushing of wings made them all look up. There, in mid-air was Simorgh Ankh with Trevor sitting safely on his broad back. He landed gently and allowed the boy to climb down. Trevor's wrist was still hurting, so he waved with his other hand. The girls stormed toward their friend and hugged him.

"Oh, Trevor are you okay. I thought that eagle had killed you," Chryséis sobbed and wiped her eyes.

"Ouch, careful, my wrist is really sore."

"Ah, good friends," the Bird God said in a deep chirp. "Shelanti, visitors to my realm. So sorry for this rough welcome. The dark sorcerer has paid with his life."

The children stared bewildered.

"A brave deed, acolyte Djehuti and my young friends when you escaped the Underworld." He nodded gracefully and closed his eyes. There was far-away growling and roars of what had to be rather large saurians.

"We must be deep in the Koh-Kaf Mountains," Djehuti said. He couldn't believe his luck that the Bird God himself had come to rescue them.

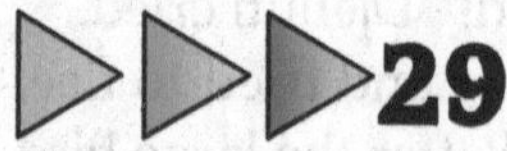 **29 THE TEMPLE OF SECRETS**

"Most Righteous Simorgh Ankh," Djehuti said and bowed slightly in front of the Bird God. "I am deeply honoured to be in your presence."

"I'm also pleased to meet you, Djehuti and young friends from the future."

The children were no longer surprised when someone said that to them and there was no reason to hide the fact from the mighty Bird God.

A long, drawn-out roar echoed between the mountains.

"Are those saurians?" Trevor asked.

"Yes, herds of ancient saurian live in the mountains," Simorgh Ankh said. "Mostly far from human settlements."

Trevor didn't like that at all. *I'm putting myself in a bubble of light and I am protected*, he thought, just as the water witch in Prydhain had taught him. Trevor suddenly remembered his first time-travel experiment and could see the rippling golden and green scales, the large steaming body.

In his mind, he was walking among sleeping dinosaurs in a shelter between tall rocks. He smelled the stench and felt the heat, picked his way around large sprawling bodies. One of them rolled over with a groan, yawning loudly baring big sharp teeth. He sprang nimbly aside and the dinosaurs didn't even move...

"Trevor, Trevor!" Chryséis shook him. "Hey, are you day-dreaming or what?"

"Emm, I think so..." Trevor said. "My wrist is still sore. Can you do something about that, Djehuti?"

"Let me see, young friend." The huge bird settled down

in all his splendid plumage while Djehuti examined Trevor's hand. "It looks broken."

"Oh no."

"Not to worry. I have a spell I can use to mend the bone." Djehuti mumbled something under his breath and Trevor squeezed his eyes closed. Then he opened his eyes again and moved his hand. "The pain is gone," he then announced.

"Without using a healing device?" Katherine asked.

"That is white magic," the Bird God said.

"Amazing. Thank you, Djehuti. Shukri, thank you very much," Trevor stammered.

"It is my pleasure to help you, athenai." the teacher of white magic answered.

"If you are ready, I will now take you to the temple high up in the mountains," the Bird God said.

"Oh, that would be just wonderful," Djehuti breathed and the children nodded.

"Please seat yourselves on my back." When they were all safely on his powerful back, the Bird God took to the sky and powerful wings carried them to lofty heights. A cold wind blew and Chryséis didn't open her eyes for a while. When she finally did, she glimpsed movement between the mountains below and it was definitely not human.

They sailed through the air, following the banks of a large river. It made its way down the mountains as a trickle that turned into a brook on the Kailas or 'Heaven Mountain' and then into a sizeable river.

"I wonder what it's like - this temple..." Chryséis said.

Katherine clung to the strong feathers next to her.

"The Bird God must be really important. Remember how people mentioned him even in the 'Pastures of Heaven?" Katherine said. "Now, that's really far from here."

"What does Djehuti want to do at the temple?" Chryséis bent to the other side and regretted it the same instant. "Phew, we are so high up. I shouldn't look straight down."

Mountain settlements came into view, but they didn't

dare look straight down. The river glistened like a broad band of crystals in the sunlight. They held tight, taking care not to tip to one side or the other, but Simorgh Ankh didn't seem to mind his load.

By the time they arrived, the sun was still sitting atop the mountain peaks and sinking fast. The 'Temple of the Bird God' was marked with the enormous statue of Simorgh Ankh, hewn from cream-coloured limestone.

One could barely distinguish it from the other rocks jutting up between the mountains. It was placed above a portal that secured the entrance to a cave and had been carved with great skill in ancient times.

Each feather was clearly visible in the fading light and stone-eyes scrutinised any intruders. The eyes were inlaid with shiny crystals and gave them a mysterious gleam.

Simorgh Ankh circled his statue twice before landing smoothly on a large platform. Djehuti helped the children climb down. They felt stiff from the cold wind and sheer effort of hanging onto Simorgh Ankh's feathery back during the flight.

The platform was secured by a low wall all around and there was a surprisingly green garden nearby. They could hear the muffled splashing of a waterfall.

The edges of the wooden portal were covered in beaten gold and the door was locked. The weathered wood was inlaid with greenish copper across both portal wings in the shape of one large eye, the 'Eye of Argus'.

You really had to know the location on the Kailas plateau to find this temple. They were in the country of Soghdiana, where the Kailas plateau was regarded as sacred. The temple on the plateau was difficult to access and only shepherds sometimes climbed into the craggy rocks to rescue a goat or lamb. They would return to their villages with fantastic stories of a house of the gods in the mountains.

They had barely reached the front of the temple when

the portal opened unexpectedly as if moved by a ghostly hand. Djehuti signalled for the children to come then led the way into the dark cavity. Meanwhile, Simorgh Ankh settled in a cosy spot by the little waterfall not far from the entrance.

"You go ahead and I will wait here," the speaking bird said and stuck his head under one wing. "I am tired from the long flight."

The children walked on bravely. A faint light fell onto sparkling crystals growing in small clusters on the cave walls. Startled birds, nesting inside took to flight as the heavy portal slowly closed behind them. Katherine looked nervous, but Djehuti did not seem concerned. The floor was slippery and one had to walk carefully.

A thin layer of unpleasantly smelling bird dung covered the entire floor. In a constant flutter, little birds moved in and out of the cave through long air-shafts. They now reached another metal-covered door. It barred the visitors from investigating the temple beyond the shimmering hall.

"Great, what do we do now?" Chryséis asked and her voice echoed a little.

"Don't know. Simorgh Ankh should have told us if there's a password to get in," Trevor said. "Djehuti should know what to do."

The door opened on creaky hinges and behind the door was a broad passage and more doors. They walked through and saw metal plaques, inscribed with strange symbols. They were fastened to the doors and seemed to be calculations and drawings of some kind. One of the drawings looked much like a space shuttle with a face. Another depicted a bowl-shaped vehicle with long robot legs on castors, seen from different angles and one of the pictures resembled an android.

This was just unbelievable.

"What is all this?" Katherine marvelled.

Djehuti was able to read the inscriptions: "It says 'The Gyelrap - genealogy of kings'." He walked to the door across the passage and read, "'The Book of Akâsa or 'Light of Nature' and 'The Book of Atharve, containing the tricks of white and black magic'."

"This temple seems to be some sort of library," Chryséis said. "Every room has its own books."

"It's not your usual type of books," Djehuti said. "These books are imprinted on stone and wooden blocks. Some of them even on very thin metal foils that have to be kept hanging in a frame. I learned about this at school, but I cannot believe that I'm really here and seeing it with my own eyes. Most of these books were brought here by the gods to be kept safe and shared with able minds."

The children had expected something else: something like statues of the gods and treasure like gold and jewels. Smoking incense and priests traipsing around noiselessly, praying before a statue of Simorgh Ankh. Things that you could usually find in a temple.

"The 'Temple of the Bird God' must be one of the hiding places, the gods chose for important books. Remember how the librarian in Kem-Oun told us about that?" Trevor told them.

"Oh, I wish I could read these books or just look at them," Chryséis whispered.

"Only initiates to the ancient knowledge are able to read and understand these books. Even then, it would take them a long time to do so," Djehuti mentioned. "There will come a time when humanity will be ready to learn from the ancient books again that are now hidden from them."

Djehuti led them into another larger hall with a high ceiling. The light was better in here and they saw golden objects, stacked into corners. It made the hall look somewhat like Ali Baba's cave in 'Arabian Nights'.

"It is a real temple with treasures, not just a library," Trevor said.

"If it makes you happy, Trevor. They probably didn't see gold as a treasure," Katherine answered him.

Chryséis was busy studying a long table and chairs made from heavy dark têrakhon in the middle of the hall. A collection of odd-looking golden animals was arranged around the back of the table. There was a sea monster next to a small-scale stegosaurus and a lumbering iguanodon; an elephant bird and a mammoth - and strangely enough - a horse. All of these animals were worked in solid gold. There were about fifty different species assembled and a round chandelier above the table illuminated everything.

"That's Shekinah, the eternal light," Djehuti explained. "The original eternal light."

The eternal light was nothing new to the time travellers. Every 'House of Life' had their own lamps and the prytaneums they had seen always housed a metal bowl with the eternal fire, but Djehuti had said that this was 'the original eternal light'!

The walls and ceilings seemed to be cut out of solid rock at near 90-degree angles. A peculiar glaze covered the surface of the stone. Unlike the rough walls of the temple's crystal-covered entrance area and even those of the Underworld, they had just escaped from.

"Who goes there?" A deep compelling voice asked.

The children looked anxiously around, but Djehuti bowed slightly in the general direction of the table and said: "Hanôk, Wise One, keeper of the secrets of the Bird God, we humbly greet you."

He bowed again and waited. No answer. "Djehuti of Innu and three young athenai of future origin beg leave to approach."

"Ah, I have been expecting you," the voice then said.

The children could now see a figure with long white hair and beard sitting in one of the big chairs. The old man's head barely reached the top of the chair's back.

Hanôk, the high priest of the Bird God, waved them

closer. The time travellers noticed wall paintings as they covered the distance through the hall. The table came up to Trevor's shoulders and the chairs could have comfortably seated thirty people. Not quite giants, but tall people.

At close range, the old man with white hair didn't look so small anymore.

"Djehuti, acolyte of Innu, named after the great God of Writing. Reports of your courage precede you and your noble companions," he said. "I am pleased that you have found your way to the temple with the help of Simorgh Ankh, the Bird God himself, built by the At-tee'kah D'At-tee-keen. The Ancient of Ancients."

"Thank you," the children said simply.

"I am the keeper of the Etana, the great bird-vehicles, in which the Gods preferred to travel through the air a long time ago. They are safely stored at the temple, waiting for the return of the gods."

"There are vehicles here?" Chryséis asked. "You mean like vimaans?"

"Not exactly the same, child. They could be used in space as well. Etanas had to be much bigger than the vimaans nowadays."

The children stood there with their mouth open.

"Where does the Bird God come from?" Trevor asked.

"He came with the gods," the old man answered patiently. "From a far-away place. The Hanôk must be replaced after his time of service, but the Bird God has seen many generations come and go."

"He must be very old then," Trevor said.

"Indeed, young friend, very old."

"What happens if the brethren of the 'Left Path' find the temple?" Trevor couldn't hide his curiosity.

"The brethren of the 'Left Path' are angry that this useful knowledge has been hidden from them. Even though they were helped by the Firbolg of the underworld, the temple has remained hidden from their grasp. Only those who are worthy are allowed in here."

"Please, can you help us, honourable Hanôk?" Katherine asked suddenly. "Thieves have stolen our backpacks in Ush-bantoun and they contained incredibly important devices. Without at least one of them, we cannot return home." Silence.

"I know. You shall all receive your answers soon. Even you, Djehuti. You have been chosen to succeed me as a servant of the Bird God and Custodian of Books," the old man said without much ado. "Besides the ancient records and Etanas, this temple also hides formidable instruments. One of them can turn any object weightless or even heavier. That's what you came for, Djehuti. A child could push a large rock with his finger, raising it to any desired height. Gigantic cities were built in such way. Even instrument to travel through time."

"Our architects will be grateful for this. And what a great honour to learn about and keep safe the books and such instruments, honourable Hanôk," Djehuti said.

The high priest of the Bird God opened the lid of a greyish flint box, set in copper and took out a narrow scroll of bark paper. The paper was covered in tightly written text and symbols. A golden seal was stamped on the parchment: a soaring bird inside a sun symbol.

"This, Djehuti of Innu, is a holy script. It contains the computations and instructions your architects in Ta Mery are searching for."

He put the scroll back into the box and Djehuti seemed to understand exactly what Hanôk was talking about.

"You shall issue a copy of this invaluable script, and take it with you back to Innu. There it shall be kept safe for yugas to come. Then you will return to the Temple of the Bird God."

"I understand, honourable Hanôk," Djehuti said. "I thank the Bird God for this priceless knowledge. Trevor stretched his neck and saw a pyramid on the paper with a lot of symbols and equations.

"I will converse with you, athenai from future times, in the morning. I believe it is getting rather late, and not being gods we need to rest."

Hanôk was not completely alone with the Bird God, then. He had helpers of his own, Dwergar, as the little people in Soghdiana were called. They went about their business in the background and the visitors only noticed them now. One Dwergar came to move the flint box and another object to another much smaller table by the wall.

The other object was a glistening, green egg in a golden holder.

"That looks a lot like a Speaking Stone," Katherine whispered. "One made of emerald."

"You're right!" Trevor said. "So that's at least one other Speaking Stone apart from the one in Caradoc."

"And it is not the only one," Hanôk told them. Of course he had heard them speak. "Let's now eat and rest until tomorrow morning," Hanôk concluded their meeting.

Some of the Dwergar took the visitors to a dining room next to the great hall and after dinner, they were shown into a chamber, clearly meant for sleeping. Feathery mattresses invited the guests. Trevor dropped onto the nearest mattress and fell asleep without having taken off his clothes or even brushed his teeth. They all slept soundly all night.

After breakfast the next day, the children were bored. Hanôk was not yet ready to speak to them, so they decided to explore the cave with their torchlights. Straight-cut pillars held up the ceilings in the rooms. They opened a random door.

"This room is warm and dry," Katherine said. "Must have a really good ventilation system."

She ran her fingers along the wall. The substance the rocked with covered with felt like glass. The Dwergars checked on them to make sure, none of the books were touched, but otherwise they had free reign. Wooden blocks, stone and clay cuneiform tablets were stacked on and around shelves. There were vellum and papyrus scrolls, covered in paintings and dense writing.

"Can you imagine, how old all that stuff must be if it comes from the 'Gods'?" Chryséis asked.

"No, I can't. But we could ask the Bird God or Hanôk about that."

Katherine was already out the door and into another room. Here, ultra-thin sheets made of metal foil were hanging in open cupboards.

"Isn't that a foil library, Chris?"

"Those must be just about the oldest written records ever. I read about libraries like that in underground caves in Ecuador."

Even scrolls with mirages were here stored in special boxes. They contained images of the first explorations by the Gods on a young planet and of their homes.

"Thank goodness these books are safe here!" Trevor said.

"Yes. Can you imagine some crazed evil giants just stealing or destroying all of this? Good thing they are hiding the books, where no one can find them."

"Look at this thing." Katherine held up a golden plaque that showed clearly – a pyramid. On the other side stood a person with a halo. A few lines of pictograms next to the figure seemed to offer an explanation of the picture. Of course, they couldn't read it.

Then a Dwergar woman walked in and said, "Please come with me, athenai. The honourable Hanôk is now ready to speak with you."

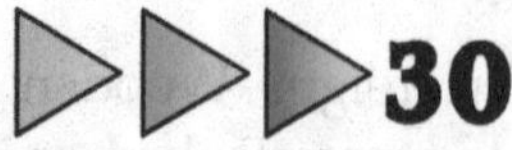 **30**   # THE MAD KING

The Custodian of Books was already waiting for them outside the Temple of the Bird God. He sat on a big green cushion atop a small platform in the garden and Hanôk looked much friendlier now than he had the night before. A thin cloud blanket diffused the sunlight on the plateau and there was no sign of the great bird Simorgh Ankh anywhere.

"Come, join me," he called them and they climbed the narrow steps up to the platform, shaded by a Zampun tree. Katherine was surprised to see Hanôk outside the cave.

"Even I need fresh air - sometimes," he explained, he explained before she could say anything.

"You are quite good at mind-reading," she said.

"It is part of my training, athenai."

"Is it not dangerous for you to go outside the temple?" Katherine asked.

"We are well protected here, I can assure you. But let me talk to you about other matters: I saw that you studied some of our most precious books and records."

"Yes, sir, I mean ..." Trevor answered. "How long will you keep the books and all the other things hidden in there? We have met so many good people since we arrived. Don't you think they should see all this?"

"Ah, so many questions." Hanôk held up his hand and smiled. "The trials on this planet are not over yet. There is peril, greater than that from evil giants and sorcerers."

Was he talking about some geological catastrophes?

"Yes to an extent," The answer came immediately. "However, greed for power and possessions all too often pushes aside the better qualities in men. Should wisdom, justice and freedom be chosen once again as the three pillars of human society, the gods may decide to establish another 'Golden Age'."

Chryséis and Trevor stared at him and lapped up every word Hanôk was saying. Katherine, on the other hand, studied a fat caterpillar that was crawling up a long leaf. Chryséis flicked her friend's knee and Katherine looked up.

"You are able to travel through space and time and put your knowledge you gained here to good use in the future," Hanôk said.

"Well, if we ever get back…" Chryséis began.

"You will. At least if you are wise and do not trust a friendly smile by those who say they know the will of the gods. You shall be taken to Minnegara where King Acarnôn holds your precious device. You will also gain back the rest of your things and thereafter leave at once."

"Will Djehuti come with us?" Trevor asked.

"Djehuti will ride on the back of Simorgh Ankh to Eridu and take a ship to Innu to complete his appointed task."

"But what about us?" Trevor was horrified that they had to continue on their own.

"You shall receive help soon, but first you must walk the last stretch of the road on your own strength," Hanôk told them.

"When are we leaving?"

"You will be leaving now." Hanôk still spoke when some of the little people brought their things to the garden.

"Are we not going to see Djehuti again?" Katherine asked. "We would like to thank him for everything."

"He is already on his way to Eridu, but he knows."

"Are you saying we must walk down the mountain from here?" Chryséis asked.

"The Dwergar will show you the way to the Minnegara Road. From there, you will make your way on your own."

So they left at once and it was a rather steep descent all

the way down from the temple. They had just reached the dusty road when the little people took their leave.

"Minnegara is this way." They pointed east. "Farewell, athenai. May the gods be with you." Hanôk had said they should make their way, so they walked, following the dirt road.

"It can't be far," Trevor tried to reassure the others.

On the higher side of the road, nomads were unpacking their beasts of burden. They ignored the children and laid out washed carpets to dry in the sun. As they turned a corner, their old friend the Djin waited quietly on a boulder by the road, shielded from the nomads' view.

The Djin cleared his throat, so the children would notice him and they children ran happily over to meet him.

"Shelanti good Djin, thank you for coming to help us," they greeted him.

"I shall help where help is due," the Djin replied. "I suppose I'm at your service once more."

"Will you take us away to the place where our time-portal finder is?" Chryséis asked boldly.

"Well… in a manner of speaking." The Djin creased his forehead. "What is it you need most?"

"We need transport. We were told that the objects we seek is with a King Acarnôn of Minnegara. Can you take us there?"

It hadn't occurred to the time travellers that they could have simply asked the Djin to produce the objects right there and then!

The Djin's eyes surveyed the area and the carpets caught his eye. He smiled and snipped his fingers. One of the thick red carpets lifted off the rocks. The nomad women were too busy to notice anything and the plush carpet began to miraculously rise and float in their direction.

"A flying carpet?" Chryséis giggled. "Get outa here!"

"Dear young friends, here is your desired transport. I wish you a comfortable journey to the city of Minnegara," the Djin said.

"This is great. We'll fly to Minnegara on a carpet!"

"Place yourselves onto the carpet," the Djin commanded. As soon as they sat comfortably, the edges of carpet rolled up and almost covered them.

And that's how the children went to Minnegara. There was a murmur and a sharp snipping sound and they felt the carpet move. Slowly at first, then faster and faster. They were swishing through the air and the feeling was exhilarating.

Trevor stuck his head out, grabbing hold of a fringe. He saw that the road they had wandered on only minutes ago, was now a narrow band below the plateau. The carpet ascended even further and Trevor fell back into the middle of their vehicle.

Then the carpet began to suddenly descend, giving the children a funny feeling in the pit of their stomachs.

There were buildings below, perched on hills – built with rocks at the bottom and topped with wooden structures. The buildings didn't look inviting, but they were now low enough to see painted cloths with hunting scenes that fluttered from the roofs. People were walking in the street and rode on elephant backs.

The carpet set down gently next to the road and unfolded itself. They were high up above a steep valley, still outside the town. At first, the three friends didn't move at all, not quite sure what to do, then Chryséis sat up first.

"I'm thirsty," she declared and took a swig of sweet spring water from the plateau. Katherine and Trevor sat up too.

"We must be in Attock now," Katherine said.

"That was an awesome ride," Trevor cried.

"I like riding in a vimaan better." Chryséis offered the water bottle to her friends.

"Come on, Chris that was totally fantastic," Katherine said.

"Okay, maybe a little."

"We have to get going," Trevor said. "Are we supposed to leave the carpet here?"

"Of course, or do you want to carry this thing all the way to Minnegara?" Katherine laughed.

As soon as they stepped off the carpet, it began to lift off the ground once more. Their miraculous vehicle rolled itself up again and dashed back west. "Cool!" Chryséis said.

They heard crunching noises and snorting and a caravan appeared on the road heading east.

"Shelanti athenai!" Trevor greeted them and the caravan came to a halt.

"Shelanti. Sain bainuu."

A family of traders were on their way to Minnegara and offered to take the children with them. They looked friendly enough in their pointy hats and felt waistcoats. Because they didn't speak Akkadian, they rather communicated with signs. The women nodded vigorously when they heard the word 'Minnegara' and moved large togoo pots out of the way; then they lifted the three children up on their tough little horses.

The caravan began to move again along the road and soon, large conical towers emerged behind the hills.

The city of Minnegara.

Strangely, the gates were unguarded and they entered the town unhindered. The caravan trotted slowly along the streets as they made their way to the marketplace. Then, the three children were on their own, once again.

"Look over there by that square." Katherine pointed to a food stall behind some low tables and chairs. They passed a group of women in stiff pleated skirts and placed themselves in front of the food stall.

The woman, who tended to the stall noticed their hungry faces and prepared a meal for them.

She opened a vat with fish fillets that were marinating in a deep red foul-smelling liquid, which turned out to be chili. After seeing that, the children didn't feel quite so hungry anymore, but they couldn't just walk away. So, they simply sat down on chairs and placed their backpacks under the table. The woman fried three fish fillets in a large pan on her zuukh stove, and the children wondered if they would be able to swallow one bite of it, but the fish didn't taste bad at all.

The woman gladly accepted the little mother-of-pearl disks Katherine handed over. She liked the unusual outlandish tender that would buy her a new yellow silk dress for sure.

"King Acarnôn's castle?" Katherine asked her clumsily.

The woman looked surprised. The castle is not a place for young children, she thought, but then she pointed to a fortress that overlooked Minnegara. One of the yaks left smelly dung right next to the tables. Chryséis sniffed and grimaced, but this was a minor annoyance compared to the things to come.

King Acarnôn was not a nice man and used to getting whatever he wanted. This morning, he had decided that he wanted another wife. Tired of the beautiful, local girls, he wished for a more exotic wife this time. The king had heard of the blonde girls in Casumir with eyes like the summer sky. They had not the most beautiful colouring, but were certainly different to the usually darker-complexioned tribes of Attock.

Although the laws of the Known World frowned upon this practice, Minnegara was far away from the civilized society.

Here, whatever the ruler wanted, he got. His giant guards were delighted to see a Casumiri female of marriageable age on the square. They approached slowly, not to frighten the maiden and her two companions.

She surely was a suitable bride for the king.

"Sain bainuu," they greeted the three strangers. "We would like you to follow us to the castle."

Needless to say that the children were a little surprised.

"That was quick," Katherine replied and stood up.

"We are looking for King Acarnôn," Chryséis shouted over the noise in the street. "Can you take us to him?"

Not exactly what the guards had expected from a Casumiri female, but at least no force was necessary. The guards proceeded to pick the time travellers up and carried them on their shoulders up the hill to the castle.

The woman at the food stall shook her head, but one did not confront the guards of King Acarnôn unpunished. So she turned her attention back to preparing more food for the Wildmen, who had taken a seat at another table.

Meanwhile, the guards entered the castle and heavy gates closed behind them. They walked into the great hall and set the children down. A man sitting on a golden chair stared at them.

This had to be the king!

Now they just had to find a way to get their stolen things back and leave this place. But that was easier said than done.

The king's herald did all the talking for him while the man on the throne cleaned his fingernails with a little golden knife and occasionally looking up at the foreigners. The children didn't understand much of what the herald had to say and instead studied the wall hanging behind the throne that was emblazoned with a black eagle's head and a red dragon.

Eventually, the herald turned arrogantly to the three friends.

"You are looking at king Acarnôn of Minnegara... and who might you be?" Luckily, they understood what he was saying.

The children already knew that nobody in Attock had ever heard of Alesia across the Atlantean Sea, so instead Trevor said, "We come from the Kingdom of America, far, far away in the west. We are Trevor, Chryséis and Katherine." He pointed to each of them.

The king was clueless and nobody really understood what the boy was saying. The king eyed the girl with the shiny hair and white skin with interest. Not very beautiful, but she will do, he thought.

"Not a bad choice," The king said without moving his eyes off Chryséis and the guards were pleased.

He stared some more, whispering to the herald.

"My Lord, the king of Minnegara, wishes to invite the young travellers to be his guests at his castle..." the herald said.

The king got up from his throne and looked short in his purple robes of state. The courtiers fell to their knees and the herald pushed the children down. They didn't like it here, but if they wanted to find the last of their TPFs, so they had to stay down, until the giant guards took them to another building.

"What's this guy up to?" Katherine asked and closed the door to their room. "Did you see how he stared at Chryséis the whole time?"

"Yeah, that kind is strange. I don't trust him as far as you can throw a cat," Trevor said.

"I hope he's not a cannibal or something," Chryséis said.

"Used to be a fine kingdom this," a voice croaked next to them. An old woman carried a bundle of washing. "Not the best king, Acarnôn is. Seems to have taken a shine to you, my girl," the old woman nodded towards Chryséis.

"Oh?" Katherine cried suspiciously.

"I'd say the king has a design to propose marriage to your young friend."

Now there was a thought! Perhaps the hag was just telling them some story.

"Marriage?" Chryséis shook herself. "Your king makes my skin crawl. And I'm only a child anyway."

"Not around here, you are not," the hag said. "I'll try to help you, but now I must go." She put the washing down and went down the stairs.

"Do you trust her?" Katherine said.

"I don't know. I hope we won't need her help," Trevor said.

Something was happening outside. The daily ritual of

taking the royal family to the dining hall for the evening meal was already in full swing.

"Now that's a sight for sore eyes," Katherine said as they looked out the window.

The king sat on a dwarf elephant and smiled down at his bowing subjects. His favourite wife rode an even smaller elephant behind him and lesser wives and concubines followed on foot, then an army of nursemaids with the royal children and a few courtiers. One of the children pulled a wooden horse on castors along on a short string…

Katherine suddenly turned around. "Where is Chryséis? Wasn't she here just now?"

"She was standing right next to me," Trevor said.

"Look over there… isn't that Chryséis?" Katherine's eyes nearly popped.

Chryséis was sitting on the arm of a giant guard behind the rest of the royal family. She looked panicked, still clutching her backpack that had their palmtop in it.

"How did they get her out of the room without us noticing?" Katherine was getting really angry.

"I don't know," Trevor said. "But we have to go and help her!"

Chryséis looked nervously around ignoring the smiles of the courtiers. That's when she saw Trevor and Katherine by the window. There was no need for a lonely escape plan or the dangerous use of telepathy. She lifted her hand slowly to acknowledge her friends and they waved back.

'See you outside…' Chryséis mouthed and grimaced. Her two friends nodded. Good, they had understood.

The king waved his bejewelled hand and said a poem in honour of his new bride. His royal court smiled benignly.

"… juicy as a plum, shining as the sun…" he rhymed in bad Akkadian and looked at Chryséis.

"Me…?" Chryséis asked.

"Yes, darling. You shall not want for anything. Once you are the sixteenth queen of Minnegara and the

Kingdom… our children…" he muttered in Akkadian.

Chryséis had to think on her feet. "Children?" She interrupted him. "In my country, I'm a princess and much too young to get married."

The king spoke to the herald. "We will ask the spirits for their permission then".

Katherine and Trevor were taken to the dining room, but were not allowed to speak to Chryséis. The herald blew a long plaintive blast on his conch horn and the banquet began. After the meal, Chryséis was taken away by servants.

What were they supposed to do now?

Soon, two invisible children sneaked out of their guest room and explored the castle grounds by this temple. They had taken their backpacks just in case they found Chryséis and the TPF. Behind the falcon mew stood the temple of the war god Xipe Xolotle. One path led to the temple from the great hall and another one led away from it towards the enormous walls that separated the castle grounds from the village and open fields on the hill.

Their situation seemed hopeless, unless they could make it outside of these castle walls.

The sun threw longer and longer shadows on the grass and stone walls when they passed the temple again. There was a large stone altar between two fire bowls and - the TPF lay on a wine-red velvet cushion on the altar next to their tiny camera!

Then they saw Chryséis. She stood to one side of the altar almost behind a pillar, dressed in her own clothes with her daypack still slung over one shoulder. And the king stood on the other side.

She was visibly seething with anger and looked staunchly down at the dark floor. A shaman approached the altar with his arms lifted up, murmuring a singsong, conjuring up the spirits of the depths.

The magical powder thrown into the flames had not produced the required green colour. The colour of betrothal. A fiery red had been produced instead. It was the colour of blood. That didn't bode well for a union between the king and the girl.

"Unfavourable. The three foreigners must be put to death instantly to appease the god Xipe Xolotle."

"You can't do that!" Chryséis shouted defiantly at the two surprised men.

"How dare you talk to a king of Attock like this?" the shaman fumed. "You shall obey the spirits."

"How dare I talk to you like this? I will tell you how I dare talk to you like this…" Chryséis continued to vent her anger in English, which left both shaman and king puzzled. But there was no stopping Chryséis now. "I'd rather chew glass than marry you, that's what…"

"Guards…!" The king called out in a haughty voice.

Two giant guards, in richly decorated brocade tunics, bowed to king and shaman, then grabbed Chryséis.

"You will take those stinking hands off me, right now…" she raged at the surprised giants. "Let go of me!" Her fury made the guards drop their hands and stare helplessly at their king.

"Take her," The king ordered coldly.

At that moment, a blast ripped through the temple. Then another. This was unexpected. The king and his guards stormed outside. They no longer paid attention to the brazen child. Their king's safety was more important. Katherine and Trevor switched their VICs off and then something else rather unexpected happened: a young man ran in and grabbed the time-portal finder off the altar.

"Hey, what are you doing, that's ours!" Trevor was not going to let him take their precious time-portal finder. No way! He grabbed the camera and wanted to lunge at him, but the confusion only lasted a brief moment, when the man saw the previously invisible Trevor and Katherine next to Chryséis. He smiled and motioned for the children to be quiet and come outside with him. There were no guards.

"How… what…?" Trevor sputtered.

"Later, athenai. Be quiet, please. We must make haste. It isn't over yet, friends," the young man said with an Alesian accent. "My name is Mishaan of Minnegara. I'll explain everything later."

"Why should we trust you?" Chryséis asked prickly.

"Chris come on, we have no choice," Katherine hissed. "Anybody who wants to help us is our friend right now."

They heard voices nearby and Mishaan signalled for them again to be quiet. "We must go," he whispered and handed Katherine the TPF.

Mishaan waved for them to follow him down the path towards the castle wall. There was no use for the invisibility capes now.

"The Lady of Cydonia instructed me to look out for you. Nobody suspected it…" he said and hurried them on.

So their old friend, the Lady of Cydonia had not forgotten about them! He gave the TPF to Katherine and said, "We must hurry before it is discovered that the blasts were a distraction. The king will not act kindly toward anyone who flees his castle."

They followed him, hearts beating wildly. Somebody from the king's retinue might see them and sound the alarm. When they reached a massive door let into the wall, Mishaan pressed down the door handle and - nothing happened.

"Oh Earthmother, help us," he said, pressed the little-used handle again and threw his weight against the door. Nothing. Then they heard a creaking noise from the outside. A key was turned in the great lock. Had they been discovered? And where was the Djin when they needed him?

Mishaan motioned for the others to stand back from the door. It slowly opened and… a head with blonde braids appeared. It was Monicia, Mishaan's younger sister. Her brother jumped forward and gave the girl a mighty fright. "Why in the name of the good Earthmother…?" He was clearly annoyed. The girl apologised meekly. She had been delayed.

Mishaan told his sister to lock the door and put the key back where it belonged when they had gone outside. Then she was to run away.

They pushed through the door just as they heard a cry: "Tuslaarai! Tuslaarai!…Help! Help!"

"We must run!" Mishaan shouted and they ran.

The young man sprinted towards a plantation of plum trees and at once, the trees concealed the group with their leaves and branches. Then they struggled through the plantation, hoping that the guards had not detected them.

"Come, take my hand," Trevor said and pulled Chryséis with him. "Careful, there's a rock." Katherine was right behind them.

Soon, there was more shouting behind them, but they didn't dare turn around and look. When the sun was sinking behind the mountains, Mishaan clambered up a grassy slope. They'd reached the foothills.

"You will find a path right there," Mishaan pointed to a thin band of hardened soil winding its way out of sight. "Run fast, but be careful. Use your invisibility capes."

How did Mishaan know about the VICs? The Lady of Cydonia must have told him. She had known that they would come to Minnegara and organised help.

"I shall return to my goats over by the orchard at once. No one will be any the wiser. Good luck and safe return to your own time. The Earthmother be with you."

"Wait!" They gave him their amulets. "They will protect you and your family," Katherine said.

"Thank you and go now before the guards come any closer," Mishaan urged them on. He put one of the amulets around his neck and the other two into a pocket of his tunic. Then he disappeared among the plum trees by the time the first guards came into sight in a cloud of dust.

The three friends stumbled along the rocky path stopping only briefly to catch their breaths. Soon, they reached a few rocks for cover.

"Quickly, Katherine. The time…portal…finder!" Trevor croaked out of breath. The dust cloud behind them grew bigger. Chryséis was the first one to push herself through the rocks and Trevor followed her. Then Katherine reached up and Trevor pulled her through the gap. They jumped to the round and hid behind the rocks.

"Hurry, press the button. The fixed point of reference," Chryséis urged Katherine, who pointed the device here and there. "Come on, work stupid TPF. Work already!"

Trevor grew impatient. "Now would be a good time!"

Katherine targeted another location and was finally successful. The wavy curtain appeared. A vortex at last!

"Over here, come quickly. The portal is opening up!" She yelled.

The king's guards had almost reached the rocky outcrop by the slope. It was the last barrier between them and the fleeing children! The guards were sure that they would return to the castle with the runaways for the king's sacrifice. But what followed next left the giant guards stunned. A glittering pulsating curtain appeared behind the rocks, then an opening circling like a cursed snake. They hesitated. Was this Tiphereth? It was surely not of this world… obeah! Averting their faces, they waited for the dust to settle, but when they looked again, there was no curtain, no snake and the children were gone. Gone to the abode of the serpent god!

*

Back in Cydonia, in the country of Alesia across the Atlantean Sea, the Lady of the citadel took a sigh of relief. She had done what she could. The children from the future were safe now.

End of Book 3

ABOUT THE AUTHOR

Evadeen Brickwood grew up with two sisters in Germany and studied cultural sciences and languages. As a young woman, she travelled extensively and many of her books are inspired by her experiences abroad. Feeling adventurous, the newly qualified translator moved to Africa in 1988 and worked for two years as a secretary and language teacher in Botswana.

The author eventually settled in South Africa, where she got married and raised two daughters. In Johannesburg, Evadeen Brickwood studied computers and management of training and worked as a corporate software trainer and as a professional translator and lecturer at WITS University. In 2003, she began her writing career with youth novels in the 'Remember the Future' series, about adventures in prehistory. Book 1, 'Children of the Moon', has been published twice in South Africa and translated into German. "The Secret of the Bird God" is the third book in time travel series. The author now self-publishes and the fourth book in the series will be the last – so far.

Her works also include the novels 'Singing Lizards', 'The Rhino Whisperer', 'A Half Moon Adventure' and the series 'Charlie Proudfoot Murder Mysteries'.

About Writing This Book

When I first planned to write the third book in the 'Remember the Future' series, I found such a wealth of information on the prehistoric climate and ancient traditions in North Africa that I got carried away and the book ballooned to over 500 pages. I faced the daunting task of having to slim down "The Secret of the Bird God" quite considerably in favour of the storyline. Storytelling seems to be a dying art in North Africa, where many 'rawis' earned their living, narrating weird and wonderful tales.

Remember there were no Google, Netflix or YouTube around and people wanted to be entertained. One of the stories resembled that of Cinderella - just imagine. Unfortunately, it had to go, but others were drastically altered and simplified for the purpose of the book. I sometimes used ancient names for places and deities, but most were invented. Libraries are interesting places in "The Secret of the Bird God" and the prehistoric books have little in common with our modern books.

The first two novels in the 'Remember the Future' series have Earth and Water as underlying themes and in the third book, it is the element of Air. All flying things play a special role; some are real, some are made-up and some are based on legend. I hope that the adventures are still as exciting to read as they were for me to write. You can look forward to the fourth book, which is already half-way completed.

Evadeen Brickwood

Can you imagine, suddenly living in the past? Not last year or in the Roman Empire, but a really, really long time ago?

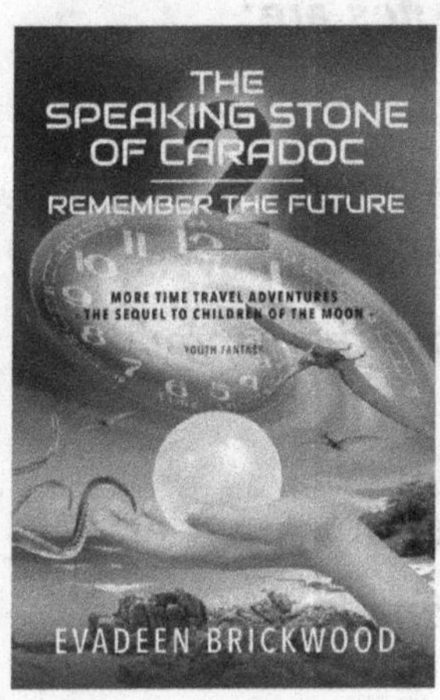

Katherine, Trevor and Chryseis embark on a ship and sail to remnants of the sunken continent of Atland.

NEW

You can now listen to readings from the first chapters
of all Evadeen Brickwood novels
on YouTube

All e-books are available from most online-retailers and as print-editions from good bookstores

The author's websites are:

http://www.evadeen.wixsite.com/youngbooks
http://www.evadeen.wixsite.com/novels
http://www.evadeen.wixsite.com/charlieproudfoot

Evadeen is also on Facebook, Twitter, Pinterest, Instagram and google+